LOST IN SPACE

"The Empire is fighting a powerful, mysterious enemy," Major Southern said. "This force called Shadow uses methods we don't understand. The people of Shadow's own world call it magic.

"You know we have representatives of Shadow's universe here at Base One. Lord Raven of Stormcrack Keep has sworn to join his efforts to ours. In just a few days we'll be sending Lord Raven and others through a space warp. I invite you to join that group. As natives of a universe different from both ours and Shadow's, you might be just what's needed to defeat this universal horror."

"No, it's not our fight," Pel said. "We only want to go home."

"We're offering you a choice. If you don't go, you're free to join the Imperial military or we'll send you to any nearby planet you choose. From then on you're on your own."

"Send us home, damn it!" Pel shouted.

The major ignored him.

By Lawrence Watt-Evans
Published By Ballantine Books:

*Forthcoming

IN THE
EMPIRE OF
SHADOW

Book Two of
the Three
Worlds Trilogy

Lawrence Watt-Evans

A Del Rey® Book
BALLANTINE BOOKS • NEW YORK

A Del Rey® Book
Published by Ballantine Books

Copyright © 1995 by Lawrence Watt Evans

Library of Congress Catalog Card Number: 94-25083

ISBN: 0-345-39786-X

Manufactured in the United States of America

First Trade Edition: March 1995
First Mass Market Edition: September 1995

10 9 8 7 6 5 4 3 2 1

FOR JULIE
BECAUSE THEY'RE ALL FOR HER

A NOTE TO THE READER

In the course of this novel, the surprise ending of the animated movie *Wizards* (1977; directed by Ralph Bakshi) is revealed. If you have not seen the film and think you might want to someday ... well, you've been warned.

CHAPTER 1

The spaceship shone vivid purple in the unfiltered light, brighter than any jewel, bright as a skateboarder's gear. Its nose and tail fins were golden; the forward fins were patterned in gold, white, and purple. At first glance, it should have been as gaudy and absurd as a cartoon.

But out there in space, with the glow of Base One's sun cutting sharp-edged division between light and shadow, with the utter black of deep space and the hard, unblinking blaze of a myriad stars behind it, it didn't look silly at all. It looked impressive, more real than reality itself.

Pel Brown supposed that this was what all those comic-book artists and movie special-effects crews had been trying for, and, limited by the media they used, had been unable to achieve. It took the reality of airlessness, free fall, and starlight to create such an intense image.

The bright colors were what did it; the bland grays and whites of NASA's shuttle or most of the movie spaceships just didn't have the same power.

Pel had never expected to see a real spaceship—not like *this*, anyway. After all, he was just a freelance marketing consultant from Germantown, Maryland, and until recently the only spaceships he'd ever known existed were the ones built by NASA or the old Soviet space program.

Three months ago he had had no idea that parallel universes were real, and not just fiction. Three months ago he hadn't met the velvet-clad thug who called himself Raven, or any of Raven's motley companions. He hadn't asked his lawyer to bail a bunch of stranded spacemen out of jail. He hadn't stepped through a portal in his basement wall into Raven's world, a universe where magic worked and something called Shadow

1

was the absolute ruler of the world. He hadn't escaped from
Shadow's monsters only to wind up in a third universe, the one
the spacemen came from, where the Galactic Empire ruled
three thousand inhabited planets. He hadn't spent weeks as a
slave working in a mine on a planet called Zeta Leo Three.

And three months ago he had had a wife and daughter, and
now they were gone, and he had been told that they were both
dead, murdered by space pirates.

Space pirates! God, that sounded like something out of the
old pulp magazines, or a low-budget movie—only they'd been
all too real, and altogether serious. They'd captured Pel, along
with Raven and the others, and sold them into slavery.

And they hadn't gone in for gaudy colors. The ship out
there was not their style at all. The colors marked it as part of
the Imperial Fleet.

This particular combination of colors wasn't quite the standard set; gold and white were unusual. The purple meant the
ship was the property of the Galactic Empire, of course; Pel
wondered what the gold represented. He guessed that it probably meant the ship carried some high official.

There were plenty of high officials at Base One already, in
Pel's opinion; he had been harassed by a few of them. A good
many of the Galactic Empire's big shots had been interested in
seeing the people from another universe.

Pel watched, vaguely annoyed, as the ship slid smoothly into
the huge airlock a quarter-mile farther down Base One's surface.

That surface was an uneasy blend of raw meteoritic stone
and riveted metal—the Imperial Military had hollowed out the
orbiting rock, and then built outward, as well. Pel's window
looked out from a bulge of asteroidal stone onto a broad vista
of sheet steel, pocked and patched as a result of collisions with
celestial debris, but untainted by any trace of rust.

Then the infinite depths of space and the long metal walls of
the station dimmed to near-invisibility and his own face leapt
out at him from the glass; someone had turned on the light in
the room behind him.

He continued to stare at the glass, at his own features super-
imposed on the universe, almost blocking it all from sight. His
nose, recently broken by the overseers at the mine where he'd
worked as slave labor, did not look quite right, and the bruises
elsewhere had left dark traces that looked like shadows, but it
was still the same face he had always had.

He was in the wrong universe, but he was still in his own body. Reality hadn't gotten *that* strange.

"Mr. Brown?" an unfamiliar voice inquired.

The clerk looked at the clipboard, then at Amy. "Miss Jewell?" he asked.

Amy dropped the magazine on the table, losing her place. The tentacular monster in the cover picture grinned lewdly up at her, ignoring the screaming girl in its coils.

Losing her place was no great inconvenience; the stories were all pretty bad anyway. Men's adventure stories weren't any better written here than back on Earth and in general were even more offensively sexist. Not to mention that the line between adventure and science fiction had been hopelessly blurred by the existence of interstellar travel and huge areas of unexplored galaxy—odd, to realize that stories of heroes fighting monsters from other planets didn't qualify as science fiction here.

The stories still sucked, though. She was very tired of evil mutant masterminds and big blond heroes.

Reading this tripe was better than nothing, but not by much. It generally took her mind off feeling lousy, but nothing more than that. When her bruises healed completely and she got back home to her three acres in Goshen, Maryland, that would probably help a lot more.

Of course, there was presumably still a stranded spaceship in her backyard. The Empire's first attempt to contact Earth, to arrange an alliance against Shadow, had ended when ISS *Ruthless* plummeted out of the sky and crash-landed there.

They'd planned on appearing twenty miles from the White House, one of the crewmen told Amy later—they didn't want to just drop right into the middle of the capital.

Twenty miles or so northwest of the White House had put them right over Amy's yard, and the moment the ship popped out of the space warp that let it into Earth's universe the crew had made the unexpected discovery that antigravity, the basis for much of the Empire's machinery, didn't *work* in Earth's universe, and there was therefore nothing holding the ship up.

It had crashed, and it was probably still there, and it was never going to fly again. The laws of physics were apparently very different in each of the three known realities.

They were different enough that something called "magic" worked in the world Shadow and Raven came from, something that had let Amy and the crew of *Ruthless* step through a basement wall into that world.

And when they'd fled into the Galactic Empire, the monsters that followed them had died for lack of that "magic," just as *Ruthless* had fallen for lack of antigravity. The three universes were *different*, all right.

Some things didn't change, though—people could still be rotten, in any universe. Like her ex-husband Stan. Like that son of a bitch Walter, who had bought her from the pirates and kept her as a slave until the Empire rescued her and brought her to Base One.

At least the Empire made an *attempt* at being civilized.

Even if, she thought with a final glance at that god-awful collection of violent, sexist, racist, imperialist adventure stories, they weren't all that good at it.

She forgot the magazine and looked up at the clerk.

"Ah . . . Miss Jewell? Or is it Mrs.?"

"It's Ms.," Amy said, perversely. Her stomach was slightly upset, as it often was lately—the food here was at least as bad as the fiction—and she was in no mood to cooperate with the Empire in its petty oppressions.

"Mrs.?" the clerk asked again.

"Ms. It's a word we use back on Earth."

"Oh. Yes, of course." The clerk noted something, then looked up again and said, "Could you come with me, Miss Jewell?"

"Why? And where?"

The clerk did not answer; instead he said, in a surprisingly definite voice, "I was told to bring you *at once*."

Amy sighed and decided not to argue anymore.

"Mr. Deranian?"

Ted ignored them, and the two men cast knowing glances at one another.

"You take the right arm," one of them said. "Be careful, though—the doctor said that besides the head wound, his ribs aren't completely healed yet."

The other nodded.

Side by side they advanced, and grabbed Ted by the arms.

"Come on, Mr. Deranian," one of them said. "Dream's not over yet."

* * *

"Miss N'goyen?"

"Nguyen," Susan said, without moving from her cot. She was lying face-down; the burns on her back no longer hurt all the time, but lying on them was still not a good idea. Her time as a slave on Zeta Leo Three had been very rough on her.

But then, having been a refugee as a child, she'd survived rough times before. She'd thought that she was finally through with all that when she'd made it through law school, passed the bar, and joined the firm of Dutton, Powell & Hough.

Obviously, she'd been wrong.

When Amy Jewell had called on her to provide legal assistance in dealing with the spaceship that had crashed in her backyard, Susan had not expected it to lead her to this.

The messenger tried again and almost managed to pronounce the name.

"What is it?" Susan asked.

"Could you come with me, please?"

Susan raised her head and looked at the messenger. "Do I have a choice?"

"Not really."

She sighed, sat up, swung her feet to the floor, and stood. "Lead the way," she said.

Pel took the seat on the far left, and Amy settled beside him. Pel noticed that she was no longer wearing heavy makeup to hide the bruise on her face; the discolorations had faded to a faint, sickly yellow tinge. Pel knew that his own injuries, too, were no longer obvious.

Ted was led in, unresisting, and seated on the far right; the fresh bandage on his head was smaller than the one Pel had last seen there, and the visible cuts and bruises had healed. There were scars, of course.

Susan, arriving last, took her place between Amy and Ted. A long-sleeved tunic hid the bandages that still covered much of her back and her forearms.

That was all of them, Pel thought, all four of them—the only living Earthpeople in the entire universe, according to the Galactic Empire.

At least, in *this* entire universe. So far as Pel knew, there were five billion others back on Earth, all blithely unaware that any universe but their own existed. And he secretly harbored hopes, despite his own better judgment, that his wife and daughter might still be alive somewhere. Their deaths had been reported to him and had been confirmed repeatedly, but he hadn't seen either of them die; he hadn't seen their bodies.

He knew, intellectually, that they were both dead, but accepting it emotionally was another matter.

Nancy and Rachel weren't here, though, even if by some miracle they weren't both dead. The four of them, Pel and Amy and Ted and Susan, were the only Earthpeople here at Base One. Pel found something peculiarly amusing in the thought that half of them were lawyers, here because they had been representing the other half.

The Galactic Empire didn't seem to care about lawyers, though. Ted wasn't representing him here, and Susan wasn't representing Amy; they were all here on their own. Pel looked around, wondering why they had been gathered.

This was a new room to them all. It was small and bare, with walls of whitewashed stone—that meant it was within the asteroid itself, rather than in the later additions, where everything was steel. The tiled floor might once have been white, too, but was now a dull gray. The four steel chairs were not particularly comfortable. The purple-painted lectern bore the lion-and-unicorn seal of the Imperial Military—but then, so did any number of objects scattered about Base One.

It looked like a small briefing room. That was, at least, an improvement on the debriefing and interrogation chambers where Pel seemed to have spent most of his waking hours for the past ten days.

The door opened, and a man in the familiar purple uniform of an Imperial officer marched past them, papers in hand, and took his place at the lectern. Pel was beginning to learn the insignia; he placed this character as a major in the political service.

That was mildly unusual; up until now they had mostly been bothered by people in Imperial Intelligence.

"Welcome to Base One," the major announced, in jovial, booming tones that were almost painful in so small a room. "I'm Major Southern."

Pel winced, not just at the tone, but at the words. He and the others had been here at Base One for over a week—Pel, without a regular cycle of sunrise and sunset, had lost track of exactly how long it had been, but he knew it was over a week. They didn't need any more welcoming speeches.

Ted grinned foolishly. "Major Southern," he said. "I like

that. Glad I thought of it. Southern, warm, friendly—a summery sort of name."

At that, *Amy* winced.

"Now, you're all intelligent people," the major proclaimed, in somewhat more moderate tones. "You all know what the situation is."

Pel glanced at Ted, who grinned back and winked broadly at him.

"We're fighting a powerful, mysterious enemy," Major Southern continued, "a force that has conquered an entire universe, and that now threatens two others."

Ted nodded, smiling happily. Susan sat in polite and motionless silence. Amy's lips tightened. Pel could almost hear her thoughts—he could imagine her muttering, "I haven't seen it threatening Earth."

"This force called Shadow uses methods we don't understand, methods that are impossible in our own universe; the people of Shadow's world call it magic, and that's as good a name as any. It's used that magic to send its agents, its spies, and its monsters into our universe. It has attempted to subvert the Galactic Empire, which has brought peace and security to all mankind—at least, in this reality."

Amy's lips twitched, and Pel could easily guess the cynical thoughts running through her mind.

All mankind, except where it hadn't gotten yet, which was far more than the Empire cared to admit—all of the little group had seen more than they wanted of the odd corners where the Empire had no dominion. And the Empire might bring security to *man*kind, perhaps, but not necessarily women. It also helped if the men were white.

Just how different was the Empire from Shadow, really? Both were imperialist; Shadow just seemed to be a little farther along in its conquests.

Of course, as one point in its favor, the Galactic Empire was run by humans; nobody knew just what Shadow was.

"You know that we have representatives of Shadow's universe here at Base One," the major said. "Lord Raven of Stormcrack Keep has taken temporary refuge here, and he and his party have fought against Shadow all their lives."

"So they say," Amy muttered, and this time it was not just Pel's imagination.

He thought this might be carrying cynicism a little far;

Raven and his man Stoddard and the two wizards had certainly seemed sincere enough.

The major either didn't hear her, or chose to ignore her. "They've sworn to continue that fight," he said, "and to join their efforts to ours, rather than to continue operating independently. In just a few days, we'll be sending Lord Raven and the others through a space warp, back into their home universe—and with them we'll be sending a squadron of our best men and a trained telepath. This combined force will be the first step in taking the battle onto Shadow's home ground, the first step in overthrowing this unnatural tyranny and freeing the oppressed people of Shadow's realm."

And probably bringing them under Imperial domination instead, Pel thought.

"I'm here today to invite the four of you to join that combined force," Major Southern said. "As natives of a universe different from both ours and Shadow's, you have a different viewpoint, you have knowledge and techniques that might be just what's needed to defeat this . . . this interuniversal horror."

"Fuck off," Pel said, unable to resist any longer. Did this beribboned idiot think they didn't know what the Empire wanted? They knew, and they weren't interested. They had all made that clear enough. "Just send us home," he said.

"It's not our fight," Amy added.

Ted giggled.

Susan's lips were a tight line; she said nothing.

"I'd been told that some of you felt that way," Major Southern said, frowning. "You're civilians and subjects of another nation—one we don't recognize, of course, but still, we realize you aren't soldiers we can order into battle. Further, you probably wouldn't be of much use if we sent you out there involuntarily. We don't seem to be getting anywhere by appealing to your patriotism and common decency—you've all turned us down. Revenge doesn't seem to have been enough, either."

"We don't know it was Shadow that sold us into slavery," Amy said. "We only have your word for that."

"Why would we lie?" The major spread his hands in a gesture of bewilderment.

"You might have staged the whole thing to get us on your side," Amy suggested. "If it was Shadow that captured us, why would it sell us? If it's after us, why weren't we killed?"

"We don't know," Southern admitted, "and that's something we'd like to find out, but we can't." He hesitated, but Amy had said her piece; no one interrupted further, and he returned to his speech.

"You won't go voluntarily, as I said," he told them, "so we're offering you a choice. Lord Raven and the rest will be sent into Shadow's universe three days from now, whether any of you four are with them or not. Those of you who don't go—well, we can't keep you here forever, living on the largesse of the Empire. You're free to join the Imperial Military; we can always use bright people like yourselves. If you're not interested, though, I'm afraid you can't stay at Base One, which is, after all, a military installation. Instead, we'll send you to any nearby planet you choose; we'll land you where you ask, and from then on, of course, you're on your own."

"Send us *home*, damn it!" Pel shouted.

The major pretended to ignore him and continued, "Of course, we can't create an interuniversal space warp just for the convenience of a handful of uncooperative civilians, but I suppose we can arrange grants of citizenship and provide the necessary papers to keep you out of jail. For brave volunteers, once the crisis is past and Shadow defeated, no reasonable reward would be refused, and opening a space warp would be considered; but for civilians who've turned down a chance to serve the Empire? Not likely."

The four Earthpeople stared at him—or at any rate, three of them did.

Ted Deranian shrugged and said, "I'll go with Raven if you like; it's all the same to me. Might make a better story that way, if I don't wake up before I get that far."

Amy let out a low moan of disgust at Ted's insistence on his delusion. Pel glanced at her, but said nothing; he understood her reaction.

Ever since the party had stepped through the magical portal from Earth to Shadow's world, Ted had been convinced that the entire thing was a dream. Beatings, torture, wounds, and the passage of days and even weeks had failed to dislodge this conviction. Almost two months had now passed since the May evening when they had passed through Pel's basement wall, but Ted persisted.

The man's exact mood varied; sometimes he seemed to be struggling to maintain his belief, sometimes he sank into near-catatonia. Right now he was treating it all as a joke that had gone on a little too long, a story that was slow in reaching the point.

It got on everyone's nerves, and Pel and Amy both feared that Ted had slipped irretrievably into insanity weeks ago. Pel suspected that the head wound he had acquired resisting the pirates aboard *Emerald Princess*, or the beatings he had received on Zeta Leo Three, might have caused brain damage, as well.

"What about the rest of you, then?" Major Southern asked, smiling.

"You're a sadistic bastard, you know that?" Pel answered calmly.

"Now, now, Mr. Brown," the major said, feigning shock. "That's no way to talk!"

No one replied. He looked them over, then stepped out from behind the lectern.

"I've said my piece," he told them. "From here on, it's all up to you."

"Sure it is," Amy said. "We get our choice of two universes—but neither one of them's ours."

The major smiled and patted Amy on the shoulder. "That's right," he said. "I'll let you think about it." He looked around the room, gave everyone a cheerful grin that was only slightly patronizing, and strolled out.

Amy glared after him, and muttered, "Where'd they find *that* stupid prick?"

Pel shrugged. "Same place as all the others, I suppose," he said. "Wherever *that* is."

Susan suddenly spoke, for the first time since entering the room.

"I'm going with Raven," she said. "And I'd advise you both to consider joining us. I don't have any power over you, Mr. Brown, but as your attorney, Amy, I strongly recommend you take my advice."

The other three all turned to stare at her.

"Susan, are you . . . what are you *talking* about?" Amy demanded.

"Amy, just think it over."

She turned and marched out.

Baffled, Pel and Amy and Ted watched her go.

CHAPTER 2

"*We've no need of them,*" *Raven repeated.*

"We don't need them here, either," General Hart replied, "and they might be useful to you. Our telepaths tell us they have the most amazing assortment of odd information tucked away in their heads; this Earth of theirs seems to make a fetish of spreading information every which way, whether it's needed or not."

"And what know they of *my* world?" Raven protested. "Not so much as a newborn babe at the nurse's breast!"

Hart shrugged. "So? My men aren't much better."

"Soldiers?" Raven waved that away, the natural gesture stiff because of the bandaged fingers of his left hand. "A soldier's a soldier, man—an they know their jobs, we'll find use for them in Stormcrack and in Shadow's lands. But the Earthfolk . . ."

"Are you bothered because two of them are women?"

Raven, pacing by the wall map, glanced at the general. "Aye," he said, "there's that, and I admit it freely. 'Tis no place for a woman, in the midst of battle."

"One of your own party's a woman," Hart pointed out.

"Elani? Nay, she's a *wizard*; 'tis another matter entire."

"Looks like a woman to me," Hart said.

Two rooms away a telepath listened in on the conversation, and on the thoughts of the participants. Proserpine Thorpe had been reading the minds of those around her, sometimes whether she wanted to or not, since her earliest childhood; she was rarely surprised by the lies and deceptions of nontelepaths dealing with one another. Even so, the cynicism underlying this particular discussion was more than she would have expected.

General Hart really didn't care about any plans to destroy

Shadow and had no interest at all in the people the mysterious evil had harmed or killed; he just wanted to get rid of all the extrauniversal troublemakers before some idiot politician or ambitious underling found some way to exploit them and make him look stupid or ineffective. He didn't really completely believe in other universes, or that this Shadow thing posed a serious threat; this whole business had happened because nobody kept a close enough eye on that overzealous geek Copley, who should never have made Major, and that pompous civilian fraud Bascombe, the so-called Undersecretary for Interdimensional Affairs—a post in the Department of Science that existed only because Bascombe had invented it and pulled sufficient strings to get it for himself.

But Copley was out of the way now, thanks to a burst appendix, and Bascombe would be harmless enough by himself once these foreigners were disposed of. If Hart had a chance to send along a couple of his own unwanted subordinates as well, that would be just fine, even if it meant losing a couple of dozen men from his command. The Empire had plenty of soldiers, after all; sending a few on a ridiculous mission was no great loss.

And he seemed quite certain that whoever was sent would be lost.

For his part, Raven cared about almost nothing *except* destroying Shadow—not so much because of what it had done to thousands of innocents, though to give him credit he did feel a certain regret and anger at such needless cruelty, but because Shadow had harmed him, his family, and his honor. Had Shadow never touched Stormcrack Keep, Raven would still have opposed it, but only from a safe distance.

That was hardly a shock; after all, Raven was, as Prossie had known for weeks, a barbarian.

As it was, though, with his younger brother ruling Stormcrack Keep as Shadow's puppet, Raven was willing to sacrifice anyone and anything, including Stormcrack itself, to defeat Shadow and avenge himself. He did not care in the least that Amy and Susan might be in danger if they ventured back into his native reality; he cared, rather, that they would be useless, and that their presence might be an inconvenience to him, and increase the risks of the party as a whole.

However, he would, in the end, agree to anything General Hart proposed, because it was General Hart who controlled access to the gate between universes—at least for the moment.

Once back in his own land Raven would be free to ignore any plans and promises made at Base One—and he intended to do just that. He thought General Hart's plan for a small, fast-moving strike force that would penetrate Shadow's fortress and assassinate Shadow to be utter nonsense. Shadow, he knew, was a magical being and if confronted directly must be fought with magic—though its creatures could be slain with sword or spear, certainly, he doubted that Shadow itself would be bothered by anything so mundane.

Raven's own plan was to gather whatever magic he could and fling it against Shadow until something got through.

To Raven, as the telepath had seen before, "magic" included not just the magic of his own universe, but any force that he did not comprehend, including Imperial science and Earthly technology.

If he took this proposed Imperial raiding party in and brought back a few survivors who would attest to the need for other weapons against Shadow, then perhaps the Empire would provide those other weapons. Perhaps, if their "science" could do nothing, they would at least provide the men and swords to dispose of Shadow's creatures.

So he was agreeing to Hart's plan, even while he knew it was absurd, in order to draw the Empire into more direct conflict with Shadow.

Prossie knew that according to the rules the Empire set for telepaths, which required the immediate reporting of any sort of treason, or deception of government officials, or other anti-Imperial thought that a telepath might accidentally uncover, she should tell General Hart—but the general already assumed that the whole thing was a suicide mission. He misjudged Raven's motives for agreeing, thought the man was acting out of some silly romantic notions of courage, honor, and chivalry, but Hart knew that the proposed attack was insane and impossible.

He was deliberately trying to get Raven and the others killed, to get them out of the way. He *liked* the idea of keeping Shadow there as the Empire's enemy; it made the military more important if there was a serious foe out there somewhere, rather than just occasional rebels and outlaws to be suppressed.

So he intended to send Raven and his companions and the Earthpeople, and a few of his own less-desirable underlings, off to get killed.

And he intended to send Prossie along. Like most Imperials,

he didn't mind at all if telepaths got killed. Almost everyone hated telepaths; that was a fact that Prossie had lived with all her life. Hart was no exception.

It was only reasonable to want to send a telepath, for communication and espionage reasons, and Hart thought that Prossie, after her previous visit to Earth, might be tainted with dangerous notions.

General Hart wanted her dead.

And as far as Prossie was concerned, that meant that he didn't deserve to be warned of Raven's plans.

Besides, even if Hart knew the lordling's true motives, his own plans wouldn't change.

Likewise, even if Raven knew Hart's own intentions, he wouldn't change his own mind; cooperation was the only way to get home to his own world.

Maybe some of the others should be warned, Prossie thought, but not these two. Aside from the uselessness of such a warning, nobody really wanted to have telepaths telling them what to do, telling them what they had misread or misunderstood or forgotten.

And for that matter, Prossie was not supposed to be listening in in the first place. She had heard her own name mentioned earlier, and had, almost inadvertently, begun eavesdropping. That was a violation of the rules; the Empire had strict penalties for telepaths who spied on innocent citizens, and even worse for those who spied on government officials. If she warned General Hart, or if she warned Raven and he let it slip to an Imperial officer, she could wind up at the whipping post, or on the operating table for a lobotomy, or even hanged.

General Hart was far more likely to order a flogging than to thank her.

Let them go on with it, then.

As for the others—well, that remained to be seen.

Prossie liked the Earthpeople, or at least three of them—Pel and Amy and Susan had such interesting, complicated minds, and so little real hatred or hostility in them. Ted's poor tangled thoughts she avoided now, but the others she enjoyed, even when Amy was feeling sick and sorry for herself. Raven's liege man Stoddard was a good person, the wizards Elani and Valadrakul were no worse than average—Elani had a noble streak under her motherly warmth that was intriguing. Prossie didn't want to see any of them killed, and she certainly didn't want to get killed herself.

But although Prossie wished the Earthpeople no ill, getting off Base One and into Shadow's realm was probably the best thing that could happen to them.

She would not say a word to General Hart.

Roughly an hour after the briefing, if that was the name for it, had broken up, while he rambled along one of the endless metal-lined corridors that laced Base One, Pel encountered Susan Nguyen and fell in beside her.

He would not admit, even to himself, that he had been deliberately tracking her down. It was just good luck, he told himself, that he had happened upon her.

Just good luck—but he did have a question or two he very much wanted her to answer.

After mumbled greetings and a few paces of polite silence, he cleared his throat. She glanced up.

"Susan, are you really going to go with Raven's party into Shadow's universe?" he asked. "You saw what sort of monsters Shadow controls—you really think this stupid attack squad is going to get anywhere? It seems to me that it's practically suicide!"

He waited for an answer and was on the verge of concluding that he wasn't going to get one when Susan suddenly said, "You've noticed that the Empire's technology is different from ours, haven't you, Mr. Brown? They've got antigravity and telepathy, but we haven't seen any sign of computers or electronics, or even radios or telephones. All the same, do you think they might know how to make bugs of some kind, Mr. Brown?"

"Bugs?" Pel blinked.

He hadn't thought about that. He chewed his lower lip for a moment, glancing along the drab gray walls.

"I suppose they might," he admitted, "but it doesn't . . ."

"Just keep walking," Susan suggested.

Pel obeyed; together, the two of them strode down the corridor.

"A telepath could hear us, anyway," Pel muttered.

"But a telepath would have to be listening," Susan pointed out, "and they really have very few telepaths."

"For all we know, they have spy-rays or something," Pel pointed out.

Susan just nodded.

A moment later, as they turned a corner, she said, "You

know, all of them are going back to their own universe, not just Raven. Elani's going."

Pel glanced at Susan, then turned his gaze resolutely ahead. "I know that," he said.

He was puzzled by the reference. He was sure Susan had some good reason for mentioning Elani and not any of Raven's other companions. Susan and Elani weren't particularly close; in fact, Pel couldn't remember ever seeing the two of them together for more than a few seconds at a stretch, or speaking to each other at all beyond common courtesies.

Elani was one of the two wizards in Raven's band, and the only surviving female; did either of those facts signify anything important?

"You know, I'd rather go back home to Earth, instead of to fight Shadow," Susan remarked. "It's a shame we can't go back the way we came."

Pel started to reply, but just then Susan turned, adding, "And here's my door. It's been a pleasure seeing you, Mr. Brown."

She stepped into her room and left Pel standing in the passageway, staring stupidly at the blank closed door.

Back the way they came?

They had arrived at Base One by spaceship. They could hardly use an ordinary spaceship to get back to Earth; spaceships couldn't travel between universes. In all the Galactic Empire, so far as they knew, there was only one space-warp generator, and it was a huge thing here at Base One, not something that could be mounted on a spaceship.

Before that spaceship they had been on another one, Pel remembered, and another before that—but before *that*, they had arrived on a worthless desert planet called Psi Cassiopeia Two through a magical portal from Shadow's realm.

Pel blinked.

They had come through a magical portal.

A magical portal that Elani had created.

And they had gotten to Shadow's realm by stepping through another, similar portal from Pel's own basement.

Pel suddenly felt very stupid.

They didn't need the Empire's gigantic space-warp machine to send them to Earth. All they needed was Elani.

Of course, the laws of nature differed drastically from one universe to the next, so none of Elani's magic worked here in the Galactic Empire, any more than his long-lost digital watch had, any more than antigravity worked on Earth. Elani couldn't send them back home from Base One.

But if they went with her into Shadow's realm, she could certainly send them home from *there*.

Now why, Pel wondered, hadn't he thought of that himself, and much sooner?

He shook his head. He'd been too busy with other thoughts to look at the situation logically, he decided. He twisted his mouth into a wry smile as he started back toward his own assigned room.

It appeared he'd be volunteering to join Raven's strike team after all.

In the next corridor, Prossie Thorpe smiled to herself. The telepath hadn't had to so much as drop a hint; Susan Nguyen had figured it out for herself, and she would let the others know. The mission would go on as planned—but not necessarily as General Hart expected.

CHAPTER 3

Pel eyed the gathered group with some dismay.

All four of the Earthpeople had eventually gotten the idea and realized that the road home led through Shadow's world; now they all stood in a little bunch to one side of the staging area. They wore hand-me-downs and castoffs; their own clothes were lost or ruined, leaving them in borrowed slacks and surplus T-shirts and old boots. Susan Nguyen had managed to hang on to her big black handbag through all their adventures, but everything else they wore came from the charity of the Galactic Empire, and in consequence they looked mismatched and scruffy.

In the center of the assembly room stood Raven of Stormcrack Keep, dramatically clad in his customary black velvet, calling and waving for order. Three fingers of his left hand were bandaged together, and his movements still had a certain stiffness to them; his arms were raised, but did not move as smoothly and freely as they ought.

It was a mystery to Pel just where Raven had gotten his clothes; when he had been taken aboard *Emperor Edward VII* for the flight to Base One he had worn only a tattered green silk bathrobe. Perhaps the Empire had been generous with him in return for his enthusiastic opposition to Shadow—or perhaps his own garments had somehow been recovered and repaired.

Beside Raven on his right stood Stoddard—none of the Earthpeople knew any other name for him, or even whether Stoddard was a family name or his given name—in a borrowed purple uniform with the insignia removed, since his own leathers had been lost or ruined somewhere along the way.

On Raven's left stood the wizard Valadrakul of Warricken,

18

and a step behind him was Elani, also a wizard. Some of their original garments, like Susan's purse, had been recovered, somewhat the worse for wear, so that Elani wore her dark red wool robe, now heavily stained and with a few tears in the fabric hastily sewn shut. Valadrakul's calf-length embroidered vest incongruously covered most of a borrowed Imperial uniform. He had worn braids and long hair before his arrival in the Galactic Empire, and had lost one braid and some skin on Zeta Leo Three; now his hair was cut short and trimmed in the bristly Imperial military style. Where Imperial soldiers were always clean-shaven, however, Valadrakul wore a full beard, which made for an odd combination.

These four, Pel knew, were all that remained of Raven's cell of the organized resistance against Shadow's rule in Stormcrack Keep's demesne; all the other members of Raven's little group were dead or lost, their remains scattered across two universes.

Of course, Raven claimed that there were other resistance groups, dozens of them, and that they formed a network that had even placed spies in the Galactic Empire and sent envoys to the Imperial Court. Pel had no way of knowing how much of that was true, but in any case, Raven's party had been cut off, and no longer knew how to contact the others.

At least, so they said.

Facing Raven was a stocky, balding man in a purple uniform, his insignia proclaiming him a full colonel. He had given his name as Carson. Behind him was arrayed his squad, some fifteen men—all of them white, of course, and most of them blond. The Galactic Empire did not believe in mixing races; Pel had learned that much during his time here. The Delta Scorpius system, where Base One orbited, was entirely reserved for whites. Pel had been told that planets and bases existed where there were blacks and Orientals and other nonwhites, either alone or in combination, but he had never seen any. The only nonwhite at Base One was Susan; even Raven, with his Mediterranean complexion, was dark enough to sometimes draw curious and uneasy looks.

So here were fifteen of the Empire's finest, which meant Aryans, in full uniform, hair cut short, tall polished boots gleaming, helmets hung on their Sam Browne belts. The fancy belts apparently indicated that they were a special elite force of some sort; the crew of ISS *Ruthless* hadn't been so equipped.

If the uniforms had been black or gray, instead of purple, Pel thought they'd have looked like fine little Nazis.

And why a group that small was under the command of a colonel, rather than a lieutenant or even just a noncom, Pel didn't know. Maybe Carson's rank was intended to impress someone. It did not, however, impress Pel.

Standing off to the side was one more person in an Imperial uniform, this one with an ordinary belt, dull-finished half boots, and the black and gold patch of a Special on her shoulder, a rather plain young woman Pel knew from his previous adventures. She had no helmet in sight, and no sidearm. Pel knew her as Registered Master Telepath Proserpine Thorpe—Prossie, to her friends.

Hers was the only familiar face in the Imperial contingent. Pel had hoped that the surviving members of the former crew of *Ruthless* would all be included—he had gotten to know them somewhat and to respect them. Especially, Pel thought, in comparison with most of the Imperial military personnel he had encountered at Base One, many of whom seemed virtual parodies of dim-witted pomposity.

The military didn't have to be like that, Pel knew; back on Earth, in the U.S., even the Marines generally weren't as absurd as the bunch at Base One.

He looked for a familiar face in Carson's squad and didn't find it. Captain Cahn was not there, nor Smith, Mervyn, Soorn, or Lieutenant Drummond.

Lampert was not there because he was still missing, last seen on Zeta Leo Three. Cahn himself was probably still in a hospital somewhere, getting his bones reassembled—he had been thrown off a rooftop on Zeta Leo Three.

And Cartwright, Peabody, and Lieutenant Godwin were dead, of course. Like Squire Donald a' Benton, and little Grummetty, and Alella, all of them dead, somewhere in the Galactic Empire.

And like Pel's wife, Nancy, and their daughter, Rachel.

So there were eight survivors from the other two universes here, and even counting Prossie as an ally, that left them a minority of the group. Carson's fifteen men—fifteen strangers—were the majority.

Pel was of the opinion that that was likely to cause trouble. Raven was certain to consider himself the leader of the entire enterprise, and from the look of it, Colonel Carson did not care to yield the point.

Colonel Carson might also have some pretty serious reservations about allowing the Earthpeople to go home. Pel thought that he and Amy could probably have convinced Captain Cahn to let them go—after all, the Earthpeople had gotten Cahn and his crew out of the Rockville jail; shouldn't he return the favor?

But Carson was a complete stranger, and his presence could be a real problem.

Still, once they were in Shadow's universe, the Imperials would no longer have their whole empire backing them up, and their blasters would not work.

Did they know that? Had they picked that up from Cahn's reports?

Pel remembered the battle that had sent the earlier group fleeing through the magical opening from Shadow's universe into the Empire's reality. Shadow had sent hordes of monsters against them, and the Imperials' blasters might as well have been harmless toys for all the good they did. Valadrakul's spells had worked, and Susan's pistol . . .

Susan's pistol.

Pel blinked, and looked at Susan.

Yes, she had her purse. The big black handbag hung from one shoulder. Despite everything, she still had it.

Carson and Raven were arguing about something, and everyone else was watching the dispute, or else busy with their own affairs. Pel leaned over and whispered to Susan, "You armed?"

She threw him a quick warning glance, then answered, not looking at him, "Yes."

He took his cue from her and did not look at her as he asked, "Loaded?"

She lowered her head slightly, in a barely perceptible nod.

A moment later, as some minor official was herding the entire party of twenty-five into the ship that would carry them through the space warp, Susan managed to step away from Ted and closer to Pel.

"Thirty-eight Police Special," she whispered. "Six-shot revolver, but I only have four rounds left. Why?"

"Just wanted to know what's available, in case we have any disagreements on the other side." He threw a meaningful glance in Colonel Carson's direction.

She nodded.

Just behind them, Amy asked, "What are you two talking about?"

Pel glanced at Ted, and at the Imperials, and said, "Tell you later."

Amy, annoyed, decided not to press the issue on the spot. "You'd better," she said.

Pel smiled. He glanced about.

His gaze fell on Prossie Thorpe and his smile vanished. If she read what he was thinking, the whole game might be up right there.

Or it might not; he wasn't sure just what side Prossie would take.

To be safe, though, he decided it would be best not to think about any of that stuff. Not about the pistol, or using Elani's magic to get back to Earth, or anything the Empire might not like. But of course, trying not to think about it was almost impossible.

If he thought about something else instead, maybe he could distract himself.

Well, here was something—just how were they going to go through the space warp? He had seen the machinery the Imperials used to generate their opening between universes, and it was absolutely gigantic—Hoover Dam would make one of the support brackets, and the Washington Monument an insulator. The resulting field was a couple of hundred yards across—and a few hundred yards away from the machinery, out in the vacuum of open space. They would need some sort of transport to reach it.

Captain Cahn's expedition to Earth had flown through the warp aboard ISS *Ruthless* and had immediately discovered, on the other side, that antigravity didn't work in Earth's universe.

Their blasters hadn't worked on Earth, either.

And their blasters hadn't worked in Shadow's realm.

Pel suspected that meant that antigravity wouldn't work in Shadow's realm, either.

So how would the whole group get there?

Was the Empire going to throw away another ship and count on Raven's wizards to send everyone back? Had they come up with some other approach?

A glider might work. The space-warp generator operated in the hard vacuum of space, but an antigravity craft with wings could use its engines on the Imperial side and its wings on the Shadow side.

"All right, folks—everybody, your attention, please!"

Pel realized he was staring at the dull gray asteroidal stone of the floor; he looked up, startled. Colonel Carson was speaking.

"We're all here, and I think we're all ready. We've got our team equipment loaded already, and if you'll all bring your personal belongings, I think it's time to board the ship and get this show on the road!" He smiled—Pel supposed the smile was intended to be encouraging and friendly, but it came out rather stiff and stupid.

Pel had very little in the way of personal belongings; unlike Susan, he had been unable to retrieve anything after his stint working the mines of Zeta Leo Three.

Not that he'd had much of anything, in any case. He hadn't carried a purse; when he'd stepped through the magical portal in his basement, planning a five-minute visit to Stormcrack Keep and a quick return home, all he'd had were the clothes he wore and the contents of his pockets. A shirt, a belt, pants, socks, and shoes; his wallet, with credit cards, and a few dollars in currency that wouldn't pass anywhere in this universe; the key to his car; and that was about it.

And even those items were all lost.

Nancy had had her purse, but she was dead and her purse was gone.

Rachel was dead, too.

So all Pel had to carry were the pair of pants he had been given at the mine and somebody's cast-off Imperial uniform.

With a sigh, he picked up the little bundle and marched in the direction Carson had indicated.

The Empire, it seemed, had decided to throw away another ship.

This one, ISS *Christopher*, was a small short-range personnel transport, smaller than *Ruthless*, perhaps seventy feet from nose to tail—certainly no more than that. It was purple and pink, but not particularly elaborate in its design or decoration—at least, not by Imperial standards. To Amy, with its fins and curves and two-tone paint job, it still looked like something out of a comic book or a campy movie.

She shivered slightly; the air of the flight deck felt thin and chilly. She knew that had to be an illusion, though; the door they had entered through had been wide open to the rest of Base One, so the air would have equalized. It was just the knowledge that the flight deck itself was an airlock that was bothering her, she was sure—that, and the general stress and uneasiness she had been living with since arriving at Base One. She glanced up at the immense outer door; that mass of steel girders and panels was all that stood between them and outer space, and in a few minutes it would be opened.

She quickly looked away, back at *Christopher*.

The entire party trooped inside and found seats in the main cabin, which was starkly utilitarian—gray steel ribs overhead, gray steel plates underfoot, and eight rows of four seats apiece, gray steel seats upholstered in worn maroon leatherette, arranged in pairs on either side of a central aisle, like some military imitation of an airliner. Three bare lightbulbs, in a line down the center of the curving ceiling, provided light.

Amy thought that *Ruthless*, from what little she had seen of it, had been far more luxurious. But then, *Ruthless* was a long-range craft, Captain Cahn had told her, and had been on a diplomatic mission.

Furthermore, they hadn't known they were throwing it away. This time they presumably did, so naturally they'd picked a less valuable ship.

There were no seat belts—Amy had noticed long ago that the Galactic Empire wasn't much on safety equipment. Personal belongings were shoved under the seats; anything large or awkward was taken to the back of the cabin, where one of Colonel Carson's men heaved it through a door and onto a shelf in the storage area astern, where the soldiers' packs and various other supplies were already stowed. The soldiers retained their helmets and sidearms, but not much else; the Earthpeople generally kept whatever they had.

Two more of Colonel Carson's men split off from the main group and trooped forward, into the cockpit; Carson himself stayed until everyone else was sorted out and seated, and then he, too, vanished through the forward door.

There were half a dozen portholes, small ones with opaque covers dogged down over them; Amy found herself seated beside one and immediately set about uncovering it.

Susan, seated beside her, watched with interest.

As Amy had suspected, the ship was already off the deck and moving slowly toward the airlock door. Antigravity was quick and silent, and the Empire, once it finally started something, didn't waste time.

The space-warp machine was out on the surface of Base

One, halfway around the asteroid. They would be out in empty space for a few minutes. Amy had traveled through space before, on *Emerald Princess* and *Emperor Edward VII*, but those were big, comfortable ships and appeared far safer than *Christopher*. She felt a twinge of uneasiness.

They stopped moving; there was no change in sensation, any more than there had been when they lifted off, but Amy could see that the flight-deck wall was no longer sliding past. For a long moment they hung suspended as air was pumped out of the chamber, the ship no longer moving forward, but swaying gently in the air currents. The process began with a distant boom that was audible even through the thick steel of the ship, and then a dull roaring that gradually faded as the air thinned.

At last silence fell; the ship was floating in vacuum, with nothing to carry vibration. Then, finally, the outer door swung open before them—Amy had to press her face against the after edge of the porthole to see it clearly, but she managed it. There was no sound, of course; the immense steel barrier moved in utter silence, swinging slowly aside and revealing the white blaze of stars beyond.

The ship began moving forward again—as always with antigravity, there was no sensation of motion, but Amy could see the airlock walls sliding by again.

Then they turned about. Amy's inner ear still registered nothing, but she saw the universe wheel vertiginously past the porthole. The open door of the airlock was replaced by an infinity of stars and blackness; then the gray steel of Base One's artificial walls appeared along one side, followed by a rough, dark stretch of the original asteroid, then by more steel.

She had hoped to have a good look at the space-warp generator, but she realized quickly that she was on the wrong side of the ship to see it clearly. Still, by repeating her edge-of-the-port maneuver, she was able to see it ahead.

It was ablaze with light. The gargantuan ring of equipment was glowing violet-white, so bright Amy found she couldn't look at it directly even when she found the right angle. Everything else vanished into the blackness of space in contrast.

The airless void gave the whole scene an impossible sharpness, a clarity that perversely made it seem dreamlike and unreal. The waking world as Amy knew it was never so stark and clean-edged.

Then the ship surged forward—still with no sensation of acceleration—and that intense light surrounded the vessel, spilling in through the port so intensely that Amy turned away, momentarily blinded. Others exclaimed in pain and surprise at the unexpected brilliance as she groped for the porthole cover and slammed it shut.

Her eyesight was almost back to normal when, abruptly, there *was* a feeling of motion.

The ship was falling. Amy could feel it. Her stomach surged uncomfortably; she clutched at her seat, wondering why the hell the Empire didn't use seat belts and shoulder harnesses.

Everyone else felt it, as well. Elani screamed; Prossie Thorpe shrieked something that might have been "Here we go again!"; and several of Carson's men swore.

To add to the confusion, the cabin lights went out, plunging them into utter darkness.

They struck something, hard; the ship rocked wildly, and Amy heard crunching and snapping. They fell again, and then again, struck something, and broke through it.

Then, with a sudden hard bump, they were down. Amy's head rocked back and forth, but she kept her seat and was undamaged. Judging by the sounds she heard in the stygian gloom not everyone was equally fortunate.

She waited for a few seconds, to be sure the ship was not going to move again; she realized that it lay at a slight angle, the artificial gravity that made it always seem level gone. It wasn't much of an angle; she didn't hear anything rolling or sliding down the slope after the first second or two.

At first it felt as if they had bounced, as if the ship were now rising, but then Amy realized that was just higher gravity. Base One had artificial gravity set at one Imperial gee—which was less than Earth's gravity. Earth, she had been told, had a gravitational field approximating 1.15 gees, by Imperial measurements.

And Shadow's conquered world was 1.3, which, she was sure, was what they were now experiencing. That heavy feeling, as if they were in an ascending elevator, was not going to go away.

Once she was convinced they weren't going anywhere, she groped her way up the wall and found the porthole. Carefully, she lifted the porthole cover slightly; light spilled in. This was not the incredible eye-scorching glare of the space warp, however; the light that now shone around the rim seemed quite manageable. In fact, it looked like ordinary daylight—perhaps a bit thin and watery, but daylight.

Amy swung the cover aside and looked out at Shadow's world.

She couldn't see much. The trunk of a huge tree, standing no more than two yards away, blocked most of her view. Turning slightly, she could see that broken branches and foliage were scattered across the ship's fin, a few feet aft of the port. The fin itself was bent and battered, its pink paint scratched and scraped, revealing black primer and shining steel. Yellow sunlight slanted down, glittering coolly on the pink paint and green spring leaves—the sun here in Shadow's realm, in what she and some of the others had taken to calling Faerie, was paler than Earth's, its light not the warmer hue Amy would have expected back home.

Although she had no reason to think she could tell the difference, the light seemed to her like morning light, rather than afternoon.

"What the hell happened?" an unfamiliar male voice demanded of no one in particular.

Amy turned away from the port and peered into the gray gloom of the main cabin.

"We landed," she said. "Hit a few trees on the way down."

"Trees?" a timid voice asked.

"Big plants," a more confident voice replied. "Some of them get to be a hundred feet tall, or more. They're what wood comes from."

"We know what trees are, idiot!" a new voice snapped.

"Not all of us, we don't," another retorted. "Or at any rate I've never seen any!"

"Well, you'll see plenty of them here," Amy called, while wondering how anyone could have grown to adulthood without seeing a tree.

Then she remembered what she had seen of the Galactic Empire—the backwater world Psi Cassiopeia Two, which was mostly lifeless desert and entirely treeless; the rebel colony on Zeta Leo Three, where she had been held captive on an immense corn farm where the only trees were a handful of six-foot shrubs near the house, obviously just recently planted; and the hollowed-out asteroid called Base One. She might have seen a tree or two somewhere besides that farm, but there certainly hadn't been very many. She had to remember that these people weren't from Earth; most of them weren't even from the equivalent homeworld of the Empire, Terra.

Maybe trees had never evolved anywhere in the Galactic

Empire's universe except Terra. Even so, she would have expected the Imperials to have exported them to all their colonies.

Well, she had expected a lot of things that didn't seem to have happened.

"Your pardon, milady," Raven said from very near behind her, startling Amy. "Might I trouble you to allow me a look?"

"Of course," Amy said, getting out of her seat and allowing Raven to lean over and peer out the port. "I'm afraid you won't be able to see much."

"Indeed," Raven agreed wryly, as he took in the sight of the immense tree trunk. " 'Tis scarcely the broad panorama that one might have hoped for."

"Any idea where we are?"

Raven shook his head. "Marry, milady, though 'tis a grand oak, 'tis hardly one I recognize—for that, how to tell one from the next, an you see but the bole, with no mark upon it save those put there by our craft's descent? The Empire's telepaths were consulted in the devising of yon opening 'tween worlds, and our goal was to arrive far enow from Shadow's demesne for safety, yet close enough to approach it in time, and perchance that's done, but that scarce names a single spot. Grand oaks such as this might be found in any number of suitable places."

Emboldened by Raven's presence, several of the others were now gathering around the port, trying to see out; poor Susan, in the seat beside Amy's, was being crowded quite rudely and was twisted almost into fetal position trying to avoid pressure on her burns.

A rush of anger swept through Amy at the sight of that. It was bad enough that the lot of them had been sent off on this stupid journey before their injuries were fully healed, but all those big, strong, healthy men crowding around poor wounded Susan . . .

"There are other ports you people could open," Amy pointed out sharply.

Before anyone could reply, the door to the cockpit swung open, and Colonel Carson appeared.

"Lord Raven," he called, "we could use you up front."

"Your pardon, milady," Raven said, managing an approximation of a bow despite having his head and shoulders wedged into the narrow space between the back of Amy's seat and a curving steel rib. He withdrew, made his way past the press of bodies, and strode up the aisle to the cockpit.

Without waiting for an invitation, Stoddard rose and followed his master.

Pel took his time undogging the porthole. After all, the ship wasn't going anywhere—not unless the Empire had some utterly uncharacteristic surprise up its collective sleeve, some way to get the thing moving in a universe where antigravity didn't work.

And he didn't really care all that much about Shadow's universe, except as a step back to Earth.

Ted Deranian was sitting beside him, watching as Pel uncovered the port. Ted was smiling foolishly. Looking at him, it was hard for Pel to believe the man had ever gotten through law school; he looked more like a village idiot than like an attorney.

Still, there was something he had said that tickled at the back of Pel's mind. It didn't really make sense unless you accepted Ted's theory that both Shadow's universe and the Empire's universe were all an elaborate dream, but Pel *wanted* to believe it.

It had been said back at Base One, when Ted had found Pel sitting alone, on the verge of tears as he thought about Nancy and Rachel.

"Don't worry, Pel," Ted had told him. "They woke up, that's all—they're back on Earth. When you get back there they'll be waiting for you."

Then he had caught himself and asked, "But why am I talking to you? You're not really here."

He had wandered off, leaving Pel furious at his insensitivity, but the idea that Nancy and Rachel were alive back on Earth had stayed, no matter how hard Pel tried to suppress it.

Maybe they were.

He knew that this wasn't all just a dream, all these strange things they had been through; he knew that Ted had it wrong, and the Empire and Shadow were real. They weren't a dream in the usual sense.

But on the other hand, this was an alien universe; Nancy and Rachel did not belong here. The Empire's universe was equally alien. Had they really, fully crossed over into these alternate realities?

What if they were all really doing some sort of astral travel?

Wouldn't Nancy and Rachel snap back into their own world when their astral selves were destroyed?

Or even if the physical bodies made the transition, was time the same here?

Pel had read plenty of science fiction and fantasy as a kid; he had seen hundreds of movies over the years. Wasn't there always something somehow unstable about someone who had been removed from his or her proper place? What if that wasn't just a literary convention, but a deep subconscious understanding of some fundamental fact about reality?

Mightn't there be some way to change the past, to make Nancy and Rachel to have never left Earth?

He and the others were in another dimension, a parallel world, an alternate reality; they were, as Amy put it, in Faerie. The very existence of such a place went against all common sense and previous experience; it threw Pel and Amy and Susan and Ted into the realm of legend, of myth, of fantasy. How could they know anymore what the rules were? Back home, dead was dead, and nobody came back—but here? Who knew? Death might be different.

Hadn't someone written a story about a land like that? "Death Is Different," that was it—by Lisa Goldstein, perhaps? About a small country somewhere where death wasn't permanent, where the dead could be seen strolling about.

What if that author had somehow known a truth about this place where Shadow ruled? After all, the worlds of Empire and Shadow so resembled the settings for any number of stories that Pel found it hard to believe it a coincidence; it made more sense to credit it to some sort of psychic leakage between universes, images from one realm finding their way into the subconscious minds of writers in another.

And if that was so, what about all those stories where people rose from the dead, where the protagonist awoke at the end home safe in his own bed, everything restored to what it was before? Were those based on truth?

What if death *was* different?

On one level he knew that was nonsense. He knew this was all hard fact; Nancy and Rachel were dead. Cartwright and Godwin and Peabody, Grummetty and Alella and Squire Donald, they were all equally real, and all equally dead, and all really dead. He had seen Grummetty's corpse himself. He had seen Cartwright bleeding as the monsters overwhelmed him. They were all dead, and would stay dead until Judgment Day.

But somewhere, in the back of his mind, where he wanted so much to believe Nancy and Rachel were alive that he could believe anything at all, he still hoped.

He swung open the porthole cover and stared out at the green and gold and deep gray of the forests of Faerie.

CHAPTER 4

Raven of Stormcrack Keep had seen many strange things in the hard, sad days since his brother had betrayed the clan and yielded the keep and its lands to Shadow. He had fled through haunted forests by night and had seen creatures there whose nature he still did not know and dared not contemplate too closely. He had lived for a time among the little people of Hrumph, the people his grandfather had called gnomes, before they were driven into exile; he had dwelt like a giant among them, and had been amazed by their ways and customs. He had fallen in with a handful of the few remaining wizards, had seen them in their own strongholds, where they lived unhampered by the dictates of the nobility and used whatsoever magic they might please. One of those wizards, Elani, had opened for him portals into the Galactic Empire, and into the world of Earth, where he had seen wonders that even the mightiest magic could not equal. He had been slave and supplicant in those other worlds; he had been beaten and abused and still bore scars and wounds not yet healed from those encounters. He had thought that nothing could faze him anymore. But now, as he stared at the men who had piloted the Imperial vessel, he discovered that he had not lost his capacity for surprise.

It was not any new marvel of science or magic that astounded him, but the depths of idiocy to which allegedly intelligent men could sink.

"Colonel," he said, "what might those two be about?" He pointed at the two men crouched beside an open panel, poking at the tangle of wires and baubles inside.

"They're trying to fix the engines, of course," Carson replied edgily.

"Be your engines broken?"

"Well, of course they are!" Carson snapped. "Why else would we have crashed?"

Raven considered this question for a moment, admiring its magnificent ineptitude. "Prithee," he asked eventually, "has none told you the nature of this realm?"

Carson glared at him. "What do you mean?"

Raven hesitated, then waved the matter away. Perhaps it would be best if he were to leave the man's ignorance intact for the moment; an opportunity might arise to exploit it at some other time. "Mayhap later," he said. "Erst, you sought my favor in some matter?"

"Yeah," Carson said, looking distastefully at the broad forward viewport. "I want to know where the heck we are. I'd figured on reconnoitering from the air, taking a look around— but then the drive quit on us. In fact, nothing seems to be working; must be a break in the power system somewhere."

"I fear, sir, that I know not where we be," Raven said. "Did they not tell you where the great portal would be?"

"They told me we'd come out around two hundred miles from this Shadow thing," Carson said. "I didn't listen to all the damn details; I figured we could straighten that out from the air once we came through."

Raven nodded. "And I've no more than that."

"You know this country, don't you?"

"Aye, for the main, an I've landmarks . . ."

"Well, then, take a look, damn it!" Carson waved at the viewport.

Raven looked.

The view here was a good deal more extensive than that from the porthole by Amy Jewell's seat, but it still revealed little more than that they were in a mature forest somewhere. Broken branches and scattered leaves were everywhere. Signs of the ship's fall were strewn in a web of sunlight and shadow; oaks towered overhead, while moss and fungus flourished below. The light was the clean sweet white of home, not the hot glare of Earth's sun, or the harsh blaze of the lights of Base One. He judged from its angle that the day was just short of midmorning.

" 'Tis a forest," Raven said, "and I and mine drew best we could a map for you ere we left, and thereon we indicated those forests we knew—and some would put us your two hundred miles from Shadow's stronghold. How to tell one forest from another, who can say? Saw you aught before we fell—a keep, a mount, any such as that?"

Carson turned and glared at one of the pilots.

"No, sir," the man replied, "we didn't have time to see much of anything. Just trees."

"There might have been mountains off that way," the copilot offered, pointing to the left.

Raven considered that, studying the angle of the sun and the patterns of the moss on the trees. "Then, an those were the Further Corydians, we might be in the West Sunderland," he said at last. "But I've no certainty."

"All right," Carson said, "if we're in Sunderland, where do we go and how will we know if we've got it wrong?"

Raven bit back a retort; he took a second to calm his voice, then replied, "An we're in the Low Forest of West Sunderland, we need but make way to the west, and in due time we should either strike the Palanquin Road, or reach the edge of the forest and the Starlinshire Downs. If it be the road, turning south will bring us in time to the River Vert; if it be the Downs, we should find landmarks enow."

Carson nodded. "And then what?" he demanded.

"And then? Why, then we strike out westward for Shadow's keep, should our plans be made and the omens favorable, and if they be otherwise, then seek we shelter with those who yet serve the cause of the Light." Raven's own plans were already made and consisted mostly of the latter choice, locating a surviving part of the resistance to Shadow's rule; he had no intention of flinging himself against Shadow's keep in some pointless, suicidal raid.

However, throwing Carson and his men into such a raid might be the best way to rid himself of a nuisance and to provide the evidence needed to convince the Empire to devise a *serious* attack. And who could say that they might not learn something from such an assault? To Raven's best knowledge, no one had been foolish enough to attempt anything of the sort in centuries.

"You can contact these others?" Carson snapped.

"Certes, I can," Raven replied, meeting his eye. He had developed the knack of lying straight-faced as a child and had never lost it, but in this case he spoke very nearly the truth. Contact could be made, though it would best be done by a wizard, rather than by himself.

"And they can contact the Empire?"

Raven hesitated. "Aye," he said, "that's within their powers." That was beyond question; the hesitation was due to uncertainty as to the wisdom of letting Carson know it.

He didn't mention that in plain truth, either Elani or Valadrakul could doubtless make contact with others in the anti-Shadow network at any time, now that they were once again in their native realm, where good magic worked as it should. In truth, Elani could most likely make contact with agents in the Galactic Empire at any time, and they could, in their turn, carry messages to the Imperial authorities.

Of course, that would most probably put an end to their usefulness as spies. Furthermore, Raven did not trust the Empire. He would communicate with it only on his own terms, not at the urging of this arrogant oaf of a commoner.

He had not yet fully settled upon his own preferred course of action to be followed once he had found a new place in the resistance. That the Empire had some fool notion of using him as native guide in their assault on Shadow's keep he knew; that he had assented to the Empire's instructions, however, did not mean he would actually obey them. He had agreed because such an agreement was his only way to leave Base One and return to his own world.

Here, though, he was in command. Colonel Carson might not have realized that yet, but Raven knew who was master here, in the natural world, away from the topsy-turvy Empire. He was the heir to Stormcrack Keep, and as such he need take no heed of such as Carson.

Carson glared at the damned foppish barbarian who called himself Raven, trying to decide whether or not he could be trusted.

He didn't *really* trust any foreigner—none of them could think straight. They all had minds as twisty as their infernal streets in those little outworld colonies or the Azean backwaters on Terra. He had been told to cooperate with this Raven, though; the savage was supposed to be sworn to fight Shadow, and it was Shadow that really scared those pissant politicians back home, especially that twit Bascombe in the Department of Science, with his fancy title that he'd made up and got his father-in-law to make official.

And, Carson admitted to himself, the people who gave him his orders might actually know what they were doing this time—though he wouldn't bet his pension on it.

They'd told him that the space warp would put him in a whole new universe, where space itself was different; he'd had his doubts, and for that matter he still wasn't *entirely* convinced that this planet wasn't just someplace off in an odd corner of the galaxy, that the space warp wasn't just a shortcut from here to there, but it did seem to operate as advertised.

They'd told him to expect equipment failures, that some of the machinery wouldn't operate in the space here, maybe most of it, and sure enough, the damn ship had fallen like a rock, the AG drive working about as well as a popped rubber. He still suspected a break in the power feed somewhere, but he couldn't prove it.

So maybe they knew what they were doing when they told him to trust this fancy-talking twit.

"We can breathe the air here?" he demanded.

"Most assuredly," Raven replied gravely.

"All right," Carson growled, "let's get out and take a look around, then, and maybe find these friends of yours."

Amy scuffed one half-booted foot through the dead leaves, enjoying the rustle that made.

It wasn't quite the same sound she'd have gotten doing the same thing back on Earth, in, say, Vermont; the air was slightly thicker here, and the higher gravity made the leaves pack down more tightly. That made it an effort to just stand and breathe, really; the tired irritability that had hounded her ever since her rescue from Walter and Beth, back on Zeta Leo Three, was still with her as well.

Still, it was good to be outdoors again after all the weeks at Base One. They had been lucky enough to arrive on a beautiful day—warm in the sun, cool in the shade—and the contrasts were delightful after the stuffy boredom of the hollowed-out asteroid. And it was good to see trees and leaves; she hadn't realized it, but she had missed them, not seeing a proper forest, or even a decent grove, since she had first arrived in the Galactic Empire.

The rich smells of black earth, rotting leaves, and growing things were absolutely wonderful after weeks of steel walls and stale air.

The forest seemed awfully quiet, though. She heard no birds, no squirrels or other animals; perhaps the spaceship's crash had frightened them away. The heavy, still air wasn't stirring anything overhead, either; the only sounds came from the stranded humans.

She looked up as the Imperial soldiers, in response to a brisk order from Colonel Carson, formed up in a line alongside the ruined spaceship, facing into a small clearing. At the sight of them, all together in their neat uniforms and silly purple helmets, it occurred to Amy that they had all been lucky that the ship had not smashed directly into one of the huge trees.

But then, the trees weren't all that close together, for the most part; a few giants had crowded out most of the lesser competition.

Even so, it appeared to Amy that they had been fortunate in falling into one of the larger gaps. Trees crowded close around the ship's nose and one side, but farther back the vessel lay in a relatively open space—open enough, at any rate, for Carson to stand there and order his men about, while the rest of the party stayed in sight but out of the way.

She saw Raven and Valadrakul exchange a derisive glance at seeing the soldiers standing in their tidy row, chests out and shoulders back.

"Popinjays," Elani muttered, "gaudy purple popinjays, ready to have the stuffing knocked from them."

Stoddard didn't say anything; he crossed his arms on his chest and watched. Pel and Susan were still helping Ted down from the ship and not paying any attention to the rest.

Amy turned and whispered to Elani, "You don't think much of them?"

"Pah!" Elani said, "soldiers such as these perished in their thousands in the wars against Shadow. The others, Captain Cahn and his men, at least showed small signs of wit; this lot, ha!"

"You haven't had a chance to get to know them," Amy protested.

Elani made a noise of disgust. "I need not," she said.

Amy remarked, "Raven seemed eager to have them along."

Elani muttered, "My lord Raven is a wise man at times, but he can be a fool, as well. Look you now and see what he thinks of these."

Amy looked at Raven, who was making no attempt to hide his disdain for Carson and company.

Well, that was fine. It might serve as a distraction.

"Elani," she said, "now that we're here, is your magic working again?"

The wizard turned to look at her. She waved a hand and something flickered briefly in the air, and then vanished.

"Aye," she said, "the craft's with me again."

Amy smiled. "Then we have a favor to ask—Pel and Susan and I."

Elani quirked one side of her mouth upward in a crooked smile of her own. "It seems to me that I might guess whereof you speak," she said. "In truth, I'd wondered when you might speak of it."

"Then you'll do it?"

The wizard shook her head. "In time, aye," she said, "for we'd have none with us who'd not be there freely, and indeed, what would we with such as your man Deranian? And yourself, a dealer in knickknacks and drapery, what have you to do with deeds of high courage and state? So aye, I'll see you home—in time, in good time. But this is no place suitable, nor have we time enow, and 'twould be impolitic to attempt this ere I have spoken to Raven."

Amy pursed her lips and reluctantly nodded. "I can see that," she said.

"And it might have risks, as well," Elani added. "There's reason to believe that the opening of the gates between worlds is what drew Shadow's eyes before, when erst you came to our land. An that be so . . . well, you'll be safe in your own realm, but those of us who remain behind . . ." She shook her head.

"I hadn't thought of that," Amy admitted.

"I had," Elani replied. "But naught of it, i'truth, for I'll have the risk, an you're quick. We'd the gate to Earth a time or two ere ever Shadow caught us at it, and all I ask is that we have at the ready a way to make good our flight when the portal again closes. For that, 'twould seem wise to know better where we stand."

Amy hesitated. "You mean you want to wait until we know where we are?"

"Certes, you have it."

Amy would greatly have preferred it if Elani had opened the portal immediately, but that evidently wasn't going to happen. She frowned, but in the heavy gravity and thick air, with her stomach uneasy, she found that she didn't have the energy to argue.

"All right," she said. "We'll wait."

* * *

Pel watched with interest as the black-garbed nobleman and the purple-uniformed colonel stood almost nose to nose, glaring at each other.

"Colonel," Raven said patiently, "imprimis, you know naught of this land. Would not it be wise, then, to heed the counsel of those who do? Secundus, is't not but common sense to dissemble, when in the enemy's lands?"

Carson glowered at Raven.

"I don't like it," he said. "I want my men in uniform. We aren't a bunch of spies."

"Are we not?" Raven demanded sarcastically. "What are we, then?"

"We are a fighting squad sent to destroy this Shadow of yours, Mr. Raven, or whatever your name is."

"And you think, then, that such a motley party as this can best a power that has laid waste twice a dozen kingdoms and brought all this world 'neath its sway?"

"I think, sir, that one properly disciplined squad of Imperial soldiers can do a better job of damn near anything than any bunch of foreign barbarians!"

Raven threw up his hands in anger and disgust. He turned away and spotted Prossie Thorpe.

"Mistress Thorpe," he called, "come hither, lend me your counsel!"

Several sets of eyes swiveled toward the telepath, who had been leaning against an immense oak and picking idly at the bark.

Prossie started and looked up, dropping flakes of bark. "Me?" she asked.

"Aye," Raven said, beckoning. "You."

Prossie had not expected anyone to notice her presence; she had no idea that she would be dragged into an argument between Raven and Colonel Carson and had hardly even been listening. She sometimes had trouble paying attention to people whose minds were closed to her, and telepathy did not work in this universe—in what Amy called "Faerie." Prossie had picked the name up in passing and rather liked it.

She still found it somewhat odd, being so out of touch with the thoughts of those around her. In fact, after the crowding at Base One, and the constant buzzing of thoughts on all sides, it was rather restful.

And it wasn't the same horrible cut-off loneliness she had felt in her cell on Earth, because here she was in constant contact with her cousin Carrie. That was the communications line between this party and the people back at Base One; it was also a natural and comfortable link between the two women. The two of them could chatter away while Prossie took in the physical sensations of this strange new world.

She had been in Shadow's world once before, but weeks ago, and in a different place. The trees here were taller, older, more imposing, the atmosphere more restful—if warmer, perhaps uncomfortably so.

It was rather intriguing to look at things, to touch things, to smell them, without having any preconceptions impinging from other minds about what the things *should* look like, *should* feel like. Prossie had really been too concerned with other, more urgent matters to take an interest in that before.

So instead of listening to the others, she was picking at the bark of a gigantic oak and enjoying the feel of it when Raven called to her.

She started and looked back at the others.

"Thorpe," Carson said, "get over here."

Reluctantly, Prossie left the oak and obeyed. Her stride was brisk and military; her expression was not.

"Mistress Thorpe," Raven said, "you can look into the minds of others, is't not so?"

"Well, ordinarily, I can," Prossie admitted hesitantly, "but not here, or on Earth. Only in normal . . . I mean, Imperial space."

"Then you cannot see what I am thinking, nor what Colonel Carson believes?"

"No, sir."

"Is that right?" Carson demanded angrily.

"Yes, sir," Prossie said.

"Well, then, what the hell did they send you for," Carson shouted, "if you can't read minds here?"

"I can maintain telepathic contact with my cousin Carrie, sir—Registered Master Telepath Carolyn Hall, that is, back at Base One," Prossie explained. "I can still handle communications with General Hart and the High Command." She did not add that he had been told all this previously; she knew perfectly well that Colonel Carson had ignored most of his briefing, assuming, as he always did, that he knew better than all the pantywaist experts and fat-bottomed generals.

Carson glared at her, and Raven took the opportunity to ask,

"But ere we left Base One, you could see into the minds about you?"

"Yes, sir," Prossie admitted warily. Although it was an interesting novelty, she was never *entirely* comfortable when her telepathic ability was blocked off, and any sort of talking to other people without it was unpleasant. This questioning, about matters she preferred not to discuss, was much worse than ordinary conversation. She had no way of knowing whether Raven suspected that she had illicitly eavesdropped on him earlier. He hadn't suspected anything at the time, but the idea could easily have come to him after the ship passed through the warp.

"And your cousin Carolyn Hall," Raven continued, "she can still see into the minds of others about her?"

"Yes, sir," Prossie admitted, "but there are strict rules to protect privacy."

Carson rumbled, muttering something that might have been a remark about it being a damn good thing. One good thing about having her head blocked off, Prossie thought, was that she could ignore the distrust and hatred everyone felt toward telepaths.

Raven nodded. "Assuredly," he said. "But then, perhaps you could answer a question of mine, as it regards the thoughts of General Hart and the others above you."

Prossie hesitated. "Maybe," she said.

"Perhaps you can tell me, Mistress Thorpe," Raven said, "why these men should have chosen to saddle me with a blockhead such as Colonel Carson."

Prossie's mouth opened, and then closed again. Someone snickered.

Had the time come to admit what she had done and tell them all the truth?

"I didn't snoop . . ." Prossie began uncertainly. Then she stopped. Her expression wavered for a moment; Raven, who had started to turn away from her to argue further with Carson, saw the colonel's expression and turned back.

She had been nervous as Raven and Carson questioned her, but Carrie, who was listening in, had thought the whole affair was thoroughly amusing. Prossie could sense her mental giggling. Carrie could afford to giggle; she was safe at home, not out here in an alien forest.

But then Raven asked why he had been saddled with Colonel Carson, and Carrie, at first amused by the question, had read what Prossie knew.

And suddenly she wasn't giggling, mentally or otherwise. Her amusement had vanished. She sent a feeler out to General Hart, and then to others . . .

By now everyone, from all three universes, was staring at the telepath, though several of them were not sure why. Pel, watching, felt a growing tension; for his own part, he had a sense of impending doom.

But then, he had felt a sense of impending doom for much of the time since Nancy's death.

Prossie's face went oddly blank as Carrie, panicking, pulled her briefly into a full linkage; then her expression returned more or less to normal.

"What troubles you, lady?" Raven asked.

Prossie hesitated, trying to think over what she had read herself, and what Carrie had relayed. Trying to decide what to say, when she couldn't read her listeners' reactions, was very difficult.

"It's a mistake," she said at last. "General Hart . . . there's been a lot of factional fighting about Shadow . . . there were several plans, and they got confused, what with Major Copley being ill. It should have been Captain Haggerty in command, not Colonel Carson . . ."

It was actually worse than that, but Prossie had had a lifetime of not telling everything she knew. She didn't relay what Carrie had just told her.

General Hart's choice of personnel and entire attitude toward the mission had been subtly affected by undeservingly trusted subordinates. Prossie had known that Hart had intended to send an officer he wanted to get rid of, but it had actually gone beyond that.

Colonel Carson had been selected by agents of Shadow as absolutely the worst possible officer for the job.

"Bull!" Carson shouted.

For a moment, Prossie thought Carson was replying to her unspoken thought, but then she realized he was simply denying that his appointment was a mistake.

Prossie felt lost without her mind reading. She knew what everyone wanted: the Earthpeople wanted Elani to send them home; Elani wanted to send them. Raven wanted to take command of the rest and take them to join the underground. Elani and Valadrakul and Stoddard trusted Raven and would support him in whatever he had planned against Shadow.

Most of the fifteen troopers just wanted to finish whatever the job was and go home; they had no idea of what they had gotten into.

And Carson wanted to prove that he was a great leader and a true man among men, but since he was not, in fact, either one, he had no idea at all how to accomplish that.

She knew what they all had wanted, up to the moment they hit the space warp—but what they intended to do about it, she had no idea. Why hadn't the Earthpeople taken Elani aside? Amy had been talking to her, but nothing had come of it, so far as Prossie could see.

Why wasn't Raven playing along with Carson, as he had with Hart? Didn't he see that the man was an arrogant fool who could be coaxed into doing anything, so long as he thought it was his own idea? If Raven didn't see it, what about Valadrakul or Elani?

Prossie wished she could take Raven aside for a few moments, or Elani, or almost any of them, but instead here she was, trapped between Raven and Carson in the most public manner possible. She regretted, now, that she had taken time to look around and admire the trees.

"It's bull, I said," Carson repeated, and Prossie realized that everyone was looking at her. She stared back at Carson. Even without her telepathy, Prossie could almost feel the hate Carson felt for her.

"Maybe I misunderstood something," she said.

"Nay, lady," Raven protested, " 'twould explain much, if this man was sent in error. 'Tis plain he's no master of subtlety and ill-fitted for our task here. What, then, shall I, as a rightful lord, take the charge? What say you all?"

"*I* say it's bloody treason, you barbaric fop!" Carson bellowed. He reached for his sidearm.

Raven stepped back and reached for his sword hilt—but he had no sword. The weapon was lost long since, somewhere back in the Galactic Empire. "Valadrakul!" he called.

Carson's blaster was out and pointed, and Prossie stared at it in horror.

Didn't they know it wouldn't work here?

Carson pulled the trigger as Valadrakul raised his hands; the wizard's fingers twisted strangely as he spoke a word.

For a moment, Prossie thought the blaster had worked after

all, as something flashed, pale and quick as heat lightning, between Carson and Valadrakul. Then she realized that the weapon was pointed at Raven, that the shimmering flare had traveled from the wizard's upraised hands to Carson's body.

For an instant the colonel stood motionless, an expression of astonishment spreading slowly across his features; then it turned to a rictus of pain, and he crumpled to the ground, still holding tight to the useless blaster.

The sound of his fall into the dead leaves seemed impossibly loud and prolonged. Accustomed to a constant telepathic echo behind every voice, the eternal hum of other minds drowning out the ordinary noises of the inanimate universe, Prossie rarely heard mere sound so clearly, but here, in this telepathically dead environment, there were no distractions. She thought she could almost hear each individual leaf crumbling, each separate impact as first one knee, then the other, then a hand and the blaster and the other hand struck, his belly and finally his face landing in the rustling detritus.

And when the sound of the impact had faded, she heard a strange arrhythmic chorus of faint clickings. At first she took it for leaves settling, but then she realized it came from the wrong direction.

She turned and saw a dozen blasters, drawn and aimed, triggers clicking uselessly against copper contacts. Carson's men were avenging their fallen commander—or trying to.

"Men of the Empire!" Raven called, his hands upraised in an orator's gesture. "Yon usurping fool is dead; drop your arms, an you'd not taste the same!"

"The hell you say," someone called.

"Raven," a quiet voice said—a woman's voice, speaking from the side, not from the line of men by the ship.

Startled, Raven turned and found Susan Nguyen standing straight, legs braced, her pistol held out before her, gripped firmly in both hands. Her black handbag, whence the revolver had come, lay open at her feet.

The barrel of the little gun was pointed directly at Valadrakul's head, from a distance of perhaps four feet away. The wizard was utterly motionless, his hands hanging stiffly at his sides.

"*This* gun works here," Susan said, speaking calmly but emphatically. "You've seen it."

"Aye, mistress, I do so recall," Raven replied warily.

"You are not going to hurt anyone else. Neither is Valadrakul. If anyone else is harmed, your wizard dies. Clear enough?"

Raven flicked his gaze to Elani; Prossie's own eyes turned to follow, and she found that Pel and Amy stood one on each side of the female wizard, each gently restraining one of Elani's arms.

"Now," Susan said, "we are all going to sit down quietly and talk this out and settle what we're going to do, and we're going to do it without any sort of violence, because the first person to use violence is going to get a bullet in his gut. Is that clear?"

"Aye, mistress," Raven said, " 'tis plain as the day. And it pleases me well—I'd no wish for strife. Yon fool drew 'gainst me, and I've no blade; am I to perish undefended by the hands of such as he?"

"You know perfectly well that blasters don't work here."

"Ah, but mistress," Raven protested, "in the heat of the moment I misremembered."

Susan did not reply to that.

She didn't lower the gun, either.

For a moment, no one spoke; then Ted Deranian burst out giggling.

"What an anticlimax!" he shouted. "No gunfight, no wizard war! My subconscious is wimping out on me."

"Shut up, Ted," Pel said.

Ted ignored him and turned to Susan.

"Lady, if you're a real person, and I didn't just dream you up," he said, "I sure hope you don't try this sort of thing in the courtroom!"

CHAPTER 5

"*But I tell you, I am your rightful lord!*" Raven shouted.

The Imperial soldiers shuffled their feet and cast uneasy, mocking glances at one another.

"The hell you say," one man muttered.

"Mr. Raven," the lieutenant explained patiently, "leaving aside that you killed the colonel, or at least your man did, and while it may have been self-defense, I'm not saying it wasn't, still, that ain't the approved procedure for promotion, and as I was saying, even leaving that aside, you aren't in the chain of command."

"And I have the word of General Hart that I *am*," Raven insisted.

"You got the paperwork, the signed orders, you let us see 'em," the lieutenant answered. "Otherwise—you don't have the uniform, you don't have the rank, you don't have anything. You're a civilian."

"I am a nobleman born!"

"That don't mean shit to us, sir. Our oath is to the emperor, nobody else. You could be the bloody King of the Franks himself, and we'd still have to tell you to call your dad and get the papers."

Pel, watching and listening from a few yards away, could see that a couple of the soldiers were not happy with that particular claim; he wondered who the King of the Franks was. He supposed it might be a title given to the heir to the throne, like the rank of "Prince of Wales" in Britain. It seemed a very odd thing to him that there would be such archaic titles in an interstellar empire.

"Listen, man," Raven argued, "your master is dead, and you are in the enemy's lands, lands that you know naught of, and

46

where I am all that you have to guide you. Your lord, the General Hart, sent you hither to aid me—me, and none other. Then is't not madness and folly to deny that command is fallen to me, that Colonel Carson is no more?"

"Mr. Raven," the lieutenant explained wearily, "you are not in the chain of command. I *am*. I was the colonel's second-in-command, and with him gone, *I* am in command. *You* are a civilian, and as long as you are, you can't possibly assume command. That doesn't mean we can't cooperate."

"Permission to speak, Lieutenant?" one of the men called.

Startled, Raven and the lieutenant turned.

The man who had spoken—Pel didn't know any of the soldiers' names yet—was leaning comfortably against a tree; now he straightened and pointed to Prossie. "We've got a mu . . . I mean, a telepath with us, Lieutenant," he said. "Why not ask *her*? Check with Base?"

"Aw, come on," someone called. "She's the one who started this and got the colonel killed!"

"No, that was the guy over there in the funny clothes," another voice protested.

"I don't mean she killed him," the first replied, "but she was the one who said things were screwed up!"

"So maybe they *were* screwed up!"

The lieutenant looked over his men, chewing his lip as he did so, then turned to look consideringly at Prossie.

"All right, Thorpe," he said, "you call home and tell us what we're supposed to do."

" 'Tis a waste . . ." Raven began.

The lieutenant thrust out a warning hand.

Susan Nguyen cleared her throat warningly.

Raven fell silent, and two score eyes focused on the telepath.

When Colonel Carson fell, Prossie had not waited for orders; she had immediately relayed the news to Carrie and told her to tell someone in authority.

Carrie had done so—she had left her cubicle and gone running for the Office of Interdimensional Affairs. Her orders were to report anything received from other universes to the undersecretary, and that included messages from Prossie, as well as contacts with the handful of psychics on Earth, or with Shadow's creatures.

The undersecretary was not in.

"It's urgent," Carrie told the receptionist.

"I'm sure it is," the receptionist replied. "Have a seat, and the undersecretary will be back momentarily."

Carrie hesitated and glanced toward the door—she made it look as if she were seeing if there were any sign of the undersecretary's approach, but in fact she was turning away so as not to stare while she read the receptionist's mind in hopes of finding out just where the undersecretary was.

The receptionist was not thinking about Undersecretary John Bascombe; she was thinking about an idealized, muscular, blond, and handsome male figure. This was the man she felt she deserved to have married, and she was convinced that she had not found him because telepaths, with their sneaking and spying, had stolen him away. There were hundreds of the dirty mutants out there, far more than anyone knew, but they kept themselves secret, only a few admitted what they were in order to get into the government where they could spy on everything better and steal all the good men away from deserving ordinary women.

It took Carrie several seconds to dig down past this depressingly familiar paranoid fantasy and locate recent memories.

"Why don't you sit down?" the receptionist asked, mentally adding, "Mutant bitch."

Carrie realized she had been staring foolishly out the door of the office. The receptionist, despite her belief in a conspiracy of evil, lawless telepaths, didn't yet realize that her thoughts had been illicitly spied on, but the idea might occur to her at any second.

"No, that's all right," Carrie said, "I'll try again later." She turned and headed back out into the corridor.

The undersecretary had been taking a long lunch and was lingering over his final cup of tea; Carrie hurried to the cafeteria, to catch him before he left.

He looked up in surprise as she entered.

"Telepath," he said, "what are you doing here? This room's off-limits for you!"

"Yes, sir," Carrie said, "but I think this is an emergency."

He put down his cup.

"Colonel Carson has been killed, sir," Carrie told him, coming to attention.

"By Shadow?"

"No, sir. By one of the wizards in his own party."

Bascombe let out a long, deep sigh. "Are you sure?"

"Yes, sir."

"Well, get out of here, anyway—no telepaths are allowed in here. I'll be out in a moment."

"Yes, sir." Carrie turned and trotted out to the hall.

She waited, and a moment later the undersecretary emerged, walking quickly. "Come along," he ordered.

She followed, but to her surprise he did not return to his own office; instead he led her down to Level Six, to General Hart's office.

Five minutes later the three of them, Hart and Bascombe and Carrie, were seated in Hart's office with the door closed.

"Now," Hart said, "tell us all about it."

"They're still arguing," Prossie told the others.

"Who is?" Lieutenant Dibbs demanded.

"General Hart and the Undersecretary for Interdimensional Affairs," Prossie replied.

"Just what are they arguing *about*?" Amy asked.

That was not easy for Prossie to answer. Carrie was relaying not just the two men's words, but some of their thoughts, as well. While the spoken debate purported to be a discussion of the best way to insure the survival of the rest of the expeditionary force, the actual subject, as both men knew, was the fact that General Hart had deliberately tried to screw up the undersecretary's project and had been caught at it. Both Hart and Bascombe knew, however, that Bascombe could not come out and say that openly—if the mission failed, he would take at least part of the blame and trying to shift it to Hart would just make him look worse.

He could, however, take Hart down with him, in a variety of ways, since Hart's sabotage had shown up so quickly. If the party had been wiped out by Shadow's forces, both men would have been able to get out cleanly—underestimating the enemy was a mistake, but an understandable and forgivable one, relatively minor, nothing at all like deliberately sending people to be killed.

So each man was now looking for a way out that would leave him blameless. Branding Raven as a dangerous lunatic or treacherous foreign outlaw was one possibility—in that case, Lieutenant Dibbs should be put in command and Raven arrested or killed. Denouncing Carson posthumously as a renegade was also a possibility, but if he had surviving family or friends that might be risky. And in either case, what should the survivors do next? Should they continue their mission and attempt to penetrate Shadow's stronghold, or should they abandon the enterprise, take shelter, and wait for rescue?

That latter possibility assumed that rescue was possible. General Hart was not at all clear on how travel between universes worked; the undersecretary had a better grasp of the subject, but did not care to enlighten a man who was, when all was said and done, his political adversary. And even knowing what he did, the undersecretary was thinking in terms of reopening the space warp and lowering a line; the possibility of using wizards' magic had not yet occurred to him.

"Whether to continue the mission," Prossie said.

Amy was seated cross-legged on dry, dead leaves, forearms resting on her knees, watching as Raven and the Imperials argued, and feeling sweat moisten the back of her T-shirt; it wasn't really very hot, and she hadn't been doing anything very active, but the thicker air seemed to make perspiration come more easily. She felt a vague discomfort in the general vicinity of her stomach, as well, and wasn't sure whether or not that could be attributed to the climate and atmosphere.

Beside her stood Elani; Amy was staying close to the wizard, who was, after all, her ticket to Earth, to peace and sanity and her own home.

As far as Amy was concerned, it made no difference at all who was in charge of the group, so long as Raven agreed to let Elani send the Earthpeople home.

Still, she could see that it mattered very much indeed to some people—with a shudder, she stole a glance at Colonel Carson's body, lying undisturbed on its bed of fallen leaves.

More death. That was not anything she wanted to see. She had managed to live forty years on Earth without seeing more than half a dozen corpses, and those were mostly at funerals; she had never seen anyone die until she had stupidly agreed to step through Pel's basement wall and take a quick look at Raven's world.

But then there had been Cartwright, killed by Shadow's monsters—though he might have still been alive, Amy told herself, when she escaped through the portal into the Empire. There had been Peabody, killed by the pirates aboard *Emerald Princess*. And others. She hadn't seen them all die, but Pel's wife Nancy was dead, and their daughter Rachel, and

Raven's friend Squire Donald, and Lieutenant Godwin, and the two little people, Grummetty and Alella. People aboard the *Princess*—she didn't know all the names. People killed in the fighting when the Empire's Task Force Umber came to the rescue.

And the two on Zeta Leo Three who had held her prisoner, Walter and Beth—they had both been hanged by the Empire. She hadn't seen that, it had happened after she was aboard *Emperor Edward VII* on her way to Base One, but it had happened, and the two of them were dead, and it was partly her fault.

It was partly their *own* damn fault, of course, for keeping slaves and abusing her and killing that other woman, whatsername, Sheila. Walter was a murderer, and Beth was his accomplice—but if Amy had kept her mouth shut, probably no one would have known that, and the two of them would still be alive in an Imperial prison camp somewhere.

If anyone asked her now, she wouldn't testify—she was over the need for vengeance and had had her fill of death. She looked at Carson's body and swallowed hard, feeling suddenly queasy.

Elani looked down at her, eyes bright.

"Is aught amiss, lady?" the wizard asked.

"I don't know," Amy replied. She felt no need to explain her misgivings. "I just don't feel very good."

"Ah, certes, you'd be home, I'll wager. Well, methinks this parley is near its end, and we'll soon be sending you hence." Elani's motherly smile suddenly dimmed. "Or be it more? Have you the Sight, lady? Is there danger?" She raised her head and lifted a hand.

Amy started to protest, then stopped.

If Elani wanted to check for danger, it might not be necessary, but it couldn't hurt.

"An they summon you home," Raven said, " 'twould be simple courtesy that I call for volunteers 'mongst your men."

"My men are under *my* orders," Lieutenant Dibbs insisted loudly.

"Ah, but you'll see that *you* might soon be under *my* orders, an your superiors so state—true?"

"Yes, sir," Dibbs agreed, "but until I get orders to that effect, I'll just do as I think best. And if we're ordered home, we go home. Thorpe, any word yet?"

Prossie shook her head. "They're still talking," she said. "I think they're planning to go on, but they haven't settled the details."

"They've said naught of who's to command?" Raven asked.

"No."

"Have you inquired?"

Prossie hesitated.

"Lord Raven," she said, "I've told Carrie that we need to know who's in charge, but she can't just interrupt a general and an undersecretary, she can't make them listen to her. They've got what they consider more important matters to settle first. If it's any help, the undersecretary wants to put you in charge, but General Hart says you should be in an advisory capacity, since you're not only not in the military, you aren't even an Imperial subject."

"Ah . . ." Raven turned away angrily, spat on the ground, then turned back. "You've no doubt of that, lady? That lying scoundrel Hart would have me play the native guide and no more, and his promises that I'd command are no more than devil's smoke?"

"I'm afraid so," Prossie said.

"In my own land, he'd have me a mere servant to this ill-born stripling?" Raven gestured toward Dibbs with the three bandaged fingers of his left hand.

Prossie nodded.

"I'll not have it," Raven shouted, "I will not and I shall not!"

"So what are you going to do about it, then?" Dibbs demanded.

The rightful lord of Stormcrack Keep turned his attention from raging at the treetops to defending his right. "Silence, fool," Raven commanded. "Hast forgotten that thy undersecretary would place me above thee? Durst address thus one who shall perhaps shortly hold thee in thrall?"

"I'm a freeborn Imperial citizen, sir, and I'll speak as I please," Dibbs retorted.

Raven grabbed at his swordless belt in frustration and cast a glance at Susan. The revolver was no longer aimed directly at Valadrakul's head, but it was still held securely in the lawyer's hands.

" 'Tis all . . ." he began.

"Raven!" Elani cried, interrupting him. "Shadow!"

Pel, who had been sitting nearby and listening to the debate, started; he looked about wildly, but saw only the downed spaceship, the cluster of people, the surrounding trees and underbrush.

"Damn!" Raven said. He, for one, clearly did not doubt Elani for a moment. "Valadrakul, wards!" he called. "Elani, where away?"

Elani pointed upward and to one side, past the spaceship's nose.

"We're under attack?" Susan asked, turning the gun away from Valadrakul.

"It's a trick, lady," one of the soldiers called. "He's just trying to get the gun!"

Susan started, and her grip on the pistol tightened, but none of the natives of "Faerie" were paying any attention. Raven was looking about for cover, glancing every so often at the sky; Stoddard was shading his eyes and looking up at the treetops; Elani and Valadrakul were both muttering and gesturing, preparing spells.

Pel got slowly to his feet, not sure just why, or what he hoped to do; he was unarmed and had no way to fight if Shadow's creatures really were approaching.

"Aye," Elani called, in a pause between mumbles, "Shadow's creatures draw nigh. Hellbeasts, carried by another, one that flies—they approach, yonder—a score, perhaps, aboard the flyer!"

The Earthpeople and the Imperials stood, baffled, or milled about in confusion; the natives were more alert. "Shelter in the ship?" Stoddard asked, nodding toward *Christopher*.

"Nay," Raven replied, "an we might be trapped within and besieged, or the vessel crushed and us thereby."

Stoddard nodded an acknowledgment; Pel, who had been heading for the door of the ship without realizing it, stopped dead in his tracks.

A better means of escape occurred to him. "Elani," he called, "can you get us out of here? Open a portal?"

Amy had gotten to her feet, as well, and was standing close beside the little wizard; she added her own voice, saying, "Please, Elani?"

The sorceress shook her head. "We've not the time," she said.

"Look!" one of the soldiers called, pointing upward.

Something big and black was moving, up above the trees,

blocking the sunlight and plunging them into shadow. Pel, watching it, thought it resembled a blimp passing overhead. Did Shadow use airships?

"All right, men," Lieutenant Dibbs called, "form up, two lines, helmets on, weapons ready."

"No," Raven shouted, "flee! Take shelter, wherever you may!"

"These are *my men* ..." Dibbs began.

"Sir," a soldier said, cutting him off, "our blasters don't work here."

Dibbs froze for a second, then said, "Damn. All right, then, we'll take cover—but in proper order. We aren't running away. Shelby, you take that end, and the rest of you form up, we'll move over there, under the starboard vane."

"Lieutenant ..." another man began.

"Move!"

For a moment, no one spoke; leaves rustled, boots stamped, as everyone did what he or she thought best to prepare for an assault. A faint humming that reminded Pel of distant insects came from somewhere overhead, and he realized it came from that dark shape.

Pel remembered his previous visit to Shadow's realm and the horrific fight near the forester's hut on Stormcrack lands, the fight where Spaceman First Class Cartwright had died; there, Shadow's creatures had burst up through the ground and come showering out of the trees from every direction. There was no safe place. The only chance to survive was flight.

He considered turning to run now, dashing off into the forest at random, but that, he realized, might just take him into the jaws of some slimy black monstrosity.

Besides, if he died, perhaps he would be reunited with Nancy and Rachel. If he died bravely, went down fighting, didn't he *deserve* to join them, wherever they were? Maybe if he died here he would wake up safely back home on Earth, in his own bed, alive and well.

But there was no point in being stupid, in making it easy for Shadow. He headed for Valadrakul and Susan. Valadrakul had his spells, Susan her revolver.

" 'Tisn't seeking us," Elani said abruptly, breaking the silence.

"Is't not?" Raven asked, startled. Pel saw that the nobleman had found a broken limb among the debris that the ship had brought down and was holding it in his right hand like a club. His bandaged left hand was empty.

"Nay. 'Tis come to study the portal that brought us hither."

Pel started to relax, then realized what that could mean. "It'll find us soon enough, then," he said.

"An it flies not on through, into Empire, aye," Elani agreed.

"Mistress Thorpe," Raven called, "can you send word, warn those who remain at Base One?"

"Of course, sir," Prossie replied, "but I can't promise they'll pay any attention."

Raven muttered a word Pel didn't catch. It sounded like an archaic obscenity.

"The flying creature is at yon portal," Elani announced, pointing upward.

"Goes it through?" Raven called.

Pel looked about and saw that the party had collected into three groups—and one individual.

One group consisted of Elani, Amy, and Ted, clustered at the base of a large tree of undetermined species; another was composed of himself, Susan, Valadrakul, Stoddard, and Prossie Thorpe, standing by the side of the downed ship; and the third was made up of Lieutenant Dibbs and his fourteen men, gathered under the ship's stubby wing, farther astern. Raven stood alone, on an upthrust root of a gigantic oak, swinging his makeshift club stiffly and watching the leaves overhead.

And Colonel Carson's body lay in the open part of the little clearing between the ship and the trees, near the center of the uneven quadrilateral formed by the survivors. Pel turned away and found himself looking at the dead officer's troops.

Dibbs had his men arranged in two rows of seven, one line facing forward, the other aft, with himself at the outer end; all of them were crouching, as the fin provided slightly less than six feet of headroom. Some, Pel saw, were clutching their blasters by the barrels; others were searching the ground for sticks or rocks.

"Are there any other weapons aboard the ship?" Pel called to the lieutenant, shifting back to the rear of his own cluster.

Dibbs shook his head.

"Nay," Elani cried. "It turns away! It senses us!"

A dozen faces turned upward.

And a moment later, a dozen assorted black-winged horrors plunged down through the green leaves, claws outstretched, fanged mouths agape.

CHAPTER 6

Valadrakul gestured, and the foremost hellbeast exploded in golden fire. Pel ducked instinctively as football-sized gobbets of black slime spattered across the ground and the side of the ship. Another flash he guessed to be Elani's doing.

The other hellbeasts came on without slowing, and before Pel could raise his head one of them struck him on the shoulders and spun him around, slamming him against the hull. Dazed, he could see nothing but purple paint on smooth metal as sharp claws or teeth—he couldn't tell which—chewed at the back of his head.

Then there came a brilliant yellow flash, and Pel could feel things sliding down his back, across his buttocks, and down the backs of his legs.

People were screaming, he could hear them, and there were other noises, gnashings and scratchings and gurglings. He heard a loud popping and realized that it was the sound of a gunshot—Susan had fired her pistol. Another flash sent spots dancing before his eyes.

He remembered the other fight against Shadow's creatures. That had been different; they had come up from beneath the ground, rather than down from the sky, and then hundreds more had come in from all sides, from the surrounding forest. There had been no warning at all, and the group there had been somewhat different—Cahn and his crew were there instead of Dibbs and his squad; the little people had still been alive; and Nancy and Rachel were there. There had been no ship, but a woodshed with a magical portal in it, and the party, hopelessly outnumbered and outmatched, had fled through the portal.

This time, there was no portal—unless one of the wizards

57

could open one, and that seemed unlikely, in the midst of battle, without any previous preparation. Pel knew nothing about how the portals worked, but he remembered that Elani had needed several minutes to open one.

If they faced those limitless hordes again, the hundreds of horrible things that had come leaping out of the forest, they were surely all as good as dead. A few might escape into the surrounding forest, but what would become of them then? They would be lost, to starve or be picked off one by one by Shadow's creatures.

Maybe, Pel thought, it was almost over. Maybe, in a few minutes, he would be joining Nancy and Rachel—either in death, or waking up again safely back home on Earth.

Unsteadily, shielding his face with one arm and bracing himself against the ship with the other, Pel turned.

Twisted fragments of monster were strewn everywhere, horribly out of place in the bright midday sun—some like the remains of a gigantic burst black balloon, some like black jelly, some like charred driftwood or burned roasts, all dark and harsh against the gentler colors of the forest. Valadrakul stood amid the debris, systematically targeting the survivors. Amy and Ted and Elani were all down, lying on the ground with hellbeasts atop them. As Pel watched, something in that heap flashed white, but the monsters continued their assault. Whatever magic Elani had attempted had not worked.

Pel's own group, by the ship, was also under attack—there were creatures assaulting Prossie Thorpe and Stoddard, and one lay dead at Susan's feet, the back of its head blown apart. Pel judged that Susan had thrust the .38 into its mouth before pulling the trigger.

A single monster had gone after Raven, who had warded it off with his club; the antagonists were now facing off, a few feet apart. It seemed to Pel that there was something unnatural about Raven's position, and for a second that puzzled him. Then he realized what it was; the natural pose for a man with a club would be to hold the weapon in both hands, or to keep his free hand up, ready to grab. Instead, Raven's bandaged left hand hung uselessly at his side.

None of the beasts had attacked the Imperial soldiers; hiding under the ship's wing had apparently been a successful ploy. Pel found himself irrationally resenting that.

And there was no second wave, no throng of monsters spill-

ing out of the trees and underbrush. In fact, this time the humans seemed to be getting the better of the fight.

Stoddard had his attacker, a thing like a greyhound with bat-
wings and elongated, tentacular forelegs, by the throat, and
was squeezing; the monster was trying to wrap its own snakelike limbs around the big man's neck in return, but its head
was twisted back so that it could not see its foe, and Stoddard
jerked it from side to side, so that it was having trouble finding
its target.

Prossie's opponent was smaller, and resembled a flying spider, or perhaps a winged monkey; at first glance it didn't look
big enough to be seriously dangerous, but Pel could see blood
on Prossie's hair and uniform as she rolled on the ground
struggling with it.

"Lieutenant!" Pel shouted. "Do something!"

Valadrakul flung out a hand, and the thing attacking Prossie
exploded.

One hellbeast had landed atop Colonel Carson's corpse; realizing at last that its prey was already dead, it turned toward
the ship and slithered forward, wings dragging behind. Pel was
not sure who it was aiming for, Valadrakul or Prossie or himself.

Stoddard began slamming his antagonist against the side of
Christopher, a steady dull thudding.

"Come on, men!" Dibbs called; he came charging out of his
shelter brandishing a thick chunk of tree limb. Several soldiers
followed; Pel, startled, saw that three or four did not, but remained where they were, huddled under the guidance vane.

Half a dozen men landed atop the slithering creature, arms
rising and falling as they pounded at it with rocks and clubs;
other men flung themselves at the two monsters that were still
atop Elani's group.

A sharp crack sounded, and Stoddard's creature went limp.
Thin liquid oozed down the side of the ship.

Valadrakul worked his magic once more, and Raven's opponent burst into ruin without ever striking a blow.

In seconds, the remaining creatures were dead, and the humans were brushing themselves off, gingerly testing wounds,
assessing the damage.

Pel had superficial scratches on his head and back, and the
T-shirt he wore had been shredded, but he was not seriously
injured. None of the soldiers had received anything worse than
a few scratches on their hands and arms. Valadrakul and Raven

were untouched; Stoddard had bruises on one forearm and a red abrasion on the side of his neck.

Prossie had received dozens of shallow slashes from the razor-edged feet of the thing she had fought and had lost enough blood to make her dizzy. She sat against the base of a tree, resting, while the others gathered.

Elani, Amy, and Ted were in a pile, under several dead monsters; it took the others a few moments to dig them out.

Ted was on the bottom and had had the wind knocked out of him, but had otherwise not visibly damaged any further than he had been before. The bandage on his head had been torn off, but the wound beneath appeared no worse.

Amy had three long gashes on one forearm, but had fended off all other attacks; she was pulled upright, dazed and panting.

Elani was dead; she had thrown herself atop the other two, and one of the monsters had torn open the back of her neck, as well as slashing at her head and elsewhere. Her hair and clothing appeared singed, though none of the creatures had used fire in their attacks. Pel wondered if some sort of acid or venom might have been responsible.

"I thought she was supposed to be a wizard," one of the Imperials muttered.

"She was," Prossie said.

"Then why didn't she defend herself, the way whatsisname did?"

"She defended Ted, instead," Amy explained dully, staring down at the dead sorceress. "She saw he wasn't moving, so she destroyed the one that went for him, instead of the one that was after her."

"I saw a flash," Pel said, "but it didn't seem to do any good."

"That was the last time," Amy said. "I'm not sure . . ."

" 'Twas her death," Valadrakul said, interrupting. "At a wizard's death the web of energies that's been woven about her through all her life comes unraveled all in an instant, and betimes there's a flash, or a display of one sort or another." He stared at Elani's remains with an expression Pel couldn't interpret—it might have been grief, or anger, or almost anything.

"Well, we . . ." Dibbs began. He cut off short and looked up, startled, as a deep shadow suddenly fell over the party, blotting out the patchy sunlight.

"What's that?" a soldier asked.

"The big one," Valadrakul said, looking up, his face suddenly intent. " 'Tis the hellbeast that carried the others hither." He raised his arms and began a spell.

"Is it attacking, too?"

No one answered, but from overhead came a sudden snapping and crunching—tree branches were being smashed aside as the thing tried to fight its way to the ground. Leaves and twigs showered down.

Pel looked up, puzzled, trying to locate the descending creature. The trees and shadows made it difficult to see just what was happening.

"Why doesn't it just come through the hole the ship left?" he asked no one in particular.

Valadrakul was too busy with his magic to answer, and no one else had a ready reply, but then Pel managed to figure out what he was looking at, and realized why. The thing *was* coming through the hole the ship had left. It still had to break off limbs.

Otherwise, it couldn't fit.

Prossie stared up at the hellbeast in weak and horrified fascination. Behind her, someone screamed, but she didn't bother to turn and look.

She had heard stories about animals of incredible size that were found on various obscure planets on the outskirts of the Empire—or even worlds that were closer in, but off the main routes. She had generally assumed that such tales were exaggerated; she knew that nontelepaths had a tendency to distort things. Telepaths had something of a self-correcting mechanism, since their memories would automatically be compared with those of the other telepaths, and even so, some events grew in the retelling, so it was no wonder that nontelepaths might blow things all out of proportion.

On the other hand, it was a big universe, and the Empire was full of marvels, so she had never completely dismissed stories of beasts the size of spaceships.

But now that she was actually looking straight up at one, she found it impossible to believe. That thing up there could *not* be real, she told herself.

A heavy tree limb plummeted down and smashed ringingly against the grounded spaceship's metal hull, leaving the opening in the treetops a little larger, giving her a better look at the thing. She stared up, ignoring the leaves, bark, and branches that fell around her.

The hellbeast was roughly bat-shaped, with a huge, bloated body the length of *Christopher* but easily twice as thick. The head was raw nightmare, with saw-edged ears the size of sails, man-sized compound eyes where each facet was a slit-pupiled green disk, and a mouth that could swallow an aircar. The clustered fangs were like swords, and the dangling purple tongue, thick as a man's thigh, writhed like a wounded squid's tentacle.

The wings were still tangled in the surrounding trees, tearing their way through; Prossie glimpsed at least four sets of claws, rather than the two that an ordinary bat would have. And the monster's shadow covered *Christopher*, the narrow clearing where the ship had fallen, and a broad stretch of forest to either side.

There was simply no way such a creature could exist in any sane universe.

But then Prossie reminded herself that she was not *in* a sane universe—she was in Shadow's realm, in Faerie, where magic ruled and science was powerless.

Regardless of what universe it was, there was still only one sensible reaction to such a monster, and that was to run. The thing might be able to smash its way through the forest, but judging by how slowly it was making its way down to the ship it would not be able to do it with any speed; she ought, she thought, to be able to escape it easily, even in her weak, wounded condition.

She forced herself up onto her feet, bracing herself against the tree she had sat beneath, and was about to flee when Carrie's mental voice called to her.

"Prossie, they want you to continue the mission, to go on to Shadow's fortress."

Prossie stumbled and looked up at the monster overhead.

She hadn't been transmitting, there was no way that Carrie could have known what was going on here, but still, the message seemed so irrelevant as to be ridiculous. A dozen dead monstrosities were scattered across the landscape, she was bleeding from a dozen cuts, Elani had been killed, and a nightmare with a quarter-mile wingspan was fighting its way down through the forest, trying to get at them—who *cared* what a couple of pompous idiots back at Base One wanted? She turned to run.

As she turned, she glimpsed Valadrakul as he flung his spell at the gigantic creature; eldritch energy flashed upward from his raised hands, and sparks flickered across the monster's belly—but that was all. Nothing exploded; no tattered bits of black monster flesh fell.

A faint whiff of something unpleasant reached her nose as she ran, but Prossie could not tell whether that meant Valadrakul's attack had singed the thing slightly, or whether it was the monster's natural aroma.

Prossie glanced back over her shoulder and saw Susan point her pistol at the thing. The lawyer looked at the weapon in her hand, then up at the descending horror; she let out a quick bark of laughter and dropped the gun in her handbag, turned, and ran, following Prossie.

Most of the others were scattering now, as well, and Prossie could only see a few of them; the rest had vanished behind the trees. Valadrakul was standing his ground, chanting; Ted Deranian was lying where he had fallen, watching everything, not moving; but all the others were departing or already gone, at paces ranging from a slow, backward-facing, step-by-step retreat to a full-tilt heedless run.

Prossie's own pace was somewhere in between; she was moving at a brisk trot, but watching where she was going and glancing back every so often. She didn't need any more scrapes or scratches, and she didn't want to leave a trail of her own blood for any of Shadow's creatures to follow. Right now, she really didn't want to think about the fight against Shadow itself, or what was happening back at Base One, or long-term plans of any kind; she just wanted to get away, to stay alive and in one piece.

Amy had panicked. When she had seen that thing coming down through the trees, had seen its shadow block out the sun, had been showered with twigs and leaves as it broke past the treetops, she had frozen for an instant, and then she had screamed, and she had turned and run.

It was all too much: Colonel Carson's death and the hellbeasts, Elani falling on top of her and dying there, and then that gigantic horror appearing overhead. She had gotten used to the relatively sane and normal life at Base One, and this succession of shocks had broken her nerve temporarily.

But only temporarily. As she stumbled across the uneven

floor of the forest she was slowed by the irregular footing, by mounting nausea, and by a wave of guilt.

She knew better. Running away didn't solve anything, that's what the counselors and therapists all said. A person must face her fears. The others were still back there, fighting that thing.

She forced herself to stop and turn around.

For a moment, as she stood sweaty and panting, her gashed arm throbbing, she could not see the monster or the ship, only trees—she had covered more ground than she had thought. In her unthinking panic it had seemed as if the creature was right behind her, just inches away; that it was not seemed somehow miraculous.

And then an entirely new sort of panic set in—she was alone, lost in the forest, wounded, with no one to help her, and no chance at all of finding her way home. For an instant, from sheer terror, she stopped breathing.

And when the sound of her own breath stopped, she could hear the sounds from the ship—wood breaking, people shouting. She followed them with her gaze and spotted first the hellbeast's shadow, then the spaceship, and finally the creature itself.

It was at that moment that Valadrakul flung his new spell; Amy could see it spilling upward from a tiny figure she had not realized was there until the orange plume of fiery magic burst forth.

The scene was so distant that it didn't seem entirely real; framed between two tree trunks, it was like a tableau, like some sort of outdoor drama staged for her amusement. The spell was a special effect, something midway between smoke and flame, vividly painted across the image but not entirely convincing. It wove upward through the air, moving not with the speed of fire, nor the slow grace of smoke, but like the ascending trail of a skyrocket on the Fourth of July.

And then it entered the creature's mouth, and something exploded, and for a moment light and smoke seemed to obscure everything. Amy had a glimpse of what looked like glowing green crystals where the creature's eyes should be.

The sound of the explosion reached her, a dull thud that echoed and reechoed through the forest; she blinked, and when her eyes were open again the monster was falling down through the air, covering the spaceship and the wizard in a lumpy black shroud.

Amy blinked again.

The wizard—that was Valadrakul.

The other wizard, Elani, was dead; with a shock, Amy realized that she still had Elani's blood on her, in her hair and on her borrowed T-shirt, smeared down her right arm, and across the back of her hand.

Elani, the wizard who had agreed to send them home to Earth, was dead.

And Valadrakul, buried under the dying monster, was the only other wizard in the group.

"No!" Amy shrieked. "No, no, no!" Her feet seemed to move of their own accord, and she found herself running back toward the clearing, the ship, and the monster just as desperately as she had fled a moment before.

Upon first spotting the hellbeast above, Raven had known instantly that this gigantic manifestation of Shadow's malice could only be fought with magic; his makeshift club could be of no effect against a beast the size of a castle.

This was Valadrakul's fight, then. Elani was fallen, and her skills had never lain in the area of combat, in any case.

"An I can serve," Raven called, "you need but speak!"

Valadrakul ignored him—and quite rightly.

A woman screamed, and Raven heard running feet. For his own part, he bethought him that a cautious retreat might be advised, lest he be struck down by the monster's struggles, all unintended. He began pacing slowly back, away from the wizard and the arena.

The first spell was launched, to no effect, but that troubled Raven not a whit; Valadrakul was but trying out his foe, using against it the spell that had sufficed to destroy the lesser beasts. Raven had seen wizards do the same upon many a previous occasion.

Debris was falling freely now, leaves and branches; Raven retreated farther. He judged that the monster was free of obstructions and stared upward, trying to determine why it did not fall, in all its fury, upon those below.

Men were shouting—undoubtedly the odious Dibbs and his underlings, but Raven spared no glance for such as they.

The beast, he could see, was gripping the great trees with its claws, holding itself aloft as it studied what lay below. It could see the sky ship, but surely knew not what it might be. Likewise could it see Valadrakul; did it know him for what he was?

If so, it might strike him down before another spell could be cast.

Raven hesitated. Valadrakul was too intrigued in his magicks to move of his own choice; should one then try to pull him thence, out from beneath his foe, ere disaster might arrive? An it might disrupt a casting, yet would it save the wizard to fight again.

Ere he could decide, another spell went up—no mere bolt like the last, but a torrent of glowing force, orange and gray, smoke and fire bound into one. It leapt up from the wizard's hands and into the beast's gaping maw.

The thing, in anticipation of the attack, had released its hold upon the trees, had drawn in its claws, and had begun to fold its great wings.

And then all happened with such speed that Raven could not follow. Valadrakul's fire caught at the inside of the monster's throat, and its head seemed to be burned out from within, the glow of the flames visible for an instant through its crystalline eyes; smoke and fire billowed forth, obscuring all; and the creature fell.

Sound and wind forced Raven back; he flung up his arms to protect his face, and thus did not see the actual impact. The rush of air knocked him back against a tree; his head struck hard against the wood, and for a moment his thoughts were scattered.

When he could see again, and understand what he saw, the spaceship was gone from his sight. The clearing, too, was gone. Valadrakul was gone, and Colonel Carson's remains, and poor Elani's. The demented Earthman, Ted Deranian, had vanished as well.

And in the place of all of them was only a great black heap.

It needed a moment ere Raven understood that that heap was the remains of the fallen bat creature.

And that Ted Deranian and Valadrakul lay somewhere beneath it.

CHAPTER 7

Pel approached the dead monstrosity carefully. The thing was obviously dead or dying; Valadrakul's fireball, or whatever it was, appeared to have burned out the entire interior of its skull, and surely even one of Shadow's magical creations couldn't survive that.

But on the other hand, with a thing that size, even a final spastic twitch of a wing could probably break a person's neck.

He saw no twitching, though. He couldn't hear if the thing was making any sounds; Amy was screaming as she ran toward him, drowning out almost everything else.

Her screaming was not particularly piercing, just loud; Pel judged that she was not so much frightened or hurt as working off accumulated tension. He ignored the screams and looked the situation over.

The body had fallen directly atop ISS *Christopher* and then slid partway down the far side, but the outstretched wings seemed to cover the entire area; the bony claws had gouged huge raw yellow chunks from the surrounding trees on the way down. Pel kicked aside a curl of bark the size of his head from one such wound; he stepped over a fallen branch and stopped a few feet from the black membrane of the wing.

It looked like thick rubber or polished leather. At first Pel thought he could see the shapes of tree branches showing through from beneath, but then he realized that those were veins within the wing itself.

He started to reach out, then stopped. He didn't really want to touch the thing.

Ted and Valadrakul were underneath it, though. They might even still be alive. Forcing himself, Pel reached out, grabbed for the edge of the wing, and tried to lift.

It was still warm, and it felt horribly like human skin with a thin coating of fine fuzz. It was thicker than he had realized; when he slid his fingers underneath he couldn't get his hand all the way around the edge to close his thumbs over the top. Prying upward with just his hands did nothing at all; the wing did not budge, and his fingers slid out from beneath.

That black fuzz was as smooth and soft as cat fur; it didn't give him any easy purchase.

"Someone give me a hand!" he called.

He tried again, thrusting his arms under the wing as far as his elbows and heaving upward. His muscles strained; his breath stopped. The veins in his face distended, and he felt as if something would burst at any moment.

The monster's wing did not move.

"You think they're still alive under there?"

Startled, Pel recognized Susan's voice. He also realized that Amy had finally stopped shrieking. He relaxed and turned to Susan, who had come up behind him.

"They might be, anyway," he said. "But they may not have much air left, if they are."

"You think it's airtight?"

Pel waved at the huge black covering. "What do you think?" he asked.

"I think you need better leverage; there are plenty of branches you could use." She, in turn, waved at the scattered debris left by the creature's descent, and the ship's fall before that.

"More men," another, deeper voice said. Pel realized that Stoddard was standing at Susan's shoulder. "Sticks are well enow, but this needs more men than one."

"You're right," Pel said.

"We're two, then," Stoddard said.

"Three," Susan corrected him.

Stoddard looked down at her from his six feet or so of height; she smiled crookedly up at him from an inch or two over five feet, her still-bandaged arms folded across her chest, and corrected herself, "Two and a half."

Pel called, "Lieutenant Dibbs!"

Dibbs had wanted to find all his men before attempting any rescue efforts; four of them had not returned yet. Only when Prossie Thorpe had reported a decision from Base One would the lieutenant agree that uncovering Valadrakul and Deranian was more urgent.

And only Prossie knew that she had lied—there had been no decision to report. The people back at Base One had completely lost touch with the situation; they were still talking about whether Colonel Carson might not be completely dead and what medical assistance might be appropriate. Bascombe and Hart were concerned with an attack on Shadow's stronghold, with setting up a proper chain of command that they could duck out of to avoid accountability if they had to. Even Carrie had not really followed the sequence of events after the arrival of the first group of hellbeasts; she was far more concerned with assurance that her cousin was safe and that there weren't any more monsters lurking somewhere nearby, about to leap out and eat everybody. No one at Base One understood about the black wing, about how big it was. No one there appreciated that Valadrakul was the only wizard left, and that magic was their only hope, both in any fight against Shadow, and as a way home.

Valadrakul *had* to be saved, or they were all trapped here, all as good as dead. And no one was listening, no one at Base One, none of the Imperials in Faerie. Pel had tried to explain, but Dibbs had almost ignored him—Brown was a civilian, a passenger, with no authority. Raven argued that the two should be freed, but he said nothing about a need for magic; he spoke only of how Valadrakul was a faithful servant and owed loyalty. Amy and Susan babbled of a common humanity that meant nothing to an Imperial soldier.

And Prossie could not speak on her own account; she was a telepath, and a woman—a mutant bitch. She had been called that all her life; she knew that that was how Dibbs saw her. No one would listen to her as herself.

But they would listen to her as a relay.

So Prossie had lied. *She* knew that Valadrakul and Ted needed help immediately, that saving Valadrakul was vital, and she had said they should be saved.

And by doing so, she had committed a capital crime. The technical term in the Imperial Articles of Service was "usurpation of representational authority by specially empowered communications personnel," and it was an offense invented as a direct result of the widespread fear and mistrust of telepaths. No nontelepath had any way to verify what a telepath reported, but telepathic communication was too valuable to leave unused; the Empire had responded to this dilemma by setting up draconian rules for all telepaths. From birth, they were trained to tell the truth, to obey nontelepaths, never to venture their own opinions—they were communication equipment, not people; spies, not soldiers.

And one reason that the Empire had only four hundred and sixteen telepaths, out of thirteen billion citizens, was that in the years since telepathy first appeared, forty-three telepaths had died for violating those rules.

If the Empire ever learned what Prossie had done, she would be the forty-fourth.

And since one of the other rules required that any telepath who learned of a violation and failed to report it was subject to the same penalty as the person who committed the original violation, she had dared not let Carrie know what she was doing.

Pel Brown had started it, asking for a decision from Base One, and Dibbs had objected; he didn't need to have headquarters overseeing his every move.

"What do they say?" Pel Brown had demanded, as Dibbs continued to protest.

Carrie was not listening in; she was still asking if there might be more monsters and ignoring Prossie's own questions.

"Carrie, calm down," Prossie had sent, trying to hide what she intended to do, "I'm fine. We're busy here right now; I'm going to break contact for now. Find me again in about twenty minutes, all right?"

"Prossie, are you sure?" Carrie's concern was touching—and also annoying.

"*Yes*, I'm sure. Now get out of my head!"

No telepath ever refused that order; it was a family rule. Carrie broke conscious contact.

"We might as well settle this," Dibbs had said. "Thorpe, report!"

"Yes, sir," Prossie had said, snapping to attention, long habit overcoming her weaknesses.

And then she had lied. "General Hart says that the survival of extrauniversal personnel is absolutely essential and must take first priority, sir! Please use all efforts to uncover Raven's man Valadrakul and the solicitor Deranian."

"Damn," Dibbs said. "I think they're making a mistake, but an order's an order. All right, Singer, Wilkins, the wizard was right by the ship, he could be under the curve of the hull—see if you can crawl in there and find him. Maybe take a couple of those branches to shore things up. Hollingsworth, Moore, you others, we've got half a dozen lumps under the wing— some of them are wood or rocks, but that one by the rib must be the colonel, and those two close together are probably the dead woman and the one we're after. See if you can pry up the edge and get a look at them."

Prossie watched with an odd mix of emotions. She admired the way Dibbs and the soldiers set out efficiently to get the job done, once they accepted an order—she'd seen it before, of course, hundreds of times, but it still amazed her that nontelepaths could work together so well without direct communication.

And tired as she was, she felt a peculiar sensation of pride and pleasure because the men were obeying *her* orders—they didn't know it, they would never have obeyed if they had known, they would kill her for it if they ever found out, but they were obeying *her* orders.

This, she realized, was the feeling of power, real power; she had never felt it before.

And tied to it was a feeling of terror. She had broken the law, the law that was all that kept nontelepaths from murdering every telepath in the galaxy. She was a criminal, an outlaw.

If Carrie ever found out . . .

Would Carrie tell, or would Carrie risk her own death sentence?

Prossie didn't want to find out. She had fifteen minutes before Carrie would call to her again; in that fifteen minutes she had to forget what she had done. She could never dare think of it again.

Not that the Empire could put her to death here in Faerie, of course. Not that Dibbs and the others could ever find out what she had done—she was their only link to the Empire. But if she ever wanted to return home, if she wanted Carrie to be able to live a normal life, she had to never again allow herself to remember consciously her crime.

At the age of eighteen, Albert Singer had signed up to be a soldier. He had enlisted because he was thoroughly bored with farming, because he liked the way the fancy purple uniforms looked, and most importantly, because he saw how much the girls liked the way the fancy purple uniforms looked. He had signed up for space service because it looked a lot more interesting than hanging around the little garrison at Cochran's Landing, and he figured it would impress the girls even more.

It had never once occurred to him that this would one day lead to crawling through the stifling, malodorous darkness underneath a wrecked spaceship and the corpse of a gigantic monster bat, shoving his way through damp earth and brittle dead leaves, trying to rescue a fat little foreigner who was probably already dead.

He couldn't see a thing, not really; a little of the afternoon light filtered in around his own boots, but the dust from the leaves was a thin haze everywhere around him, grit had gotten in his eyes, and there wasn't anything to see, in any case. He sneezed, spraying warm goo on his upper lip and the back of one hand, and could hardly wipe it off. The entire front of his uniform, chest to toe, was becoming coated with dirt—he could feel it, could feel the cool moisture and the grainy texture.

He belatedly decided that he should have taken off his boots; the shiny finish was going to be ruined, and he thought he'd have been able to crawl better without them.

He pushed with his toes and elbows, forcing himself deeper into the narrow passage. One shoulder brushed against the steel of the ship's hull; the opposite knee rubbed against the furry, rubbery flesh of the dead monster.

Why the hell did the lieutenant have to pick *him* for this? And why had he not argued when Wilkins had said to go in first? Good old Ronnie Wilkins was squatting back there watching, not doing a damn thing except staring into the dark, where he probably couldn't even see the bottoms of Singer's boots anymore.

The first part had been easy, crawling under the ship's starboard guidance vane, but this part . . .

Singer coughed, without meaning to, and hoped very much that he wasn't going to cough up anything that would wind up smeared on his chin or his uniform. The dust from the leaves was ghastly.

As much to clear his throat as anything else, he called, "Anyone in here?"

To his utter astonishment, a voice called back weakly, "Aye, lad."

Not only was the bearded foreigner still alive, Singer realized, but he was conscious and only a few feet away.

"Hold on, sir, we'll get you out," Singer said, trying unsuccessfully to sound reassuring. Then he coughed again. The powdered leaves felt like ground glass scraping the back of his throat.

He saw something flutter indistinctly in the dimness ahead, and suddenly his throat cleared. He swallowed experimentally, and everything worked.

Singer remembered that the man ahead was supposed to be a magic-worker of some kind. "Did you do that?" he asked.

"Aye," the voice replied. "An it please you."

"Thanks." Singer shoved himself forward again, then stretched out one arm and found he could touch Valadrakul's embroidered vest.

Then the roof fell in, or seemed to; the blackness that was the dead monster's wing suddenly sank in, pressing down on him, and Singer found his face pressed into the dirt beneath. "Hey," he managed to shout, his voice muffled.

Wilkins heard him, and called in, "They're lifting it off the other one, the loony with the head wound. They were picking it up, and everything shifted."

"Well, tell them to hurry up, for God's sake," Singer called back.

"Right." Wilkins turned away and shouted something, but Singer was no longer listening; he was trying to see through the gloom ahead of him.

"Are you okay?" he asked.

"Aye, lad," the wizard answered.

"Can you move?"

"After a fashion, aye," Valadrakul replied. "My head is free, 'neath the ship's hull, like your own. And I can move hands, arms, and all, despite the weight of the flesh atop. But alas, one of the beast's bones lies across the back of my legs, and holds me fast. An that be moved, I'd be free."

"You can't lift it?"

"Nay."

"I saw you doing those fire tricks before; you can't burn your way out?"

"Nay, I'd but set myself afire, as well. A blade might serve, but I've none, mine was lost long since."

"A blade . . ." Singer mentally cursed himself for not bringing a knife. He had one, of course, a standard military-issue combat knife, but it was in his pack, inside the ship, and the ship was underneath the dead monster.

Then, abruptly, the thick layer of flesh above him shifted

again, this time pulling up and away. Twisting around so that his helmet was out of the way, he looked up at it, and realized that the rest of the squad must have heaved the wing out a little.

He still couldn't see much, though. His flashlight was in his pack, aboard the ship, as well. Another stupid mistake. At least he wasn't the only one who had made this particular mistake; as far as he knew, everybody, even Lieutenant Dibbs, had left his pack aboard ship.

He peered into the darkness. The dust had settled, and his eyes had adapted; he could see the wizard's face as a pale, colorless blur.

He had room now to get up on his knees, his back pressing up into the creature's wing; he did, and leaned forward, groped ahead until he was able to grasp Valadrakul's hand.

"Maybe I can pull you free," he suggested.

"Mayhap you can," Valadrakul agreed. "An you haul, I'll push."

Singer grabbed the wizard's arm in both hands, braced himself, and said, "Ready? Heave!"

They heaved.

Nothing happened. There wasn't enough room for Singer to really dig in his heels, and his grip was on Valadrakul's sleeve more than on the arm within.

Someone shouted, back out there in the world of light and air; Singer glanced toward the opening, then decided to ignore it. It couldn't have anything to do with him or the trapped foreigner.

" 'Tis the ankles that hold me," Valadrakul said. "And the thing's wing bone."

"Maybe if I dig down underneath?"

" 'Tis a sound idea, methinks," Valadrakul agreed.

Singer took a deep breath, cupped his hands, and started burrowing.

Pel watched as Ted got unsteadily to his feet.

"Are you all right?" he asked.

"Guess I got the blanket over my face," Ted said, looking back at the huge black wing. "Or maybe a pillow. Maybe I pulled it down off the bed—I think I must've fallen out long ago."

Lieutenant Dibbs snorted with disgust; Pel didn't blame him.

Ted's persistance in his delusion had long since passed the point of evoking sympathy, concern, or even amusement.

Pel had long ago run out of ideas for dissuading Ted, though; nothing worked.

Dibbs and the civilians watched as the soldiers heaved at the wing, trying to pull it out, away from the ship, as much as possible. The soldier who was helping in the attempt to free Valadrakul—Wilkins, was it?—had said that his companion was having problems, being squeezed in there.

That would not do. They *needed* Valadrakul, needed him badly.

So the soldiers were trying to give Valadrakul and his rescuer a little more room. They were too far under to have the wing lifted off them completely, the way it had been lifted off Ted, but it should be possible to stretch it a little tighter, so it didn't hang down so heavily upon them.

Pel thought it was a very good idea. "Can I help?" he asked.

Dibbs looked at him, at the tattered remnants of his shirt and the blood and dirt smeared on his face and body, then turned back to his men. "No, sir," he said flatly. "We're doing fine."

Pel didn't argue, but he wondered just how fine Dibbs was actually doing. His commanding officer had been killed—and, Pel realized, Dibbs was now, under orders, trying to rescue the man who had killed Carson. Four of his men had vanished during the panic as the bat-thing approached; they still had not returned. His supplies, other than the useless sidearms, were all aboard the ship, which was inaccessible—and for that matter, the ship had crashed, stranding them all in an alien universe.

Pel reminded himself that this universe was just as alien to the Imperials as it was to the Earthpeople.

It would be perfectly reasonable for Lieutenant Dibbs to be feeling some pretty serious strain. Pel decided not to push the man about the rescue efforts, or anything else, just yet.

As Pel decided this, one of the soldiers happened to look to one side. Startled, he pointed and shouted. Equally startled, Pel turned.

A rather shamefaced Imperial soldier was stumbling out of the forest, toward the dead monster and the buried ship. His helmet was gone, and his face smeared with something.

Well, that was one of the four, anyway; Pel glanced surreptitiously at Dibbs's face, and caught an expression of intense relief.

Then it vanished.

"All right, Sawyer," the lieutenant shouted. "It's about time you got back! Get over there and give the others a hand!"

Dirt sprayed into Singer's face; his eyes had closed immediately, but not fast enough, and now they stung horribly. Dirt was blocking his nose; he huffed most of it out. He could taste the earth in his mouth, on his tongue and lips; he spat out as much as he could.

"Your pardon, good sir, a thousand times, I beg your pardon!" the wizard said hastily. "I am shamed and dishonored to have discomfited you, who sought to rescue me—and who did so! Look you!" He wiggled his newly freed, booted foot.

"No problem," Singer muttered, wiping away dirt. "Let's get out of here."

"Aye," Valadrakul agreed fervently, "with a good will!"

CHAPTER 8

"*You cannot see it,*" *Valadrakul remarked, gently probing* his jaw, "but 'neath this beard, all my chin's but a single bruise, by the feel."

He stood a few feet from the corner of the tail assembly that was the only exposed portion of ISS *Christopher*; his long black vest and borrowed uniform were smeared with grime. Still, he was smiling.

Lieutenant Dibbs, a few feet away, was not. "All right, they're out," he said. "And Sawyer's back, so that's one out of four. Now, can I find the rest of my missing men, Thorpe, or has Base got some other stupid order?"

"I'm sorry, Lieutenant, I've been out of contact," Prossie replied, not mentioning that this was deliberate and entirely her own idea. "Should I ask?"

"Don't bother," Dibbs answered. "If they aren't calling us, then there can't be anything very urgent and maybe we'll do better if we don't have a bunch of bigwigs watching over our shoulders."

"I don't see how we could do much worse either way," someone muttered.

Dibbs whirled to spot the speaker.

Before he could say anything, someone else interrupted.

"Whoe'er spoke has the right of it," Stoddard said, startling everyone. "Scarce in this land a second hour, and we'd seen Elani die, seen your Colonel Carson die, lost three men to the forests, and been found by Shadow. All this, and we've yet to say who's to lead and who's to follow, yet to say whither we go, yet to step a dozen paces from this sky ship, save we flee in panic. I've my fill of it."

Prossie turned, startled; she had never heard Stoddard make so long a speech.

"Not to mention," Singer pointed out, "that all our supplies are in the ship, and we can't get at them with that dead whatever-it-is draped across everything."

"Stoddard, hold tongue," Raven snapped. "We've had misfortune, aye, but 'tis no fault of any of us gathered here. That Carson was a fool was none's fault save his own, and he's paid the price that folly must bring. All else follows upon Shadow's magic, that told it to yon sky portal ere we were well through it, and how to counter that, how to prevent?"

"I'll *not* hold tongue," Stoddard said, "for I've words to say. Ask me not of how to counter Shadow, for I'm but an honest warrior, but ask rather yon corpse that was a wizard, and wise in the ways of magic." He gestured at Valadrakul. "Ask likewise this, that stands before us, brushing dust from his garb with no thought that Shadow must still seek us."

Prossie's mouth opened in astonishment; she had never before heard Stoddard defy Raven in even the slightest degree.

Valadrakul, too, looked at Stoddard, startled. "I am ever aware of Shadow's threat, man; what wouldst have me do?"

Stoddard turned. "Hast no wards, no warnings, naught that might guard us?"

"Nay, I've none," Valadrakul replied angrily. "Magicks are not all as one, and I've no spell that would stand 'gainst Shadow."

"Then of what use art thou?" Stoddard demanded.

" 'Gainst Shadow itself, little more than any man," Valadrakul retorted, "yet I've spells that serve us well enow in other regards!" He waved at the gigantic remains that covered the ship.

Stoddard looked at the dead monstrosity and seemed to soften and shrink. "Aye," he said, "aye, wizard, I've wronged thee. Your pardon."

"Freely given, Stoddard," Valadrakul answered.

"Fine, so that's settled," Dibbs said.

"Nay," Stoddard said, " 'tis not settled; yet do I say, I've had my fill. An we do no better, I'll depart. This is mine own world, not Earth nor Empire, and should I go, who's to say me nay? Now, you who would lead us, my lord Raven and Messire Dibbs, Mistress Thorpe who speaks for the Empire, what do you propose to do?"

Prossie decided that this would be a very good time for

Carrie to reestablish contact; weren't the twenty minutes up yet? Surely, they must be! She tried to listen, despite the mental wool that this universe stuffed in her head; she strained, threw her senses open . . .

And jumped when Carrie's greeting came through.

"Prossie," she asked, "what's happening?"

Prossie quickly ran through the basics: attack survived, monsters slain, three men deserted, ship at least temporarily inaccessible, Elani dead. Carrie already knew Carson was dead.

"I'll take my orders from Base One," Dibbs was saying, "but personally, I think the whole thing's a disaster from the start, and once I find my other three men we should just go home. They can try again later, with a better-equipped force—I mean, our guns don't work, our ship can't fly, we've got a dozen of us out here fighting with rocks and sticks."

"And what if there be no home that one may flee to?" Raven asked angrily. "I've no welcome at Stormcrack, much as I might wish it otherwise."

"Not my problem," Dibbs said, shrugging.

"Flee, then," Raven said. "Flee, and be damned. I and mine will struggle on."

Dibbs glanced meaningfully at Stoddard.

"In time," Raven said warningly, "your emperor and all his empire will come to see the need to destroy Shadow. I pray to the Goddess that that time will not come too late."

Prossie listened approvingly.

She agreed with Raven that Shadow must be destroyed; she had seen enough of Shadow's horrors, both firsthand and in dozens of memories, to have no doubts of that.

But she agreed with Dibbs, too; this expedition had been a farce, doomed from the outset, and the best thing to do now would be to call it off before anyone else died, to send the Earthpeople home, let Raven and his people rejoin their underground, and then go back to Base One and start over.

The only question was whether the Empire would agree that there was a need to start over, rather than to abandon the entire thing. Without Raven there at Base One, prodding them, the generals and politicians might decide to wait and see what happened.

"Listen, Raven," Dibbs said, "you're back in your own land, and you can go on with your resistance movement. And if I'm told to, I'll help out. But do you really think that a dozen strangers are going to make a big difference against something that plays with monsters like that?" He gestured at the gigantic wreckage of the bat-thing.

"Methinks you've changed your position," Raven remarked, his head cocked as he eyed the lieutenant.

"I sure have," Dibbs said. "That thing convinced me. My men are tops, but we're out of our league with stuff like this."

"Then perhaps we're agreed," Raven replied.

"I know *we* are," Amy interjected, seizing the opportunity. "We want to go home, Raven—Pel and Susan and I. We're no use here. Send us back to Earth."

Raven turned, startled.

"So hasty, mistress . . . Are you certain, then?"

"We all are," Pel said, stepping up beside Amy. Susan was a few feet behind; Ted had wandered off to inspect one of the trees.

"I've no wish to keep you 'gainst your will," Raven said. "I promised you could return to your homes, and I meant that promise—but are you certain that you're of no use here? Mistress Susan, that device you carry—methinks that's of good service."

"The gun?" Susan tugged at the strap of her purse. "Raven, I only have . . . well, it's very limited. If you send us home, though, we can give you lots of guns, lots of ammunition— better stuff than this."

"Aye? Truthfully?" Raven eyed her thoughtfully.

"Absolutely," Pel said.

"Then indeed, 'twould be folly to keep you," the nobleman said emphatically, "and I'll be sending you to your Earth at the first hour I may."

"Why not *now*?" Amy demanded. "Tell Valadrakul to send us!"

Raven turned to the wizard, who held up his hands. "Messires, mesdames, methinks you mistake the situation," Valadrakul protested. "I've no power to send you home."

The three Earthpeople present stared at him in outraged silence. Somewhere a bird whistled, the first that Prossie had heard since her previous visit to Faerie.

"Why *not*?" Amy demanded. "You're a wizard, aren't you?"

"Oh, aye, I'm that," Valadrakul agreed, "but I know naught of the portal spell."

"*Elani* knew it!" Pel shouted.

"Indeed she did," Valadrakul affirmed. "And she mastered it well, caught it in the structure of her magicks. But I know it not; the webs of my work are otherwise. I'm learned in the spells of fire and destruction, magicks that send forth the raw energy of magic in fiery outbursts; likewise, I know the spells that send forth and draw in in other ways and have caught the strands of those in me. But the spells that shape worlds, that link the several realities, those I ken not a whit."

"But Elani did!"

"Aye; in that, she was far my better. The worse for us, that she's no more."

Prossie heard all this with growing unhappiness. She had not consciously known that only Elani knew the portal spell, but somehow she felt none of the shock the Earthpeople felt; perhaps she had telepathically sensed the truth, on some subconscious level, back at Base One.

Still, it was very bad news.

And while Valadrakul was admitting his impotence, Carrie had received Prossie's report and was relaying parts of it to General Hart and Undersecretary Bascombe. Prossie suspected, from the flavor of Carrie's thoughts, that it was not going over well.

That was no surprise. Hart and Bascombe did not want anyone coming home bearing tales of incompetence.

Well, it looked as if they might not have anything to worry about; without magic, it appeared that no one was going to leave this universe. The Empire's own space warp was up above treetop level, where they couldn't get at it. Dibbs and his men were not going home any time very soon—and neither, that meant, was Prossie.

"Raven," Amy demanded, "where can we find another wizard who knows the portal spell?"

"I've not the slightest notion," Raven replied. "Wizardry is none of mine."

"Valadrakul?" Pel asked.

The wizard frowned deeply, then winced as the movement affected his injured jaw.

"The brotherhood of magicians is scattered and broken in these sad times," he said. "A handful survives here, another there, but we've no central councils, no trustworthy messengers, canny or otherwise. For the most part, we dare not use the greater lines of power, for those are Shadow's. The portal spells are likewise Shadow's; they were stolen from Shadow, and taught quickly to those few who could learn them well, who could draw down those strands from the web of powers; there was Elani, and likewise Taillefer, who served us betimes, but of others, I know not. 'Twas thought unwise that any should know too much of others' skills, lest we be captured and questioned by Shadow."

Prossie nodded slightly to herself; she had known that. While the wizards didn't follow the system of revolutionary cells as carefully as the other members of the resistance did, they did keep plenty of secrets.

"This Taillefer," Pel asked, "where can we find him?"

Valadrakul considered that carefully.

"You don't know," Amy said. "Do you?"

"Nay," Valadrakul admitted, "I do not."

The Earthpeople accepted that, but Prossie, watching Valadrakul carefully, wondered if the wizard might be concealing something. She was no expert at reading facial nuances, really, because she had never had to resort to such crude methods in her own universe, but still, something seemed wrong about Valadrakul's answer.

Could she be remembering something she had learned from Valadrakul's mind earlier, without realizing it?

"Well, damn it, if you can't find him, we better start looking for him!" Amy shouted.

"You go right ahead," Dibbs said. "Meanwhile, I'll be rounding up my men and calling for pickup. Wilkins, Moore, Dawber, I want you three to take a look around, see if you can spot any sign of where our missing men went. Stay in sight, we don't know what's out there; you see anything moving, you call it in, don't play hero."

"Right, Lieutenant," Wilkins said. He picked a direction and started walking; the other two Dibbs had chosen followed him.

"Uh . . . permission to speak, sir?" Prossie said uneasily, glancing after the three.

"What is it, Thorpe?" Dibbs stepped away from the rest of the group, and Prossie followed.

"I'm not sure there's going to be a pickup, sir."

"You aren't," Dibbs said. "Why not?"

Prossie hesitated, wishing she felt better and stronger; what she really wanted to do was curl up somewhere and rest, not argue.

But she had to warn Dibbs if she could.

The real reason she was fairly sure there would be no pickup was that Bascombe had shown her once before that he felt no compunction about abandoning a failed mission, rather than risking further complications; the undersecretary had left Prossie and the rest of Joshua Cahn's crew in jail on Earth without a second thought, and in that case there hadn't even been evidence of incompetence or mismanagement, where the current expedition had been a disaster right from its inception.

Telling Lieutenant Dibbs this did not seem like a good idea, though. He didn't like cynics—and for that matter, he didn't like telepaths. A telepath accusing a superior of callous political gamesmanship was asking for trouble.

"Technical reasons, sir," Prossie said.

Lying really wasn't very hard at all, she was finding, despite all her years of training.

"Go on."

"The Department of Science has confirmed earlier theories, sir—antigravity cannot operate outside normal space. This world we're on is not in normal space; that's why *Christopher* went down. And any rescue ship would lose all lift, too. We'd need a vehicle that can fly in the distorted space here, and Base One hasn't got any. So they *can't* pick us up."

"You sure of that, Thorpe?"

Prossie hesitated. She had sinned once; she would resist the temptation this time. "It's not relayed, sir; it's my own conclusion," she said.

Dibbs nodded slowly. "Got a reason they can't just drop a *rope* through that space warp up there, telepath?" he asked sarcastically.

"No, sir," Prossie answered truthfully. She had no idea whether a rope was possible or not. She could see no reason that it would not work, but then, she didn't understand space-warp science. If the warp was as open as that, wouldn't air from Faerie be boiling off into Imperial space right now?

She didn't know. Maybe a rope would work.

But she was quite sure nobody would be sending one.

"As you wish," Raven said, with a tight little smile. "We'll away, then, in pursuit of Taillefer. For that, we must make our way westward, as there lies the fastest route from these woods, to clear air where Valadrakul's spells might best work, to summon his compatriot, that a portal to your Earth might be opened. An you be safely home, we'll arrange a thousand of these 'guns' be sent. Then see we will whether the things of Shadow can withstand them!"

"You'll not be marching hence to beard Shadow in its lair,

then?" Stoddard asked. "If this be Sunderland, Shadow's hold lies to the west."

"Nay," Raven answered. "What good of that, with a band such as this—fools and fainthearts and women, with only you and I and the wizard that would stand fast? We fare west only to be free of the forests."

Stung by Raven's words, Pel said, "It's not my fight, you know—there's nothing wrong with my running away. And I'll do you a lot more good buying guns back home than getting myself eaten by monsters here."

Raven turned to face the Earthman, caught sight of his battered and bloody appearance, and hesitated. Then he smiled ruefully. "True enow, friend Pel," Raven admitted, "and you've my apology that I spoke ill of you."

"Where are you going to get a thousand guns, Pel?" Amy asked. "And where are you going to get a thousand men to use them?"

"I'll buy them," Pel replied. "A few at a time."

"I'll help," Susan said.

"And for men," Raven said, "perhaps the Empire has better than our friends to offer." He waved his bandaged hand at Dibbs and his men. Dibbs was talking quietly with Prossie; the others were chatting among themselves, leaving the Earthpeople and the natives alone.

Amy looked at Pel, at Susan, and at Dibbs, then shrugged. "I guess you're right," she said, "and what do I care, anyway? As long as I get home."

Pel frowned.

Getting home was what he cared about, too. He intended to keep his promise to buy guns, but then, why shouldn't he? If he didn't, Raven and a couple of oversized swordsmen like Stoddard might walk out of his basement wall at any time and drag him away on more idiotic, dangerous, deadly adventures.

And when he got home . . .

The house would be empty, just him and Silly Cat—wouldn't it? Nancy and Rachel wouldn't be coming home with him.

Unless Ted was right, in which case they already *were* home, waiting for him.

He knew they weren't; he knew they were dead; he really did know that.

But he had to *see*. He had to see for himself. He had to get home and see.

* * *

"All right, Thorpe," Dibbs said. "Unless we get orders telling us otherwise, we're going to sit right here and wait for a pickup. That clear?"

"Yes, sir." Prossie knew better than to argue. If she were to suddenly manifest an order from Bascombe or Hart at this point in the argument, Dibbs probably would reject it outright. Maybe later, when the men started to get bored, she could "receive" an order to move on.

Or maybe she could leave without Dibbs and the rest and go with Raven and his group instead; certainly, they would be more interesting companions.

That thought was treasonous, she told herself; she didn't dare think it.

Dibbs turned away and shouted, "Raven, all the rest of you! We're staying right here until Base One sends someone to get us. Anyone who wants to stay, that's fine with us. If the rest of you want to go, we won't stop you—it's your world, you're not Imperial citizens."

"It's not *my* world," Susan said quietly; Dibbs ignored her.

"Messire Lieutenant," Raven said, "methinks you might best reconsider. I'll not ask you to join us if you've no wish to, but in all true compassion that the Goddess bids us, I'd warn you that this place be perchance more dangerous than you realize."

"This place," Dibbs replied, "is where the space warp comes out."

"Aye, so 'tis, and therefore of interest to Shadow; would you face more such as this?" The nobleman gestured at the dead monster.

"You think more are coming?"

"Aye, so I do."

"Well, I don't," Dibbs said flatly. "And if they do, we'll take shelter."

"And what can shelter you from such as that?" Raven was clearly trying hard to be reasonable and persuasive; Prossie wondered why, since she was fairly sure he didn't particularly want Dibbs and his men along anymore. Could it be honest concern?

That was a frightening thought, that there was something so fearsome approaching that Raven would worry about what it might do to other people.

More likely Raven was afraid that if Dibbs and company

stayed here at the ship they would somehow interfere with his own schemes against Shadow.

"We'll be safe enough in the trees," Dibbs said. "We can take care of ourselves."

Raven considered for a moment; Stoddard and the Earthpeople all watched him. Valadrakul was studying the dead monster; the soldiers were looking in various directions.

"An it please you," Raven said at last, "I'd ask a favor. Could call for volunteers, that would come with us?"

"Lieutenant," Prossie said, before Dibbs could reply, "Base One agrees with Raven that there's a risk here."

No one at Base One had said any such thing. Prossie had once again yielded to the temptation to play God, to alter the facts to suit herself—or at least to exceed her authority and lie.

Prossie could sense that Carrie, who had not been paying much attention, was suddenly much more interested. Prossie tried to ignore her questions. Did someone here say that? Did I relay that? I don't remember anything like that, Prossie . . .

Dibbs did not like what he heard, either. He frowned at Prossie.

"I'm not going anywhere," he said.

"But volunteers?" Raven asked, his tone almost wheedling.

Dibbs glanced at his men, then yielded. "All right," he said, "you can take volunteers. I doubt you'll get any."

"I'll go," Prossie said immediately. "Base One will want to stay in touch with the advance party." It would get her away from Lieutenant Dibbs and, she hoped, eliminate any further temptation to lie about relayed messages. More importantly, it would get her away from the space warp; she was now convinced that Raven was sincere in his warning and that this place was a death trap.

"Wait a minute, Thorpe," Dibbs protested. "What am *I* supposed to do for communications, then?"

"With all respect, sir, you won't need any, if you're just waiting right here. And Base One can send messages through the warp if they have to."

Besides, Prossie thought, she wasn't reliable anyway. She had lied about messages more than once already. The farther she got from Lieutenant Dibbs, the less likely she would be to do it again—and the less likely she would be to think about it, and perhaps let Carrie know what had happened.

She tried not to let those thoughts come clear; she didn't want Carrie to hear them.

Carrie wasn't receiving, though, she was sending, objecting to Prossie's decision. Prossie hadn't cleared it; she hadn't even asked anyone at Base One; how could she volunteer for anything that way? Telepaths didn't do that! Telepaths didn't choose for themselves! And who had told her that there was any danger?

Then Spaceman Singer said, "I'd like to go, too, sir," and suddenly everyone was distracted; Prossie felt a surge of relief that she was no longer the center of attention.

But she dared not think about it, dared not enjoy the relief; Carrie would notice. Instead, she forced her mind into a receptive blank and passed the scene in the forest on to Carrie without comment, as mindlessly as she could, struggling to be only a camera.

"Do we wait until morning?" Pel asked, as he carefully felt the scratches on the back of his head; they were scabbing over. He tugged a lock of hair out of the congealing blood and winced at the sharp pain that resulted.

"Nay," Raven said. "And spend the night here, with that?" He gestured at the dead bat-thing. "More, 'tis by night and the dark that Shadow's strongest. We'll depart as soon we may."

"It's already well after noon."

"And I know it well, friend Pel; think you I'd not? It may be we'll not get far, but every pace we put betwixt ourselves and this place will be a pace away from wasting our lives."

Pel nodded. "Right," he said.

"Who all is coming?" Amy asked.

"Well, we are," Pel said, indicating himself, Amy, Susan, and Raven. "And Valadrakul, and I think Stoddard . . ."

"Aye," Stoddard said. "I've no wish to linger in this foul spot."

"And three of the soldiers . . ." Pel said.

"Three?" Amy asked. She turned and saw only one Imperial trooper standing near. Dirt was smeared down the front of his uniform; he had obviously hit the ground at some point, but nothing appeared torn or bloody. He had his helmet tucked under one arm.

"That's right," the soldier said. "Me, and Ronnie Wilkins, and Bill Marks. Four, if you count Miss Thorpe."

"So where are the others?" Amy asked.

"Ronnie and Bill are arguing with the lieutenant," the soldier explained. "I'm not sure where Thorpe went."

" 'Twill do no good," Raven said. " 'Tis plain Messire Dibbs's mind is set firmly in its course."

"That's why I'm over here with you folks," the Imperial agreed.

"What about Ted?" Amy asked.

Pel frowned, and glanced at the lawyer, who was standing to one side, alone, gazing idly at the dead bat-monster. "I don't know," he admitted.

"We better take him," Amy said. "He'll get killed if he stays here. The lieutenant isn't going to want to look after him."

"I don't know," Pel said reluctantly. "He's pretty far gone. He could really slow us down . . ."

"Pel Brown, how can you say that?" Amy shouted. "If he doesn't come with us, he'll *never* get home to Earth! And getting home is probably the only chance he's ever got to recover, and you know it!"

"It's not a hell of a great chance," Pel shouted back. "If we drag him along, maybe *none* of us will get back!"

Amy prepared to shout a reply, but Pel raised a hand to forestall her. "You're right, you're right," he said, "I know that. We have to bring him. Stoddard, could you go bring him along, please?"

"I'll go," Susan said quietly.

"Together, then, lady," Stoddard said.

As if echoing the Earthpeople's shouts, a loud argument broke out just then among the Imperials; startled, Pel and Amy turned to see two soldiers marching angrily away from their companions and toward Raven's group.

A third hesitated and then followed. This one had no helmet, Pel noticed.

The pair marched up; the shorter of the two addressed the soldier who was already there.

"You better be right about this, Al," he said. "The lieutenant says that he'll let us go and won't try to stop us, but if Base One calls it desertion, he won't argue with them, either."

"Lord Raven," the first soldier said, "this is Ronnie Wilkins. And beside him there is Bill Marks."

"And your own name, good sir?" Raven asked.

The soldier smiled. "Guess I forgot to say; I'm Albert Singer."

The fourth soldier, the one who had followed Wilkins and Marks, cleared his throat. He stood behind and between his companions, speaking over their shoulders. Pel recognized him as the man who had been missing for an hour or so after the hellbeasts had attacked.

"Excuse me," the soldier said, "but are you people serious about it being dangerous here? That this dead monster's going to attract more?"

"Aye, and indeed we are," Raven answered. " 'Tis a thing of Shadow, and where one falls, a dozen follow."

"In that case . . ." He glanced back over his own shoulder, then turned toward Raven again and said, "In that case, I'd say I'm coming with you." He held out a hand. "My name's Tom Sawyer."

Pel started.

Raven made no move to take the soldier's hand, so Pel stepped forward and shook it warmly. "Tom Sawyer? Really?" he asked.

Puzzled, the soldier nodded. "Spaceman Second Class Thomas James Sawyer," he said.

"Tom Sawyer," Pel repeated, grinning foolishly. "I'll be damned."

The soldiers and the Faerie folk were all staring curiously at Pel; Amy shoved him.

"It's not so strange as all that," she said. "Now, come on, let's get out of here. We have a wizard to find."

"Right," Pel said, dropping Sawyer's hand and turning to Raven. "Which way?"

CHAPTER 9

Something rustled in the dark leaves overhead; Pel started and looked up.

"Probably just a squirrel," Wilkins said somewhere behind Pel; he looked upward, as well.

Pel turned at the comment and realized that Sawyer had his blaster drawn—for all the good that would do him, here in Faerie.

Sawyer was next to Wilkins; Marks and Singer were a step ahead. The four Imperial soldiers had stayed close together, talking mostly with each other, as the group proceeded; Pel didn't suppose he could blame them for that, for wanting to stay with their friends and compatriots while trapped in this alien reality. He had noticed, though, that they seemed to avoid Prossie Thorpe—wasn't she an Imperial, too? Her uniform had been somewhat slashed up by Shadow's hellbeasts, but she still had the proper purple blouse and slacks, and the insignia on her shoulder.

Of course, for himself, he avoided Ted, who was a fellow Earthman, but that was different. Ted was . . . well . . . damaged. Prossie wasn't. And she was a woman, too; why would soldiers avoid a woman, especially one with those peekaboo tears in her blouse? It seemed out of character.

This stupid Imperial prejudice against telepathic "mutants" was probably responsible.

Pel glanced at Prossie; she seemed content to walk with Stoddard and Amy and Susan. Raven and Valadrakul had moved on a few paces ahead of the others; then came Ted, herded forward by Stoddard and the women. Pel, not inclined to talk just now, was close behind; he had taken off the remains of his borrowed T-shirt, since he hardly needed it in the warm, damp evening air of the forest, and wore only purple pants and black boots. The sweat was starting to dry on his back, though; what he would do when the air cooled further he didn't know. And he thought he might be developing a blister on his right foot; the boots were a fairly good fit, but unfamiliar, and he wasn't used to walking so much.

Behind him, the Imperial soldiers brought up the rear, still fully dressed and wearing boots and helmets—except Sawyer, of course, who had lost his helmet. Pel wondered why they weren't stinking of sweat.

Maybe they were, and he just didn't smell it over the rich, heavy odors of the forest.

"What're you planning to do with *that*?" Wilkins said, pointing to Sawyer's blaster.

"Nothing," Sawyer replied defensively, holstering the weapon. "Just habit."

"You really think it was just a squirrel?" Marks said uneasily.

Wilkins shrugged. "Or a bird, or something."

"It's getting hard to see what's up there," Marks pointed out. "How do you know it wasn't one of those black things?"

"Because if it was, it would have attacked us already," Wilkins said.

No one had an answer to that; Pel turned away, and they all marched on.

A moment later, Wilkins stubbed his toe on a tree root hidden in fallen leaves and swore quietly—though Pel doubted it had actually hurt, through the heavy boot the soldier wore.

"Hey, Raven," Singer called.

Ahead, Pel saw Raven and Valadrakul stop and turn.

"It's getting dark," Singer called. "The sun's been down a good half an hour, at least. When are we going to make camp for the night?"

"Yeah," Amy said, loudly. "I'm tired. It's been a long day."

That, Pel thought, was an understatement. They had gotten out of bed that morning in Base One; now they were in the forests of Faerie, Elani and Colonel Carson and a score of Shadow's monsters were dead—and it had been a very long day literally, as well as figuratively, since they had departed Base One in late afternoon by the artificial local time and arrived in Faerie around midday, going by the sun.

Amy added, "And we've been walking forever. My feet are killing me."

Pel could sympathize with that. The Imperials were all soldiers and presumably accustomed to marching, while the Faerie folk came from a world where human feet were still the primary form of transportation, but Pel and Amy, at least, weren't in the habit of walking when they could drive. Pel wasn't sure about Susan or Ted; they didn't seem inclined to complain.

Susan never seemed inclined to complain about anything, of course, and if Ted had had anything to say about pain in his feet, or tired legs, he'd probably have attributed it all to twisted bedsheets or something else suited to his insistence that he was dreaming.

Raven looked at Valadrakul, who made a gesture with his hands that Pel couldn't interpret.

"As you will, then," Raven said. " 'Tis true we've put a league and more behind us, but I'd thought to fare on until the night grew too deep. The darkness draws fast o'er us; perhaps 'tis best we stop."

"Nay," Valadrakul said, "not yet. Shall we not find water ere we rest? There's no sign of stream or brook here."

"Oh," Amy said.

"No water?" Ted asked, startling everyone. "More nightmare, I guess. Haven't done thirst in a while."

Pel clenched a fist and wished he could reach Ted with a good punch on the nose.

"Oh, shut up," Amy muttered wearily.

"Can't the wizard get us water, somehow?" Sawyer called.

"Would that I could," Valadrakul called back. "I can, perhaps, take game, that we might have our supper, but water is beyond my powers."

"Maybe we better keep walking, then," Susan said quietly.

"I *can't*," Amy protested. She dropped abruptly, to sit cross-legged on the ground. "I can't go any farther."

"As you will, then," Raven said. "We'll camp here."

"What about the water?" Wilkins asked. "We crossed a stream a ways back."

"We'll not retrace our steps so far!" Raven said, shocked. "Surely, we'll find water nearby and can fetch it hither, if the women can go no more."

Pel looked around as the others spoke and found himself agreeing. There had to be water around here somewhere, didn't there? Where did rainfall here *go*?

He looked at the slope of the land. "That way?" he said, pointing to the left, where the ground dropped off somewhat.

"Aye, of course," Raven answered. "Wouldst join me, friend Pel?"

Pel just wanted to get off his feet, but he couldn't let himself be seen as a whiner or shirker. "I don't have anything to carry water in," he replied.

"Then these others? An they've naught else, surely those helms they bear will hold water."

Pel turned and saw Wilkins shrug and remove his helmet. "If you want," the Imperial said. "I'm in no hurry to wear the thing again, anyway, and it should be dry by morning."

"I'll get firewood," Pel offered, feeling a bit guilty.

"A fine thought, friend Pel. And if the ladies would clear a space that the fire might be set . . . ?"

"We will," Susan said.

A thought struck Pel. "Valadrakul," he said, "we saw something up in that tree a little while ago." He pointed upward.

"Ah," the wizard said, smiling. "And you think it might serve to feed us?"

Pel smiled back. "It might."

Twenty minutes later, when Raven, Wilkins, Marks, and Singer returned with three helmetfuls of water, Stoddard was midway through skinning a fair-sized opossum, and Pel was tending the campfire Valadrakul had, by means of his magic, lit. Amy, Ted, and Susan had brushed away branches, leaves, and underbrush, and were sitting around the fire; Sawyer, bearing a good-sized tree limb, was standing guard, after helping gather wood.

"A fine sight to return to," Raven remarked.

Pel eyed the half-skinned, slightly scorched opossum.

"Well," he said, "it could certainly be worse."

Amy awoke shortly before sunrise, her back stiff from sleeping on the hard, dewy ground and her feet still sore from the long day's hike; she felt chilled, and her stomach was churning. The overripe scent of decay was in her nostrils. She sat up slowly, then suddenly sprang to her feet—or tried to. She got as far as her knees before the remains of her share of the roast opossum came up.

She retched several more times after her stomach was emptied.

When at last she was able to stop heaving and straighten up, she found the rest of the party awake and staring at her in the dim predawn light.

"I never ate 'possum before, okay?" she said, glaring around at them.

No one answered; embarrassed, most of them turned away and set about getting themselves up, since there was obviously no point in going back to sleep.

Susan, however, took the three steps necessary to reach Amy's side and knelt beside her.

"Are you all right, Amy?" she asked.

Amy nodded. "I'm okay. Really."

"It's just the food, you think?"

"What else could it be?" Amy asked, hopelessly. "I mean, it's not as if I've had anything decent to eat in months, now." She laughed unhappily. "It's hard to believe I'm looking back on that cheap pizza we ate at Pel's house as the last good meal I had."

"Some of the food hasn't been bad, just different," Susan said. "You'd get used to it."

"I don't *want* to get used to it," Amy said. "I want to go *home.*"

"I know," Susan said quietly. "Me, too."

"Everything's tasted *weird.* Even when I know what it is, and it's something normal, like chicken, it'll taste funny. The whole time we were in the Empire, everything tasted funny. And here in Faerie, what do I get to eat, after an entire day of running around being chased by monsters? Dirty water and one-twelfth of a 'possum. What kind of a meal is that?"

"An improvised one," Susan said. "It'll get better. When we get to civilization, or whatever passes for it here, we'll have real food again."

"If it doesn't poison us," Amy muttered.

"It won't poison us," Susan said. "We're all human beings, even if we do come from three different worlds. Anything they can eat here, we can eat." She smiled. "Did I ever tell you about when I first came to the U.S., and they gave me a cheeseburger? I'd never eaten cheese before, my mother called it rotten milk. I couldn't imagine how anyone could eat that stuff. But I had to, if I wanted the beef it was on, so I peeled off what I could, and ate the rest, and then I waited to get sick from eating spoiled food. And nothing happened to me, of course."

Amy gestured unhappily at the mess on the dead leaves. "I wasn't so lucky," she said.

"It's probably just strain," Susan said. "It's rough on everybody, getting stranded here all over again and worrying about Shadow sending more monsters after us. And you'd hardly even recovered from what happened on Zeta Leo Three when they sent us here."

At the mention of her enslavement Amy lost control again, and bent over, retching. She brought up a thin stream of clear fluid, nothing else.

Susan put a reassuring hand on her back, and with the other scrabbled in her purse and came up with a somewhat used tissue, which she offered.

Amy accepted the crumpled paper and wiped her mouth, then stared at the result distastefully.

"I've ruined your Kleenex," she said, "and you probably don't have any more."

"I still have a couple of others," Susan said. "It doesn't matter."

"I'm sorry, anyway," Amy said. "And I've got to find the little girls' bush." She got to her feet. "Thanks, Susan," she said.

"All part of the service," Susan said, smiling. She, too, stood.

As Amy ducked behind a tree in search of privacy, Susan noticed Prossie, standing quietly a few feet away, watching. The men were going about their own affairs—many of them undoubtedly doing the same thing Amy was, while others were fetching water or clearing away the campsite.

"Is there anything I can do to help?" Prossie asked uncertainly.

Susan glanced after Amy, then shrugged. "I don't know," she said.

"I didn't want to intrude," Prossie explained, a little ashamed that she hadn't done anything for their stricken companion.

"Oh, go ahead and intrude," Susan said. "After all, there's just the three of us with all these men."

Prossie hesitated.

She wasn't from the same universe as Susan and Amy. Besides, she was a telepath, a mutant, unfit for the company of normal humans. But right now Carrie wasn't communicating, and this world of Faerie was so silent and strange with her telepathy cut off.

"Thanks," she said.

"No breakfast," Pel remarked, as he splashed his face at the stream and wished the water were cleaner and warmer.

"Not unless you can spot us another 'possum or something," Wilkins replied.

"I was hoping to see a fish or two, maybe, now that there's better light," Pel said.

Wilkins considered the stream, then shook his head. "Doesn't look too likely," he said.

"No," Pel agreed. He shivered and wished he still had a shirt.

"The sooner we get moving, the better," Wilkins said, seeing Pel's actions. "Let's fill these helmets and get up there." He was holding his own helmet as he spoke and gestured toward the other with it.

Pel picked it up. "Whose is this?" he asked.

"Bill Marks's," Wilkins answered. "Al keeps hold of his, and Sawyer's is missing."

"Right." Pel scooped water from the stream, and together the two men headed back up the slope.

The entire party was regrouped and moving by the time the sun was a handsbreadth above the horizon.

"I'm hungry," Ted said. "I wish I could wake up and get myself a snack."

No one bothered to hush him this time; Sawyer remarked, "I'm hungry, too."

"I don't think I could keep anything down if we had it," Amy said. Susan eyed her uneasily, but said nothing.

They walked on; Amy could hear someone's stomach growling, while her own seemed to be tying itself in painful knots. She felt tired and ill.

Of course, she hadn't felt *good* since *Emerald Princess* was captured by pirates. They'd starved their captives on the journey to Zeta Leo Three, and then after the one meal there everyone had been hurried through the showers and put on the stage for auction, all nervous, even terrified. She'd been tired and scared, and Walter had bought her and taken her back to his farm, and then he'd raped her, and beaten her, and for all the weeks she lived with Walter and Beth she had been abused, over and over.

And then she'd been rescued and flown to Base One aboard *Emperor Edward VII*, and she'd mostly recovered there, the bruises were healing, she was sleeping better, but she still felt tired all the time, still felt sour and irritable—and then, before she could get over it, they'd sent her off to Faerie.

She hoped it was just strain and fatigue.

But as she walked through the forests of Faerie she remembered poor little Alella, and Grummetty, the little people from Hrumph who didn't like to be called gnomes, the little people who had died because their bodies didn't work right in Imperial space.

What if *her* body didn't work right in Faerie? What if she had been uncomfortable in the Empire as much because the nature of space itself was wrong, as anything else?

Susan had said, that morning, that they were all human beings, regardless of which universe they came from—but what if she was wrong, and they weren't the same at all?

That was a terrifying idea. She hadn't watched Grummetty and Alella fade away; she hadn't had the nerve to face it and had left all the nursing to Nancy Brown and little Rachel—she felt guilty about that now, especially since Nancy and Rachel were dead, and she also selfishly regretted that she didn't know more about how it had worked. How could she tell if the same thing was happening to her?

None of the other Earthpeople seemed to be troubled by any such effect, though.

At least, not yet.

"I wonder what Lieutenant Dibbs and his men have to eat," Susan said, stepping neatly over a tree root that, a moment before, Ted had stubbed his toe on.

"There are supplies in the ship," Prossie said. "Maybe we should have taken our share before we left."

"We couldn't get at them," Singer pointed out. "That monster's wing covered the door."

"By now Dibbs probably has that thing propped up like a front porch," Wilkins said. "They'll be fine."

"They've no water within a hundred yards or more," Stoddard pointed out.

"There's some water in the ship, too," Sawyer said. "At least, I think there is."

"They'll be fine," Wilkins repeated.

"They why the hell are we here, instead of there?" Marks demanded.

Wilkins glared at him. "Oh, shut up," he said.

CHAPTER 10

They struck the road around midmorning and emerged from the forest shortly after noon.

Not that it was much of a road, by the standards of either the Earthpeople or the Imperials. Pel had noticed the four soldiers exchanging derisory glances when Raven called the narrow path a highway. He had sympathized, but had kept his mouth shut; Raven knew this world, and the Imperials didn't.

"Do you know where we are?" Pel asked Raven, as they all paused, blinking in the bright pale sunlight, atop the gentle slope that led down to cultivated fields and half a dozen crude huts. Rolling farmland stretched out before them almost as far as they could see, broken by streams and occasional small groves and ending in a grassy ridge topped by a massive structure Pel could not make out clearly.

The air had warmed again, and a trickle of sweat was running down his back and into the waistband of his pants.

"Not as exactly as I would choose, friend Pel," Raven replied, scanning the landscape. "This must surely be the Starlinshire Downs, and behind us the Low Forest, but this road we follow is not the Palanquin Road—'tis not of the size to be that. Thus we must be well to the north, but I'd know no more than that until we find landmarks or ask the dwellers here."

"My lord?" Valadrakul said quietly.

"But ah, look you, friend Pel," Raven said, turning suddenly, his hand on the wizard's shoulder. "Look you all, we've no need to limit ourselves to means natural, for we've a practitioner of the arcane arts with us! Speak, then, Valadrakul— where are we now, and where may we find he that we seek, your compatriot Taillefer?"

99

"I know not, my lord, but a spell can tell me, an you allow me a moment."

" 'Tis safe, my friend, e'en in this realm of Shadow?"

Valadrakul spread empty hands. "Who can say, when we know not the extent of Shadow's power? At this moment, we might yet be pursued by creatures keen to avenge those we slew beside the sky ship, and perchance even the merest trace of an incantation will draw disaster upon us. But 'tis only the very simplest of magicks, and I've practiced its like many times before, without mischance."

"Thus, wilt know our whereabouts?"

"Aye, and more," Valadrakul answered. "Though I know not where we be, yet I sense that this place is a goodly one for magicks and that hence can I send word to Taillefer through the currents of the air and ether. It might chance that such a message Shadow will feel likewise, but 'tis only a small risk; ne'er has Shadow troubled itself with the signals that we lesser magicians send each other betimes."

Raven hesitated, then nodded—Pel noticed that he didn't bother to look around at any of the others, let alone to consult them.

"Go, then," Raven told the wizard, "work thy wonders—methinks 'twill give the ladies a needed rest. And if thou canst discover us whence our next meal may come, as well, surely shalt thou have the gratitude of us all!"

It seemed to Pel that Raven and Valadrakul were getting carried away, their phrasing becoming more flowery than ever for no good reason, even while their peculiar Australo-Brooklyn accent grew stronger. Pel didn't like that. Any time Raven began to talk too much, it meant trouble.

But the man in black did have a point; a glance at Amy convinced Pel that she did, indeed, need a rest. She looked terrible. She hadn't thrown up again since that morning, but her face was pale, and she appeared to be on the verge of collapse. Susan was keeping a solicitous eye on her; Pel was relieved that someone was.

The four Earthpeople and Prossie settled to the grass in a group; the other four Imperials settled a few feet away. Raven and Stoddard remained upright, roaming along the slope, studying the countryside.

And Valadrakul crouched on the slope, muttering, working his magic.

* * *

Amy was ravenously hungry, but at the same time she doubted she could keep anything down if she ate it. She felt achy and exhausted; her feet throbbed. The stop for Valadrakul's magic had been very welcome indeed.

She wondered what was wrong with her. There were so many things it could be.

Stress, hunger, weeks of bad food—that could be it. The others weren't visibly suffering, but stress didn't affect everyone the same way. Ted Deranian wasn't exactly suffering, but he'd snapped completely. And Pel Brown had become sort of detached since his wife and daughter were killed; that might be his way of dealing with the strain.

Susan, of course, could cope with anything; Amy was convinced of that. She'd been through it all before, as a child in Southeast Asia.

And the others—well, they were different. The Faerie folk were in their own world, they were *used* to dealing with Shadow's monsters and all the rest of it. The Imperials were all soldiers, even Prossie; they'd been trained for hardships. And they'd only been out of their own reality for a day and a half, not a couple of months.

So maybe it was just stress affecting her. Stress, and the thin air, and the heavy gravity, and the heat, and the humidity, and the weird washed-out sunlight.

She liked that idea, the idea that it was just stress, much better than the other possibilities. If this space wasn't quite right for Earthpeople to live in, then finding a way home wasn't just a way to get back to normal, it was a matter of life and death.

But none of the other Earthpeople were showing any symptoms that she could see, so she hoped that that wasn't it.

If it was, then she was the most sensitive. If the others *did* start showing symptoms, then she would be the first to die.

Right now, she felt as if she might die if she didn't get a few days' rest and some good food.

There were other possibilities, of course, and in a way those were even more frightening. What if she'd contracted some alien disease somewhere? What if she'd caught something from her rapist, Walter, back on Zeta Leo Three? She'd been free of him for weeks—heavens, he'd been *dead* for weeks, hanged on her testimony—but how could she be sure she hadn't picked up something from him? Who knows what loathsome alien diseases he might have had?

Oh, hell, who needed anything alien? If he had syphilis or

herpes or something, that would be bad enough, though she didn't think her symptoms fit either of those.

What if Walter had AIDS? Did AIDS exist in the Galactic Empire? In the space movies on the late show they never talked about things like that.

And what were the symptoms of the early stages of AIDS? Despite all the scare stories on TV, she didn't have any idea. Feeling tired and sick and nauseated didn't seem very distinctive. And didn't AIDS usually take years to appear?

That brought a terrible thought—could she have gotten AIDS from her ex-husband and have had it all along, for the past year and a half? Despite all their arguments and accusations, she had no idea whether Stan had ever really been unfaithful, whether he might have picked up the virus somewhere.

This was all silly, though, she told herself; it wasn't AIDS. It was more likely to be mononucleosis, or that "yuppie flu," or something. She could have caught *anything* on Zeta Leo Three. Or on Base One.

And that was all the more reason to get home to Earth. Somehow, she doubted that modern medicine was easily come by here in Faerie.

Valadrakul was crouched a few yards down the slope from her. "How's it going?" she called.

"Don't bother him," Prossie said, from where she sat just behind and to Amy's left. "He's working magic, or whatever you want to call it."

Amy glanced at her, startled.

"He needs to concentrate," the telepath explained.

"Are you reading his mind?"

Prossie grimaced. "No," she said, "I can't, here. Telepathy doesn't work any better here than it does on Earth."

"But I thought . . . weren't you relaying instructions from Base One?"

Prossie nodded. "That's right," she said, "but only as a receiver; it's my cousin Carrie who does the sending."

"Oh, that's right, you said that." Amy waved a hand at herself and said, "I forgot."

Prossie shrugged.

"So, is Carrie sending anything right now? Does she have any news about Lieutenant Dibbs?"

Startled, Prossie stared at Amy. "How could she have any news about him?"

"Well, if they sent a rescue party, or something."

Prossie shook her head. "They're not sending any rescue party," she said. "If there were any chance they'd do that I'd probably have stayed there myself."

Amy frowned. "Then what's going to happen to those men?" she asked.

"I don't know," Prossie said. "I hope that eventually they'll have the sense to leave. Or maybe we can send Taillefer to help them, after he's sent you Earthpeople home."

"That sounds good," Amy agreed.

"What I'm afraid of, though," Prossie said, "is that Shadow's going to send more monsters, and more, and more, until Dibbs and his men are all dead. That's what Raven's expecting, you know; that's why he fled, but didn't argue more about everybody coming."

"I don't understand," Amy said uneasily.

Prossie picked up a pebble and tossed it down the slope. "It's simple enough," she said. "Shadow knows something's happened back there at the clearing where we crashed, right? It sensed the space warp, and it sent those creatures to investigate, and we killed them all. So it'll be expecting a report, and it isn't going to get one; what'll it do then?"

Amy stared at her.

"It's pretty obvious, isn't it?" the telepath said. "It'll send another force, a larger one. And if that doesn't work, it'll send a third, and a fourth. It'll send trackers, too, in case whatever it's after has left."

"Then they'll be coming after us," Amy whispered, suddenly terrified.

Prossie shook her head. "No, they won't," she said. "Or at least Raven doesn't think so. He thinks that they'll find the ship and Lieutenant Dibbs and the rest there, and they'll kill them all, and it'll never occur to Shadow that there were more, that the rest of us got away."

"Is that . . ." Amy began. Then the implication sank in. "But that's . . . that's horrible . . ."

Prossie grimaced. "Raven set them up," she said. "A decoy, so we could get away."

Amy glanced at Raven, standing farther down the slope, showing no sign at all of a troubled conscience.

"He did ask for volunteers," Prossie said unhappily. "He gave them a chance."

"Do you know for sure that that was what he was doing?" Amy asked. "Did you read his mind?"

Prossie shook her head. "I told you," she answered, "I can't read minds here."

"You're just guessing?"

"You can call it that if you like."

That was exactly what Amy liked; she didn't want to think of Raven as being as callous and calculating as Prossie claimed. She swallowed, then changed the subject. "So what *is* your cousin Carrie saying? What's happening back on Base One?"

"Not much," Prossie said, a trifle uneasily.

"Oh," Amy said.

Her stomach cramped.

"I wish Valadrakul would hurry up," she said. "And I wish . . . oh, the hell with it. I wish I were safe at home and this was all *over*, that's what I wish!"

"Me, too," Prossie said.

Prossie watched as Amy lay back on the grass and closed her eyes. The Earthwoman had a hand on her belly and winced occasionally at some internal discomfort.

There were advantages to being cut off, Prossie thought; she couldn't feel Amy's discomfort, whatever it was, at all.

And of course, being in this other universe made it possible to keep her contacts with Carrie to a minimum, as well; Carrie had not yet been forced to realize that Prossie was deliberately disobeying orders, that Prossie had lied, and had given false reports.

And she didn't know that Prossie had willingly let Raven set Dibbs and the others up to be sacrificed, in order to preserve the group he led, the group Prossie was in.

Of course, the brass back at Base One had sent the entire expedition out as a sacrifice to save face for themselves, but Carrie would expect better of a fellow telepath, wouldn't she?

Prossie knew that Carrie suspected something was very wrong, beyond what had been reported; Prossie suspected that Carrie knew Prossie had gone rogue.

That's what it was, of course; that's what she had done. And that was one more reason, aside from her increased chances for survival, that she was very glad that she had gone with Raven's group. If she had stayed with Dibbs, people would have asked her questions, demanded she relay orders, and her treachery would have been revealed. With *this* group, no one bothered her—even the four soldiers seemed to have forgotten that she was a telepath, that she could talk to Base One at any time. She could keep her secrets.

She could never go back to Base One, though. She could probably never again risk reentering the Galactic Empire anywhere.

She would never again be able to live in her own reality, and that meant that she would never again have her full telepathic ability. She would always be able to touch the minds of her family, back in the Empire, but no one else.

That was a frightening and lonely thought, in a way, but it wasn't all bad. She would never again have to feel the fear and hatred of others, would never be forced to share in someone else's pain or sick terror. She had been mulling it over for hours now, as they traveled, and she was beginning to reconcile herself to the idea.

She didn't think much of Faerie as a place to live, though; she thought Earth would be much more enjoyable. When the others got their space warp, their magical portal, open, she would go through it with them.

"Prossie?"

Carrie. Prossie looked up; no one was watching her.

"What is it?" she sent.

"You've been ignoring me. All today and last night, and even before that. I don't think you even heard some of what I sent."

"I probably didn't," she admitted. "I was thinking."

"Prossie, you're in trouble. I can't get answers out of you. General Hart and Undersecretary Bascombe are both . . . well, they say they're furious, but they're relieved. They can write off the whole mission if they lose contact with you. They've already written off that poor lieutenant and all those men. They can't admit that, of course, but it's true—and Prossie, they'll blame it on you. They'll say that the crazy mutant bitch screwed up communications and got everyone killed. And if they need a scapegoat on this end, they'll get *me*. Prossie, I'm really scared about this."

Prossie hesitated, then said, "Carrie, it's okay. Don't worry about me. Save yourself, Carrie—tell them I really have screwed things up. Tell them anything you like—anything *they* like. Let them blame me. I really *did* disobey orders."

"Prossie, you didn't, did you? Have you gone *crazy*?"

"Maybe I have. You tell them whatever you need to tell them to get yourself out of trouble, Carrie, and don't worry about me—I won't be coming back."

For a long moment, Prossie heard only with her ears, only the gentle near-silence of the Faerie hillside—a light wind rustling leaves, Wilkins muttering something, a distant bird's call. She hadn't heard many birds in the forest, but now one was singing somewhere.

Then Carrie asked, "Are you really sure?"

"I'm sure."

Before either of them could transmit more Valadrakul made an unexpected noise, a sort of great wheezing sigh, as he let his breath out all at once.

All eyes but Amy's turned toward the wizard, but no one spoke as the man got slowly to his feet and turned to address the rest of the party.

Amy, Prossie noticed, stirred, but did not sit up.

For a few seconds, no one spoke.

"He is bespoke," Valadrakul announced. "Taillefer is called, and he comes. We're to meet him at yon ruin, at nightfall." He pointed to the misshapen edifice on the ridge ahead.

"Prossie, what's happening?" Carrie asked.

"Nothing," Prossie said. "It's not important anymore. Don't worry about it."

The contact wavered as Carrie floundered for something to say, for the right way to respond.

"You're really leaving the family?" she asked at last.

Prossie frowned. She hadn't thought of it that way, but of course, that's just what she was doing.

"Yes," she said, "I really am."

"Then good-bye, Prossie."

"Good-bye, Carrie—but hey, I'd still like to hear from you sometimes, you or any of the others. If you can't find me here, check on Earth, too."

"Earth? But, Prossie . . ."

"Good-bye, Carrie."

"Well, come on, folks," Pel said, marching down the slope. "We've got to get there by nightfall."

CHAPTER 11

"We've no need to rush headlong 'cross the vale," Raven said, as the party splashed through the small stream at the foot of the slope. "A meal would do us all good."

"Where are we going to get a meal?" Pel asked, looking about. "I don't see any shops or restaurants or anything."

Stoddard stared at the Earthman; Raven let out a bark of laughter.

"Hardly, friend Pel," Raven said. "These slopes are the Starlinshire Downs, deep in the heart of Shadow's domain, and to the best of what I know, there's neither village nor keep nearby. Yet are there people, and the customs of hospitality surely have not been forgot entirely, even here."

Amy shuddered. "This is Shadow's territory, then?"

"Aye," Stoddard said sourly, "all the world is Shadow's."

"And this part fell to Shadow centuries past," Raven added, "yet surely some semblance of decency must remain."

Pel looked about, startled. "This land's been under Shadow for hundreds of years?" he asked.

"Aye," Raven said, looking at the Earthman with sudden interest. "What of it? Think you of aught that might aid us, then?"

"No," Pel said, "it's nothing important." He blinked, rubbed his nose, and gazed about.

The surrounding landscape was not at all what he would have expected after centuries of rule by an evil wizard. In the movies and stories, when evil fell over the land everything died, everything was dead and black and gray. Clouds were supposed to blot out the sun, if the sun still rose at all. The countryside was supposed to reflect the gloom and despair of its people.

This place didn't. The sun still shone—a bit pale and watery, but bright enough. The grass was green, the trees bore leaves, the crops were growing in the fields, and most of the huts they had seen from the slope, while primitive, had looked reasonably clean and well kept; Pel remembered noticing that the thatch on one was obviously fresh and new.

Of course, he had only seen the outsides of the houses, and only from a distance.

Still, Pel didn't think that Mordor had looked like this. There was no stink of evil in the air here—neither brimstone nor blood nor burning oil—but the smell of raw earth and things growing. No suspicious smoke rose anywhere, nor did ominous fires glow in the distance. The air was a little chilly just now, but there was no soul-deadening cold or exhausting heat, and he was comfortable enough without his shirt; in fact, the occasional breezes felt pleasantly stimulating on his bare back. Shadow obviously wasn't up there with Sauron or Lord Foul or Skynet as a despoiler of countrysides.

On the other hand, Shadow did just fine at creating and sending monsters, he remembered.

At least, if it was really Shadow that sent those creatures. What if they were just ordinary beasts that had happened along, and Raven and his crew blamed Shadow unfairly?

Well, no, Pel admitted to himself, they were scarcely *ordinary* beasts. They were clearly unnatural in their appearance, and they had attacked without reason and fought to the death where ordinary animals would have turned and fled. They probably *were* Shadow's doing—whatever Shadow was.

Raven and his people always spoke of Shadow as if it were an individual, but was it really? Was it a person, a force, or an organization?

Pel didn't know and was not at all happy that he didn't.

As he had been thinking this, the party had continued on, up the west bank of the stream and farther along the little road. Now, suddenly, they halted.

"Here," Raven said, pointing with his bandaged hand, "here's the house that will give us to eat, an any human hearts remain in these lands."

Amy winced as Stoddard pounded on the door of the cottage—if "cottage" wasn't too generous a term for the place. "Hovel" perhaps went too far the other way, but it certainly wasn't anywhere Amy would have wanted to live.

Even so, it seemed rude to hammer like that when they had come seeking the occupant's charity.

The door opened, and a frightened face peered out at them—a woman's face, thirtyish, Amy thought, and not attractive, with unkempt hair and coarse skin.

"Open, in the name of the Goddess," Raven said. "We are famished and claim hospitality by the ancient laws."

The woman glanced up at Stoddard's raised fist, resting on her door, and seemed much more impressed by that, and by Stoddard in general, than by Raven's words. She opened the door, staying behind it.

Stoddard and Raven and Valadrakul marched boldly in; the others hesitated at first, but then Wilkins shrugged and followed, with Sawyer and Marks and Singer close behind.

Ted went next, then Pel, and the three women brought up the rear, Amy last of all.

She found the cottage's main room jammed; it had never been meant to hold so many. The Imperials and Earthpeople were standing near the center, milling about in a crowd that practically filled the available floor space, while the Faerie folk had found their way to an alcove that, Amy realized, must be the kitchen.

At the other end of the little house was an earthen hearth before a crude stone chimney and mantel. A rough trestle table and benches stood beside the hearth; Sawyer and Singer were crowded against the near end of the table, leaning up against it.

Pel was standing a few feet from the table, staring at it—or under it, Amy realized. As she watched, he closed his eyes tight, and stood, swaying slightly, with them shut. Puzzled, Amy glanced under the table.

Hiding beneath it was a child—Amy couldn't be sure whether it was a boy or a girl—who stared out at the strangers with frightened eyes. The poor thing wore a dull brown sacklike garment and nothing else, had mousy brown hair hacked off unevenly at shoulder length.

The child didn't really look anything like Rachel Brown, but Amy knew that that was who Pel was thinking of. Uncomfortable, Amy looked up, away from the child, away from any memories of Pel's dead daughter.

Above the table was a loft. The central portion of the cottage was open from dirt floor to thatched roof, but the kitchen alcove and the hearth area both had plank ceilings. Another child sat in the loft, this one, dressed in faded blue, almost certainly a girl; she clutched a baby in her arms. For a moment Amy thought the baby might just be a doll, but then it waved an arm.

No one who lived in a place like this would have a doll that could wave its arms, Amy was sure. She swallowed.

The space above the kitchen alcove was smaller and lower, and appeared to be used for storage; at any rate, there were no children to be seen there.

The woman closed the heavy door, the bang and the sudden dimness startling Amy.

"Ah, Goodwife," Raven called. "We claim but a single meal. What would you give us?"

"We have nothing to give you," the woman said, her voice high and unsteady, her tone flat.

"Oh, come," Raven replied. "I see much here before me—fruits and grain and vegetables, and surely that keg holds ale."

" 'Tis not for you," the woman insisted. "We've children to feed, and our taxes are not yet paid." Amy noticed that she didn't seem to have quite the same accent to her speech that Raven and Valadrakul and the others did.

"And what of the Goddess's decree that all Her children owe hospitality to one another, whenever they might be wanderers upon the land?" Raven demanded.

"We pay no heed to the old faiths," the woman replied. "We heed only Shadow's orders."

"And what does Shadow say, then, in how one is to treat travelers?"

"Know you not, then?" The woman stood, hands on her hips, eyeing the intruders.

"I'd hear it from you," Raven answered.

"Shadow commands that we feed and shelter those who come on Shadow's business, and to deny all others," the woman told them, "but not when that would risk our own lives, for they are not our own to sacrifice, but are Shadow's, and valued more highly than whatever else might be stolen from us. Better to lose a year's crops, and Shadow's tax thereupon, than a lifetime's, and there are many of you, while I am alone here, save for my children."

Amy glanced up at the loft again, at the children there. Pel, standing near, still had his eyes tightly closed.

She wondered if Shadow could use its magic to spy on this somehow, here in its own territory. Would Shadow, whatever it was, feel the instinctive desire to protect those children that she felt? Did their mother have any way of informing Shadow of the presence of intruders?

"And you admitted us, then, in fear of your life?" Raven asked the peasant woman.

The woman gestured in the direction of Stoddard and Valadrakul. "That," she agreed, "and in hopes that you might prove yourselves to be servants of Shadow."

"You do disgrace to your ancestors and your spirit, in this sad acquiescence to that evil power and the renunciation of the true faith and its customs," Raven said.

"And you prove yourselves fools, to oppose the Shadow that shades the world!"

Amy, already uneasy, had listened to this exchange with mounting discomfort. Now, as the woman and the three intruding natives of Faerie glared at one another through the little crowd, she called, "Raven, let's get out of here, if we're not welcome." She didn't mention anything about the possibility of drawing Shadow's attention, but she thought that Raven would see it.

If Prossie was right about why Raven had left Lieutenant Dibbs back at the ship, then Raven certainly ought to have that in mind.

"Nay," Raven said angrily, "by the bleeding Goddess, I say you nay! We've a right under the ancient law, and we'll take a meal here before we go!"

"She's got a right to her own home," Amy protested. "It'd be stealing!"

"I don't care about that," Sawyer said, before Raven could say anything more, "but I might worry about her men getting back. She's got a husband, at least, or there wouldn't be that baby up there."

Amy bit back a comment about the naïveté implied by that comment; there wasn't necessarily a husband anywhere—but there certainly *might* be one.

"We can handle a husband," Wilkins said, "if it's only one."

"Aye," Stoddard agreed, "an it's but one; what, then, if that one brings friends?"

"Then we'll take what we can carry," Raven said. "I'll not leave here without our due."

Amy watched unhappily as the men of Faerie and the Galactic Empire picked through the contents of the kitchen alcove, but she did not protest further. It was stealing, no matter what ancient rights and privileges Raven might claim, stealing from a woman and her children—but Amy was hungry, very hungry, and the woman wasn't arguing anymore, and there were seven men doing the stealing, compared with two men, four women, and a few children who were not—and Amy was fairly sure that if it came down to open conflict, Susan and Prossie and perhaps even Pel would side with the thieves, while Ted would be useless to either faction.

Pel might be useless, as well, lost in his grief; he was still standing with eyes closed.

She stood and watched and wished she could think of something to say to comfort the woman they were robbing, but nothing came.

She was sure that the woman would report their presence to Shadow, if she could—but then, she probably would have reported the presence of strangers even if they hadn't robbed her.

And ten minutes later, when the entire party was moving again, across the valley toward the ruin where they were to meet Taillefer, Amy ate the raisins and dried apples and sticks of hard-baked bread that were her share of the booty without complaint.

She did not so much as glance back at the cottage, where the woman still stood in the open doorway, watching the thieves depart.

They had finished their meal as they had started it, while walking. The intermediate stage, when they had settled briefly by the roadside to sort out their loot and prepare anything that required preparation, had lasted no more than fifteen minutes, at most, Pel was sure.

Of course, he had no way to check; digital watches didn't work in either Faerie or Imperial space, and his was long gone, anyway. He relied on his own time sense, which he knew was not particularly good.

Still, he was sure that they were moving again less than half an hour after the robbery—despite Raven's claims, Pel could not help thinking of the way they had acquired their meal as a strong-arm robbery.

He almost wished he had joined in, though, and taken a shirt. He hadn't seen any, but there had probably been some, somewhere.

He hadn't seen any because he hadn't wanted to look.

He tried very hard not to think of the girl under the table, not to associate her and her mother with Rachel and Nancy.

Maybe they would realize, when they thought about it, that Pel and the others hadn't taken very much; maybe they wouldn't hold the robbery against him. Maybe they would accept that it had been a necessity.

Robbery or not, it was done, and the party was well along the dirt track that Raven insisted on calling a highway, passing farms and fields on their way to the ridgetop ruin. This time the Earthman had not hung back; instead he walked in the front, with the three natives of Faerie.

"We don't have any hereditary nobility with special privileges back home," Pel remarked to Raven as they walked. "Not anymore, anyway."

The nobleman glanced at the Earthman, but did not break stride or comment.

"I'm not complaining, I was as hungry as anyone," Pel continued, "but back home, taking that woman's food would have been outright theft."

" 'Twas hospitality, not theft," Raven snapped. "The custom is required by the Goddess who brought forth all life and has naught to do with the patents of nobility."

"Well, but it was because you're a member of the nobility that you thought you were entitled, wasn't it?"

"Nay, of course not; these lands are not mine, nor am I brought here to guest, nor are you my retinue, that I'd have the right to feed you." Raven paused, then remarked, " 'Tis clear that your homeland's customs are not as our own, friend Pel— hospitality to travelers is a religious duty put upon us by the Goddess, and any who walk Her green earth are entitled, merely by virtue of being Her children, to the boon of a single meal from any who dwell upon the land and share in Her bounty. 'Tis this right and duty that I sought to claim, not some privilege due my gentle birth."

"Oh," Pel said, comprehension dawning. "It's a sort of tithe, you mean?"

"Aye, a tithe indeed," Raven agreed, nodding. "I'd not thought you had the word. A tithe and a duty, yet one that that woman sought to deny us, so debased has this realm become under Shadow's rule! Yon wife placed her duties to Shadow above all common duties to the Goddess—a greater disgrace to Shadow I cannot imagine."

Pel suspected this was hyperbole; he could think of a great

many things worse than abandoning the customs of traditional religion. He decided against saying so, however.

He squinted at the sun as it descended steadily toward the ridgetop before them. The sky was reddening about it, the wisps of cloud were edged in golden fire—it promised to be a spectacular sunset.

There was nothing abnormal or threatening about it at all, nothing reflecting Shadow's alleged presence.

The lands to either side were green with the lush growth of spring, save where fresh-tilled fields showed rich and black, clean-edged and tidy squares set in the landscape, as if to break the monotony of green. Pel could see men and women and even children working in the fields, here and there; although none were near enough for a good hard look at their faces, they all seemed to be going about their business cheerfully enough. He saw no whips, no tears; backs were bent with labor, but not, so far as he could see, with undue hardship. The people didn't appear to be suffering any more than peasants anywhere might suffer, be it medieval Europe or some Third World country in Africa or South America.

Yet this land was under Shadow's rule, had been under Shadow's rule for centuries, and the Faerie folk spoke of Shadow as this hideous monster, this unspeakable evil. When Pel had first heard Raven's story he had immediately associated Shadow with Tolkien's Dark Lord, Sauron; with Donaldson's Lord Foul; with Bakshi's Blackwolf; with all the evil powers of fantasy films and novels.

By those standards, this land should have been a blasted wilderness, all ash and stone; the people should be crippled by floggings and torture; the skies should be black with unnatural clouds.

None of that fit.

Not for the first time, but far less idly than ever before, Pel wondered whether Shadow might be less a villain than it was a victim of bad press.

Despite the meal, despite the prospect of rescue and a return to Earth that lay ahead, Amy found herself wearing out quickly. She struggled to continue, to keep up with the others, but she felt weak and sick.

At least, she thought, she was able to keep down the stolen food. She pushed on, placing one foot ahead of the other, but the mound of brush and vine-wrapped stone atop the ridge seemed to be taking forever to draw any nearer.

The sun was reddening in the west and the sky darkening, they were finally at the foot of the ridge itself, and Amy was on the verge of collapse when Pel dropped back from the main group, coming even with Amy and Prossie, who had fallen behind.

"Hi," the Earthman said. "You two doing okay, back here?"

Prossie glanced at Amy, who was in no hurry to answer. She shrugged and said, "I'm fine, I guess; I've been thinking, and keeping Amy here company."

"I'm okay," Amy said. "At least, I think I am. Tired, but otherwise I'm okay."

"Not throwing up anymore?" Pel asked.

Amy grimaced at this grotesque lack of tact. "Not throwing up," she said. "Not feeling real good, maybe, but not throwing up."

"I've been thinking about this Shadow thing," Pel said. "I think maybe I had a wrong idea about it."

Amy had been staring at her own feet, willing them to keep moving; now she looked up at Pel. "What sort of wrong idea?" she asked.

"Well, I'd been thinking of it as really being this all-encompassing evil that Raven claims it is—a big supernatural force, like in a horror movie or something. Like Sauron in *The Lord of the Rings*."

"Yeah, so? Maybe it is. Raven seems to think so." She jerked her head in Valadrakul's direction. "And we know there's real magic here."

"But if it *were*," Pel said, "then would everything here look so *normal*, here in Shadow's own territory?" He gestured at the evening sky, the darkening fields, the looming ruin atop the ridge.

"Normal," Amy said, glaring at him. "The sun's the wrong color and everyone talks funny and we all weigh about half a ton and I'm getting sick for no reason, and we're going to meet a wizard, and you're saying everything's too *normal* for you?"

"No, I mean ... I mean if this is Shadow's country, shouldn't the skies be dark?"

"They *are* getting dark," Prossie pointed out.

"No, I mean all the time," Pel persisted. "Shouldn't it be a wasteland, all smoke and ash?"

Amy stared at him, then shook her head. "You're being silly, Pel," she said. "This isn't some stupid movie, like that one, *Wizards* . . . did you ever see that? It was an animated film . . ."

"I saw it," Pel said. "That's the sort of thing I was thinking of. I mean, we've fallen into a story like that, haven't we? Wizards and Galactic Empires and all the rest of it, it's all a story—so why isn't the bad guy acting the part?"

"How do you know he isn't?" Amy said. "How do you know who the bad guy *is*? This isn't a story, Pel; this is real life."

"Then you don't think Shadow's really evil?"

"I didn't say that," Amy protested. "I don't know anything about Shadow. It could be just as bad as Raven says."

"But then why doesn't the countryside show it?" Pel asked, waving an arm at the farms behind them.

Amy sighed. "Pel," she said, "suppose someone popped you through a magical portal into some nice, quiet rural area in Germany in 1943—would the skies be dark? Would the landscape be all twisted and evil?"

Pel frowned. "I guess not," he said. "Not necessarily, anyway, if it was someplace that wasn't getting bombed and away from the camps. But Hitler wasn't a wizard, there wasn't anything supernatural about him."

"So maybe Shadow isn't supernatural evil incarnate," Amy said. "So it's not Sauron. It could still be Hitler."

"Or it could be nothing much. Maybe it's *Raven* who's Hitler—or Napoleon returning from Elba."

"And it could be that we don't have any idea what's going on, and we shouldn't worry about it, we should just all go home," Amy replied, exasperated.

Pel looked uncomfortable and didn't answer. Instead he turned away, and the party continued silently up the ridge in the gathering twilight.

CHAPTER 12

"*And where is he, then?*" *Stoddard demanded, directing* his question equally to Raven and Valadrakul.

Valadrakul shrugged. "I know not," he replied. "He gave a sign for nightfall, I am certain; thus, I understood he would be here by nightfall."

"He will come, I am certain," Raven said.

"Night has fallen," Stoddard pointed out, gesturing at the darkening sky overhead. Stars were beginning to appear.

Pel, standing a step or two away from the Faerie folk, looked up at the sky and shuddered.

The stars were wrong. The constellations were strange, and the pattern and groupings just didn't seem natural. He remembered what Valadrakul had said once, that the stars here were not unimaginably distant spheres of gas, burning by atomic fusion, as they were at home; instead, they were mere thousands of miles away and burned by magic.

That shouldn't really make any difference, he told himself. After all, that was what people had believed back on Earth, for thousands of years. They had learned better, eventually.

But Valadrakul said that the wizards here had gone up and *looked*, that they *knew* the stars were small and near.

Something dark moved across the sky, and Pel blinked. He stared.

Then, as he watched, the dark object suddenly flared into light, and Pel saw that it was a man, a man holding a staff, and the end of the staff was ablaze with something that wasn't quite flame and wasn't quite sparks.

"We must give him time," Valadrakul was saying. "Perchance some delay has befallen . . ."

" 'Scuse me," Pel said loudly, "but is that him?" He pointed.

117

Raven and most of the others whirled, or at any rate snapped their heads around quickly; Stoddard turned more deliberately.

"Aye," Valadrakul said, " 'tis him; Taillefer a' Norleigh." He raised a hand, and a yellow glow shone from his palm, casting a weak and uneasy light over the entire party as they huddled in the ruined castle.

The flying figure was approaching rapidly; now, seeing the light, the man waved, and adjusted his course to head more directly for Raven's party.

"Can *you* fly?" Pel asked Valadrakul.

Startled, the wizard glanced at him, then turned his attention back to his incoming compatriot.

"Aye," he said, "an some, though none so well as yonder."

"I haven't seen you do it," Pel said.

"I've had no need," Valadrakul answered.

Pel's mouth opened, then closed.

No need, perhaps, but wouldn't flight have been useful against Shadow's hellbeasts? Wouldn't it have been useful in scouting ahead, in finding food and water, in insuring that at least one member of the party would be at the ruin by nightfall? Pel could see a dozen ways in which flying might have been convenient, yet Valadrakul's feet had always remained firmly on the ground.

If nothing else, wouldn't it be a way to avoid blisters and aching feet? Pel's own feet were certainly suffering, and he assumed that Valadrakul's hurt, too.

Still, he reminded himself that he shouldn't pry. It wasn't any of his business. If Valadrakul didn't care to fly, he presumably had a reason; there might be a cost he didn't want to pay, or some danger inherent in it.

Or maybe, despite his claim, he just couldn't fly, any more than he could open the interdimensional portals; wizardry was obviously not all a single skill. There was nothing wrong in that, either, and Pel could hardly question Valadrakul's power or value, since the wizard's magic had saved Pel's life when the hellbeasts had attacked.

And then Taillefer was coming in for a landing, not in a slow upright descent like a movie superhero, but in a headlong tumbling plunge; at Raven's direction Stoddard and the four Imperial troopers were preparing to catch him, Stoddard at the point of a *V*, the soldiers two on either side of the big Faerie native, obviously a bit unsure of what they were doing.

"I'd aid, as well, an I could," Raven said, holding up his bandaged hand, and calling to the others. "Friend Pel, here, stand you ready by the side. Ted Deranian, would take this side with me, and be my other hand? And the women, though you be frailer, stand to the rear and watch, lest any fall."

Pel stepped up, taking a position behind Wilkins and Sawyer, not at all sure what he was doing; then, before anyone else could react, before anyone could ask any questions, Taillefer came plummeting into the wide end of the *V*, headed straight toward Stoddard.

"Catch you him!" Raven and Valadrakul called in near-perfect unison, as Stoddard stepped forward, arms out and knees bent, and the four soldiers thrust out their hands.

The flying wizard hit Stoddard hard; Pel could see that he had curled up as best he could, and Stoddard had positioned himself to have an arm under each shoulder, but still, Taillefer's head drove into Stoddard's belly hard enough to knock the wind out of the big man. The wizard's legs flew up, and the Imperials grabbed at them.

And then Stoddard and Taillefer and Singer were all in a heap on the broken flagstone floor of the ruin, and the others were all crowding around at once, trying to help them up.

All except Amy, that is, who was leaning against a broken wall, looking sick.

The ruins had been a castle. That had not been obvious at all until they actually reached the outer wall and fought their way through the entangling vines, but once they were inside, even Amy could see that the structure had once had a central mass, an encircling wall, and guardian towers at the corners.

It had obviously never been a graceful fairy castle like the one at Disney World, or the one that crazy Bavarian king had built on a mountaintop; from the look of it, this had been a practical and very ugly fortress, with thick walls of heavy gray stone, few windows, and little in the way of comforts or ornamentation.

Whatever it had been, however, not much remained. The curtain wall, as Raven called it, was broken down into rubble in several places; the courtyard was overgrown with weeds and thornbushes; the roof was gone entirely, the supporting arches and columns broken off short. The great hall had one side missing, the other three jagged remnants.

Oddly, the tower at one end still stood, apparently almost intact, though it was hard to be sure through the thick layer of ivy that covered it. That tower, and the adjoining mass of stonework, had been what they had seen from afar, what they had steered for.

When they had reached it, though, no one had shown any inclination to enter the tower or most of the rest of the structure; they had simply gathered in the ruined hall, where the remains of a stone floor had kept the undergrowth from getting out of hand.

When the men had begun arguing about why Taillefer wasn't there yet, Amy had almost suggested that perhaps he was, maybe he was in the tower somewhere—but then she had thought better of it. She didn't want anyone to go in there; she didn't want the group to be split up into search parties. She just sat down and waited; if this Taillefer was in there, he'd come out sooner or later.

And he hadn't been in there; instead he'd come falling out of the sky. Amy had stood up when Raven called for help, but the move had upset her delicate stomach—except her stomach had never been delicate back on Earth.

It was delicate now; she struggled to keep down the supper they had stolen from that poor woman and her children, and as the wizard tumbled into the others and knocked them sprawling, like some horribly unfunny clown act, Amy stood by, off to the side, making no move to help. As she watched the men get to their feet, she thought it was a miracle that nobody had broken any bones, and that Stoddard hadn't gotten a concussion from whacking his head on the stones.

At least, she hoped no one had a concussion; in the sickly yellow glow from Valadrakul's hand and Taillefer's staff, none of the faces looked particularly healthy.

"And look what the wind's blown us," Raven called cheerfully, using his good hand to help Taillefer up. "Come you, one and all, and greet him who is come to aid us in our hour of need!"

Amy stayed in her place by the wall; she didn't want to bother greeting the new arrival. With any luck, he'd be creating a portal back to Earth in a few minutes, and she could go home and make an appointment with her doctor and never see Taillefer or any of these other people again.

She couldn't help looking at them, though.

Taillefer was short for a man, no more than her own height, and fat—not really obese, but thick and rounded everywhere, the sort of fat that Amy associated with the word "stout." He was dressed in black, a long fur-trimmed coat over a black tunic and black tights, with gold rings on his fingers, and more gold rings on the carved five-foot staff of dark wood he held in one hand. The rings on his fingers looked ordinary enough, but the gold bands on the staff were glowing dully.

Wizardry at work, Amy supposed. She didn't much care anymore; she just wanted it all to be over. At this point she found it more amazing that he hadn't whacked anyone with the staff when he came plunging down out of the sky than that the gold fittings glowed.

And why had he done that plunge, anyway? Why hadn't he just landed by himself? This was the wizard they were trusting to send them home, she thought sourly, a magician who couldn't land on his own two feet?

Singer helped Taillefer brush off the dust, then slapped at the dark smudges on his own uniform; the purple fabric looked dark and ominous in the yellow light.

Amy shuddered. She was starting to get the creeps. Pel had been complaining about how Shadow's country didn't look evil enough; what about this place, then, this ruined castle, with its dark stone walls and black shadows and nasty thorns and vines growing everywhere? In the entire place she hadn't seen a single flower, or an honest blade of ordinary grass. What about right here, where even the silly Imperial uniforms could look threatening?

But that was the peculiar light, and that came from the two wizards, who were supposed to be on the good guys' side.

"The blessings of the Goddess to you all," Taillefer said, in a surprisingly high-pitched tenor and with an accent distinctly different from the peculiar Australian–New York intonation of the other Faerie folk Amy had met. "My brother Valadrakul, I greet you; for the rest, come, let us know one another! Pray, someone among you, make us a light, that my fellow wizard can cool his hand, and I my staff."

"I'll fetch something," Stoddard said; he turned away and began looking for dead brush.

While he and the Imperials set about building a fire, Raven stepped up to Taillefer and announced, "I am called Raven of Stormcrack Keep, and I welcome you to this place, whatever it might be." He held out a hand.

Taillefer clasped the hand and smiled. "Ah, Lord Raven, as you would surely have it," he said, "I've heard much of you.

But know you not what this place is, then? Did not my brother in the arcane arts tell you that much?" He turned to look at Valadrakul.

"I saw no need," Valadrakul said, "and we'd more urgent concerns."

"Indeed, I daresay you did, yet 'tis worthy of note where we meet, is't not?" Taillefer grinned in a way Amy did not find comforting.

"Where are we, then?" Raven asked, a trifle annoyed. Stoddard looked up from the armful of brush he and the Imperials had collected.

"Why, this is Castle Regisvert, none other!" Taillefer's grin broadened, then slipped somewhat as most of his audience failed to react.

Stoddard and Raven reacted, however; Stoddard's face went blank, as if he had just decided not to believe what he was being told, and he continued stacking the firewood.

Raven started, then looked about at the ruins with new interest. "Truly, say you?" he asked.

"Aye, truly," Taillefer said.

Prossie and the four Earthpeople still didn't respond, since none of them had ever heard of any Castle Regisvert. Two of the Imperials paused in their efforts.

"So what?" Wilkins asked.

"Why, know you not the tale?" Taillefer asked, astonished.

"We're not from around here," Wilkins answered dryly.

"Then gladly I'll tell it," Taillefer said, his grin returned. " 'Twas in the days of old, when Shadow's reach was yet limited, when darkness had not yet fallen upon all the lands, yet strife was widespread, for those who opposed the encroaching evil were not united; aye, in truth, that's the damning disgrace of all our people, and all that was needed for the triumph of Shadow that so oppresses and shames us now . . ."

"Excuse me," Amy called from her place by the wall, "but I don't think this is the time for stories."

Affronted, Taillefer turned to glare at her. " 'Tis no mere *story*, wench, but the true history of this place."

"All the same," Pel said, "maybe it can wait. Amy isn't well, and we'd like to get her home. And I want to get home, too, and probably the Imperials do. And we should get Ted there to a doctor."

Ted giggled.

Susan said nothing, Amy noticed; she just stood by and watched.

"Ah, and is this why I was summoned hither?" Taillefer asked. "Has Valadrakul told you that I might bear you to your homes?"

Valadrakul cleared his throat. His still-raised hand was still glowing, but the glow dimmed perceptibly.

"Indeed, I've a fine gift for wind-riding," Taillefer said, "and I might well bring another, though I doubt me I can carry any but one at the time."

" 'Tis not wind-riding we ask," Valadrakul said, lowering his hand. Only the faint fading glimmer of Taillefer's staff and the dim light of the stars overhead remained to illuminate the scene.

"And what then is it?" Taillefer asked. "That sign sent me told me that I was called, and by whom, and to what part of the world, but naught else. What would you have of me, Valadrakul of Warricken?"

A thin tongue of flame flared up in the stack of brush, as Valadrakul worked his magic with a gesture. "Before we talk of that," the wizard said, "let us exchange names, as you said we should. You know me well of old, and Raven has spoken his name; know then that he who stands yonder is Stoddard, of Raven's household, most faithful of all." He pointed to where Stoddard stood, faintly visible in the still-weak firelight. "And of all you see here, good Taillefer, only we three, Raven, Stoddard, and myself, are from this realm."

Taillefer cocked his head slightly. "How mean you, Valadrakul?"

Valadrakul sighed. "I mean that this good man, Pellinore Brown, and likewise Ted Deranian, and these ladies known to me as Amy and Susan, came to us from a land they call Earth; and that these others, Messires Wilkins and Sawyer and Singer and Marks, and Mistress Thorpe, are from the Galactic Empire."

Amy couldn't see just where the wizard pointed as he named all the names and wished that they had some proper light—even just a flashlight. The fire was growing, and that would help.

The glow of his staff lit Taillefer's face, though, and Amy could see that he was considering them all for a moment, looking about in the darkness.

For a moment, firelight flared, as a particularly dry bit of kindling caught; then it flickered and died down.

"And that would account for their garb, I would suppose," Taillefer said at last, "but that yourself, Valadrakul, and him you name Stoddard, wear the same. And lo, Vala, your hair is much transformed; had you fleas, perhaps, that would not yield without this butchery?"

"We have sojourned in the Galactic Empire," Valadrakul explained, "and there were forced to make do with what attire came to hand." He put a hand to his head. "As for this, 'twas but the result of misfortunes that bear no retelling here and now."

Taillefer nodded thoughtfully. "And Elani? For surely, 'twas she who sent you thither?"

"Dead," Valadrakul replied bitterly. "Slain by Shadow's black beasts."

Amy's stomach lurched, and she called, "Can we get on with it, please?"

Taillefer threw her a glance, then turned back to Valadrakul. " 'Tis a grievous loss you speak of," he said, "and when time more freely permits, I'll mourn her as she is due. Erstwhile, howsoever, he that you called the Brown Pellinore spoke of going home. Home to this Earth, is it?"

"Aye," Valadrakul said.

Amy could hear Wilkins and the others trying to help the fire along, could hear the bits of wood scraping on the stone floor and the muttering of their voices, but she could no longer see their faces. Someone was cursing under his breath, but she couldn't tell who it was.

"And you'd have me open the portal, then?" Taillefer asked his compatriot. " 'Tis for this that you summoned me and sought my aid?"

"Aye," Valadrakul replied.

"And you'd have it here in Regisvert, I suppose? Do you think me mad, Vala?"

"The place was of your own choosing, Taillefer, that it might be readily found by us all; I'd no mind as to where the portal might be."

"What's wrong with right here?" Amy demanded.

Taillefer turned a disdainful stare her way, his face ghostly in the gloom. "Methought you'd have none of the history, woman," he said.

"I don't need any lectures," Amy snapped. "What's wrong with here?"

Valadrakul sighed and turned to her. The darkness hid his features. "Four hundred years and more agone," he said, "this Castle Regisvert was hearth and stronghold for the Green Magician, sworn foe to Shadow. 'Twas built upon this spot because here the currents of magic are strong, the flow of power rich and full; and as was ever the case that drew the attention of Shadow, who one dire night came, and, after a famous battle of eldritch skill and might that lasted for many days, Shadow struck down the Green Magician, threw down the castle to ruin, and drew the powers of this place into its own web. The magic yet runs strong here—but likewise it is yet linked close to Shadow, and as any touch upon the strands of a spider's web will draw the spider's eye, yet will any spell worked in this place draw Shadow's gaze."

"You tell it briefly, and without interest," Taillefer said, "yet is that the essence of the tale, and of my reasoning."

"Then we'll go somewhere else," Amy said. "We don't care where you open the portal, we just want to go home."

"And I've no doubt you desire it," Taillefer said, "but I'll have none of it. Go where you will, yet I'll not conjure you home."

Wilkins, squatting, looked up from the fire; Stoddard, who had been standing impassively nearby, unfolded his arms from across his chest.

Ted giggled hysterically. "I knew it," he said. "I'm *never* going to wake up from this one. I must be comatose, or maybe dead."

And Amy's stomach betrayed her again; she bent, clutching her belly, and threw up most of her stolen supper.

CHAPTER 13

*R*aven frowned and glanced at the black-haired Earthwoman, the one called Susan. She was tending to her sick companion, and her black bag rested on the ground beside her. The madman, ted-Deranian, was leaning against a broken wall, staring at the stars. Pel the Brown and the witch-woman Thorpe were dividing their attention between their fallen comrade and the wizards, while the four soldiers had eyes only for Raven, Valadrakul, and Taillefer.

Stoddard was standing back, beyond the fire, but Raven had no worries where Stoddard was concerned; the man had been true all his life, the most faithful helpmeet any could ask for.

And Valadrakul had returned to his customary silence; he was standing there, looking first to his compatriot in the mystic arts, then to his liege lord, and saying nothing.

None stepped forward to confront this rogue Taillefer, who sought to betray the cause. That was a leader's duty.

That was *his* duty.

And he'd no wish to shirk that duty; he would be only too glad to berate the scoundrel, to demand an explanation, to demolish the fool's every argument against doing as they asked. Yet it would not do to be overhasty. He had expected a tumult of protest when the wizard spoke his defiance and had bethought himself to enter as the voice of calm reason, quieting the roil; the woman Amy had put an end to that by her illness, puking on the holy stones of Castle Regisvert like an overfed bitch. To speak up whilst her condition was unknown would have been seen as unseemly.

But her attendants were about her, and it would scarcely do to leave Taillefer too long unchallenged.

"Look you, wizard," Raven said, trying to sound calm and

126

reasonable, "wherefore say you this, that you'll not conjure the portal to the realm called Earth?"

"And I'll not," Taillefer answered coldly. " 'Tis reason enough."

"Play no games with *me*, Taillefer," Raven snapped. "Say then, why you will not conjure as we ask."

"Because, O Raven, I love my life and would not see it early ended. Much as I appreciate that all must in time return to the breast of the Goddess, yet am I in no hurry to do so."

"Nor are we, wizard," Raven retorted, fighting down anger. "What does this with the conjuring?"

Taillefer sighed ostentatiously. "See you, Lord Raven," he said, "who has conjured this spell that you ask me to perform? Why, imprimis, there is Shadow, who created it, by what means we know not, for Shadow's ways are unknown to us. An it was human once, we might well doubt that it is yet, and it has lived these many centuries, it draws upon such unlimited powers, it binds together a web of powers and magicks the like of which no mortal has ever known. That Shadow survives the conjuring between worlds means naught for such as myself."

"I know that . . ." Raven began.

Taillefer held up a silencing hand. "Secundus," he said, "there was Quarren, who sought the title Light-Bearer, and who bethought to lead all the wizards remaining in crusade 'gainst Shadow. 'Twas he who first stole the secret of the portals, brought it from Shadow to the light, as it might be said. You well know what befell him."

"He died," Raven said. "I can scarce deny it, he was slain by Shadow. Yet the conjuring of portals was in no way the cause, Taillefer."

"Ah, but know you that in certainty, you who call yourself Raven? And remember, tertius, was Elani of the Scarlet Cloak, who stood among your companions 'gainst the rule of Shadow. And where is she now, O bird of ill omen?"

"Dead likewise, in truth," Raven admitted. "But see you, Taillefer, she died not from the conjuring of a portal, but from merest mischance, that we should be in that forest when Shadow's hellbeasts passed by."

"Say you so, then?" Taillefer shook his head. "An you do, I say you lie. 'Twas no mischance, methinks."

"And I say 'twas just that, wizard," Raven replied, glaring. "I was there by her side; were you?"

"Nay," Taillefer admitted, "yet do I know that which you do

not. You and Valadrakul and Elani, you were gone many days, O Raven, vanished from the face of the land—to the Galactic Empire, 'twould seem, from Vala's words. There were reports that hinted at such, from our agents—and yes, I bespoke them, I opened the portals as you would have me do. And every time I did, Shadow's creatures descended upon me, swiftly and with deadly intent, until I dared not do so again. Shadow's reach is long, Raven, and it has ways of knowing that we do not; perhaps it feels tremors in its web, perhaps it sees in ways we do not. Whatever the means, I doubt me not that Shadow *knows*, upon the instant, when any lesser being dares open the gates between worlds. When my compatriot told me that Elani was dead, slain by Shadow's beasts, I knew in an instant that she had conjured one portal too many, and I'll not follow her down that path."

Raven glowered at him. " 'Twas not quite the way of it, wizard," he said. "True, that perchance the beasts were drawn by a gate between worlds, but 'twas none of Elani's conjuring. The mages of the Galactic Empire, those they call scientists, opened the portal."

"What matter, then?" Taillefer demanded. "You see my point; 'twas the gate that drew Shadow's attention, whosoever conjured it."

"Yet have you, by your own words, conjured portals and lived to tell of it."

"Indeed, for I fled instanter, when attacked."

"Then do this the same!"

Taillefer shook his head. "Nay, Raven. I have gone too oft to the well and fear that the bucket must soon give way. These last conjurings were each for but an instant, and each guided to a particular ally in the Empire, yet I scarce won away." He drew back a sleeve and held up his left arm, displaying deep, half-healed wounds, plainly visible even by firelight. "And that was in Old Dunleigh, seven score miles from here, and five score further from Shadow's keep. Here, with no friend upon the other side to guide the spell home, with the need to see half a dozen men and women transported . . . I'll not risk it. E'en should I open the gate, it might well deliver these to the wrong spot in yonder realm—I might send them to Stormcrack when I sought Starlinshire, as it were, or leave them in some blasted wasteland, or drop them in the sea, an I take not an hour or more to guide it. And an hour, when every second draws Shadow's ire closer?"

"Yet 'twould be the right world, and surely, the journey home come be made . . ."

"Nay, Lord Raven," Taillefer said, "be you not so sure. Know you, that in the realm these call Earth, there are many worlds? And that in some, the air itself is poison, if there be air at all?"

Raven turned to Pel, who was standing close at hand. "Is't true?" the rightful lord of Stormcrack Keep demanded.

Pel had not been expecting the question; he had been standing close by, listening intently but silently, hoping that Raven would find some way to talk Taillefer around—certainly, Pel had always found Raven persuasive—but he had had no intention of getting into the argument himself, for fear of messing things up.

But when he was directly questioned, he could hardly stay out. He couldn't answer immediately, though; puzzling out what Taillefer meant took a few seconds. "Do you mean the other planets?" he asked. "Mars and Venus and like that?"

"Aye."

"But I thought you could only open a gate to places where people spoke English . . ." Pel let his sentence trail off, suddenly realizing how stupid it sounded.

"Nay, 'tis the miracle workers of the Empire, who speak without voice, who can locate only those minds that speak the Good Tongue," Taillefer said. "The spells of Shadow can open gateways unto any realm whose existence is known beyond doubt—that is, any realm of which certain arcane characteristics are known. But where in that realm the portal opens, who wist?"

Valadrakul spoke up. "Friend Pel, though we esteem you greatly now, think you that we had *chosen* your cellars as our point of entry? Had we the fullest choice, we'd have emerged in the audience chamber of a king or prince. And think you that we *chose* that foul desert whither Elani sent us, when Shadow's beasts o'ercame us at Stormcrack?"

Pel was flustered. "But she said . . . she was in a hurry . . ."

"As would I be," Taillefer pointed out.

"Listen, if you could be sure it was on Earth, on land," Pel said, "we'd take it—at least, I would. We'd get home eventually." He glanced at the others for support.

Ted shrugged; Amy nodded, Susan frowned, then shook her head, once, a sharp little negative jerk.

"*I'd* take it," Pel insisted.

"And what of the rest, who would be left behind to face Shadow's anger?" Taillefer asked. "Not to put too fine a point on it, what of myself?"

"You could come with us," Pel suggested, not very hopefully.

"Oh, aye," Taillefer replied sarcastically. "Plunge myself into an unknown corner of a realm where all my spells and powers are for naught, where I know not a thing of the ways and customs; a realm that, alone of the three known, has no way to reach the others, so that never could I return?"

"But why would you *want* to return?" Pel asked desperately. "This world's ruled by Shadow, isn't it? Our world isn't; it's not bad at all, really." He had intended to argue further, but he stopped abruptly when he saw the expressions not just on Taillefer's face, but on Raven's and Valadrakul's, as well.

"Man," Taillefer said, "this world may seem unpleasant to *you*, yet is it my world, my homeland, and I'll not abandon it to Shadow, not leave it in its hour of need."

"Nor will I," Raven said.

Pel looked at Valadrakul, whose expression convinced Pel that he didn't need to hear what the other wizard had to say. The Earthman sighed.

"You won't do it?" he asked.

Taillefer shook his head. "That I won't," he said.

Amy heard it all, heard first Raven, then Pel argue with Taillefer. Her stomach had calmed, and she was in no danger of vomiting again; she was ravenously hungry and felt weak and sick, but she was not going to throw up for a while. She sat against the ruined wall of the castle, surrounded by shadows and gloom, and listened to the men debate the rest of her life.

And she was losing the argument. If someone didn't do something, it sounded as if she would be trapped in this horrible fairy world forever.

Raven, much as he wanted his guns and soldiers, appeared to have abandoned the argument to Pel. Pel was trying, but he argued like a man, all rationalizations and confrontations, and he was obviously losing. Taillefer felt his life was at stake; he wasn't going to be swayed by that sort of logic.

"But why would you *want* to return?" she heard Pel ask.

"This world's ruled by Shadow, isn't it? Our world isn't; it's not bad at all, really."

Amy didn't need to hear; she knew the answers. If anything, Pel had just convinced Raven to switch sides, rather than Taillefer. "Susan?" she said quietly.

"Yes?"

"You have your bag?"

Susan took a moment to consider that.

"I don't think it'll work," she said, "but I'll try it if you want."

"Please," Amy said.

Susan sighed, then pulled her bag up where she could reach into it more easily.

Then she had her little revolver in her hand, the .38 Police Special; she glanced at Amy, who nodded.

"I don't think it'll work," Susan said again, as she rose, pistol ready.

The men had not noticed anything, as yet; Pel was asking the plump wizard, "You won't do it?"

"That I won't," Taillefer replied.

Susan cleared her throat, then raised the pistol, gripped tightly in both hands, and pointed it at Taillefer.

"Wizard," she called, her finger tight on the trigger.

Raven turned at the sound of the Earthwoman's voice, expecting nothing more from her than a plea for mercy; it took a second before his eyes adjusted to the dimness, but at the sight of the weapon in her hands his jaw dropped.

Quickly, he caught himself, composed himself.

"Aye, mistress?" Taillefer asked, as he, too, turned. "What would you, and what is this you point at me?"

"This thing I'm pointing at you is a weapon from Earth," Susan explained. "It's commonly called a handgun. If I pull the trigger, it'll blow a hole right through you—ask Raven and Valadrakul, they've seen me use it to kill Shadow's creatures. It's what Raven wants from Earth—we've promised him a supply of guns to use against Shadow."

"Ah," Taillefer said, eyeing the revolver with interest.

"Now, we're going to ask you again whether you'll open the portal to Earth," Susan said, "with the understanding that if you refuse, I'll blow your head off. Will you open the portal?"

Taillefer hesitated, then turned to Valadrakul. "Does this device what she says?"

"Aye," Valadrakul said, blinking at Susan. For a moment, Raven thought the wizard intended to say more, but in the end he left the single word to stand alone.

Thoughtfully, Taillefer turned back to face the Earthwoman. "See you, mistress, the position you put me in," he said. "An you make good your threat, I perish. An I accede to your demands, then too do I perish, but at Shadow's hands rather than yours. Either way, I am dead. If 'tis Shadow that slays me, then mayhap others die with me. Now, consider likewise what you'd accomplish; an I refuse, and you slay me, you do not gain what you seek, for there's none but I who can do it. An I yield, you may yet see Earth, but I die, and there shall be none who can restore the portal for the delivery of the weapons you say this worthy who calls himself Raven seeks; thus, Shadow triumphant, my people forever enslaved. I'd not have that weighing upon my soul in the afterlife."

"I don't need an argument," Susan said harshly. "I need a decision."

"And I say that you shall have one, in a moment—if you see it not yet. Think you, if you slay me, you shall be forevermore trapped in our world; if you refrain, the chance shall remain, so long as I live, that some way shall be found that I may safely send you home."

"You're refusing, then."

"Aye, mistress; I refuse you."

Slowly, Susan lowered the pistol. Then she shrugged, and said to Amy, "I told you it wouldn't work." She turned away.

And Raven let out his breath.

He had not realized, until that moment, that he had bated it.

Nor had he realized, until the danger was past, that he had thought Susan would shoot. Yet it was with surprise and wonder that he saw her put the weapon away and saw Taillefer standing unharmed.

Had it been he himself who held the weapon, and who held Susan's position, Raven knew that Taillefer would now be dead.

Which would, as Taillefer had said, be a disaster.

This bore some thought.

"Maybe you should have wounded him," Pel suggested quietly, leaning on one elbow. The stone pavement of Castle Regisvert was cold beneath him. "If you'd put a bullet in his leg, say, maybe he'd have believed you, not called your bluff."

Susan, lying nearby, raised her head and shook it no; Pel could just barely see the movement in the darkness. "Too risky," she said. "What if he bled to death, or the wound got infected? No, it was all bluff, and we lost."

"So what do we do now?"

"We go to sleep, Mr. Brown. It's late; it's been a long day. You heard Raven and Wilkins and Taillefer. We'll talk it all out tomorrow, by daylight."

"But how do we get back to Earth?" Pel heard his own voice rising in pitch; he realized that he must sound almost hysterical.

That was reasonable; he *was* almost hysterical. He *had* to get home. He had to get out of this fairy-tale world, this pulp fantasy story he had found himself in, back to the sane and normal world of lawnmowers and income taxes and marketing consultation, back to the world of Nancy and Rachel. He couldn't stay in Faerie; he simply couldn't take it.

And his only way back was Taillefer, and Taillefer was refusing to cooperate.

How could he go to sleep?

"How do we get back?" he repeated, a bit more quietly.

"I don't know, Mr. Brown," Susan said. "I don't know, and no one here knows. You're tired, we're all tired, we're distraught—get some sleep. It'll help."

"But what . . ."

"Maybe Taillefer will be braver by daylight; had you thought of that? People are like that sometimes—*everybody* is, whether they admit it or not. It's easier to take risks by daylight. Go to sleep, Mr. Brown."

Pel hesitated, then rolled over, and tried to sleep.

It was easier than he had expected.

CHAPTER 14

*A*my sat up, stretched, then immediately leaned over and threw up—or tried to; her stomach held nothing she could bring up.

Susan awoke at the sound; Amy saw the attorney's eyes, closed a moment before, open and watching her. Pel, on Susan's other side, stirred.

Taillefer, already up and about, turned and looked at her with interest.

"What ails you, woman?" he asked.

"I dunno," Amy muttered, wiping her mouth with the back of her hand.

"Have you a fever, then?"

Amy shrugged; Susan, who had felt Amy's wrist and forehead the night before, answered, "No fever I could find."

"Is't bad food, perchance? What had you to eat, of late?"

"Garbage," Amy muttered.

"The same as the rest of us," Susan replied.

Taillefer considered that. "Well, betimes a poison may strike one and pass another by, yet . . . how long has this troubled you?"

"A few days," Amy said, wiping her hand on a clump of grass.

"Has it . . . your pardon for my coarseness; has it troubled your bowels?"

Amy shook her head. "Not really. Not yet, anyway."

"Feel you weak and weary, perchance? An so, did that come ere the vomiting?"

"I've felt rotten for weeks," Amy agreed. "But it's just this place—I need to go home!"

Taillefer shook his head. "I think that's not the cause, mistress."

Amy glared up at him. "Oh? Is this something people get here? You recognize it?"

Taillefer smiled crookedly. "An I read the signs aright, mistress," he said, "'tis something that women must surely 'get' in every land, be it here in the True World, or in the Galactic Empire, or on your Earth. Are you wed?"

For a moment, Amy didn't understand what Taillefer meant; the sudden question seemed to come from nowhere, to be completely irrelevant.

Then she saw the connection. The anger drained from her stare, to be replaced with shock.

"Oh, my God," she said.

Pel returned from the bushes still blinking sleepily as he buttoned his pants; he wished the Galactic Empire had developed the zippered fly, but they apparently hadn't. He looked up to see that Amy was crying, and Susan was comforting her—again.

Pel frowned slightly. Whatever was bothering Amy, she didn't seem to be taking it well. It didn't seem to be getting much worse—or any better.

He had heard her asking Susan whether she thought it could be the same thing that killed Grummetty and Alella, that her system was somehow incompatible with this entire universe; he didn't see how that could be it, since no one else was affected, and he certainly hoped it wasn't that.

Well, whatever it was, there wasn't anything he could do about it except help her get back to Earth. The sooner the whole group sat down together and figured out how to do that, the better.

Amy and Susan were sitting against the east wall of the great hall, in the shade; Ted was still asleep nearby. Taillefer and Valadrakul were talking quietly over toward the northeast corner. Raven and Singer and Prossie were doing something together in the sunlit center of the hall, shadows stretching far out to the west—Pel hoped they were getting breakfast. Wilkins and Marks and Sawyer were moving about over at the south end, where thornbushes had grown up through the broken floor.

Stoddard was nowhere in sight; Pel guessed he was out gathering firewood. The morning air was chilly and damp, fragrant with mosses and weeds, and he still had no shirt; a fire would be welcome.

But there was no need to wait for that; if everyone but Ted was awake, it was time to start discussion.

"So what are we doing?" Pel demanded loudly, of no one in particular.

"Getting breakfast, I hope," Wilkins replied. "We've been trying to catch something here—might be a woodchuck, if you have those here."

The two wizards looked up from their colloquy. "Perchance I might lend a hand," Valadrakul said.

The animal was a badger, not a woodchuck, and managed to claw Singer's arm before being clubbed into unconsciousness by the butts of four blasters and a chunk of wood; it was finished off by Wilkins, who cut its throat with his pocketknife.

Pel watched the operation with morbid interest, but did not help beyond lending moral support; he was not yet accustomed to killing his own food. It seemed like a very messy business—not that he saw much of an alternative here.

He did help build the fire, though.

The meat was edible, at least some of it—Raven cut out the portions he said were fit to eat, and left the rest. Even when properly cooked, however, it wasn't very pleasant eating, and the relatively good parts did not go very far when divided a dozen ways. The smells of blood and dew-wet badger fur lingered, which didn't help Pel's appetite any.

For the rest of the meal Taillefer had a pouch of hard biscuits he shared out, while Sawyer and Marks brought water from a nearby spring.

As they ate, Pel kept looking for Stoddard's return, but there was no sign of the man; when he suggested that a share be set aside for him, Raven simply shook his head.

Amy ate her share quietly, without complaint, and kept it down—she seemed more interested in the biscuits than the meat, however.

The entire party was gathered around the cooking fire in a circle, more or less; the three women were seated together on one side, between Ted Deranian and Albert Singer, while the other men were arranged in no particular order. Pel found himself between Sawyer and Valadrakul; Raven was seated on Sawyer's other side, Taillefer just beyond Valadrakul.

When everyone had eaten, and had brushed crumbs from

their hands and clothes, and Valadrakul had collected the offal and gnawed bones in a heap on the dead animal's hide for later burial in sacrifice to the Goddess the Faerie folk worshipped, Pel asked loudly, "Should we get down to business now, or should we wait for Stoddard?"

Raven glared silently at him; Valadrakul looked up from the badger skin to say quietly, "Messire Brown, speak you no more of Raven's man. Stoddard left in the night, whither we know not, without leave nor notice. We can but assume that he has left Raven's service, as did so many others, and that we'll not see him more."

Startled, Pel turned to Raven for confirmation; the nobleman nodded, once.

It had never occurred to Pel, despite Stoddard's complaints, that Stoddard would *really* desert.

"Oh," he said. Then he recovered himself. "Well, then, let's get on with it!"

"On with *what*?" Wilkins demanded.

"On with deciding what to do next, of course," Pel said. "Taillefer says he won't open the space warp for us, and we don't seem to be able to force him—so how do we get home?"

"Maybe we don't," Wilkins growled.

"And you'll all be made welcome by those of us who yet resist Shadow's foul dominion," Raven said. "Live you among us, and join our fight!"

"I say we go back to the ship," Marks said. "Maybe they've sent a rescue party. Or maybe the lieutenant's got some plans of his own."

"We can check that easily enough," Susan said. She leaned forward to speak past Amy, to Prossie. "Did they send a rescue party?"

Prossie had been sitting quietly, not listening, not thinking, but just *being*; it was something she had never really done until very recently. All her life, back in the Empire, no matter where she was sent, no matter where she lived, she had had to either listen, or to actively shut out the constant background noise of other minds; she had never, ever been able to sit and to do absolutely *nothing*, to neither think nor heed the world around her. The Empire did not allow telepaths that sort of isolation; telepaths were watched and guarded, always kept aboard crowded ships or in crowded military installations or in crowded cities. Telepaths, even should one somehow find herself far away from all ordinary minds, were always in contact with the far-flung network of their clan, always open to the common chitchat of their sibs and cousins; even their dreams were shared, built up of the gossip passing back and forth around them and the images that drifted through a shared unconscious.

In Prossie's brief stay on Earth she had been too frightened by the strangeness of mental silence, too lonely, too worried about what would become of her, to really appreciate the virtues of solitude. A jail cell on an alien world, she thought, was hardly the best place for a young woman to look into herself.

And at first, here in Faerie, she had been too busy worrying about survival, too concerned with the politics of Base One, too involved with events—and she had had Carrie, sending to her, listening to her, keeping her in touch.

But since she had cut herself loose, told Carrie to break off, she had begun to drift inward, to look down into the depths of her own mind, depths that she had never really acknowledged to exist until now.

She knew, of course, that minds all exist on multiple levels, sometimes in parallel and contradictory consciousness— she had seen for herself that people could believe things at the same time they saw them for nonsense and never notice the discrepancy; she had seen that the same person could feel love, hate, and indifference, all at once, toward something. She had known that there were layers of memory and emotion, piled up upon each other ever since infancy, though she had always been forbidden to dig down into all that accumulated experience.

But she had never, before this, thought that there must be such layers in her *own* mind. She had never, before this, tried to explore those layers.

But during the walk across the Starlinshire Downs, the wait for Taillefer at the Castle Regisvert, she had begun to wonder. She found herself thinking of things, almost at random, that she had not thought of in months, or years—and for the first time in her life, she couldn't attribute it to leakage from the thoughts of those around her.

These odd bits of thought, and of memory, must be coming from *her*.

And when she reached that realization, she began to deliberately *look* for them, to search her own memories, her own feelings—as she had been forbidden to, back in the Empire, where the government wanted all their telepaths to be nothing more than communication devices, with no thoughts or desires of their own.

She had never thought of that as something *bad* before. She had been trained to think that the Empire had been merciful and kind in not simply killing all the telepaths, as a danger to the state—or simply allowing hostile mobs to kill them. Everyone she knew had told her that, had *believed* that, and it was almost impossible for her to disagree when she could see that belief in the minds around her. That the Empire had done so because they found telepaths useful she had always known and accepted; that was the price of survival.

But it wasn't *fair*. She had been denied all her own thoughts.

And, she discovered as she slept on the cold stone floor of Regisvert, her own dreams, as well. Her dreams that night were fragmentary and uneasy; her mind was not accustomed to constructing its own, without outside influence.

When she awoke she tried to remember those dreams and could not; she sat there, groping to recover images, as the soldiers trapped and butchered the badger. She ate silently, letting her own memories drift up from wherever they had been buried, enjoying the sensation of not thinking, not listening, but just being herself.

And then she realized everyone was staring at her, that someone had asked her a question.

Susan repeated, "Did Base One send a rescue party?"

Prossie blinked and said, "I don't know." Recovering quickly, she added, "I've been out of touch; should I see if I can make contact and ask?"

She saw some of the others glancing uneasily at one another; she saw Wilkins making a familiar, hated gesture to Marks, the clawed finger-wiggling sign used to tease telepaths, the sign that meant "freak" or "monster."

"If you could," Susan said.

"I'll try," Prossie said. She sat up straighter and closed her eyes—which was just for show, not necessary, but it seemed to be called for in this instance.

She didn't say anything to Wilkins, didn't acknowledge his gesture, but inside she hated him with an intensity she had never before allowed herself, a hate that was hot and crawling in her skull, a hate that was the cumulative effect of a thousand memories collected throughout her lifetime, from infancy right up to now, of being loathed just for what she *was*, regardless of what she did, or *who* she was.

Maybe she wouldn't try at all; why should she help Wilkins and his like? How would anyone know?

But it had been Susan who asked, not Wilkins. Prossie wondered why anyone cared, why they thought of it just now—she hadn't been listening to the conversation at all, she realized.

But whether she tried or not made little difference, really; it was up to Carrie, and as she sat, mind open and receptive, she realized that Carrie wasn't listening, wasn't sending, wasn't there at all as far as Prossie could tell. No one else made contact, either.

She opened her eyes and started to speak, then caught herself.

Why were they asking about rescues?

The only possible reason was that they were hoping to go back to the ship and be rescued themselves.

There were monsters back there. Shadow would have taken an interest in the ship by now. To go back there would be insanely dangerous. And even if by some miracle the Empire really *had* sent a rescue party, which they had certainly had no intention of doing when she was last in contact with Carrie, Prossie did not *want* to go back and be rescued.

"No rescue," she said. "They've decided not to risk it. We're on our own."

It was a lie—but who cared? These people would never know unless they returned to the Empire, and Prossie would never go back there, never go back to the hatred and oppression, the rules and limits, the constant barrage of thought.

Right now, though, she thought she had better pay closer attention to what was being said.

"I just want to go home," Amy said.

"Me, too," Pel said.

"I want to wake up," Ted said. "I'm tired of this."

"Same thing," Pel told him.

"I'm not real interested in staying around here, either," Wilkins said. "The question is, what can we do about it?"

"If nobody's rescued the lieutenant," Sawyer asked Prossie, "what *has* happened to those guys?"

"I don't know," Prossie said. "I don't have any way to find out; they're cut off, no communications." She looked Sawyer in the eye.

Sawyer frowned, obviously unhappy with the answer—or with Prossie's behavior.

"I'd send you all home," Raven said, "if 'twas in my power. Alas, 'tis not. Think you, then, on what you'd have in the stead of that—would you join me in the fight 'gainst Shadow? Though in truth I'd rather the weapons of Earth, yet would willing hands be welcome e'en without."

"You won't reconsider?" Pel asked Taillefer.

The wizard shook his head. "Nay," he said. "To open a portal would be to die at Shadow's hand, and I've no wish to die."

Pel looked at him, then back at Raven, then around at the others, at Ted and Amy and Susan, Ted with his bandaged head, Amy leaning weakly against Susan, who stood clutching her big black purse. The wizard Taillefer, the only one here who could get them out of this storybook world and back home to Earth and sanity, but too afraid of Shadow to try; Raven, who wanted guns to fight Shadow; Ted, who thought he was dreaming; poor sick Amy; Susan, with the revolver in her purse . . .

Suddenly, the pieces fell into place for Pel, as he stared first at Susan's purse, then at Taillefer and Valadrakul.

Wizards.

Or rather, he corrected himself, *Wizards*, the movie by Ralph Bakshi.

While he had been thinking of all this as something out of a story ever since Grummetty first stepped from the basement wall, ever since he first heard Raven speak, up until now he hadn't settled on just *one* story. He had thought of Tolkien and "Twilight Zone" and a dozen others, but none of those had shown him a way out, back to real life.

Wizards was another matter.

Of course, this *wasn't* just a story, this *was* real life, but still . . .

And there was something else. Taillefer was the only one *here* who knew the portal spell, but there was someone else who knew it even better, someone who just might not be quite the villain it was painted.

Of course, convincing anyone else to try that would be difficult. The gun was easier.

"Listen," he said, turning back to Taillefer, "if Shadow were dead, you could send us home, right?"

"Aye, surely," Taillefer said, mystified. "Were Shadow dead 'twould be as a new dawn, and all would be different indeed;

I'd have no fear of its creatures, if any even survived. More, methinks the death of Shadow would wreak great change upon the flow of magic through all the world, and all who study the arcane arts would find new strengths to draw on, were Shadow's web sundered. A portal would be but the least of spells, surely, and gladly would I perform it."

"Friend Pel," Raven said, "an Shadow were dead . . . welladay, 'twould be glorious beyond measure; 'tis the end I've sought all my life. But how to achieve this miracle? Shadow's life has spanned centuries; it draws unnatural vitality from its nets of power, that it ages not. How then, think you to end this? A blade is as naught; no spell can touch Shadow; no mere mortal can hope to outlive it."

"All right, Shadow can't be killed by anything from this land, but what about a weapon from another world?" He pointed at Susan.

Raven followed Pel's pointing finger, and Pel knew from his expression that he had understood Pel's plan immediately.

So did most of the others.

"Would it work?" Susan asked. "I mean, it's just a bullet, this isn't any sort of big magic."

"It might," Pel said.

"And how would you administer this 'bullet,' Messire Pel?" Taillefer asked. "Need you enter Shadow's fortress? I'd not risk a farthing 'gainst all the gold in Goringham for your chances, then."

"We'd need to get pretty close, yeah," Pel admitted.

" 'Tis not to be done, then," Taillefer said, with clear finality.

"No?" Pel demanded, challengingly. "How do you know? You ever *tried* it?"

"I yet live, do I not?" Taillefer retorted. "No, I've not made the trial."

"Then how do you *know*?" Pel repeated. "*I* say it's worth a try—at least, for some of us." He hesitated, then plunged on. "In fact," he said, "I think it might be time for some of us to go see Shadow even *without* the gun. After all, if *you* won't send us home, maybe *it* will!"

Raven stared at Pel, mouth open in dumbfoundment; Taillefer stared for a moment, then burst out laughing.

"Oh, foolish man," he said, when he could speak again, "think you that Shadow will do your bidding, an you walk up to the fortress and ask ever so politely? 'Oh, please, destroyer of kingdoms, ravager of nations, master of all the world, send me home, though I've nothing to pay, and no reason to give that you'll not better to strike me dead this instant.' Is *that* what you'd say, brown one?"

"Something like . . . no," Pel said. He put his hands to his hips and glared at the wizard. "No, *not* like that. Listen, *you* may be a sworn enemy of Shadow, but *we* aren't." He waved an arm to take in both Earthpeople and Imperials. "All we know about it is what we've heard from *you*, and from your friends. How do we know Shadow's any worse than you are? And who says we have nothing to offer it?"

"You speak treason," Raven said quietly, his hand falling to where his sword hilt should have been.

"You're calling me a traitor?"

"Aye . . ." Raven began.

"Traitor to *what*?" Pel demanded, cutting the aristocrat off short. "I'm a citizen of the United States of America. I'm not one of your underlings, *Lord* Raven! And even if I were—where's Stoddard this morning? For that matter, where's Donald a' Benton, or Elani, or Grummetty, or any of the others? Isn't Shadow the government around here? Seems to me that *you're* the fugitive from the law, and anyone who follows you and doesn't have the sense to give up like Stoddard did is just buying an early death. Where's my *wife*, Lord Raven? Where's my daughter? They're *dead*, from following you . . ."

"They're slain by *Shadow*, Pel Brown," Raven countered. "Would you join your wife's murderer, then?"

"*Who says* it was Shadow?" Pel shouted. "*You* do, and your buddies in the Galactic Empire! *I* don't know who killed her—hell, I don't even know she's really dead, I just have your word on it, yours and the Empire's—*I* never got to see them! *I* didn't see the bodies!" He had stepped forward, as had Raven; the two of them stood with their noses an inch or two apart, shouting in each other's faces.

"Pel," Susan said, putting a hand on his shoulder.

Pel fell silent, but stayed face-to-face with Raven, glaring down at the shorter man, for a long moment. At last, though, he backed away.

"I don't care what you say, Raven," Pel announced, "or any of the rest of you, for that matter. Prossie says the Empire's abandoned us, and Taillefer won't send me home; well, the only other person—or *thing*—that can send me home is Shadow, so I'm going to go *see* Shadow, and if I can't make a deal with it, I'll do my damnedest to kill it, and if I do *that*, my price is Taillefer's portal spell. So I'm going looking for Shadow. Now, who's coming with me?"

He looked around at the faces, at expressions of confusion, dismay, and even fear.

"You're mad," Taillefer announced loudly.

"I'll come," Susan said quietly. "At least for now. You may want the pistol, after all."

"Makes no difference to me," Ted said with a shrug. "I'll come."

"Whaddaya think?" Wilkins asked, turning toward Marks and Sawyer.

"I'll go along for now," Singer said.

"I'm in," Marks said.

Sawyer hesitated. "Whatever you guys decide," he said.

"Then we go," Wilkins concluded.

Amy listened to Pel and Raven argue, listened to the soldiers make their decision. When Susan said she would go with Pel, Amy felt as if something had fallen out from beneath her insides somewhere—how could Susan say that without even a glance at Amy, to see what she thought? Susan was betraying her.

No, she wasn't, Amy corrected herself; Susan was looking after herself. She wasn't really a *friend*, after all—they'd been acting like friends for weeks, but that was because they were the only two American women around; they didn't have anyone *else* to talk to. Susan wasn't really her friend; Susan was her *attorney*. She had to remember that.

And Susan was right, anyway; they had to go to Shadow. If Taillefer was right, if Amy was really carrying Walter's child—she thought she must be, she realized now that she hadn't had her period since early in her captivity on Zeta Leo Three, and a baby would have to be Walter's, since she hadn't been with another man in almost a year—then she had to get *home*, back to a civilized world, where she could abort it, or put it up for adoption, or do *something*. She didn't want her dead rapist's child. And she didn't want to go through pregnancy and labor and childbirth in this stupid primitive world, this place out of some horrible old fairy tale where for all she knew leeches were the latest thing in medical care.

And she wasn't a young woman; she had no business having

a first child at her age. She was used to being childless; she liked it; she didn't *want* a child.

And if she did, she wouldn't want it to be by that sadistic bastard Walter.

She had to go to Shadow with Pel, even if it meant risking death, because just *staying* in this world meant risking death. She could catch a plague, she could die of something in the water, she could bleed to death.

She had to get home, by any means possible.

"I'll come," she said.

Prossie had begun to drift away into her own thoughts again, but when she heard all the different voices speaking up, saying whether they would accompany Pel Brown, she listened. She thought back to what she had heard without paying attention.

Going to confront Shadow—that was insane! She had seen and heard memories, back at Base One, from Raven and Valadrakul and Elani and Stoddard; even allowing for added coloration, she knew from those memories that Shadow was cruel and ruthless, willing to commit atrocities to further its ends or remove those who opposed it.

But they were all going along—Susan and Amy and Bill Marks and all of them. If she didn't agree, she would be left behind, with Raven and the wizards, the only foreigner among them.

That would be awful.

And maybe she could convince the others to turn back. Maybe they would come to their senses.

"I'll go," she said.

If she hadn't been trained since childhood not to venture her own opinions, she would have added, But I don't like it.

Raven watched with annoyance as voice after voice spoke up, hand after hand raised, agreeing to accompany Pel Brown on his mad errand.

He didn't really have any great *need* for this oddly assorted group, but he was reluctant to let them go heedlessly and needlessly to their deaths without some further attempt to save them, perhaps to win some benefit from all this disastrous series of events.

And of course, the lot of them might come to their senses when they learned just what they had taken upon themselves. When they saw Shadow's fortress and realized that none could penetrate it to confront Shadow itself, the survivors might well be valuable additions to the forces of resistance.

They might also, in their madness, learn something useful of Shadow's defenses—surely not enough to allow them to enter Shadow's keep, but something that could be turned to use someday, by those wiser and mightier than themselves.

"All of you are fools," he said, "and I feel I must accompany you as far as I dare, that I might do what I can to save you from your folly."

Taillefer watched with mounting astonishment as one after another in the party announced his or her intention of bearding Shadow in its lair, of marching in wide-eyed innocence to certain destruction.

When even Raven and a reluctant Valadrakul agreed to go along, at least for some part of the way, Taillefer flung his hands up.

"May the Goddess preserve me!" he shouted. "You have, every one of you, lost your senses! I'd call on the Goddess to save you all, if I thought it possible even for Her! And as 'tis not, I'll take my leave of you all, lest this madness be catching! Go, then, and die, and I'll pray for your souls!" He spread his arms and spoke the Word of Power he had prepared, and the wind rose, filling his cloak.

He felt the air pressing him upward, felt the currents of power beneath this place, power that led to Shadow, he knew, but power that he could turn to his own ends, at least for now. He drew upon it to conjure the wind that roared about him.

He grew lighter and lighter, until at last the air, and the magical power behind it, lifted him off his feet.

A moment later the others watched as the wizard literally blew away, up into the sky, bound for his distant home.

CHAPTER 15

"**Y**ou're sure there's no magic ring, no mystic gem, or something?" Pel asked Raven as they walked down the western slope, away from the thorn-covered ruins of Castle Regisvert and down into a broad green valley. Gray clouds hung on the horizon before them, but where they walked the sun shone warmly. A bird sang somewhere in the distance, and the rich scents of late spring filled the air. "Maybe Shadow keeps its heart in a bowl somewhere, or something like that?" he suggested.

Raven shook his head. "I've heard naught, in all my days, of any such device. Shadow draws its power from the magic that flows through earth and sky, and weaves that into its web; it needs no rings nor jewelry, any more than does our own Valadrakul."

"Does Valadrakul weave these same currents, then?" Pel inquired, looking back at the wizard.

"Indeed, he draws 'pon them," Raven agreed, "though not as Shadow does; Valadrakul and the other free wizards, as they tell me, make their magic but from the crumbs that fall from Shadow's table, as it were. They weave no webs outside their own bodies, hold no elaborate traceries at the ready, own no patterns save those in their own minds, but instead pluck away what they can when chance allows, and shape the magicks within themselves." He hesitated, then added, "Ah, in truth, I've most probably made nonsense of it, for 'tis none of mine that we speak of here, friend Pel. If you'd have it right, you'd best speak with Valadrakul, and not myself."

Pel nodded, and dropped back a pace to where the wizard walked.

147

Valadrakul turned and stared silently at the Earthman as they marched a dozen steps farther down the highway.

Pel realized that this was the first time he had deliberately and directly addressed Valadrakul in normal conversation, and he wasn't sure just how to begin. At last, though, he said, "You're a wizard, right?"

Wilkins, a few feet away, snickered.

"Have you not seen for yourself, Pellinore Brown?" Valadrakul replied.

"I suppose, yeah," Pel admitted. Wilkins snorted, but Pel ignored him. "So tell me about wizards."

Valadrakul blinked, then smiled crookedly. "You'd have me open to you all the secrets of my kind, the mysteries we hold dear, the teachings I struggled for a dozen years to absorb, here as we walk? Think you, perhaps, that what you ask might not be so simple as that?"

"Yeah, well," Pel said, annoyed, "I didn't mean that. I mean, tell me why, if you're a wizard and Shadow's a wizard, why Shadow's so much more powerful than you are."

"And who told you, I pray, that Shadow is a wizard?"

"Didn't you . . ." Pel hesitated. "Or maybe it was Raven—I don't know, but *somebody* told me."

Valadrakul didn't reply, and angrily, Pel demanded, "All right, if Shadow isn't a wizard, what *is* it?"

" 'Tis Shadow," Valadrakul said with a shrug. "It needs no other name, for there's no other like it, nor has ever been. What in truth it is, no one knows."

"Didn't one of you tell me that it started out as an ordinary wizard?"

"Perhaps," Valadrakul admitted.

"Then *did* it start out as an ordinary wizard?"

"So 'tis said. And perhaps 'tis true. 'Tis no wizard now, though—not as we use the word."

"So what happened, then?" Pel asked. "How come Shadow's so incredibly powerful, and the rest of you wizards aren't?"

"Good question," Wilkins said. "Took you long enough to get it straight, though."

Pel glared at him for an instant, then turned back to Valadrakul.

The wizard looked thoughtfully at the ground for a moment, and the entire party moved onward a few yards before he spoke again.

"Raven spoke to you of the flow of magic through the world," Valadrakul said at last.

Pel nodded.

" 'Tis not exactly a flow, you understand—nor is it precisely in *this* world. The exact nature . . . well, you've not the understanding." The wizard glanced up at Pel.

"All right," Pel said. "Explain it however you can, don't worry about getting all the details right."

Valadrakul nodded. "As you wish." He gazed about at the surrounding greenery. "If you think of the sources of nature's magic as springs, from which flow not water but the invisible energies that we wizards wield, you will have but a poor understanding, for the flow is not as water, nor as light, nor as any other thing in the commonplace world. It permeates all the world, yet varies throughout, from the faintest of traces in one spot to a bursting torrent in another. And when a wizard draws upon it, it is not consumed—the well cannot be emptied. There are flows, but they are not streams—more oft, they're loops, spinning endlessly. And there are points, and lines, and patterns."

"All right," Pel said, "I think I have the idea."

Valadrakul nodded. "Well," he said, "a wizard such as myself, such as all modern wizards, can draw upon whatever energy might be found in the place where that wizard stands, and no more. I can sense these energies, but only dimly; they are not as light to me, but as, perhaps, faint sounds—I can perhaps tell you, that way there is a great power source, but I cannot tell you how far, nor its exact nature, nor can I in any way draw it nearer. At most, if I find a locus I remember, I can perhaps use its peculiar nature to my advantage—as when I used what might be described as a line of magical energy to send a message to Taillefer."

"Okay," Pel acknowledged. "I think I get it."

"Of old, though," Valadrakul continued, "there were wizards who had a greater understanding of these forces, who could perhaps see them, and map them, and distinguish the patterns in them. This higher art, these pattern wizards, these are now thought to be lost—though I'd not swear that none might still lurk in the odd corners, hiding from Shadow. 'Twas pattern wizards who provided much of the art that we lesser wizards use; they were more powerful than we, and for that reason Shadow has made every effort to obliterate them, lest they be a threat to its dominion."

"So Shadow was a pattern wizard?" Pel asked.

Valadrakul shook his head. "Nay," he said, "listen further. 'Tis said that long ago, there was yet a third tier among those who wield magic—those who could not only perceive the patterns, but could *alter* them, could alter the flow of energy, could divert one stream into another, could weave the threads of magic as if they were merest wool, could form matrices of magic that they carried about with them—not the mere patterns of spells trapped within their minds, as we yet do in our small ways, but great intricate webs of the raw stuff of magic itself, that might be formed into whatever spells they needed. They had no need to make do with what powers were at hand, but could draw to themselves whatsoever powers they needed, through these matrices they held. Matrix wizards, these magic-weavers were called."

"And Shadow was a matrix wizard?" Pel asked, remembering what Raven had said about Shadow's webs and networks.

Valadrakul nodded. "Aye," he said, "the greatest of them. And Shadow built about itself a structure that stretches out to embrace all the magic in this world—it gathered in all the lines to itself, drew down the wells, absorbed the matrices of all other matrix wizards, and left nowhere untouched. If another somehow learned the lost art of the matrix wizards and sought to draw into himself even the slightest part of the world's magic, Shadow would sense it, would feel the tug upon its web as a spider feels a fly's struggles. Should that happen, Shadow would reach out and strike down whoever had dared to tamper with its networks." He sighed. "Indeed, 'twould seem that that's why Taillefer would send you nowhere—the portal spell impinges upon Shadow's matrix, tugs at its web, as it were."

"Oh," Pel said. The explanation made sense, he supposed. Or did it?

"Wait a minute," he said, as they trudged onward. "If Shadow's linked to *all* the magical energy in the world, doesn't it feel something any time *any* wizard works *any* magic?"

"A good question," Valadrakul said. "But alas, we've no good answer. It may be that Shadow senses it as we sense the distant hum of insects, as something always there and not worth the trouble to stop. It may be that our spells are so weak that Shadow sees them not at all, as you and I cannot see the stars in the sun's daylight." He shrugged. "We know not the truth of the matter."

"Oh," Pel said again.

He was hardly satisfied, but how could he demand that Valadrakul tell him something the wizard didn't know himself? Shadow's true nature would have to remain a mystery.

The idea that she might be several weeks pregnant with Walter's child was appalling, but somehow it was a relief, too—it was an explanation, and one that fit all the facts. What's more, it was one that Amy understood, more or less, and one with a definite end in sight. AIDS could take years, other diseases could be sudden or chronic, but pregnancy was nine months, at most, give or take a few weeks.

And it wasn't a death sentence. Childbirth was dangerous, certainly, especially if she couldn't get back to Earth, but she wasn't going to follow Grummetty and Alella and die horribly in a matter of days.

At least for the moment, having an answer, any answer, was better than nothing. And crying all over Susan and Prossie had helped, too.

Perhaps as a result of her lessened worry, perhaps just because her pregnancy was progressing past that point, she was feeling better. She still felt heavy and clumsy in the stronger gravity of Faerie and still tired easily, but her stomach was no longer cramping, and she felt no urge to vomit.

Thank God, she thought, for small blessings.

And being able to think about something other than her own insides and the possibility of imminent death brought her to wondering just what she and the others were doing. Yes, they had to get back to Earth—but were they really just walking right into Shadow's home territory, marching right up to Shadow's lair? Wasn't that, well . . . suicidal?

Did Pel know what he was doing?

She had voted to do this herself, she knew that, but she was having second thoughts now. At the time of the decision she had been panicky, desperate to do anything that would get her home; now she was thinking a bit more clearly.

Would this get her home, or would it get her killed?

And if it would get her killed, what should she be doing instead?

She glanced at Raven, but he appeared to be lost in thought, and besides, he was a liar and a thief, not to be trusted—she thought he meant well, that he was sincere in thinking that everything he did was justified by the need to defeat Shadow, but still, she couldn't trust him.

Valadrakul was better, but he was explaining something to Pel. And those two were the only natives of Faerie left in the party—Elani and Squire Donald were dead, Stoddard and Taillefer had abandoned the group.

Raven kept talking about Shadow as if it were some ultimate evil, and Pel always thought he meant it literally, like some monster from the fairy tales, or a movie villain, but Amy didn't think she believed in stuff like that.

There were real villains, though, lots of them, and if she couldn't quite believe that Shadow was Evil Incarnate, she could believe that it was the local version of Adolf Hitler, or Stalin, or Pol Pot, or the Ayatollah Khomeini. The woman in the cottage had told Raven some of Shadow's rules, and they'd sounded like something Hilter or Stalin might have come up with.

Well, then, what if she thought of herself as having somehow landed in Nazi Germany? What would she have done?

She'd have tried to get *out*, of course—across the Alps to Switzerland, like the von Trapps, or to England or somewhere.

Except there *was* no Switzerland or England here. Shadow had won its war and conquered the entire world.

So what then?

There was an underground, of course—Raven was proof of that. She had already seen the underground, by traveling with Raven and Valadrakul, and talking with Taillefer, and they'd made promises to get her home, and then they hadn't been able to deliver.

Well, to hell with them, then. She wasn't going to join the underground and become a freedom fighter if they couldn't keep their promises. And it didn't look as if they stood any chance of winning the war, anyway.

Undergrounds never won their wars without outside help, anyway—she was pretty sure she'd read that somewhere.

But to return to her analogy, here she was, in the Faerie equivalent of Nazi Germany, with no way to get out of the country to Switzerland or England. She was going to stay in Germany unless Hitler himself decided to send her home, so she was on her way to Berlin to ask.

Was that going to work?

Well, it might; she wasn't the local equivalent of a Jew, so far as she could tell, or otherwise fodder for the concentration camps. If there *was* an equivalent to the Jews, from what

Valadrakul had said she supposed it was wizards. She certainly wasn't a wizard.

She was a foreigner, of course, and Hitler had hated foreigners, but he hadn't just killed them out of hand.

And besides, there was no point in carrying the analogy *too* far.

So they were going to Berlin to ask a favor of Hitler, more or less—and if that failed, Pel wanted to try to assassinate him.

What were the odds of getting away with that?

Probably nil. She just couldn't imagine a bunch of lost American tourists walking in and killing Hitler, which would be the equivalent.

And she couldn't see how they could hope to destroy Shadow, whatever it was, *and* get away with it; despite what Pel seemed to think, this wasn't some silly adventure story. Things like that didn't happen in real life.

But maybe Shadow would send them home.

And what else could she do?

Well, if she were in Germany, she could just settle down somewhere, find work, or someone who would take her in, and just hope nobody reported her to the Gestapo as she got on with her life. She didn't suppose there'd be much call for an interior decorator in a place like Faerie, but she could find something to do, she was sure. And she wouldn't even have to learn the language—the people here spoke English.

When they came to a town, she decided, she'd do that, she'd settle down and make the best of things. Not a farm—she wanted nothing to do with rural life. But sooner or later, surely, they'd find a place with shops and some semblance of civilization, and she could stay there. The others could go on to Shadow's fortress if they wanted, and if Shadow agreed to help they could send for her, but she didn't want to walk in there with them.

She'd have the baby to worry about, of course, if she settled down and stayed.

Well, maybe that wouldn't be so bad; she could claim to be widowed, that she'd left her home because she couldn't manage alone with the baby coming. And just because it was Walter's child didn't mean it would be a monster; she could bring it up properly, and it would probably turn out fine.

And it might die, anyway.

That was a horrible thought, she told herself, but she couldn't help it. Her situation was so awful—trapped in an alien, uncomfortable, hostile world, carrying her rapist's child—that she thought a little morbid speculation was entirely justified.

She looked ahead, at Raven and Pel and Valadrakul, and decided she wouldn't mention anything to them yet. They might not approve. Time enough when they found someplace she could stay, some suitable little town or village.

That woman's cottage had been primitive, but Amy didn't think it was too uncomfortable, really. If she could find a place no worse than that, she thought she could stand it.

She wondered if Prossie or Susan would be interested in staying with her.

The land undulated, Prossie decided. It was a fancy word, but it fit. The countryside was an apparently endless series of gentle-sloped ridges, and their path led them up and over each one. The westward slopes, the ones they went down, seemed longer and steeper than the eastward sides; that meant they were gradually descending these ripples, coming down from the forest, and that eventually, if they continued, they would reach either the sea or the flat plain of the coast.

It also meant, though, that most of the time they couldn't see where they were going, but each time they topped a ridge the whole world would suddenly be spread out before them, a green expanse of small farms, groves, meadows, orchards that seemed to go on forever, arranged in the rows formed by the ridges—or rather, Prossie corrected herself, the Downs.

From each summit they could see a new valley, and then the tops of the succeeding ridges, fading away in the distance. The horizon was lost in mist from the first few ridgetops, but as the day progressed and the air warmed the mist receded and vanished. From the next two ridges everything was sharp and clear—but then the air began to grow hazy again as the temperature continued to rise. Dark clouds hovered on the western horizon, far ahead of them, but drew no nearer.

There was a pleasant sort of repetition to it all. Prossie supposed that eventually they would arrive somewhere, but she was in no particular hurry; she had been on perhaps a dozen worlds in her lifetime, and despite the high gravity this was one of the most pleasant she had yet encountered. The spaceborne habitats and bases where she had spent most of her time weren't even in the running.

Also, the long walk gave her time to think, to meditate, to remember, and to just *be*.

She thought back to her childhood, remembering when she had first realized that she was a distinct individual. She knew, from reading other minds, that normal babies began to differentiate themselves from their environment when they were just a few weeks old and had a pretty good grasp on the concept of "I" by the time they were toddlers; telepathic children, though, had a rougher time of it. Distinguishing their own thoughts from those around them, and from the network of other telepaths, was not easy.

Prossie had been slow; she had been almost four when she finally got a firm grip on which thoughts were her own and which came from outside. The key had been when she finally learned to close out other minds.

By then she had learned any number of things that normal children didn't encounter until much later—she knew about sex, from several different viewpoints; she knew about death, and addiction, and lust, and grief; she knew about the dark, sick thoughts that lurked below so many minds.

And she had accepted all that as parts of herself, because she was part of all humanity, a link in the chain of telepaths that bound her species together. She knew that people didn't speak about those darknesses, the raw lusts and searing pain, but it wasn't until years later that she really understood why. She heard people thinking, over and over, that their thoughts were wrong, were different from everyone else, but she had known it wasn't true.

It was so much easier to just accept it all, the foulness and shame and guilt, along with the joy and beauty and peace, and to not think about any of it, to not distinguish any of it as "good" or "bad." It just *was*. It was in everyone, in varying degrees.

Except, of course, in herself, since she was a mere passive receiver, a relay, a servant of the Galactic Empire, not responsible for anything except performing her duty.

But now, thinking back, she knew that she had the darknesses in herself, too. That disgusting Bascombe, the Undersecretary for Interdimensional Affairs, hadn't had a second thought about sending his own people out to die, just to help his own reputation, and she had, somewhere in the back of her mind, thought she was better than that, that she would never have done such a thing—but hadn't she left Lieutenant Dibbs and the others to die? Paul, who had raped her back on Zeta Leo Three, had been awash in fantasies of power and abuse, and she had never done anything like that—but she had never had the chance, and hadn't she deliberately lied to the people here, to manipulate them into doing what she wanted, and hadn't she enjoyed the feeling of power it gave her?

And after all, hadn't she betrayed her own family and her Empire?

But then, her family and Empire had virtually enslaved her from infancy, in their own way just as much as Paul had when he bought her at auction and took her to his home in chains.

Did that make her treason acceptable?

Perhaps it did, but it was still a betrayal. Certainly, her little crimes weren't as bad as Bascombe's or Paul's or the Empire's, but she was no pure little innocent.

And now that she was alone in her head, she could look at that, could take the time to consider her own motives and see just what was lurking down there in the back of her mind.

And she was discovering, as she walked across the Starlinshire Downs, that she had the same drives as anyone else—power and pride and sex and fear and anger, the need for love, the need for acceptance, all tangled together into her own individual mix.

She was thinking about her reasons for serving the Empire so willingly for so long, the fear of punishment, the acceptance by her family, the pride in her work, when she felt Carrie's presence.

She blinked, then almost stumbled on the latest upgrade.

"Are you all right, Prossie?" Carrie's thoughts were tinged with worry—nothing serious, just concern for Prossie.

"I'm fine," she thought back, "just fine." To her own surprise as much as Carrie's, her reply carried an edge of annoyance; she had already become accustomed to the mental isolation, the partial sensory deprivation, and she had been enjoying it. The sudden contact came as an intrusion on her own meditations.

"What about the others?"

Prossie looked around as she topped the rise. "Wilkins and Marks and Sawyer and Singer are all fine; the Earthpeople are alive, anyway, and seem to be functioning. Raven and Valadrakul are the only natives we still have with us."

"What about Lieutenant Dibbs and the others?"

"How should I know?" The edge of anger was stronger and

more obvious than ever, Carrie could hardly miss it, but Prossie didn't care. "We left them back at the ship; you know that."

"You haven't heard anything more?"

"No."

"What about that wizard who was going to send people home?"

"Didn't work out," Prossie replied. She wasn't really paying very close attention anymore; she had just looked out across the valley before them and realized that this time they weren't just going to pass more scattered, isolated farms.

This time, a town stood in the center of the valley. She couldn't see very much; the afternoon air was hazy and humid, wavering in the heat, but the collection of stone and wood structures half a mile or so away was definitely a town.

"So what's happening, then?" Carrie demanded. "Where are you going? You're walking; I can sense that—where to?"

"We're going to Shadow's fortress," Prossie said, studying the town. The highway widened out to form the main street; another road crossed at the center of town, and a few narrow back streets filled in the rest.

For several seconds Carrie didn't reply; when she did, she said, "Prossie, that's crazy."

"I know," Prossie said, taking her first step down the slope. "But it should make General Hart happy, shouldn't it?"

CHAPTER 16

*A*my smiled weakly at the sight of the town. She hadn't smiled much lately; it felt surprisingly good.

It wasn't much of a town; she doubted the whole thing covered more than about two dozen acres. Still, it was something more than a farm. The buildings lined the main street pretty solidly for a good two hundred yards, with more houses scattered across the surrounding area; she could see signboards hanging above doorways, which meant businesses, and there appeared to be a square at the crossroads, which seemed to imply some sort of local government. A platform was set up in the square, with people on it—Amy couldn't make out any details, but that seemed a pleasantly homey feature.

She thought she caught the scent of woodsmoke, but she wasn't sure; and even if she did, she couldn't be sure it came from the town.

It wasn't Goshen, Maryland—but then, Goshen was just a spread-out bedroom community, a sort of annex to Gaithersburg and Rockville, themselves more or less suburbs of Washington. Amy couldn't expect anything like that here. This town was probably the best she could reasonably hope for.

Besides, her feet hurt too much, and she was too tired, to go any farther.

Now she needed to decide just when to tell the others that she wanted to stay here, not to go on and beard Shadow in its lair.

She glanced around, at Raven and Pel and the others. Raven was frowning angrily, though Amy had no idea why; Pel was staring at the town like a baby studying a new toy, trying to see every bit of it at once. Susan had the wary

158

look of a prowling cat; Prossie had on one of her distant expressions, and Amy wondered whether she was talking to someone back in the Galactic Empire, or whether she was just woolgathering.

The other Imperials weren't paying much attention to the town at all, but simply walking on, chatting among themselves. Ted, as usual, wasn't paying attention to anything at all, and Amy couldn't see Valadrakul's face from where she walked.

Nobody was saying anything, which suddenly struck Amy as somehow wrong. This was the first town that any of the Earthpeople or the Imperials had ever seen in this stupid world of Raven's; didn't it deserve some sort of comment?

"Raven," she called, "what's the town called? Is that whats-it, Starlinshire, that the Downs are named for?"

Raven turned and glowered at her for a moment before remembering his manners.

"Nay, lady," he said, " 'tis but some lesser town, the local market, perchance; Starlinton be greater by far."

"Do you know its name?" Amy persisted.

Raven shook his head. "Nay," he said. "Who's to know every hamlet and village?"

"I just thought you might, where it's on the highway," she said.

" 'Tis in Shadow's inner domain, and that's all I wot," Raven answered, turning his gaze forward again.

The road curved as it descended the slope, and trees grew along the verge, so that once the party left the ridgetop Amy could only catch occasional tantalizing glimpses of the town; each time an especially good view presented itself she would pause and stare, then hurry to catch up to the others.

Every time they passed a farmhouse, Amy thought it might be the outskirts of town; every time, she knew she was being foolish to be disappointed when it was not, but she was disappointed all the same.

The sky was beginning to darken, as well, and the already-thick air seemed to be growing heavier; Amy wondered if they might be caught by a storm before they could reach the town and shelter.

At last, however, one house was followed closely by another, and then another, and then by a smithy—the open-sided building with the open-hearth forge at the center was very much like those Amy had seen in historical re-creations at

Jamestown and Sturbridge Village, and at Renaissance fairs. The fires were banked, however, and the smith nowhere to be seen.

Three large dogs were chained just below the big bellows, however, black dogs of a breed Amy didn't recognize; these beasts watched the party intently as it passed, obviously ready to defend the smithy against any thieves or invaders. Amy was unsure whether she heard one growling, deep in its throat; whether she did or not, none of them barked, nor made any overtly hostile move.

She could smell them, a hot, doggy smell that she did not care for. She could see muscles tense in the nearest dog's fore-legs.

These were serious watchdogs, she decided, not pets. She was careful to stay on the highway and not take so much as a single step on the smithy's grounds.

This was hardly a warm welcome to the town she hoped to make her home. This did not appear to be the sort of place where people left their doors unlocked.

But then, most people didn't leave the doors unlocked in Goshen, either.

Beyond the smithy was a row of houses, small and old but reasonably well kept. Two old men sat on a bench out front of the third one, staring at the group of strangers.

Amy realized that her party must make a curious sight, with only Raven dressed in anything resembling the local garb—and at that, his velvets were the attire of a nobleman, and there was no sign of a castle or palace or manse anywhere in this town, so even he was out of place. Valadrakul wore his embroidered vest, but over an Imperial uniform, and with his hair cut short, where every other native of Faerie Amy had seen wore it long. The five Imperials were all in their gaudy purple uniforms, now somewhat the worse for wear—especially Prossie's, with the ruined sleeves and the slashes in the side. The four Earthpeople were in old, ill-fitting slacks and T-shirts—if that; poor Pel was bare-chested.

Which probably made him the least alien of the lot, Amy thought. And even bare-chested he was hardly intimidating; Pel Brown was no Arnold Schwarzenegger, by any means. He was taller than any native of Faerie Amy had seen with the single exception of Stoddard, but he was also pale and flabby and narrow-shouldered.

"Should we ask them for directions or anything?" Amy heard Pel ask Raven quietly.

"Nay, why trouble them?" Raven replied. "I'd sooner we sought an inn or public house, that we might eat a decent meal for once and wash the dust from our throats and perhaps even from our clothes. When that's done, our hosts will surely tell us if our road's the one we seek."

Pel nodded, and the party marched on past the seated pair in uneasy silence. The four soldiers stopped talking, for once, and no one else spoke, neither visitor nor native.

Past the two on the bench the highway turned a corner, around an immense oak tree. From that point on the road became a street, lined with houses and shops—though the shops had none of the broad display windows Amy would have expected and were distinguished from the houses mainly by signboards and what was behind the windows, rather than anything about the architecture. Doors and windows were all closed, many shuttered. The houses were relatively crude—rough-hewn heavy wooden cornerposts and lintels exposed, the walls between the posts some sort of yellowish, not-very-smooth plaster that reminded Amy of Bavarian postcards, or beer ads, but without the traditional German decoration. Some walls were patched, some stained, some speckled with mildew or just with dirt. Not a single structure in sight stood more than two stories in height, and many were only one.

The signboards did not have writing on them, but only crude pictures—this one of a loom, that of pottery; Amy supposed, with regret, that most of the locals couldn't read. Maybe, she thought, she could make a living teaching reading and writing—but it still didn't bode well for quality of life here.

The highway had become a street, but it had by no means straightened out; it turned and twisted its way through the town, for no reason that Amy could see. There were no sidewalks, no front lawns, very few trees—and those trees there were just as likely to be in the center of the street as along the side. The buildings were built wall to wall, broken every three or four houses by a narrow alleyway; most of the alleys were closed off with gates, either of wood or black iron. The whole place smelled of cooked meat and cabbage, of dust, and of urine.

The entire place should have been quaint, Amy thought, but mostly managed to be ugly, instead. She wondered whether

Shadow had anything to do with that, or whether it was just the prevailing style in this world.

She also wondered whether those re-created villages and medieval towns back on Earth had been prettied up; none ever looked as ugly as this.

There were people on the street, but most of them, upon spotting the strangers, stepped aside, pressing themselves against walls or ducking out of sight completely, into doorways and alleys. No one invited conversation.

This was not, Amy decided, a friendly place—but maybe that was just as well; if people here minded their own business, then they wouldn't bother her, once she settled in, would they?

Besides, if Shadow was the local equivalent of Hitler, *every* town was probably like this.

Then they rounded the next corner and came in sight of the town square.

For a moment the party became utterly disorganized as most of the group stopped dead in their tracks, while a few—Raven, Valadrakul, Wilkins, and Marks—kept going. Ted and Susan veered to one side, rather than simply stopping; Ted began babbling quietly to himself, while Sawyer said softly, "Oh, my God."

Amy stood and stared.

The platform in the town square was a gallows, a square perhaps a dozen feet on a side, raised seven or eight feet above the street. At either side a post rose well above the platform, supporting one end of a crossbeam.

Three men were hanging from the beam—three corpses, rather. At first, Amy thought that the nooses had been made with extra rope, and that that was what dangled down past the dead bare feet, but at last her mind acknowledged what her eyes were reporting—that the three men had been disemboweled, their bellies sliced open from breastbone to groin, and that those were loops of rotting intestine that dragged on the wooden planks below.

And the black haze around them wasn't in her mind; it wasn't a sign that she was on the verge of fainting. It was a cloud of flies.

The smell, which had been merely an unnoticed unpleasant whiff a moment before, hit at the same moment as the realization of what she was seeing, and she almost vomited. Perhaps because she had been toughened up by her earlier bouts of nausea, or perhaps for some other reason, she managed to fight it down—a small personal victory, but one she appreciated.

When she could think more clearly again, one thought repeated itself over and over in Amy's mind as she forced herself to walk on down the street.

She wasn't staying here. She wouldn't stay here. She couldn't stay here.

At first it appeared that they might have to physically drag Amy to get her into the grubby little tavern, and Pel didn't really blame her—the place faced on the town square, which would have been reasonable enough if it weren't for that bloody gibbet standing there with those hideous rotting things hanging from it. Pel was none too enthusiastic about going anywhere near it himself; quite aside from it being a sickening sight, the stink had made him gag, and he was amazed no one had thrown up.

Raven was far less patient; while the others stared at the corpses, or struggled to say something about them, the velvet-clad aristocrat shrugged and said, "And what would you, then? Shadow deals with its foes thus; 'tis no surprise. 'Twas ever so." He pointed out the tavern, with its sign of a foam-topped beer mug, and urged them all onward.

Susan nodded and seemed to accept the situation without further comment, but Pel noticed that she carefully avoided looking at the dead men.

Ted, on the other hand, stared at them openly, swallowing occasionally, and then remarked, "I never realized what a sick mind I have. I wonder if that's what they'd *really* look like? And smell like?"

Valadrakul ignored the whole matter and simply waited for the others to get on with it. Prossie looked ill, but said nothing and followed Raven's lead into the tavern.

Wilkins started to make a joke about how the hanged men resembled beads on a string, but when he saw the looks on his companions' faces he decided not to finish it. Marks darted quick little glances at the gibbet and said nothing. Sawyer went white, looked quickly at the others, then hurried to the tavern door.

Singer muttered, "Poor bastards," and thereafter kept his head down.

Amy, though, stood frozen in the street, refusing to approach. Raven, standing in the tavern door and waving the others in, saw her and began, "Friend Pel . . ." He pointed, but didn't finish the sentence.

Pel nodded, and hurried back up the street. He took Amy by the hand and said, "Come on. Let's get in off the street."

She shook him off and took a step backward, all the while staring at the hanging viscera.

"Come on," he repeated, catching her arm again. He almost said something about getting a decent meal, but caught himself; given Amy's recent bouts of nausea and what she was now looking at, it was a wonder she wasn't already vomiting, and the mention of food might be the final straw.

She shook her head.

"Look, I want to get out of here as much as you do," Pel told her, "maybe more—but if we're ever going to get *any-where*, we need to go through this town and out the other side, past that . . . past that. And we need to get some f . . . some supplies. And I think maybe we need to talk some more. So come on into the tavern with us, and we'll find someplace away from the windows, where you can't see . . . can't see anything."

Amy hesitated, then said, "I'm not staying here."

"Of course not," Pel agreed. "Come on."

She swallowed, nodded, and came.

Once inside the tavern, Pel found Raven standing by a table near a window and said, "I think we want someplace quieter." He jerked his head toward the open shutters, hoping Raven would take the hint.

Raven did. "Indeed," he said, "so public a place as this is scarce fit for the ladies among us. Your pardon, all, I beg, that I'd not seen this sooner." He turned and led the way to a large table in a back corner of one of the other of the tavern's three rooms.

The entire operation, however, was not particularly large, and even from this rearmost area anyone who wanted to could see out through the archway, the front room, and the windows on the square.

A large man in a grubby apron had stood by, watching, as the party squeezed themselves into the back room, crowding two tables and occupying all but one of the dozen chairs there; when everyone appeared settled, he approached.

"What can I fetch you?" he asked, none too politely.

"Drink," Raven called in reply. "Whatever you have that's fit to be drunk."

The innkeeper, or whatever he was, grunted. "First I'd see the color of your money," he said.

Pel had been anticipating a cool drink, maybe some decent food, and at the innkeeper's words his stomach knotted in frustration. They didn't *have* any money.

Raven frowned, glanced at Valadrakul, and then began to say something, but before he got the first word out Susan had hauled her big black purse onto the table and was rummaging through it.

Raven paused, staring at her.

"Susan," Pel said, "I don't think . . ."

Then he stopped, as she hauled out a wallet and unsnapped the change compartment.

Pel felt suddenly foolish; he had assumed that Susan was going to pull out her pistol and demand a meal at gunpoint, which would hardly have been a good idea—even with a gun, they were eleven against an entire town, without even mentioning Shadow. Furthermore, the locals might not even recognize the little revolver as a weapon.

Susan pulled out two quarters and silently held them up. The innkeeper squinted.

"Silver, is it?" he asked.

Susan tossed the coins on the table, still without a word. The innkeeper reached to pick one up, and Raven's hand shot out, catching him by the wrist.

"Our drinks first," the nobleman said.

"I'm no thief," the innkeeper said, "but I've not seen coins the likes of these before, and I'd study them, to ascertain their worth."

Reluctantly, Raven allowed the man to pick up one of the quarters. He rubbed it between thumb and forefinger, ran a finger around the milled edge, and looked it over.

Pel waited, wondering what the man would make of the copper sandwiched between layers of whatever the silvery metal was—Pel knew perfectly well that there wasn't much actual silver in modern American coins.

"Most peculiar," the innkeeper said, "and whilst 'tis surely worth something, changing it's not to be simple."

Susan fished more coins from her wallet.

In the end, eleven mugs of lukewarm ale cost a dollar and fifteen cents in coin, leaving Susan's change compartment almost empty.

* * *

Amy sipped her ale and stared out the window, ignoring what little conversation was going on around her. The sky had gone gray and the daylight was dim, but it was still far brighter than the tavern's interior, and the gallows stood out vividly.

Those three men had been hanged and disemboweled —hanged by the neck until dead. The evisceration was just an extra; they had died of hanging. Their necks were twisted, their features puffy, their tongues thrust out and swollen; flies were crawling on their faces, on the dark protruding tongues. Their hands were out of sight, presumably tied behind their backs. And Amy couldn't forget the smell that came from them, a thick, heavy odor she never wanted to smell again.

She didn't think this had been the sort of quick, one-snap-and-it's-over, break-the-neck hanging that she had always heard about; she thought this had been slow strangulation. She shuddered and sipped at her ale and wished she had something else to drink.

She had never seen a hanged man before. It wasn't like the movies or TV, where the person still looked like a person, just hanging; the features were distorted, and the body and legs seemed somehow thin and stretched.

That might have something to do with how long they'd been hanging, of course, or with having their guts pulled out. The ale suddenly tasted sour at the thought, and she put her mug down.

She wondered why the three had been hanged; were they murderers? Or rapists, perhaps? Was rape even considered a serious crime here?

Or maybe a crime didn't *need* to be serious to merit hanging, here in Shadow's country. Maybe they were up there because they'd stolen a few apples, or a loaf of bread, or talked back to the local magistrate. Maybe they were hanging there just because Shadow didn't *like* them. Had they done anything as serious as Walter and Beth had?

She swallowed, not drinking, but just trying to keep down what she had already drunk.

She had sent Walter and Beth to their deaths at the hands of Imperial troops, and she suddenly found herself imagining the two of them hanging side by side like that, on a gallows, necks twisted, faces discolored, tongues lolling, bodies stretched. She could see just what Walter's face would have looked like, a parody of what she had seen so often when his features flashed and distorted with anger or lust.

But he was a rapist and a murderer; he had killed that other girl; he had beaten Amy repeatedly. He had known what would happen if the Empire ever caught him. He had brought it on himself; nobody had told him to keep slaves, to rape women, to strangle poor Sheila, whom Amy had never met, whom Amy had replaced. He'd thought he wouldn't be caught, that he could get away with it forever, but the Empire had come looking for Amy and the other Earthpeople, and she'd told them what Walter had done, and he'd been hanged for it.

Hanged, with his face congested with blood, his tongue swollen and protruding, body limp and lifeless, no longer a human being but just a *thing*.

Amy shuddered.

That dead thing back on Zeta whatever-it-was had fathered a child on her, too, which only made it worse. What kind of a human being was it who did things like that?

And Beth, who'd been hanged as well, even though she was a slave, the same as Amy had been—the Empire never knew that, had taken Amy's word for it when she said Beth was guilty, too. Plain quiet Beth, who'd helped Walter abuse Amy, and who had mostly stayed out of Walter's way the rest of the time. What kind of woman had she been, to help her master, her captor, against another victim?

But then, Amy knew she had heard of such things before. Patty Hearst had helped the SLA, hadn't she? Amy remembered the name for it, for hostages coming to help their captors—the Stockholm syndrome. It happened all the time.

And it wasn't new. The Sabine women had sided with the Romans against their own brothers and fathers, hadn't they? Why should Beth have been any different? Why side with a loser?

Because it was *right*, Amy answered herself. Because siding with the abuser was *wrong*; it was evil; it just encouraged more abuse.

Would *she* ever have helped Walter with someone new? *She* had resisted—why couldn't Beth?

But of course, Beth had been there for years, not just weeks. Maybe she had fought at first; maybe she had resisted just as much as Amy had, until it finally sank in that resistance did no good. No Imperial troops came to rescue Beth, the way they had saved Amy. Beth had seen Sheila die for fighting back.

What did it matter, anyway, Amy asked herself. Walter and Beth were dead, and nothing could bring them back. If Beth hadn't deserved hanging, it was a little late to worry about it. Beth had given up and had died for it, and that was too damn bad, but why was Amy worrying about it? So there were three dead men hanging in the town square—nothing could bring *them* back, either, and what business was it of hers, anyway? She didn't know anything about it.

She did know that she wouldn't be staying in this town, though. She wouldn't stay in a place where those corpses could be left out there. Why hadn't they been cut down and decently buried?

They were meant as a warning, of course, and as far as Amy was concerned, they'd worked—they'd warned her away from this place, once and for all. Anyone who could stay here would be accepting things like that, would be as bad as Beth.

And, Amy reluctantly realized, the same was probably true of anywhere Shadow ruled. She couldn't just settle down, not here, not anywhere.

But walking into Shadow's fortress was suicide, and wasn't that wrong, too?

There was no way out. There was no right thing to do. She was trapped.

She sipped more ale. She wanted to cry, but fought back the urge—not here, not now, not in this town.

Later she intended to cry, but not now.

"What do you suppose they did?" Pel asked, nodding toward the window as he picked at a splinter in the tabletop.

Raven shrugged. "Doubtless they irked Shadow somewise," he said. "As you'd do, by troubling it in its fortress."

"You don't think we should do that, do you?" Pel asked unhappily.

"Nay, I do not," Raven said.

"But what *else* can we do?" Pel asked. "It's our only way home, the only way we can get you your guns, the only chance we have. There are only eleven of us; we can't fight all Shadow's monsters and magic by ourselves."

"Yet that's just what you attempt, is't not?"

"No, it isn't," Pel insisted. "We aren't trying to *fight* them, we're trying to get *past* them, to destroy Shadow itself. Like

Frodo and the Ring. Or like assassinating Hitler to end World War II."

Raven shrugged. "These names mean naught to me."

"Frodo's from a famous story about war against an evil magician—a lot like Shadow, from your description."

"But a mere story?"

Reluctantly, Pel nodded. "But Hitler was real," he said.

"And was this Hitler assassinated, as you propose?"

"No," Pel admitted.

Raven said nothing, but his expression was plain for Pel to read. Raven clearly thought both Pel's examples were silly.

And Pel had to admit that he had a point; this was real life, not Tolkien's Middle-Earth—but then, this wasn't Earth at all, and the only experiences Pel had ever had with other worlds had been in books and movies, and in all of those, a few brave and determined people *could* destroy the all-powerful enemy and save the world.

In the real world, nobody had ever assassinated Hitler or Stalin or Napoleon, but how hard had anyone tried? And if he remembered his history right, someone *had* assassinated Caligula, and who knew how many other tyrants had been destroyed before they had reached Hitler's level?

Besides, what *else* was Pel supposed to do?

"Well, what alternative are you offering us?" he demanded. "Just how do *you* propose to defeat Shadow and send us home?"

"In truth," Raven said, "I know not. I would have us find shelter, that we might take what time we need in gathering our forces, that we might await whatever opportunity the Goddess might send—for surely, She will not allow Shadow to rule forever, in despite of Her."

"I don't believe in your Goddess," Pel answered. "We have a saying in my world that God helps those who help themselves; those who simply have faith and wait usually wait forever, if you ask me. And if someone *does* save them, it's other people who *weren't* waiting, not God—or your Goddess, either."

Pel didn't want to wait, sitting around the way he had at Base One, with nothing to do but remember his dead wife and daughter, sinking in morose helplessness. He needed to *do* something. He had set a goal of getting home to Earth, and that was what he intended to do.

Besides, what did he have to lose? Nancy and Rachel were dead; if he got himself killed as well, so what?

"Then you insist on going on?" Raven asked.

"That's right," Pel said.

CHAPTER 17

"*If this Shadow's so tough with its magic,*" *Wilkins asked,* looking around at the scattered bones, "why hasn't it spotted us and sent a bunch of its monsters after us?"

"It probably hasn't noticed us yet," Pel muttered unhappily, as he trudged on down the highway. He looked straight ahead, at the tree-lined highway, trying not to see the bones below or the clouds overhead.

"Well, why the hell *not*?" Wilkins demanded, stopping in his tracks. "It noticed *these* people!" He kicked at a skull fragment.

"We don't know that," Pel insisted, pausing reluctantly. "Maybe it was wild animals or bandits that killed them."

"Bandits?" Wilkins picked up a thighbone. "Something sucked the marrow out of this, Brown—what kind of bandits would do that?"

"Animals, then," Pel said. "Come on, let's keep moving; I don't like it here. *Whatever* did this, it might come back."

"I never heard of any animal that would do anything like this," Sawyer said, joining the discussion.

" 'Twas most likely Shadow's beasts," Raven said, leaning his bandaged left hand against a tree by the roadside. "This looks very much in their fashion."

"Which is what I said in the first place," Wilkins pointed out. "So why hasn't Shadow sent the beasts after *us*?"

"It did, back at the ship," Amy said, not very confidently.

"But not *since* then," Wilkins argued.

Amy shrugged; she was obviously struggling to hold down her lunch. Her bouts of nausea had become far less frequent over the last few days, but she still had trouble when they came across something unpleasant.

171

Human bones scattered across the highway were definitely unpleasant. Pel had no idea how old these were, or how long they had actually been there, but he didn't think they had been brought there from somewhere else; it looked as if a small group of people had been killed and torn to pieces right there on the spot.

"Maybe they did something to attract attention," Pel suggested. "Used magic, maybe."

"Brown, *we've* been using magic," Wilkins shouted. "Back at the ruin, that twit Taillefer was bloody *flying*, and why didn't *that* attract Shadow?"

"I don't know," Pel said. "Maybe we were just lucky that time." He frowned.

"We've been using magic over and over again, Brown," Wilkins insisted. "Our tame wizard here's lit us a fire with his fingers every night."

"We'd no need, had we funds to pay an inn, or had Shadow not done away with all laws of hospitality," Valadrakul pointed out. "But as it is, we've no tinderbox, no other way to make fire. Would you eat your food raw and sleep unwarmed?"

"It's better than getting ripped apart, like whoever these people were," Marks snapped.

"But we *haven't* been," Wilkins said. "And I want to know why."

Raven said, "Perhaps the Goddess protects us."

"Shit," Wilkins replied.

Pel didn't say anything more; he just turned and marched onward.

For five days now they had been off the Starlinshire Downs and onto flat country that Raven assured them was a coastal plain; they had marched on across Shadow's countryside, passing through towns and villages without stopping, since they had no more coins to spend. No one spoke to them; children, and sometimes adults, ran and hid at the sight of strangers. Even those who spotted them stealing food never called out or protested; they turned away, or simply watched, without intervening.

Most of the towns had had gibbets in the square, and most of those gibbets had been in use, with corpses of varying age. Some had been fresh, as if the travelers had only just missed the execution; others had been little more than bone and blackened skin. Most were men; some were women; and in one village four children had dangled there, naked and eviscerated—three girls and a boy, none older than twelve.

Pel no longer argued that Shadow might just be the victim of hostile propaganda.

The travelers had grown quieter, gloomier, and more nervous with each new atrocity, and the weather had not helped any; the bright sunlight and greenery of Castle Regisvert were only a memory, and they had been walking beneath a heavy overcast since shortly after that first town, where they had wasted Susan's handful of coins at the inn.

Pel almost wished it would rain and get it over with, but it didn't; the clouds hung oppressive and unmoving overhead, growing steadily thicker and darker, but never releasing so much as a drop of rain. Wind rustled ominously in the leaves, but at ground level the air was still and thick and heavy and smelled of mold.

Pel waited for a moment longer, but Wilkins seemed to have said his piece.

"Come on," Pel said. He started walking. Raven straightened up and joined him; the others followed.

"You know what it is," Wilkins said. "We're walking into a trap, that's what it is. Shadow *wants* us to come to its fortress and save it the trouble of hunting us down. If we turned back, we'd probably have the monsters after us in a minute."

Pel turned to argue and saw Susan and Prossie staring at Wilkins intently as they walked; they obviously thought the soldier was on to something.

"That's ridiculous," Pel said.

"Why?" Wilkins demanded belligerently. "What's ridiculous about it?"

Pel's mouth opened, then closed.

What *was* ridiculous about it? It made far more sense than Pel wanted to admit.

And what would he do if it were true? To turn back would be to invite attack. True or false, he had to continue.

He turned forward again and kept walking.

Prossie glanced up from the half-eaten chicken leg she held and noticed that Wilkins was, for the moment, alone; he was sitting to one side, leaning against the base of a rather unhealthy-looking tree and gnawing on a chunk of poultry, while most of the others were clustered close around the fire.

She rose to a half crouch and took a quick few steps over

to the tree, staying low, as if there were enemies out there watching, ready to shoot—and for all she knew, there were.

She wished she could still read minds; the freedom of mental silence, of being out of the Empire's net, was still new and strange and wonderful, but it was also horribly frustrating to not know what anyone was thinking, to not know if there were people out there she couldn't see. She was unaccustomed to knowing less than the people around her.

It wasn't really frightening anymore, but it was frustrating. And lonely.

"Spaceman Wilkins," she whispered, as she squatted beside him.

He looked up. "Yeah, Thorpe?"

"May I talk to you?" She didn't look him in the eye; nontelepaths never liked it when telepaths looked directly at them—as if the eyes had something to do with mind reading.

Wilkins put down his chicken and wiped greasy fingers on his already-filthy uniform trousers. "*You* need to talk, telepath?" he asked belligerently. "About what?"

"Yes, I need to talk," Prossie said, annoyed. "I can't read your mind here."

"That's what you *said*, anyway," Wilkins acknowledged, his tone a little less hostile. "So what do you want?" He glanced at the neckline of her uniform, and she realized that squatting as she had might not have been clever. "If it's what I think," Wilkins said, leering, "I don't know—there's not much privacy, and I never screwed a mutant freak before. You noisy? Mind if the others watch?"

"That's not what I want," Prossie said, refusing to rise to his bait; she guessed that he wanted an angry response. "I just want to talk to you about something you said earlier."

"Maybe I don't want to talk to a mutant," he replied, a challenge clear in his voice.

Prossie stared at him for a moment, wishing she could see whether he was joking, just what mix of fright and anger and hate and resentment and lust he was feeling. His expression was a peculiar one, not quite smiling, a little tense—she had never been good at reading expressions, since she had never had to be. She had always just read the thoughts behind the face.

She couldn't do that now, though, and she finally decided to get directly to the point.

"Do you really think we're walking into a trap?" she asked.

He glanced past her at the others, then back to her, and asked, "Why?"

"Because I don't want to die," she answered bluntly.

"Everybody dies," he said, looking down and picking up his piece of chicken. Whatever emotional game he had been playing with her seemed to be over. "The only questions are when and how."

She smiled bitterly. "True enough, Spaceman, but if I get a choice, I vote for much later, and of natural causes."

"So you don't get a choice," he said, taking a bite of chicken, still not looking at her.

She actually thought for a moment of snatching the food from his mouth, but the remnants of her lifelong conditioning held; she didn't touch him, but she didn't leave, either.

He chewed and swallowed, took another bite, chewed and swallowed, then looked up and found her still there, staring at him. He stared back for a moment, then tossed the rest of the chicken aside.

"What do you want, Thorpe?" he asked. "Who are you spying for now?"

"I'm not spying for anyone," Prossie said. "I'm just trying to stay alive."

"And what if I don't believe that? You've always been a spy; maybe you say you can't read my mind now, but that doesn't mean you've stopped spying. You can still talk to Base One, right? You can still report on whether I've been a good little boy, still loyal to His Imperial Majesty? Well, maybe I don't want to give you anything to tell them. Maybe I don't know who you're working for back there, whether you're a good little soldier or some politician's flunky, and I just don't want to get tangled up in anything."

"I'm not spying for anyone," Prossie insisted. "I can still talk to my cousin, yes, but I haven't heard from her for two days now, and I don't tell her everything, and she's loyal to our family and the Emperor, nobody else. If you think we're working for General Hart or Undersecretary Bascombe, we're not. And I'm just asking for *me*, nobody else."

"So what do you want from me?" Wilkins asked.

"I just want to know why you think we're walking into a trap, and whether you know of a way out."

"I think it's pretty obvious why I think it's a trap," he said. "If this Shadow is as all-powerful as these people say it is, wouldn't it have to know we're here? I mean, even if it doesn't know anything from its magic, or whatever it is, we've been passing through town after town, in broad daylight, and if it's got *anything* better than messengers on foot, there's been plenty of time for a message to reach it. Valadrakul got a message to that flying nitwit somehow, and I'm pretty sure I've seen smoke used for signaling, so I figure Shadow knows we're here—but it hasn't come after us."

"Maybe it doesn't care," Prossie suggested.

Wilkins shook his head. "You think it's that kind of a thing? Then what were all those people hanged for? What spread those bones around the highway back there? If those were all murderers, the whole region would have been depopulated by now. If they're thieves, you'd think they'd have learned— Raven said this has been Shadow's turf for a couple of centuries now. About the only thing I can think of that people just can't learn to do, even if it gets them killed, is to keep their damn mouths shut—so I think Shadow's the kind of boss who takes loose talk seriously and doesn't stand for any kind of loose ends. It wouldn't allow a bunch of foreigners to stroll across the countryside any old way they want—not unless it was watching them somehow, and they were doing just what it wanted."

Prossie nodded. She had learned the word "paranoid" from the Earthpeople, and it seemed to fit what Wilkins described; it also matched her own perceptions of Shadow.

"So maybe it's not exactly a trap," Wilkins said. "Maybe it's not going to kill us; maybe if we turn back we'll just find a bunch of cops who'll take us in for questioning, instead of those black animal things. Maybe when we get there it'll offer us all a chance to join its side, maybe go back to the Empire as traitors, saboteurs—I don't know. I do know that either it's tracking us and knows perfectly well where we are, or else Raven and the wizard have been lying to us, and we don't know a damn thing about what's going on here."

"Makes sense," Prossie admitted.

Wilkins studied her, then asked, "So, Thorpe, you can still call Base One, right? You can tell them whether to send reinforcements, or try to pick us up?"

"I can ask Carrie to pass on a message," Prossie agreed, "but that's it. They'll probably ignore it."

"That's about the only way we're going to get out of this, though—if they send in someone else. If you *tell* them that it's a trap, won't they listen to you?"

Prossie hesitated.

"Listen, Wilkins," she said. "There's something I didn't tell anyone—I don't know if you know all the rules we telepaths have, some people do and some don't, but we have rules about what we tell who of what we read, and I'm not supposed to tell you this, but the hell with that."

"What?" He eyed her warily.

"We were set up. I don't know the details, I didn't get it all, but Bascombe deliberately screwed up this whole expedition just to get rid of those people." She waved a hand at the others, sure that Wilkins would understand that she meant the Earthpeople and Faerie folk. "He was listening to Shadow's spies back there at Base One when he picked Carson for command. And when things started going wrong, he and General Hart decided that they want us all dead, so there won't be any evidence that they screwed up. *That's* why I've been so sure we weren't getting rescued."

Wilkins blinked. "Why didn't you tell the lieutenant, back at the ship?"

"You think he'd have believed me? A mutant, telling him he can't trust his own superiors? Lieutenant Dibbs, we're talking about."

"So why are you telling *me*, then?" Wilkins asked. "Why should *I* believe you?"

"Because you figured out that we're being set up again— that Shadow's watching us. So maybe I think you're smarter than the lieutenant. And maybe if you know a bit more, you can figure out how we can get *out* of this."

For a moment the two stared silently at each other; then Wilkins said, "Yeah, I can see what you mean." He glanced over at the others. "Problem is, there are a couple of things we don't know here."

"What?"

"What Shadow wants with us," Wilkins said, "and *which* of us it wants."

" 'I wish the damn clouds would either break up or rain,' " Sawyer said angrily to Pel. "You had to say that."

Pel glared back at him; it wasn't worth trying to talk over the constant patter of the rain, or the splashing as they slogged through the mud. His stolen shirt, taken from a farmer's hut two days before, clung damply to his back and dripped down his wrists; he almost regretted its acquisition.

"Think you he tempted the gods, then?" Raven asked, peering out from under the dripping cloak he held over his head.

"Something like that," Sawyer agreed. He had stolen another farmer's cap that morning, but it was clearly not doing him much good in the steady downpour.

Raven shook his head. "The foolishness of you pagans," he said. "To think our mere words could thus affect the Goddess's scheme."

"You're calling *me* a pagan?" Sawyer exclaimed angrily. He stopped and grabbed Raven by the arm.

Raven turned and struck at Sawyer without thinking; Pel saw him start to wince, and then suppress it, as his mostly healed but still tender fingers hit Sawyer's wrist.

Sawyer saw it, too, and let go. "Sorry," he said.

" 'Tis naught," Raven said. "I spoke ill of your faith; 'twas rude of me."

By now the entire party had stopped; Pel and Raven and Sawyer had been at the front, and the others were now gathered about them, sinking into the mud of the road.

"Oh, come on," Amy said. "If we keep going maybe we can find somewhere to get out of the rain." She turned and trudged onward; she limped slightly, thanks to popped blisters, but seemed to be over her illness. Susan followed her lead, tugging at Ted's wrist to make sure he came, as well.

Prossie, who had been near the center of the line talking to Valadrakul, turned to look over the party, and Pel saw her frown.

Sawyer, too, noticed her expression, and looked over the rest of the group.

"Hey," he said, "Where's Ron?"

"Who?" Pel asked.

"Ronnie Wilkins."

Amy and Susan and Ted kept walking, unaware of the consternation as the others all turned and looked around.

"He's gone," Marks said, sounding very surprised. He took off his helmet to look around better and blinked as the rain drenched him.

"When did you last see him?" Pel asked.

The others glanced at one another.

"At that last village, I guess," Sawyer said, "just before it started raining."

"He was with us when we left the village," Singer said unsteadily; he was cradling his swollen left wrist in his right hand. The badger scratches he had received back at Castle Regisvert had become infected, and Valadrakul's crude attempts at treatment had done little good; Pel had thought it amusing, or ironic, or at any rate worthy of note, that scratches left by an ordinary badger had turned out to be septic, while the various wounds he and Prossie and Amy had gotten from Shadow's hellbeasts were all healing cleanly.

Maybe ordinary germs couldn't live on Shadow's unnatural creatures.

"I did a count," Singer added. "I *know* he was with us."

"He was here," Marks confirmed.

"How long after that, though?" Pel asked.

Singer shrugged. "That was the last time I saw him," he said. "He was way at the back." He looked at Marks. "I thought he was talking to you."

"He was, for a while," Marks agreed. "But then he said he wanted to think, so I left him alone and came up to talk to Sawyer."

"I remember that," Sawyer said. "So no one's seen him since then?"

No one had.

"D'you think the monsters got him?" Sawyer asked. "Shadow's things? Or maybe something else, some other magic?"

Singer snorted derisively; Raven smiled.

Valadrakul shook his head. "I doubt 'twas Shadow."

"I think he must've just left," Pel said. "He decided not to come with us and didn't bother to argue about it."

"He decided not to walk into a trap," Prossie said quietly. "Not when he isn't one of the ones it wants."

The others stared at her for a moment; then Marks said bitterly, "And the son of a bitch didn't ask me to come with him, either!"

"Or any of us," Sawyer pointed out.

"Probably figured he had a better shot by himself," Singer suggested wearily. "Probably right, too."

"Well, he's gone, now," Pel said. He turned without another word and began marching onward, following Amy and Susan and Ted.

"We aren't going to try to find him?" Singer asked.

"Why should we?" Pel called back over his shoulder. "He's a big boy; he can take care of himself."

"And where would you seek him?" Raven asked. " 'Tis a

broad land, and he's had time to conceal himself where'er he would."

Singer blinked at him, then said, "Yeah, you're right." He trudged after Pel.

After a moment's hesitation, the rest came close behind.

"I'm going to bunk," Marks whispered.

Prossie turned, startled.

"Like Ronnie," Marks explained. "He was right; why should we *all* get killed? This Shadow thing probably just wants Raven and his wizard pal, or maybe the Earthpeople."

Prossie glanced around. They were in open country now, a low, grassy plain where no trees grew, much of it too sodden to farm; the highway wound its way along the higher, drier portions, past the dreary little farms that mostly seemed to raise various sorts of berries. They hadn't passed anything resembling a village for several miles, and their last meal had been nothing but stolen raspberries—sweet, but not very satisfying.

"Where will you go?" she asked.

"I don't know," he said. "It all looks pretty much the same, so who cares?"

Prossie was considering that when Marks asked anxiously, "So, Thorpe, are you with me?"

"Who else are you asking?" Prossie asked.

"Nobody," Marks replied hastily. "I mean, I figured you and I, we could make like we're married, if anyone asks . . ."

She knew what he meant. Prossie looked at him more closely, considering.

Bill Marks was hardly her idea of the perfect mate; he was of medium height, not particularly well built, with a receding chin and a bad complexion—not really ugly, but not anyone's image of handsome, either. She didn't doubt for a minute that he wanted to carry the fiction of a marriage a little further than answers to questions from nosy natives. The notion did not particularly appeal to her. With the right person, maybe, but not with Bill Marks.

Hell, he didn't even call her by her first name.

"What about Singer and Sawyer?" she asked.

"What *about* them?" Marks asked, flustered.

Prossie looked him in the eye, then turned and looked at the others, a dozen yards ahead.

"Well, you know," Marks said, a little desperately, "Singer's got that bad arm, and besides, the more of us there are, the more likely we'll be noticed, you know, by Shadow or someone . . ."

"Never mind," she said. "I think I'll take my chances with the rest of them, at least for now. You go ahead, and good luck!"

Marks hesitated. "You sure?" he asked.

"Yes," Prossie answered firmly.

She was sure of her decision—but she wished she were sure she was right.

Pel turned, startled, at a tap on his shoulder and found Prossie Thorpe just behind him.

"Mr. Brown," she said quietly, without preamble, "I was wondering just what your opinion was on Wilkins."

"My opinion?" Pel glanced around; no one else seemed to be paying any attention. He had half expected to see Nancy glaring at him for talking to another woman this way, but Nancy was dead; she wasn't with them. "My opinion is that he's gone," Pel said. "What do you mean, my opinion?"

"I mean, do you think he got away safely?"

Pel shrugged. "I don't know. He probably did, but I don't know any more than you do. Maybe less, if your telepathy can tell you anything."

"Not about that," Prossie said. "I still hear from Base One sometimes, but they've written us all off as lost."

Pel nodded. "I'm not surprised," he said.

"So do you think Wilkins was right, that he did the right thing by turning back?"

"Or aside," Pel said. "We don't know *where* he went, remember."

"But do you think he was right?" Prossie insisted.

Pel shrugged again. "Who knows?"

"He thought we were all walking into a trap, you know," Prossie said.

"So he said," Pel replied.

Prossie nodded. "He talked to me about it a little; he figured that Shadow might want you, because the warp came out in your house, and Raven because he's the lord of Stormcrack, and Valadrakul because he's a wizard, and so on, but that it wouldn't have any use for a bunch of ordinary Imperial soldiers."

Pel thought that over. "He might've been right," he admitted.

"So what about the others?" Prossie asked. "I mean, I'm a telepath, so maybe I'm one of the special ones, too, but what about Marks and Sawyer and Singer?"

"What *about* them?" Pel asked, trying to figure out what Prossie was leading up to."

"What if they turned back, instead of going on with the rest of us?"

Pel shrugged; he started to say, "It's a free country," then remembered where he was. "They can do what they please," he said. "I'm not their jailer."

"But do you think it would be safe?"

Pel gave her a startled look.

"I mean," Prossie explained, "Wilkins thought that if we turned back, *then* we'd find Shadow's monsters waiting for us, that it was only leaving us alone as long as we stayed headed in the right direction. So if someone it wanted turned back, he would be running right into the monsters. So do you think Marks and Sawyer and Singer would be safe?"

"Why are you asking *me*?" Pel demanded. "*You're* the telepath! And Raven's the expert on Shadow. I'm just . . . I'm just me."

"Raven lies," Prossie said. "You know that; he'd tell me whatever he thought would be best for him. I think I can get an honest answer from you."

Pel looked at her, puzzled. Her eyes were green, he saw—he had never noticed that before. Her hair was a dull brown, her face ordinary.

"You want an honest answer?" he said. "Fine; I honestly don't know. I don't know what's going on; I'm just trying to muddle along. I want to go home. I want my wife and daughter back. Beyond that, I don't care what happens, to me or anyone else. If those guys want to go back to the ship, or go hide somewhere, it's fine with me."

For only an instant, her eyes met his; then she dropped her gaze to the ground, and he was sure he had offended or frightened or embarrassed her somehow. He started to frame an apology, then stopped; he had nothing to apologize for.

Maybe she was just shy. Or maybe she was trying to flirt with him.

He wasn't interested in flirting; he was a married man—or at least, he still thought of himself as one. It was too soon after

Nancy's loss to look elsewhere—or maybe he was just too tired, or too scared.

And even if he hadn't been, Prossie Thorpe wasn't exactly what he was looking for in a woman. He looked down at his own muddy boots.

She turned away without saying anything more.

Raven was satisfied with their progress—or at any rate, with the speed of it; the direction was not what he would have chosen. Marching to Shadow's fortress still seemed to him the height of folly.

And now they were but a day away, he thought, as he peered out into the blackness of the surrounding night, and that day, if the tales spoke truth, to be spent all upon the causeway across Shadowmarsh, with nowhere to turn or hide. They had seen the marsh spread before them as the sun sank, and that was why Raven had called the night's halt where he did.

Might he not best serve his land and his people and his cause by slipping away and leaving these foreigners to their own devices? If they were to perish at Shadow's hands, 'twould be a sad loss, but there had been many such losses over the years.

And this was the final moment, the time when he must decide. He had debated the matter with Pellinore Brown over their meager supper, and the Brown remained unyielding—he was bound for Shadow's keep.

Some might accuse a man in Raven's place of cowardice, did he now flee—but what of that? Was he not outcast now? He would know it was not fear, but prudence and hope for the future that guided his steps.

Still, to be marked as coward, even wrongly . . .

He had got that far in his thinking when a cry sounded; instantly, Raven was on his feet, once again cursing the fate that had left him without his sword.

"Help!" a man's voice called, as from a distance. "Oh, my God . . ."

Raven snatched up a brand from the dying fire and waved it, that the air might brighten the sparks; it flared briefly, but the flame did not linger, and he saw naught but startled faces and muddy boots.

"It's Marks," the man Singer said; he, too, raised an impromptu torch in his good hand and headed for the sound.

The voice cried out again, wordlessly, as Singer and Raven

ran up the highway to the east, away from Shadowmarsh. Raven saw that the others, to their shame, stayed behind—even Valadrakul, who, though a wizard, Raven had thought to be a man of honor and some small courage.

The cries stopped well before Raven and Singer reached their source.

When they did reach Marks's body, it was far too late to lend any aid beyond a decent burial; his dead eyes gleamed orange in the feeble torchlight, staring up at the black clouds above, but his face was black with dirt and blood. His throat and chest had been torn open, and Raven knew at a glance that even the finest healer could not have saved him.

"Damn," Singer muttered. "What did it?" He raised his torch, brighter than Raven's own, and waved it about. "Where is it?"

"Shadow," Raven told him, lowering his own brand.

"Are you sure?" a female voice asked.

Startled, Raven whirled, and found the woman called Susan standing a few paces down the road, her black bag open on her shoulder, her hand within—ready, Raven supposed, to bring out in an instant that magical weapon of hers.

He smiled slightly. At least *one* of the foreigners had courage—and the skill to use it, to have followed so silently!

"What else?" he asked her. " 'Tis surely another warning—more bones by the roadside for any who would follow us."

"Why just him? Why not all of us?"

Raven turned back for another look at Marks.

"See you," he said, "he sought to flee; we are surely a good quarter-mile from our camp. This man had turned back upon the path."

"And Shadow doesn't want us to do that," Singer said.

"As you say," Raven agreed. "Shadow would not have us turn back."

"You don't think it's a coincidence?" Susan asked. "After all, as far as we know, Wilkins got away safely."

"Insofar as we know," Raven agreed, "but how far is that? And more, the rules may well have changed since Wilkins turned aside; we were not then so near to Shadow's hold."

Susan nodded, the motion just barely visible in the darkness. "So we go on," she said flatly.

"Indeed," Raven agreed. "In the morning, we go on."

In the morning, they would march into the jaws of death, where only the Goddess herself could save them.

And perhaps the Goddess *would* save them; perhaps she had wearied of Shadow's importunities and would somehow use Raven and his companions as her tools for defeating it.

Or perhaps they would all die, and their souls return to the Goddess's womb. That was death, and Raven did not seek death—but how was he to avoid it, now?

Perhaps, Raven thought later, as he settled to sleep, they should have brought Marks's body back with them, should have buried the poor man's remains and returned his flesh to the Goddess as well as his soul—but no one had suggested it, no one had argued, and the rain had begun anew.

Scores of men had lain unburied in the war against Shadow; one more would matter not.

And Raven knew that on the morrow, he might well be yet another.

CHAPTER 18

"*That's it, isn't it?*" *Amy asked, pointing.*

Raven nodded wearily. "Indeed, 'twould seem to be. Understand you, I've not been here until now, I've never seen Shadow's keep ere this, but in truth, that we see before us fits every tale I've heard."

Amy had somehow assumed that Raven must have seen Shadow's fortress, but of course, there was no reason he should have. She stared, trying to make out more details.

The rain that had fallen off and on for the past two days seemed to have finally stopped for good, but the air was still thick and damp and hazy. She saw a heavy gray structure built around a central tower that rose in uneven steps, with odd jogs and turrets here and there; it resembled a storybook castle rather more than Stormcrack Keep or Castle Regisvert had, but broader and uglier; no one would ever call this thing "soaring" or "graceful."

She couldn't make out windows or doors with any certainty, nor those things like teeth that ran along the tops of castle walls; that made it very hard to get a clear idea of the size of the fortress.

"How much farther is it, then?" she asked, glancing down at her aching feet.

"Probably farther than it looks," Pel said.

Amy, remembering a few long walks through American cities toward buildings that were visible but distant, nodded as she looked around.

This was no city, though; the gray mass of Shadow's fortress rose from a broad marshy plain that looked almost equally gray. The highway was literally a high way here, a band of yellowish earth built up about two feet above the surrounding

186

reeds and grasses; it was bare, lifeless dirt, no grass or weeds along the verge.

The marshes to either side looked dead, Amy thought; she supposed that was an illusion, that the reeds just weren't as green as the ones she was used to. The dull light that seeped through the thick overcast didn't help at all; it seemed to leach the color out of everything. The place reeked of brine and decay, smothering in the warm, dense air.

To the north she could see wooded hills, and perhaps the clouds were thinner there, because the forests were green enough. Looking back, the higher, drier plain behind them wasn't as drab, either—the trees and the farmers' fields showed color, and even the thatched roofs of the scattered houses, and of the last village they had passed through, were brighter than what lay ahead.

The marsh really *was* that sick, flat color, she decided, and she remembered how, back on the Downs, Pel had argued that the countryside didn't look like it was ruled by evil magic.

She didn't remember even the mudflats of New Jersey being as ugly as this, though—though they did smell worse. "Is this more what you had in mind?" she asked Pel.

"What?" Pel started, and looked puzzled.

"I mean this place—is this the sort of place you'd expect an evil wizard to live?"

Pel glanced at the distant shape of Shadow's fortress, at the miles of dun marshland.

"Yeah," he said. "I guess it is."

It certainly seemed to fit the part to Amy. Maybe most of the rest of the bizarre things that had happened since Captain Cahn's spaceship fell in her backyard hadn't fit the stereotypes, but Shadow's fortress looked just fine as an evil wizard's castle, even if it wasn't built in the shape of a skull or anything as silly as that.

"What's that on the road?" Singer asked, pointing with his good hand.

Amy dropped her gaze from the fortress to the highway and saw what Singer meant—something dark lay on the road ahead, not moving.

"Someone dropped a pack, maybe," she suggested.

"Raven?" Susan asked.

The nobleman turned up his palms. "I know no more than do you," he said.

They trudged onward, but all of them were now moving

more cautiously, watching the dark mass on the highway. Amy couldn't decide if it was black or a very dark gray; the poor light didn't make it easy to distinguish.

And its color didn't really matter, anyway.

The thing was about three feet long, she judged, and almost featureless; it looked a little like a huge empty boot, or an irregularly shaped stovepipe. She had no idea what it was, or what it was doing there—until, when they were perhaps ten feet away, it moved.

It lifted one end and swung it to point at the approaching travelers; the end split open, revealing long rows of sharp white teeth. Amy could still see no eyes, no nostrils, no other features, but the mouth and the teeth were unmistakable. The thing was alive, and hostile.

"A Shadow thing," Pel said.

"Kill it," Sawyer said, drawing his blaster.

Raven's hand dropped to his empty belt; Singer hesitated, hands clutching; Susan shifted her purse but did not reach in.

Valadrakul raised a hand, then paused.

"No magic," Raven warned him. "Not when Shadow's keep looms before us."

Sawyer clicked the trigger of his blaster a couple of times, then turned to stare helplessly at the others.

"Save wizardry, we are unarmed, my lord," Valadrakul pointed out.

That wasn't literally true, Amy thought, remembering the pistol in Susan's purse, but she didn't correct him; it was close enough to the truth.

Instead, she asked, "Do you think that's the one that got poor Marks last night?"

"No," Singer said flatly. He didn't explain, and after a moment's hesitation, Amy decided that she didn't want him to.

For a moment, the nine of them stood in silent confusion; then Ted—Ted Deranian, of all people—marched forward.

"This is stupid," he said. "It looks as if I'm not going to wake up until I get through this whole stupid thing, right up to the showdown, so let's get on with it. I'm not going to let some stupid refugee from *Aliens* stretch it out." He walked up to the monster and kicked at it.

"Go on, get out of here," he said. "You're in the way."

The creature twitched away from Ted's foot, then seemed to hesitate, open jaws wavering.

Then it closed its mouth and slithered away, off the highway and down into the marsh.

"Come on," Ted said. "Let's get this *over* with!" He stamped onward, toward the fortress.

The others, by unspoken common consent, hung back.

"We're unarmed," Pel said. "We're walking into Shadow's fortress unarmed and out in the open."

" 'Twas your own proposal," Raven pointed out.

"I know," Pel said, "and you told me at the time it was a stupid idea, and you were right." He hesitated, as if trying to gather the will to turn back.

That was too much for Amy. She wanted to get this all over with. If she was going to die, then she would die, and maybe it would serve her right for sending Beth to the gallows, but she wasn't going to turn back the way Bill Marks had, she wanted to at least face whatever they were up against. "What *else* are we going to do?" she demanded angrily. "Even if it lets us? Do you want to go back and live in some village where they hang *children*, Pel? Where no one talks to us? Or go back to Raven's friends, who don't have the nerve to work a spell to send us home?" Unconsciously, she rested one hand on her faintly bulging abdomen.

"I wonder if maybe Taillefer could *teach* the portal spell to someone?" Pel asked. "Someone who could use it and step through with us?"

Amy stared at him, angrier than ever. "*Now* you think of that?" she shouted.

"Don't forget about Ted," Susan said quietly, pointing. Pel's lawyer was a hundred feet away, marching on toward the fortress.

"Valadrakul," Pel said, "*could* Taillefer teach someone to work the spell, without using it himself? Without Shadow noticing?"

The wizard considered the question, but before he could reply, Singer said, "I don't think it matters."

The others turned to him.

"Why not?" Pel demanded.

"Remember Bill Marks," Singer said. He pointed, back along the highway, and the others turned to look.

On the road behind them were half a dozen of the stovepipe-shaped monsters, sprawled across the highway; as they watched, another slithered up from the marsh.

"I don't think *those* are going to let us kick them aside," Singer said.

"Wilkins was right all along," Prossie said. "It's a trap; Shadow *wants* us to come to it, and if we don't we'll all wind up like Marks."

For a moment, they all stared at the creatures; then Pel shrugged and said, "Well, if we don't have a choice, we might as well get going."

He turned and marched ahead, following Ted.

Amy stared at the monsters.

"Come on," Prossie said, touching her arm.

Reluctantly, Amy turned.

"We might as well get it over with," she agreed.

Just as Pel had expected, the fortress was larger and farther away than it had looked; they had first spotted it in the morning, but dusk was falling by the time they finally approached the gates. He was soaked with sweat; so were most of the others. The day was not actually all that hot, but the humidity and the high gravity made it an exhausting march.

Raven had judged their entire journey to be around two hundred miles, once everyone had agreed on what a mile was, and Pel now appreciated just how much that was. Two hundred miles was about the distance from Washington to Philadelphia, about four hours by car, nothing much—but it was a damnably long way to *walk*, through forests and over ridges and across the plain and then through this soggy, unpleasant marshland.

And Pel would much rather have arrived at Philadelphia than at Shadow's fortress; he amused himself for part of this final leg of the journey by trying to remember the exact phrasing of the appropriate W. C. Fields quote, and although he had no way to check it, he finally settled on, "Frankly, I'd rather be in Philadelphia."

They weren't in Philadelphia, though; they were approaching the fortress.

In a way, that didn't seem quite right; they hadn't had enough adventures along the way. They hadn't really had *any* adventures since leaving Castle Regisvert; petty theft wasn't much of an adventure. Wilkins's disappearance hadn't been very dramatic; Marks's death hardly qualified. The whole two-hundred-mile walk had been pretty dull.

In the stories, the journeys were never so boring—or was that just because the authors left out the dull parts?

No, any epic quest was supposed to have real challenges along the way—goblins and monsters, not just rain and irate villagers. And the adventurers were supposed to defeat the menaces through wit and strength and other traditional virtues, not by just trudging onward, day after day.

They hadn't even *seen* the monster that had killed Marks. And while Valadrakul had defeated the giant bat-thing with a spell, that was a long time ago, and far away, and hardly seemed to count.

But this wasn't a story, this was real life, and Pel supposed that if anyone ever wrote it all down, the long dull walk would be relegated to a line or two of scene-shifting.

In any case, challenges met and menaces defeated or not, they had reached Shadow's fortress.

The marsh came right up to the towering stone walls, but the highway led directly into an open gate. The entire thing was built on a gigantic scale; the outer wall was at least as long as a city block, and Pel judged it to rise ten stories or so—a hundred feet high. The towers were not visible from directly below the walls, but he had seen from the highway that they were clearly at least three or four times as high. Pel hadn't thought simple masonry, with no steel frame, could support so high a tower—but then, it probably didn't; Shadow's magic probably held the thing together.

Just like all those Hollywood movies, he supposed; if by some miracle they *did* play out the traditional heroic adventure and managed to kill Shadow, that whole immense tower would probably fall in and crush them all.

That never happened in the stories—the heroes always got out in time, though the villains might get crushed. Pel didn't care to trust to that sort of thing in real life.

They had no choice, though; a glance back showed him that the highway behind them was sprinkled with those crawling giant-slug-with-teeth monsters. And although Singer had said those weren't what had killed Marks, *something* had killed him—Raven and Singer and Susan all agreed on that. They couldn't turn back; they had to go on in and finish up the story, even if it meant dying.

And maybe dying wouldn't be that bad. If there was an afterlife, maybe he'd see Nancy and Rachel again; if Ted's theory was right, he'd be back on Earth. Maybe Marks was back in the Galactic Empire even now, back with his family, if he had any.

Pel was suddenly bothered that he had no idea whether Marks had had any family. Wilkins would have known, but Wilkins was gone, too—maybe dead, maybe not.

Marks was definitely dead. Elani was dead. Carson was dead. Nancy and Rachel were dead. If Pel died, he would at any rate be in good company.

And whatever death might mean, at least if Pel died he would be out of Shadow's power and out of Raven's world, this whole ghastly thing would be over for him.

And he might or might not die. If they *were* in a story, and one of them was the hero—Raven seemed like the traditional candidate—then that one could expect to win through alive somehow, but the rest of them could die; sidekicks and spear-carriers were always expendable.

And it was always possible that they were just one of the earlier expeditions doomed to fail, so that some later hero might avenge them. Or perhaps the men would be slain and the women imprisoned, for later rescue.

Or maybe it wasn't a story at all, maybe real life didn't work that way. It certainly hadn't worked out well for somebody, he saw; there were more dead bodies, like those in the towns and villages, hanging by their necks from the parapet above the open gate.

Pel had thought he'd gotten used to gibbets and scaffolds and bones and corpses, so at first he didn't really pay much attention when he realized that there were people hanging there; he just tried not to look. The fading light made that easier; so did his sore feet, as they kept his attention elsewhere.

After all, this was Shadow's headquarters; why would it be any different from the rest of Shadow's realm?

Then he heard Sawyer say, "Oh, shit."

He turned and saw the Imperial soldier staring up at the dangling corpses. Without meaning to, without thinking about it, Pel looked up at them, too.

He swallowed hard.

He had thought he'd gotten used to gibbets and scaffolds and bones and corpses, but this was different.

This time he knew them.

There were six men hanging there, each with his belly sliced open and grayish loops of his intestines torn out and draped across his legs and feet—Shadow apparently wasn't interested in originality in its executions. Six men, and Pel recognized them all. Second from the left was Lieutenant Dibbs; Pel couldn't put definite names to the others, but all wore the remains of the purple uniform of the Galactic Empire, and all their faces, twisted and discolored as they were, were familiar. Of the six, useless blasters still hung on the belts of three. One even wore his helmet.

As Pel watched, they swayed gently in the wind; one swollen hand brushed lightly against the damp gray stone of the castle wall.

If Dibbs had thought this was a story, he'd probably thought he was the hero, and now he was nothing but a warning to anyone who came after him.

Pel realized that he had stopped walking, that the entire party, even Ted, had stopped, that all nine of them were looking up at the dangling corpses.

"Now what?" he asked. He swallowed; his throat was suddenly dry.

"Now we go on," Raven said angrily. "We've yet no choice."

"That's the lieutenant," Sawyer said.

"That changes nothing," Raven answered.

"Where are the others, though?" Singer asked, craning his neck to see the faces. "Where's Dawber? Or Moore? Or Smallwood, or Twidman?"

"Wilkins isn't there, either," Prossie pointed out.

"They're probably hanging around the other side," Sawyer said.

"Why would they be on the other side?" Amy asked bitterly. "We were coming in this way, and Shadow knew it—it hung them up there to tease us."

"Maybe there wasn't enough left of the others to hang up there," Susan said quietly.

"Oh, thanks, lady," Sawyer growled. "You really know how to cheer a fellow up!"

"Or maybe Shadow's just playing with us, trying to make us wonder about the others," Amy said.

"Or maybe they really got away," Pel suggested. "Maybe Shadow's not as omnipotent as it would like." He didn't say anything about it out loud, but he found himself wondering if perhaps Wilkins or one of the others might be the actual hero of the tale. Maybe Spaceman First Class Ronnie Wilkins would appear at the last moment, guns blazing, to save Pel and the others from Shadow's clutches—if he had guns that could blaze here. Blasters couldn't.

Sword flashing, then.

Pel tried to imagine Wilkins with a sword; the image wouldn't come. Instead, he saw him with a switchblade. It seemed more his style.

Ted had stared up at the corpses with everyone else, but had said nothing; now he shrugged and strolled forward, toward the gate, boots crunching on the gravelly road. The sound drew everyone's attention.

Pel didn't mind staring at Ted; he was happy to be distracted from the corpses.

For a moment, no one spoke, as Ted stepped through the open arch onto the stone floor beyond. The crunch of gravel turned to scuffing as he stepped into shadow.

"Our mad friend has the right of it," Raven muttered. "We'll learn nothing more out here; 'tis within that our fate awaits."

"Maybe yours," Sawyer said, stepping back, "but I've had it. I'm not going in there. I'm not the one it wants, any more than Wilkins was."

"How do you know?" Amy asked.

"Because I'm just another soldier," Sawyer said. "I'm nobody special." He pointed to Valadrakul and said, "He's a wizard," then indicated Raven and continued, "and he's some kind of prince or something. Thorpe's a telepath; you're pregnant—you're all special somehow. Your crazy friend has visions, maybe that's important. Mr. Brown—well, I don't know, because I don't know anything about him or the world he came from. That other woman hardly ever says anything; I'm not even sure of her name; she could be *anything*. But Singer and me, we're just a couple of packhumpers and shipjumpers. It let Wilkins get away—why shouldn't it let me go, too?"

"It didn't let Dibbs go," Pel pointed out. "Or Marks."

"It killed Marks so the rest of you wouldn't turn back," Sawyer said. "And maybe the lieutenant put up a fight or something. Look up there, though—there are six of them, out of what, eleven men we left back at the ship? *Where are the others?* Shadow let them go, I tell you, because they weren't important!"

"You're guessing," Pel said.

"We're *all* guessing," Sawyer retorted, "all of us, all the time! We don't any of us have the first idea what the hell is going on here. We don't know what Shadow *is*, or what it wants, or anything, all we can do is guess—and I'm guessing that it doesn't want me, and I'm staying out here."

Pel glanced at the others.

"Let him stay, if he would," Raven said.

"What difference does it make?" Singer asked. "If Shadow wants him inside, it can get him inside." He pointed at the giant slug-things.

Pel looked, back at the monster-speckled highway, then up at the dangling soldiers, then into the gloom beyond the gate. The sun was down, the light dying, but the darkness within the fortress was still far deeper than that without; there were no lights anywhere to be seen.

This was not how Pel had pictured it. Oh, the fortress was suitable enough, the marsh reasonably appropriate if a bit on the drab side, and the dead bodies were a fittingly macabre touch, but the gathering darkness, unbroken by torchlight, didn't seem quite right—it wasn't the shadowy, sinister darkness of dungeons or of midnight, but the soft dimness of twilight, the sort that doesn't scare anyone but just gradually convinces everyone to go home for dinner.

Pel wished he *could* just go home for dinner, and find Nancy and Rachel waiting there for him. He was *trying* to get home—but of course, Nancy and Rachel wouldn't be there.

And the gentle darkness didn't seem right for an assault on the villain's headquarters. The fact that poor mad Ted had gone on ahead, was already almost out of sight in the gloom, didn't seem right. That they were virtually unarmed, no swords, no armor, no secret magic, didn't seem right. That they were walking openly into the front gate, aware that Shadow expected them, didn't seem right—shouldn't they be sneaking in by some secret passage, scaling a back wall, crawling in through the sewers? They had no plan, no organization . . .

And no choice. One of the slug-things was crawling up onto the highway less than a yard behind Sawyer's feet.

"Let's go in, then," Pel said. "And maybe Tom Sawyer'll change his mind when those Shadow things start crowding him." He pointed.

Sawyer whirled and saw the creature behind him. It opened its maw and showed him its teeth, but Sawyer did not retreat.

"I'm not going," he said, still facing the slug. "The rest of you, go on if you're going, and when you're in there, maybe this thing will leave me alone."

"What will you eat?" Susan asked abruptly, startling everyone. "We've had nothing since breakfast, and it's a long way back to the last village."

"Don't remind me!" Amy said.

Pel sympathized; he was hungry, too. He thought he must have lost twenty pounds since he first stepped through his basement wall; he *never* seemed to get enough food, or any *good* food, anywhere in Faerie, nor even in the Galactic Empire before it.

"I'll manage," Sawyer said, still not looking at the others. "It's not *that* far."

The thought occurred to Pel that Sawyer *meant* to die, out here—that he preferred being eaten by those slug-things to facing Shadow itself.

Or maybe not. Pel didn't know and decided he didn't want to ask.

"What the hell," he said, turning back to the gate, "maybe at least Shadow will give us a last meal."

He marched forward, into the darkness of the gate.

CHAPTER 19

A my had expected something to happen when they were all inside the fortress—the gates to slam shut, or the Shadow things to surge up and attack poor Sawyer, or lights to spring up, or *something*—but nothing did. She shuffled on into the blackness, hands out before her to fend off stray furniture, feet sliding along the stone flooring.

"Ted?" she called. "Are you there?"

"Shut up!" Ted answered furiously. "I think I'm waking up! I don't see anything anymore!"

"That's because it's *dark* in here, you idiot!" Pel snapped.

Amy giggled nervously and glanced back at the huge gateway. It was still wide open; she could only vaguely make out the gates themselves, grayish shapes to either side. Sawyer was clearly outlined against the dimming sky; he was standing there, facing away from her, in a sort of crouch, as if expecting an attack from the stovepipe things.

She couldn't see anything attacking, though.

"Now what?" she said.

"Damned if I know," Pel said.

" 'Tis an excellent question," Raven's voice answered; Amy could see nothing of him in the darkness. She could see Sawyer, and Pel was a shadowy figure to her left, but the others were invisible now.

She could hear footsteps, but couldn't identify them all— were they all here? Was anyone *else* here, lurking in the darkness?

She wondered what sort of room they were in; it seemed to be large, judging by the sounds, and since no one had reported bumping into any walls or other impediments. The air was cooler than outside and seemed a little drier, a little less of a dead weight pressing down on her.

Then she heard rustling—not clothing, but a different, drier sound. Unbidden and unwanted, the thought of rats immediately leapt to mind.

They had seen a few rats along the long walk, but never very close, and never when they were inside, in the dark, in a strange and forbidding place.

"What's that?" she asked, dropping her voice to a whisper.

Then a light sprang up suddenly, off to her right; Amy started.

"It's me," Susan said, holding up a lit match and a twist of paper. She lit the paper, shook out the match, and held up her impromptu torch. "I thought we could use some light."

"You had *matches*?" Amy said, astonished. "And you never *told* anyone?"

"I only had about three left," Susan replied. "They were in my purse. Valadrakul seemed to do just fine lighting fires, so I figured I'd save them until we really needed them."

Two or three voices spoke up at once; one of them was Amy's, asking, "And you think we need them now?"

"My thanks, mistress," Valadrakul said. "I'd no stomach to try my magic here in Shadow's own keep."

Amy didn't bother arguing with Susan about it, though it still didn't seem *fair*, somehow, that she had had matches and not told anyone. Instead Amy peered around in the darkness, trying to see where they were. The paper was burning quickly, and not casting much useful light; Amy tried to take in as much as she could before it burned away.

They were in a huge chamber of bare stone, fifty or sixty feet wide and at least twice as long, the ceiling invisible in the darkness above—and they weren't alone. A ledge or balcony ran along either side of the immense room, about ten feet up, and on those two ledges were crouched dozens of vague black shapes, shapes with heads and legs and claws, with eyes and gleaming teeth.

Monsters.

"Are they statues?" Singer asked. The tone of his voice made it clear that he didn't think so.

"They're moving," Pel answered.

"I'm not sure that proves anything here," Prossie said.

"They aren't attacking," Singer said, a bit more hopefully.

Then the flame reached Susan's fingers, and she dropped her

paper torch to the floor; it flared as it fell, then went out on impact.

"'Tis my guess," Valadrakul said in the renewed darkness, "that Shadow retains these creatures ready here, to be sent hither and yon as the whim strikes it. Were we to be slaughtered, surely 'twould have begun."

Amy turned, looking for anything that might reassure her, but the only things she could see were the last few sparks dying by Susan's feet, and the dim gray arch of the entrance. The light outside had died away completely, full night had fallen—and Sawyer seemed to have vanished; she couldn't see anything of him.

"Now what?" Pel asked.

"We wait," Raven said.

"What, until *morning*?" Amy demanded. "No way. I couldn't *stand* it. Susan, light another ma . . . hey!" A thought struck her. "Matches *work* here? Aren't they technology?"

"Of a sort," Pel agreed. "Susan's gun works, too, remember? But my watch didn't. Some things do, some things don't."

"Blasters don't," Singer said bitterly. "If they did, we wouldn't have any problems."

"Antigravity doesn't, either," Prossie added. "Nor telepathy." When Singer started to object, she corrected herself. "At least, not properly; I can only communicate with telepaths back in the Empire."

Amy stared at the doorway, wondering what had become of Sawyer. The others all seemed to be here; she had heard Raven and Valadrakul and Pel and Susan and Singer and Prossie . . .

But Ted hadn't said anything since he told her to shut up, and she hadn't seem him when Susan burned her bit of paper.

"Ted?" she called.

No one answered.

"Ted?!" she screamed.

Again, no one answered; the others all fell silent, listening.

Amy could hear rustlings and scratchings from the creatures on the ledges, could hear the breathing of some of her companions, could hear a faint, distant splashing from somewhere out in the marsh—and somewhere, far off toward the interior of the fortress, she heard footsteps, boot leather on stone.

"He's gone on ahead," she said. "Into the darkness."

"Into Shadow," Raven replied.

* * *

Pel wasn't sure why Amy was so certain that Ted had gone on ahead, but it seemed reasonable enough. Ted believed this wasn't real—or at least, he *said* he believed it wasn't real, and acted as if he believed that—which meant that nothing could hurt him. He therefore wasn't afraid of anything, and he wanted to get it all over with. Why *wouldn't* he have gone on ahead?

Pel had been too concerned with his own worries—Nancy and Rachel and his own attempts to get home—to worry much about Ted, but he had decided back at Base One that Ted's disbelief was a defense mechanism, a way to keep from breaking down completely. Convincing himself that it wasn't real was a way to avoid going into a state of perpetual panic; Ted had always wanted to be in control of his surroundings and didn't deal well with surroundings that didn't cooperate.

Whether the disbelief was genuine, or just a front Ted put up, Pel wasn't sure, and it didn't really matter, because Ted was tough and stubborn enough to act as if he disbelieved no matter what. Pel had proved that to his own satisfaction weeks ago.

Maybe, Pel thought, Ted had decided that whether it was real or not, it was all a story, and he was the hero. Pel could understand that; he'd thought the same way sometimes. If Ted thought of himself as the hero, then he was destined to win out, no matter what.

To Pel, though, Ted looked more like one of those pitiful innocents in a Hollywood movie who gets killed to show the audience just how rotten and nasty the villain is, to show that this is not a game, that there will be blood and death and violence.

"Ted!" he shouted. "Wait!"

"Shut up!" Singer snapped. "Listen, you two, all of you, stop yelling!"

"But . . ." Amy began.

"We're standing in this thing's headquarters, unarmed, in the dark, defenseless, with monsters lined up on either side of us, and you people are *yelling*," Singer said angrily. "Do you *want* to get killed?"

"Think you that Shadow cares?" Raven asked. "What are shouts to it?"

"Noisy, that's what," Singer retorted. "Why go out of our way to anger our host? Didn't we come here peacefully, to ask it to send us home?"

Pel blinked in surprise—not that blinking made any difference, in the darkness.

They had, hadn't they?

After what had happened to Bill Marks, after seeing Dibbs and the others hanging over the gate, after all the corpses and monsters, Pel had forgotten that it was possible to think of Shadow as anything but the enemy.

"What about Ted?" he asked quietly.

"Let him go," Singer said. "There's nothing we can do anyway, is there?"

"True," Pel reluctantly admitted.

"So what do we do now?" Amy asked.

"We wait," Raven repeated.

"Or maybe we ask Shadow politely for some light," Singer suggested. "Or to send us home."

"You think it can hear us?" Pel asked, peering around into the darkness.

Then, abruptly, before Singer could answer, light blazed; blinded, Pel threw an arm over his eyes. Even through his closed lids, the light that poured around the shielding arm was intensely bright.

Then, gradually, it dimmed, and after a moment Pel risked opening his eyes, arm still raised.

The floor was made of blue-gray flagstones, joined so well that the seams were almost invisible. His boots, Imperial military issue, were muddy and badly scuffed; the cuffs of his purple uniform pants were frayed and stained. The light was still bright, but bearable.

Cautiously, he raised his eyes and lowered his arm.

Something was glowing overhead—not the ceiling, which was now visible perhaps fifty feet up, but something several feet below the ceiling, something long and straight that ran from the wall above the gate down the length of the room—if it was a room. Pel looked around.

He and most of the others were standing near one end of a chamber that was perhaps fifty feet wide at floor level, but at least sixty by the time it reached the blue-painted ceiling, thanks to the setbacks on either side where the Shadow things stood. However, it was not at all clear whether it was a room or a corridor, because the length was easily a hundred yards, and the far end was not a wall, but a gigantic staircase leading upward.

The walls were pale gray stone, unadorned—granite, Pel

guessed. The floor was unbroken by rugs, carpets, rushes, or any sort of inlay or decoration. The ceiling was hard to make out beyond the glowing rod, or beam, or whatever it was, but it appeared to be plaster, painted the color of the sky in a baroque fresco, that warm, rich blue that made such a fine background for cherubs and chiffon-draped nudes.

Pel couldn't see any cavorting nymphs here, though—just blank blue. The whole place had a rather barren, unfinished look to it. The intense color of the ceiling didn't seem to go very well with the natural gray of the walls.

The light source was an utter mystery; Pel had never seen anything remotely like it. It was as if there were an invisible tube full of glowing gas running the length of the chamber, then vanishing into that immense stairway.

Ted Deranian was more than halfway to the stairs, Pel saw; everyone else was clustered near the door.

Everyone else human, anyway—there were all those creatures on the ledges, too. Some looked almost normal—panthers and apes—while others were tentacular horrors, or just *things* that Pel couldn't describe. They ranged from the size of a cat—assuming there weren't others he couldn't see that were even smaller—up to a gigantic creature near the gate that could only be called a dragon, so large that it appeared to have some difficulty squeezing onto the ledge.

All of them, even in the brilliant white light, were black. Some were flat grayish black, some were glossy black, but all were black, except for eyes, claws, and teeth. Even the dragon was shiny black, from its pointed snout to its snakelike tail, its taloned feet to its batlike wingtips, scales glistening darkly.

And as Pel watched, the dragon moved.

All of the Shadow creatures looked alive, all of them seemed to be breathing, their eyes open and alert, but the others were motionless—or at least staying where they were; a few twitched or shuddered, a few heads turned, claws shifted slightly.

The dragon, though, was stretching its foreclaws and wings, and black horny claws rasped loudly against stone.

Everyone turned at the sound; Pel saw that Raven was rubbing his eyes and waving his head, as if still blind from the flash, while Singer and Amy were blinking. The others seemed to be okay as they turned to look up at the dragon.

It stretched its neck out over the edge of its ledge and peered down at the humans below; Pel could look directly into its greenish-gold eyes, could see the odd frill, or tendrils, or whatever it was that dangled from the monster's chin, and the hard ridges above the eyes.

Then it slithered down from the ledge.

Singer made a dash for the doorway, but the dragon was faster; the soldier stopped dead only a foot or so from its flank as it interposed itself between the humans and their only exit.

"Damn," Singer said, as he backed away. It was the first word any of them had spoken since the flash.

"Now what?" Prossie asked.

The dragon hissed, but made no threatening moves; it simply sat there, between the humans and the door.

"I think," Pel said slowly, "that this is just another version of those slug-things—making sure we can't turn back."

"But Sawyer's outside," Singer objected.

"I suppose he was right," Pel said. "Shadow didn't care about him—but it wants the rest of us."

"So what do we do?" Amy asked.

Pel shrugged. "We go on," he said. "At least now we can see where we're going."

Amy's feet hurt—but then, they had hurt for days now. A year ago, she would have said she could never walk two hundred miles, not if she had all the time in the world and her life depended on it, and especially not when she felt so heavy and tired all the time, whether it was from the gravity here or because she was pregnant. She would have said she could never walk so far.

But now she had done it, and as a direct result, her feet ached. It seemed unfair that even after reaching this stupid fortress, she still had to walk farther. Why wasn't Shadow right there at the front door, waiting for them?

It was probably trying to impress or intimidate them, making them walk down this ridiculous huge room lined with monsters; she didn't see what other possible use such a place could have.

Amy had no intention of being impressed or intimidated, though; she thought the room was ugly, was nothing in comparison to, say, the main hall at Union Station in Washington, even if it was a lot longer. And they'd seen plenty of monsters already—the stovepipe things, and the giant bat, and the others they had fought at the spaceship, and the ones that had attacked them back at Stormcrack the *first* time they saw Faerie. She wasn't particularly surprised by more of them.

At least this time they weren't trying to kill her.

That dragon, though, was crowding them.

It didn't actually push anyone, but as they moved forward, it moved along with them, its talons scratching on the stone floor like fingernails on a blackboard, and it wouldn't retreat—if they tried to turn back it stopped and stood there watching them, lashing its tail like an angry cat's, or like a snake squirming, blocking them. If someone tried to go around it it would lunge, and scamper, and cut off whoever it was that had tried to escape.

Singer and Raven had tried to split up and go around both ends, which was when the party had learned that the dragon's tail was prehensile, capable of tripping a man and then picking him up, and also when they had discovered that the dragon's full, extended length was at least fifty feet—it could stretch itself across the entire width of the hall.

It was also amazingly fast.

Amy hadn't tried to turn back; for one thing, that would mean abandoning Ted, who had vanished up the stairs. She trudged on.

At the foot of the steps, however, she stopped and stared upward, dismayed.

The climb had to be a hundred feet—a ten-story building and then some. That bar of light ran right through the center, though she couldn't see any sort of projector. Someone was sitting at the top, with the ragged remains of a bandage on his head—Ted, waiting for them.

It looked as if he *had* to wait; the stairs seemed to end at a wall.

It didn't make any sense; this was a completely stupid way to arrange a building, she thought. Why weren't there any side passages? Why did everyone have to go up these stairs? How did anyone get into the rest of the fortress?

It was absurd—but it was here, and very solid and real, and she didn't seem to have much of a choice. She sighed, and started climbing.

The dragon was asleep at the foot of the stairs, curled up like a gigantic cat; as Pel mounted the last few steps he looked down past the light beam at it, bitterly certain that if any of them tried to go back down the creature would awaken instantly.

He wondered what had happened to Sawyer; had the slug-things gotten him, or had he found a way past, or was he still standing out there, waiting, slowly starving to death?

Of course, Pel felt as if he weren't all that far from starvation himself. Singer's canteen and Raven's water bag, stolen three days before from a farmhouse on the road, kept thirst under control, but none of them had eaten a bite since their rather meager breakfast of assorted berries that morning.

Less than a day without food, that was nothing, he tried to tell himself, but his stomach disagreed.

You'd think, he told himself, that he'd be used to it by now. He hadn't eaten properly for weeks. Back home he'd always taken food for granted—oh, let's eat Chinese tonight, let's grab a burger, what about a pizza?

He thought that right now he would be ready to strangle a man with his bare hands if it would get him a decent meal.

Maybe Shadow would feed them eventually—or maybe it would starve them all to death here atop the stairs.

Pel had no intention of starving—if that began to look like a real possibility, he'd go back down and let the dragon make a meal of him, or maybe jump into the light beam—Valadrakul had warned them all, in his archaic phrasing and barbaric accent, that it would fry anyone who touched it, cook them instantly, that it was basically the same sort of magical zap that he had used against the monsters back at the spaceship, but, in the wizard's phrase, writ large.

No one had cared to test the wizard's claim; they had all stayed well clear as they passed it.

Being *above* the light made everything on this upper part of the climb look strange—faces were lit from below, so the nostrils stood out, as if they were all in a low-budget horror film. The stairs were shadowed, making it harder to climb if one looked down. And the space at the top of the stairs was almost dark.

Pel mounted the final step and stopped.

It wasn't *completely* dark here, by any means; they could all see the wall, with its ornate door, just a few feet away, on the other side of the landing at the top.

The door wasn't anything like the gate below, which was easily at least fifteen feet high and ten feet wide, but this door was still big—maybe ten feet high and five feet wide, Pel guessed. It was red decorated with gold, rather like decor in a Chinese restaurant—Pel wished he could stop associating things with food.

Ted was sitting cross-legged on the bare stone floor in front of the door, waiting; the others were standing along the top of the stair, or just now coming up. Poor Amy was the last; she was panting. This was nothing a woman in her condition should be doing, Pel thought angrily.

He was panting, too, he realized.

Tired, hungry, thirsty, virtually unarmed—they were in *great* shape to confront the all-powerful Shadow.

If, of course, they were going to. If they weren't going to just sit here and starve. If they weren't going to wander on through some interminable maze. If they weren't all going to be killed instantly—after all, if Shadow could create that light beam . . .

How had he ever got into this? Pel reached down to give Amy a hand up the last three steps, and tried to figure that out.

He hadn't gone anywhere or done anything stupid. He'd just been down in his own basement, minding his own business, when this all began happening around him.

And now his wife was dead; his daughter was dead; Elani and Grummetty and Alella were dead; all those Imperials had died for nothing.

When this was over, they'd probably *all* be dead.

Why was he still going on? What good did it do? Why had he bothered to come this far?

Heroes did this sort of thing in the books he read and in the movies he watched. They fought on against impossible odds as their friends died around them, until at last they defeated evil and saved the world—but he was no hero. He wasn't going to save any worlds. He was just going to die.

Well, everybody dies eventually. He might as well get it over with.

He turned to face the door just as it opened.

CHAPTER 20

*A*my closed her eyes to catch her breath as she mounted the final step and let go of Pel's hand. She wondered whether that light bar might be radioactive, whether it would do anything to her unborn baby—though even if it did, she really hoped that wouldn't matter, that she'd be able to abort the thing soon.

Although right now it seemed more likely that she would die and take the baby with her.

Suddenly it seemed as if everyone was shouting, and reluctantly, wearily, she opened her eyes.

The doors were opening, and light was spilling out, bright moving multicolored lights that flashed and sparkled every which way—and which seemed to create shadows between them, as if the differing lights canceled each other out in places, creating darkness. The glare blazed in every color she had ever heard of and several she hadn't, painfully bright; she closed her eyes again and raised a guarding hand. If the light bar wasn't dangerous to be near, something here probably was—in all that chaos there had to be some kind of nasty radiation. If it wasn't radioactivity maybe it was ultraviolet or lasers or something, and she'd get skin cancer or cataracts or her hair would fall out.

And there were sounds—rushings and rustlings, like storm winds, or like some sort of machinery warming up. The dead air of the landing stirred to life. She smelled the electric bristle of ozone, and other scents, metallic and harsh, that she couldn't place.

"I'm not going in there," she said, more to herself than anyone else.

"Ted is," Pel told her.

She opened her eyes slightly and squinted, trying to see through the glare, and sure enough, with one arm shading his eyes, Ted was staggering through the big door right into the lights.

"Oh, damn," she said. She hesitated. "All right," she said, after a second or two, "I guess I *am* going in there." She couldn't have explained her decision very coherently to anyone else, but she knew it had something to do with Bill Marks, torn apart on the road; with Tom Sawyer back there with the stove-pipe monsters; with Elani, who had died protecting her, and with dead Beth on the gallows because Amy had said she deserved it. Amy had reached the point where she thought she was less afraid of her own death than of feeling responsible for any more of the stupid, pointless deaths of others.

She wondered if Pel felt any of the same thing; he was right there beside her as she walked the few steps toward the door. Was he, too, thinking of Marks and Sawyer and Elani? Or was he remembering his poor wife and their little girl, horribly murdered by people who *might* have been sent by Shadow? Was he thinking about revenge, or was he just getting ready to die, to be with his family? Amy had no way of knowing; it was hardly something she could ask him, as even after the weeks of traveling and waiting and traveling together he wasn't much more than a friendly stranger.

And what about Raven, or Valadrakul, or Al Singer? What about Prossie and Susan? Ted still thought it was a dream, he wasn't worried, but what about the others? Was it courage that drove them forward? All of them were moving, all of them were approaching the door, and Amy wondered *why*. Weren't any of them scared?

She had to stop in the doorway; the flickering glare was too intense to continue. The moving air brushed across her face like fingers, like wings, like blowing leaves, sometimes warm, sometimes cool, sometimes gentle, sometimes sharp as wire. Shadow and color shifted too fast for her to see anything clearly.

Ted had gone through the door, and Pel, and Raven, though Amy didn't know how they could stand to do it. Prossie and Susan and Singer were just behind her, still outside; Valadrakul was at her side.

"What *is* all that, anyway?" Amy asked.

"Magic," Valadrakul said. "The raw energies of Shadow made manifest."

"If it's Shadow, shouldn't it all be *dark*?" Amy asked. She inched forward, took her first step into the chamber beyond the door; her arm was across her face, and colors seemed to ripple and flare on all sides. Pink and orange and electric blue swept across her arm, coloring everything she saw. The air felt oddly stuffy now, as it pressed against her, and she couldn't decide if it was warm or cold.

"It could be dark, if Shadow so chose," Valadrakul told her. His voice sounded unsteady.

Startled, Amy glanced at the wizard.

He was trembling.

The air of the room seemed somehow *compressed*, Prossie thought as she lingered in the doorway.

She didn't like the look of the place at all; the shifting, glaring colors made her think of alarms and beacons and a dozen other sorts of warning, all going off at once, or of some sort of huge machinery going berserk. If the warp generator back at Base One had run wild, she thought it might have looked something like this.

No warp generator had ever run wild, though. Prossie knew what various other kinds of machinery would do when they failed—she had scanned through the memories of engineers any number of times, either directly or secondhand, and had seen what happened when antigravity drives imploded, when blasters melted down, when everything went wrong. It was a standard part of the follow-up to any disaster in the Galactic Empire to let the telepaths loose on everyone involved so as to find out what went wrong and who was responsible.

And none of those disasters had ever looked anything like this.

A warp generator malfunction probably wouldn't either, she told herself. No warp generator had ever run amok, but Prossie had read the memories of scientists who thought they knew what it would do, and none of them had seen it being this varied and colorful.

Of course, scientists tended to think of such things in terms of numbers and schematics, not light and color.

Whatever was happening here, she didn't like it, and didn't understand it, and she didn't want to face it alone.

"Carrie!" she thought, trying desperately to project, knowing as she tried that in this unnatural continuum, in Faerie, she couldn't.

She could only hope that Carrie was listening.

Light shows, Pel thought. It was all a light show. Like the trip sequence in *2001: A Space Odyssey*, or when the ark is opened in *Raiders of the Lost Ark*, or any number of scenes in various other special-effects spectaculars.

Except that this one was different because it was all around, not confined to a screen; he wasn't sitting in a dark theater, he was walking *through* the lights and colors, he thought he could actually *feel* them, and whether he could or not, he could certainly feel the air, and smell and taste it, and it had a weird, static-electric, closed-in feeling even though it was moving.

And the lights weren't flashing in some ill-defined sound-stage void; as his eyes adjusted he could catch glimpses of a solid room behind the glare, a colonnaded chamber with gilded decoration on white walls—he couldn't see whether the walls were stone or plaster or what, the light was too bright.

No movie was ever so bright, so intense.

The lights moved and shifted, but there were patterns to them, and they seemed to focus on the far end of the room. He couldn't look directly at whatever occupied that space.

Was that Shadow? If so, it seemed horribly misnamed.

It *ought* to be Shadow, though; they had gone through the whole stupid quest, they had fought monsters and thirst and hunger, trudged hundreds of miles, seen half their companions dead, and finally reached and entered the fortress of the enemy. In all the stories, that meant it was time to confront the Evil Power.

Was this it, then?

All that light and color—*was* Shadow misnamed? Was this some other being or force entirely, one that would send them home? One that could bring Nancy and Rachel back to life? One that would make this whole thing just the dream Ted still said it was?

For all Pel knew, this wasn't Shadow, but God. The blinding light seemed more appropriate to God's glory than to a being called Shadow.

Whatever it might be, this was definitely the payoff, the climax of the whole horrible adventure.

Behind him, he heard Amy and Valadrakul talking, but he didn't pay much attention. His ears were starting to ring, though he didn't know why; the whooshings and rumblings and flappings that had accompanied the colors died away suddenly, so that besides the two voices, neither of them speaking loudly, the only sounds were the tapping of boots on marble, the shuffle of feet and rustle of clothing, and labored breathing from someone nearby—maybe Ted.

"Are you all right?" Amy asked, her voice concerned; startled out of his thoughts about Shadow, Pel turned to see who she was asking.

Valadrakul was trembling violently; Amy could see his beard quivering, and his now-ragged embroidered vest was almost slapping the frayed knees of his purple Imperial pants.

"What *is* it?" she demanded, on the verge of panic. She had never seen Valadrakul visibly frightened or upset before.

"'Tis Shadow," the wizard said, almost gasping. "'Tis the matrix. Look you, how 'tis composed—ah, so splendid! Look you, how majestical! What glory is here before us!"

"It's a lot of bright lights," Amy said uneasily. Perhaps the wizard wasn't scared after all, she realized; perhaps it was something else.

"Nay, you look, but you do not *see*! You've not the eyes, you who know nothing of the arcane arts!"

"Tell us, then, what *you* see," Raven said, stepping up close behind Valadrakul. His left arm shielded his eyes; his black clothing seemed to absorb the light, to be the only solid and unchanging thing in the shifting images.

"The matrix," Valadrakul said. "The heart of Shadow—and what name is that, for this is no feeble shadow, but power incarnate! See, each light a strand of the web, woven gloriously together—why, that beam we passed on the stair, I see now how it fits!" Suddenly, the wizard was striding forward into the room, into the light and color; Amy reached out, tried to catch him as he passed, and missed.

"Look you all," he cried as he marched, "whosoever sits at the center, upon that throne, there is the center of it all! I could no more construct a matrix such as this than a sparrow could swim, but oh, I see how it works, I see what every finest fiber must be! You, who sit there, let me try, I beg you—for but a moment, but the merest instant, give me your place!"

"Who sits *where*?" Amy asked, squinting, trying to see through the glare. She could see no one sitting anywhere; Ted was only a vague, dark blur, and Valadrakul, too, was fading into the brilliance.

"Fool," a voice said, a voice none of them had heard before, rich and loud, but not particularly deep. "The matrix does *my* will, not thine, thou pitiful semblance of a wizard. It centers not upon this seat, but upon *me!*"

The words came from somewhere farther in the room, deeper in the blaze of light, beyond Ted and Valadrakul, but Amy still couldn't see anything of the speaker.

"Oh, but let me share it," Valadrakul pleaded. "I could learn so *much* . . ."

"*Too* much, perchance," the voice said. "Begone, wizardling; another step, and perish."

"Oh . . ." Valadrakul began. He stepped forward, hands outstretched, reaching for the glory he saw before him.

And then he burned; the initial golden flash was scarcely noticeable amid the lights, but Amy had been watching Valadrakul, staring at him, and the flames were plain enough.

After the flames, the blast struck the wizard and flung him backward, directly toward Amy; she let out a noise, a choking, gasping noise that might have been a scream had she been able to breathe more deeply before it came out.

An instant later a flash of pure white, pale and almost lost in the polychrome glory of Shadow's presence, burst from the flying remains of Valadrakul—Amy remembered the flash when Elani had died, when her magicks had shattered, and knew that Valadrakul, too, was dead.

The body skidded to a halt by her feet, and Amy looked down through flickering colors at the blackened remains of the mage Valadrakul of Warricken.

His vest was reduced to a few scorched threads; the Imperial uniform had held up somewhat better and was still mostly intact, but every bit of it was charred black, not a trace of purple remaining. A few beard hairs were still sizzling, and the stench of burning hair made Amy gag even before the blackened ruin of the wizard's face registered on her consciousness.

Something white showed through at one spot, and when Amy realized she couldn't tell if it was exposed bone or exposed eyeball she turned away and decided against bothering to keep down whatever wanted to come up.

Very little did come up, though; a thin spatter of yellowish fluid, nothing more.

* * *

They were all dead, Pel decided as he looked at Valadrakul's smoking remains. The wizard had been blasted just as effectively, and a good deal more quickly, than the Nazis in *Raiders*.

Which meant that while this was plainly Shadow, and not a merciful God, this Shadow, to all intents and purposes, was as powerful here as God.

They were all dead. There was nothing more to lose. He turned back to face Shadow, if that was what sat before them in that polychrome glare, and asked, "What did you do that for?"

For a moment, everything was almost silent, save for odd unidentified rustlings, like those that they had heard when the doors first opened, and a faint popping and hissing that Pel realized with a shock was the sound of Valadrakul's corpse cooling. The quiet was so total that it seemed as if the surviving humans were holding their breath, and Pel supposed that some of them were.

The shifting labyrinth of light and color seemed to slow and dim slightly.

"Durst thou address me thus, then?" Shadow's voice asked; Pel thought he heard a note of amusement.

"Why not?" Pel replied. "You've got us; we're all dead anyway."

"Think'st so?" The amusement was definite now, and the voice was higher than Pel had realized.

Pel didn't bother to answer, and Shadow continued, "I'truth, some among you might yet live to see daylight more."

"Well, that's up to you, isn't it?" Pel said. "Any whim that strikes you, there isn't anything *we* can do about it, is there?"

"Nay," Raven shouted suddenly, lurching forward, his still-bandaged fingers raised in a defiant gesture. It occurred to Pel, apropos of nothing, that they ought to be healed by now. " 'Tis the duty of all free men, of all who love the Goddess, to resist this thing!" Raven called. "Friend Pel, yield not your soul to it!"

For an instant, Pel thought that they had finally arrived at the climax of the story, that Raven, the storybook hero, had found some secret weakness, some way to resist Shadow's power. He would draw a magic sword and cut through Shadow's spells, or fling some prepared spell of his own.

Then he realized that that wasn't it at all; this was no simple story. Raven had no secret weapon; he had merely cracked under the strain and done something stupid, not something heroic. He had done something stupid, and he would die for it. If there was any hero here, it wasn't Raven after all.

And Pel didn't really think there was any hero. Not after Valadrakul's death. This was real life, and in real life last-minute rescues didn't always come, sometimes innocents died horribly, and sometimes the good guys were slaughtered. Real life didn't need to be fair, or just, or satisfying; where was the justice in a plane wreck or an earthquake?

Innocents and good guys died meaningless deaths all the time.

He didn't really know anything about Raven's past, didn't know if Raven was an innocent or a good guy, in any sense of the terms, but right now it looked as if Raven was about to die a horrible and meaningless death.

He was. Pel turned as Raven's velvets flared up, in a blaze of fire and spark; black smoke billowed upward around the man's burning black hair into the golden shafts above, spilling into the light like ink into clear sparkling water. The swarthy skin reddened, then blackened, then disappeared.

There was no shock wave like the one that had flung Valadrakul's corpse at Amy's feet, and although the self-proclaimed rightful lord of Stormcrack Keep had time to give a brief, anguished cry before the flames consumed him, there was no recognizable corpse, but merely a flurry of black ash.

"I'd worry not of souls, little man," Shadow told the smoking, drifting remains and the shocked survivors. "I deal not in souls; the flesh of this world is enough to concern me."

Pel stared for a moment; he heard Singer make a strangled noise somewhere nearby. It occurred to him that Raven had been the last of their native companions; everyone who still stood before Shadow came from either Earth or the Galactic Empire.

He doubted that would make any difference if they ran afoul of one of Shadow's whims.

One by one, Al Singer thought; it's picking us off one by one and there isn't anything we can do about it.

This was not what he'd joined the military for. This wasn't anything he'd ever imagined.

And he couldn't even fight back. Oh, he still had his blaster, but it wouldn't work here except for whacking someone over the head, or maybe cracking nuts.

He glanced at Prossie Thorpe, the expedition's Special—but *she* didn't work here, either, or at least that was what she said. She couldn't call for help, couldn't read the enemy's plans. She could maybe still talk to Base One, but they couldn't send help in time, if at all—and what's more, they *wouldn't* send it.

Colonel Carson, Lieutenant Dibbs—the officers hadn't been much use on this expedition. And Thorpe said that General Hart had written them all off.

What kind of military solidarity was that? The Empire was supposed to stand behind its men, protect its troops just as the troops protected the Empire.

It looked like that was just another lie, like Father Christmas or virgin brides.

He was beginning to wish that he'd never joined up, had never seen little Laura Bailey mooning over the fancy uniforms at the port, and had never decided that the best way to get into her pants was to sign away a couple of years of his life.

It wasn't fair, the six of them up against this . . . this *force*, this *thing*.

And they didn't even know what it was.

"Hey," he called, "if you're concerned with flesh, why don't you show yourself, anyway? Do you need all these colors and lights? Are you afraid to let us see you? Are you that ugly? Is that why you killed the wizard, because he could see through this stuff?"

"Wouldst see me unveiled?" Shadow asked, and Singer thought it sounded surprised.

He remembered some of the stories he'd heard as a kid, whispered around a campfire or read aloud by the hearth, about unspeakable monsters—but he didn't care. He was tired of not knowing what was going on. He wanted to see the thing.

"Well, yeah, why not?" he demanded. "You think we'll go mad at the sight, like in the old stories?"

"I'd hope not," Shadow said. "As you will, then."

Abruptly, the colors faded away, the buzzing in Singer's ears was gone, and the blazing lights faded to a soft golden glow from somewhere overhead. His head hurt; whether he had developed a headache in the glare and simply not noticed, or whether the shift had triggered it, he wasn't sure.

He blinked, his eyes trying to adjust to this sudden change, and then took a good look at what the chamber *really* looked like.

The walls were white marble, ornamented with gilded carvings, behind twin colonnades—but some of the gilt was flaking away. The floor was covered in faded carpets, most of them dark red patterned with darker blue. Before them, in the center of the room, was a low stone dais, and on the dais was a dark wooden throne, the straight back and arms carved with strange flowers and impossible beasts.

Slouched in the throne was a woman.

She was fat, but not obese; aging, but not yet old; unattractive, but not really ugly. Her hair was long and dark brown and somewhat disheveled, spilling over her shoulders in tangled curls; her face was soft, with an unhealthy pallor. She looked to Singer as if she should be sitting behind the counter in some inexpensive shop somewhere, shortchanging customers and chasing children away from the candy.

Someone giggled. Singer heard Pel mutter, "Pay no attention to the man behind the curtain," but he had no idea what the Earthman was talking about.

"*You're* Shadow?" Singer asked.

"Indeed, I am," the woman said, and it was the same voice, though not quite as loud.

This was Shadow.

This frumpy, middle-aged woman was the all-powerful Shadow.

"Oh, come on," Singer said.

"Judge not by appearances, child," the woman chided him. "The matrix yet stands, and I am yet at its heart, though thou seest it not; I've but rendered it invisible, not impotent."

"But you're just an old woman!" Singer blurted.

And in his last instant, as he saw the old woman frown, he knew that she really was Shadow, that he had seen Raven and Valadrakul killed for displeasing her, and that now *he* had displeased her. Just because the lights were gone, that didn't mean her power was.

His last thought was to wish that he had never seen Laura Bailey at all, because then he wouldn't be about to die so stupidly, in this horrible alien place. He didn't have the time to think anything more profound.

He didn't even have time to think that at least it was quick.

* * *

Pel watched Singer die, as Raven and Valadrakul had died; the flames seemed more impressive now that the light show was gone.

When only smoldering ash remained, he turned back to Shadow. "Was that necessary?" he asked.

Shadow shrugged. "Necessary or no, 'twas my wish," she said.

"And that's all that matters, isn't it?"

"Aye." Shadow made no attempt to keep the self-satisfaction out of her voice.

"Can we get this over with, so I can wake up?" Ted asked.

Shadow glanced at Ted, at the filthy remnant of bandage on his head, then asked Pel, "Is he deranged?"

Pel hesitated, trying to think which answer would be least likely to reduce Ted, too, to charred fragments.

They were all dead anyway, and maybe he would wake up back on Earth, and he couldn't second-guess Shadow, anyway; he didn't know enough about her. There wasn't any reason to lie. "I'm afraid so," he said.

"Amusingly so?"

"Sometimes."

"Then he lives; I've need of amusement betimes."

"Is that why you brought us here, then?" Pel demanded. "For your amusement?"

"In part," Shadow answered.

"And the three you killed weren't amusing enough?"

Shadow waved a hand dismissively. "What amusement in a hedge wizard who thinks he might wield my power? Many of them have I seen, i' these many years, and all in the end I've slain. And a displaced lordling, in his towering rage? Scores have I seen and slain. The soldier, in truth, was new, but scarce new enough; in these past few days I've seen his like a dozen times over. You saw his companions at the gate, an you troubled to raise your eyes."

"We saw," Pel agreed. "So you'll kill us all, one by one, when we bore you or annoy you?"

"Perhaps," Shadow said, "but perhaps not. I did guide you here, as thou sayest, and 'twas purposeful. Serve me well, and thou shalt live, each of you."

Pel puzzled for a moment over the pronouns in that sentence until he realized that Shadow was using "thou" as singular and "you" as plural; he supposed it made sense. Raven and

Valadrakul hadn't used "thou" at all, that he could recall; it was confusing.

Then he forced himself to stop thinking about such trivia. She had just said they might yet live.

It was a story after all. It was real life, but it was following the stories. He recognized it now. This was the part where the villain explained herself, where she revealed her whole evil plan and offered them a chance of some kind, and the hero was supposed to refuse it.

Raven hadn't been the hero—he had died, while the villain still lived, so he hadn't been the hero; heroes could only die while heroically saving others, they couldn't throw their lives away in stupid frontal attacks that left the villain untouched.

Who was the hero, then?

He glanced at the others—at Amy Jewell, clutching her belly and looking nauseated; at Ted Deranian, standing to the side looking bored and impatient; at Susan Nguyen, hanging back warily; at Prossie Thorpe, confused and frightened.

It might be Susan; it might even be Amy. Either of them could be the unexpected hero, the ordinary person who finds unseen strength—Susan with her history of suffering, Amy with her unborn child for inspiration.

Somehow he couldn't see poor mad Ted in the hero role, nor quiet Prossie with her muffled telepathy, her military pose not hiding her general vagueness.

Amy or Susan might fit, but the most likely candidate was himself. He was the one doing the talking, after all. He was the one who had insisted they come here.

He didn't feel very heroic, but then, he'd heard that heroes usually didn't.

Well, if he was the hero—and he still wasn't convinced— he might as well carry on with the role.

"All right," he said, "let's hear about it."

CHAPTER 21

*A*my was impressed with Pel's courage, to stand there and argue with the woman who claimed to be Shadow, or at least to represent Shadow. She wasn't sure it was really very bright, but it was certainly courageous, after three out of eight of them had been murdered.

She couldn't believe how calmly she was taking it, that the three had been . . . had been *fried*. She had been traveling with those people all this time, and now they were *dead*, horribly dead, burned; she wanted to scream and cry and faint, but she didn't dare even do that, because the thing that had killed them was still here, all around, and if she did anything it might kill *her*.

And she did not want to die.

Yet Pel was talking back to it—he was brave, but maybe stupid.

She had resisted Walter, but she had known when to shut up, so as not to be killed; she hoped that Pel knew as much.

And for now, she wasn't going to say anything. She didn't want to die.

No one else was saying anything anymore, either; were they all as terrified as she was?

Ted was crazy, so he didn't count.

She glanced back at Susan, who was still on the narrow landing beyond the door, not in the throne room at all, and saw her slip a hand into her purse.

Amy remembered that Pel had talked about emulating Bakshi's *Wizards*, where the evil wizard was ready for any sort of magical attack, so the good wizard pulled out a pistol and blew him away. She remembered the Arab swordsman in *Raiders of the Lost Ark*, too.

219

Shadow, despite her power, just looked like an ordinary woman; maybe, if Susan shot her, she would just die like an ordinary woman. Maybe she would die, and Amy would live. And if there was ever going to be a time to use that pistol, Amy had to agree that this must be it—but shouldn't Susan get closer? She couldn't be sure she'd hit the woman at all from way back there, let alone kill her with the first shot—and Amy didn't think she'd have time for more than one.

Maybe Susan was waiting for a distraction; well, Pel was providing that, wasn't he?

"Let's hear about it," Pel said.

That was an invitation to a speech if Amy had ever heard one; maybe the Shadow woman would get talking and forget herself.

Still, Susan was too far away. Amy unobtrusively beckoned her forward, as Shadow said, "I have lived long, little people from realms beyond this world; my magicks have given me years beyond measure, have kept me from aging. I grow, not weary, but bored, and seek distraction."

"What, so you just want to talk?" Pel asked.

That didn't seem very likely; this awful woman would scarcely have driven them here with her monsters just to chat. She probably had something gruesome and disgusting in mind, something worse than anything Walter had done.

Amy hoped that Shadow would die before she could do whatever it was, instead of after, as Walter had.

Shadow laughed, a very unpleasant laugh. Amy turned quickly, ignoring Susan, keeping her attention on the horrible woman on the throne.

"Nay, fool," Shadow said. "I seek to explore new worlds. I've my fill of this one."

She hadn't noticed what Susan was doing—either that, or she didn't care. Amy wondered if Shadow could read minds. Prossie couldn't, here in Faerie, but maybe Shadow could. If so, she knew what Susan had in her purse and was just toying with them all.

Maybe, Amy thought, I'd better not think about it.

Instead, she tried to concentrate on what Shadow was saying, to involve herself in that—though she hoped it wouldn't matter what Shadow wanted.

Pel frowned. "So where's the problem?" he said. "You're the one who can open those magical portals, right?"

Amy shook her head. Pel was being stupid. He wasn't leading Shadow on well enough.

"She wants native guides," Amy suggested. "People who can show her around, keep her out of trouble." She had moved around to one side a little, hoping to draw Shadow's attention away from Susan. She didn't really think that was what Shadow wanted; she just wanted to keep that nasty old woman talking.

"Near the heart, wench," Shadow answered, "but not to the meat of it."

"So tell us, then," Pel said. "At least, if it's something where we need to help you consciously, and you don't just need a bunch of blood sacrifices or something."

"If it's sacrifices," Amy added, trying not to sound too upset with the idea, "I think we'd just as soon not know." She tried very hard not to look back to where Susan was creeping through the door, nearer to Shadow's throne.

"And what need would I have of *your* blood that would not be served by another's, more easily had?" Shadow asked.

"So tell us about it," Pel repeated.

The villains in the stories never needed so much coaxing, Pel thought; they'd start babbling about their plans at the drop of a hint. How was he supposed to play the hero and find a way out, if Shadow wouldn't explain what it—or she—was up to? He smiled expectantly at the flabby, blowsy, drab woman that was Shadow.

She hardly looked the part of a world-conquering wizard, but this wasn't Hollywood.

"Know you aught of matrices?" she asked.

"No," Pel said. "At least, not the way you mean it, not if you mean magic ones."

Shadow nodded. "Indeed, magic," she said. "A matrix is a gathering of magical forces, a construction of magicks, a framework."

"Valadrakul said something about webs," Amy said. Pel glanced at her; she seemed to be getting more talkative, all of a sudden.

"Aye," Shadow agreed, "a web, or a net—i'truth, a matrix can be likened to many things, all in some way truthful, yet none a complete description. And there are some—or there *were*—who had the talent for the weaving of them."

Pel nodded encouragingly; she was finally telling her story.

Shadow settled back in her chair. "This was centuries past," she said, "long ere your fathers' fathers were born. There were those of us in the world who learned the making of matrices, and we were friends, and teachers, and students, and rivals, one to another, and sometimes we were bitter enemies. We twined our magicks, erected our structures thereof, each after his own fashion, but each learning from the others.

"Thus it was, for many years, for centuries before my own birth; how it began was lost in the past. Magic was loose and wild in the world, free for the taking, so that any person who could speak the words of a simple charm might use it, but only a few of us, only a very few, had the talent for binding the wild magicks and building matrices that we could take with us, that we could send forth, that we could use for purposes more profound than mere kitchen spells.

"Yet the matrix wizards of that time were mortal and died, and when each died the matrix he had built crumbled, and the magicks bound therein burst free. See you the way of it?"

"I think so," Pel said. It seemed clear enough.

"See then, in time, certain discoveries were made; a method was found whereby a wizard's matrix might be taken from him intact and bound to another, should the binder be present when the wizard failed. Further, 'twas learned how one could turn magic upon one's own aging and stave off the ravages of time; a matrix wizard need not grow old, should he attain sufficient mastery."

Pel nodded.

"But see you, then, what this meant," Shadow said, gesturing dramatically. "We had the time to gather to ourselves *all* the magicks, to bind and bind and bind until the wild magicks were no more, until only matrix wizards, or those we permitted to tap our matrices, could work even the simplest spell or cantrip. And further, when that was done, there was no way to gain more, save by the usurpation of another wizard's matrix—and most commonly, by another wizard's murder, for how else to wrest away a well-made matrix? That rivalry that had always been present, that competition amongst us, turned deadly, and we began to entrap one another, to slay one another, to form alliances and partnerships, only to betray one another when better alliances offered." She sighed. "Perhaps were better that had never been, but nonetheless, thus it became."

"I understand," Pel said.

He thought he did, too. Like animals fighting over a prize

until only one survived, the matrix wizards had killed each other off—and the survivor wouldn't be the best or brightest, but the most vicious killer of the lot.

And here she was in front of him, presumably.

He wished he could see how to use this against her. Had she built her matrix around a magic ring, or something? There *had* to be some flaw in her power.

"I was called Shadow," she said, "because I kept ever in the background; I'd been a timid child, and change was slow in coming. Yet I was no fool, and I chose my allies and my betrayals carefully, so that in time, I controlled the greatest single matrix ever held." She waved a hand, and brilliant colors rippled through the air for a moment, a reminder of her power. "I took this fortress for my own, slaying the wizard who held it before me, because 'twas in this place that the natural lines of power were strongest. I built my matrix ever larger, in my own time and quietly." She sighed. "But of course, the tallest tree is the one every woodsman wishes to hew down, and my power became too great to conceal. The other matrix wizards banded against me and spread lies among those who could no longer wield magic, and among those who could tug at the stray ends of it, as it were, but who could not weave their own webs. They made me out a figure of terror and evil; they turned my own name 'gainst me, named me Shadow as 'twere the shadow of death; they spoke of this marsh as a damned, dead place, when i'truth 'tis but an ordinary marsh; they noted my dislike for the sun and the rains I summon and made of this something twisted and dark."

Pel could read mounting anger in Shadow's face; these were obviously not happy memories for her. Maybe he could use that somehow. Maybe he could psychoanalyze her into impotence or surrender—except he wasn't a psychiatrist; he was a marketing consultant.

He wondered how much truth there really was in her story and how much was marketing.

"I'll not deny," she said, calming somewhat, "that I was not, perhaps, the most pleasant of neighbors; 'tis true that I slew those peasants who displeased me, as I do yet, but this was the common practice among the matrix wizards at our height. Why this should be turned against *me*, when all did it . . ."

She caught herself, paused, then continued, "Yet it was. Even that sanctimonious fool who called himself the Green Magician slew half a dozen lovers, yet he turned the peasants against me. Nor was he the worst; the Light, as they called themselves, were all hypocrites and liars—yet their words did their work, and ere I knew it, my reputation was that of the wolf, the scorpion, the vilest beast upon the face of the land. And all, all because I dared to build to myself the mightiest matrix of them all." She paused for a moment, then shook her head in remembered disbelief of such injustice.

"So . . ." Pel said, hoping she would give some clue he could use.

"*So,*" Shadow snapped, "in time, I was *forced* by such perfidy to destroy *all* the other matrix wizards and add their matrices to my own, until at last I controlled all the magic in the world—or at least, I had it at my beck, for in truth the matrix is so vast that I cannot control it all for every moment. Thus, the little wizards of today can pick at it betimes, snatch away a splinter here and there for their petty spells—but what of it? 'Tis naught to *me!*" She waved away the whole matter. "Yet the lies about me persisted, and those poor magicless fools, the peasants and most especially their silly lordlings, still struggled 'gainst me, so that in time I was forced to extend my domain over all the mundane world, as well as the magical. I would suppose that the late claimant to the barony of Stormcrack told you some of that."

"A little," Pel agreed.

"He and his kind existed by my tolerance," Shadow said. "Never were they worth the bother to exterminate."

"I can believe it," Pel said wryly—and honestly. He had not found Raven and his companions very impressive as revolutionaries. He'd seen no signs of a real organization, of intelligence gathering, or of anything but a willingness to oppose Shadow.

And what good was that, if Shadow was as powerful as everyone said?

"At any rate," Shadow continued, "I found myself mistress of all the world—and I grew bored. For centuries, I had schemed and fought, always expanding my power—and now I had reached the limits; there were no foes left worthy of my attention, no new lands to conquer. So I drew in to myself and sought some new entertainment. I experimented with magic; I reached out with senses beyond your poor comprehension— and I succeeded! I found . . ." She turned to Prossie. "I found thy Galactic Empire, with its spaceships, its machines, its telepaths, its many worlds, its myriad wonders and delights, and *there*, I thought, there I saw the solution to my boredom."

"Oh," Prossie said uneasily. Pel glanced at her, then back at Shadow.

He supposed that Shadow meant she intended to conquer the Galactic Empire; that seemed like the sort of thing an all-powerful evil wizard would want to do.

Though to be honest, Pel couldn't really see the point in it when she already ruled an entire world.

Shadow nodded. "First to tour," she said, "and then perhaps to conquer, to play with, to amuse myself with entire worlds—*that* would be an entertainment worthy of me, and one that would last for centuries!"

Pel grimaced.

Boredom as a motive for an interuniversal war of conquest? Not hatred, or anger? Not revenge, or power-hungriness? Just plain old boredom?

Well, why not? When one had centuries in which to become bored, when one already had so much power that there were no other challenges left, why not?

"Carrie," Prossie screamed silently, "do you *hear* this?" She was on the verge of panic, she *knew* she was on the verge of panic, but she couldn't help it. She was trapped and alone here, without her family to support her.

"I hear it," Carrie answered, "but what can I *do* about it? Hart and Bascombe won't listen to me; they don't care."

"She wants to play with whole planets," Prossie said desperately. "How can they not care?"

"Because they won't believe it," Carrie replied. "They can't think on that scale. Besides, why hasn't she already *done* it, they'll ask, and you don't have an answer."

"I might in a few minutes," Prossie replied. She was having trouble accepting Carrie's apparent indifference; this was her *cousin*, her friend, a person she'd shared her thoughts with over and over. It was true Prossie had deliberately left the family, given up her ties to the Empire, but even so, how could Carrie be so uncaring?

It was as if, to Carrie, she was no longer a telepath at all.

She knew that some of her distress must be leaking through, that Carrie knew what she felt, and she waited for Carrie to give her some sort of reassurance.

Carrie replied with the mental equivalent of a shrug.

* * *

Now, Pel thought, they were getting to the traditional villain's pitch. They'd gone through the whole self-justification speech; now Shadow could get to the point.

He wondered again how much of her story was true.

"So what does that have to do with *us*?" he asked. "Why didn't you just go invade the Galactic Empire, if that's what you wanted?"

"Because I *can't,* fool!" Shadow shouted. "Think you I'd be here now, could I?"

"Oh," Amy said, "I get it. Magic doesn't work there."

"Ah," Shadow said, pointing at Amy, "*one* among you has some wit!"

"So you can't conquer the Empire directly," Pel said.

"But you sent your creatures," Prossie pointed out. "You could send more, couldn't you?"

"Aye, my creatures," Shadow agreed. "I can send whatever spies and servants I please, and hearken to their reports when they return—and what of it? They tell me of marvels; I would *see* those marvels for myself! Conquest, when I know not what there is to conquer? I can create homunculi; I can raise the dead to fight for me, and i'truth I think I could lay waste all the Empire and claim it for my own, in time—but what sort of ruler would I be, unable to set foot upon my own land? How could I call those lands my own, if I could not see to them?"

Pel blinked.

"Can you really make whole armies of those things?" Prossie asked.

"Certes, I can," Shadow replied. "Do you doubt it?"

"Oh, well, it's been seven years, and all the Empire ever found were scouts and some dead monsters . . ."

"And 'tis all I've sent, thus far, those and my spies, but 'twas no true test of my powers, woman—I have not yet begun. I sought to learn what could live in that unnatural realm of yours; i'truth, the forms that abide well there are sore few!"

"But wait a minute," Pel said. "If you can send whole armies there, why can't you go? Even if your magic doesn't work there, you could go visit, then come back, couldn't you?"

"Ah, now we reach the kernel. No, fool, I cannot. For think you, if I leave this world, and take my matrix not with me, what befalls? And if I open the gate and step forth, but remain not here to hold the gate open, how shall I then return?"

Full understanding of Shadow's dilemma abruptly dawned on Pel.

"Oh," he said.

"*Now* you see," Shadow said. "And see you this also, I even thought that perhaps I might yield up the matrix and go forth to dwell forever among the Empire's worlds, with an army to serve me and keep me strong—until I bethought of the passage of time. For what is it that preserves me from senility and death, but the matrix I hold? The Empire's not worth my very life!"

"You mean, like, you'd instantly age a thousand years, or however old you are, without your magic?" Amy asked. Pel immediately thought of movies again—*Lost Horizon* and others, where immortal villains had done just that, fading to dust when their magic was lost.

Shadow snorted in derision. "Nay," she said, "this age of mine is no seeming, but truth. I'd be there as I am here. Howsoever, I'd not *remain* so, but would age as others do, would grow old and in the fullness of time, as the traditional phrase of those with little understanding would have it, I would die. Die! I, face death? I'd not have it, when by staying here I have eternity."

"An eternity of boredom," Pel pointed out.

"Exactly," Shadow agreed. "Wouldst choose death o'er ennui? I'd never."

"I still don't see what you want from us, then," Amy said. "We can't play native guides if you can't go there."

"I think I see," Pel said, with sudden comprehension. He couldn't really believe he had this right, but he couldn't come up with anything else Shadow could want.

And if he was wrong, it wouldn't be the first time.

Startled, Amy turned to him. "What?"

"She wants someone to hold the door for her until she gets back," Pel said.

Shadow nodded. "Precisely," she said. "To hold the door, and to hold the matrix ready, that I may resume it upon my return; if there's none holding it, 'twill crumble, and the wild magicks will be freed again."

Pel couldn't believe it would be this simple. There had to be something wrong with this. Shadow must have safeguards in mind, or some sort of trickery.

"But I . . ." Amy stammered, "you mean you want one of *us* to . . ."

"I would make one of you a matrix wizard in my place, and in my service," Shadow said, with a nod.

CHAPTER 22

Shadow did not give anyone time to protest—not that Pel had any intention of protesting. He supposed some of the others might have said something, if Shadow hadn't gone on speaking.

"See you, none from *this* world can serve; the ability to hold a matrix is lost here. Those who e'er could do so, so they did, and so in their time they all, save me, died," Shadow explained.

"You can't make a whatchacallit, a homunculus, to do it?" Pel asked—not that he really thought Shadow wouldn't have tried that long ago; he was just trying to clear away all doubts, to satisfy his own curiosity and tie up loose ends. It was plain that they were nearing the end of the story, when one of them would be offered Shadow's power.

He wondered who it would be, and whether he or she would accept, and what the consequences would be. Which would be better, to accept or refuse?

This was real life, he reminded himself; he couldn't rely on the most dramatically satisfying conclusion.

"Nay," Shadow said, "no homunculus nor other creation, nor either a dead man, for while I can instill therein a semblance of life, indistinguishable by any normal means from any mortal born, yet some certain spark is lacking. Perhaps 'tis true that the Goddess lives and blesses each infant with her gift, and 'tis this gift that lacks; I know not, neither do I care. I know only that 'tis lacking."

Pel trembled slightly; she had said it again, that she could restore the dead to life—and indistinguishably.

"So if none of the locals can do it," Amy asked, "how do you know *we* can?"

229

"Thinkest I'd not have tried thee?" Shadow answered. "Each of you has been tested and found fit. The Stormcrack lord was not, of course, and the wizardling could have held only the fraction, not the whole. None from the Empire save this one have the gift—yet all the four from Earth do. Perhaps 'tis something in the nature of the worlds whence you come, or perhaps 'tis mere chance, but whatever the reason, so 'tis."

"Maybe it's connected to telepathy, somehow," Pel suggested. "I mean, if Prossie has it but none of the others did."

"You're really sure that no one from your own world can do it?" Amy asked.

"Sure enow," Shadow replied. "Further, an I found one who had somehow escaped destruction, or one born a throwback to times past, how could I trust such a one? For in this land, whoever holds the matrix of Shadow is supreme, and whether it be me or another matters not a whit. You, though—thou and thou and thou—this place is not yours, and what wouldst have here?"

"You don't think any of us would be interested in ruling a world?" Pel asked. Ted giggled; the other Earthpeople ignored him, but Pel was uncomfortably aware how stupid his question sounded.

Still, he felt he had to ask it; he had to know just what the terms were, and why Shadow thought she could make her plans work.

"Not *this* world," Shadow said. "Look you, whosoever I choose shall have of me whatever he will, save that it endanger me not. Wouldst go home, to thy native land? Thou shalt be there instanter, upon my return. Wouldst have power there? Shalt have slaves sent thither to do thy bidding, whole armies, an thou wishest it. Riches untold for the asking, whole worlds at thy feet—for I have riches and power without limit and shall not stint my faithful servants."

"It sounds good," Pel said slowly. He couldn't resist any longer; he had to ask straight out, "but how do we know we can trust you?"

Shadow glared at him, and flickers of light and darkness obscured her features; bands of color chased one another across the walls, and the air seemed to hum silently.

"Thou durst ask?" Shadow demanded.

"I . . ." Pel's voice caught in his throat.

"Thinkest thou on thy choice, fool!" Shadow shouted. "To

trust, and perhaps win wealth and glory, or to refuse, and surely die!"

Pel hesitated.

"And knowest thou," Shadow added warningly, "if thou considerest betrayal on thine own part, that though I shall have not my matrix and the power gained thereby, yet shalt thou have my hand 'gainst thee as long as thou livest, and all my knowledge turned 'pon thy destruction. Thou shalt have the matrix, aye, but shalt have the knowledge to wield it? Shalt have the experience to defy me, and mine own foes in this land, and surely the Galactic Empire as well?"

"So we couldn't use the matrix anyway, you're saying," Pel said, relieved—Shadow's immediate moment of fury seemed to have passed, and besides, he could now see some of her reasoning, which was reassuring.

He much preferred to have the catches out in the open, where he could see them.

"Oh, in this and that, in those appliances requiring neither skill nor finesse, thou might bludgeon a way to thy end," Shadow told him, "but think not that the mere grasp on power without comprehension shall gain thee what I struggled centuries to learn, to compile and constrain to my will."

"But if we go along, you'll send us all safely home, and make us rich?" Amy asked; Pel heard both eagerness and doubt in her voice.

"Nay, 'tis thus not assured," Shadow said, "I'll but grant the whims of the one that serves; the fate of the others shall be for the one to determine."

"Well, I'm sure that'll mean we all get sent home," Amy said, glancing worriedly at Ted.

"If you're telling the truth and don't change your mind," Pel heard himself say.

He didn't know just why he had said it; he didn't *really* want to antagonize Shadow. This was his chance to have Shadow's power at his disposal.

If it was true.

"Look you, then," Shadow said, waving an arm.

The air to one side of the throne rippled oddly, like the air above a hot stove. A dull pressure made Pel's ears ache. He was unsure what he was supposed to look at; the rippling didn't seem to be *doing* anything. He started to say something, then stopped; Shadow was still working at whatever it was, her hands moving in odd, brisk little clutching gestures. Her control of the glare of the matrix was slipping as she was distracted, so that shafts of colored light flitted about, and blobs of shadow rolled suddenly across Pel's field of vision, vanishing before he could focus on them.

For what seemed like an hour, Pel and the others waited for whatever it was Shadow was doing to be complete; a tension grew, and Pel was unsure whether it was entirely emotional, or whether some force was literally charging the air around him.

Shadow's face was lost behind a silvery-pink glitter, and blue sparkles were spattering across the ceiling, when the ripple vanished from the air and she spoke again.

"See you here, then," Shadow said, "a portal to a worldlet in the Empire. Step through, telepath, and in that place shalt thou be able to hear my thoughts, and to know the truth of what I say, and to so testify to these others."

Prossie stared at the spot where the air had wavered as a rabbit might stare at a wolf; her eyes locked on it even though there was nothing there to see.

Here she was being offered what she had never really expected, a chance to return to the Empire.

Could she take it?

After all, she had broken the law; she had betrayed her trust; she had given up her family. If she stepped through, her own family would denounce her and see her condemned to death; she knew that from her last contact with Carrie, from Carrie's indifference to Prossie's danger. If Prossie stepped through and remained in the Empire, she would be hunted down and slain.

But if she refused, Shadow might well kill her here and now.

Reluctantly, she took a step.

"Takest thou a goodly deep breath, telepath," Shadow said.

Prossie looked up at her, startled.

Shadow smiled cruelly. "Thinkest me a fool?" she said. "Beyond is no world of men, but a bare, bitter rock, with scant air and none that might be breathed by such as thou; thou shalt have but a moment there to look into my soul, and then must thou return or perish."

Prossie blinked. She remembered anew what she was dealing with. This was no ordinary wizard; this was *Shadow*, the cruel overlord of Faerie, the being who had threatened the Empire, and who had sent monsters and saboteurs to destroy anyone who opposed her. Shadow would think nothing of sending a woman out into the void without a suit, without even a breath-mask—but Prossie could not take it so lightly. She had known a telepath, a great-uncle, who had been present when a ship's hull was breached, and Prossie trembled at the thought, at the stolen memories of men dying in vacuum, of lungs straining for air that wasn't there, of the fierce pressure behind bulging eyes, of sweat and saliva boiling off into the emptiness.

And she remembered something else.

"Wait a minute," she said unsteadily. "No one can read your mind; we tried. My family, I mean—the other telepaths. Reggie died trying."

"Ah, then that was no false tale concocted by the Empire's storytellers?" Shadow asked, and Prossie thought she could see a nasty little smile behind the deep orange glow that hid Shadow's face at that moment.

"No, it's not a tale," Prossie said, gasping, on the verge of panic. "It was true! I read it!"

"Fear not, little thought-thief," Shadow said. "I'd not destroy thee thus. When thou'rt beyond yon gate shall I put aside what I can of the matrix, so that thou might see into my soul without harm."

"You can do that?" Prossie asked, grasping desperately at the hope.

But she still didn't want to read Shadow's mind, and she still doubted she could—to locate a single mind from another universe, in the time she could hold her breath, while exposed to a hostile environment?

And she was just getting comfortable with herself; she didn't want to be plunged into a mind like Shadow's, a mind centuries old and full of foulness and treachery, a mind that was not troubled by the gutted corpses over the fortress entry, not troubled by the fiery destruction, just moments before, of three enemies. Prossie did not want any part of that.

But she didn't want to die, to be the fourth one of the party burned to ash, either.

"An I cannot clear the way enow," Shadow said, "do not force thyself unto madness, nor death, but return straightway; we'll find other means."

Prossie still hesitated—until she saw Shadow begin to frown.

* * *

Amy watched Prossie walk fearfully toward the portal, and she wished there was something she could do, some way to take away Prossie's fear, or to make it unnecessary for her to go—but what could she do? Shadow had told Prossie to go, and disobeying Shadow meant dying.

Maybe if she said she'd believe Shadow without Prossie's word, that she'd take the silly matrix—but she *didn't* believe Shadow, any more than she had believed Stan when he said he wasn't angry, or Walter when he said he wouldn't hurt her, or Beth when she had said she was just as frightened as Amy was herself. She couldn't believe a bully anymore; they always lied, always, and Prossie's report wouldn't change anything, because the bullies believed their own lies.

If only someone could do something to make Shadow stop . . .

She glanced back at Susan, who had crept into the room long minutes before, virtually unnoticed. She was moving so *slowly*. Susan's hand was in her purse, closed around something, and she was inching closer to Shadow from the opposite side while Shadow watched Prossie, while Pel watched Prossie, while Ted stared vacantly at no particular part of the whole scene.

Why hadn't Susan shot Shadow while it—or she, whichever—was conjuring up this portal to the Empire? Shadow had been distracted, at least slightly; was Susan expecting a better chance?

Amy blinked, as realization struck.

Susan *was* hoping for a better chance—and she might get it. When Shadow conjured the gateway, it was very much involved in its magical matrix—the colors had been visible, though not the blinding glare they had all seen earlier. And the matrix would almost certainly be able to stop a bullet, even if Shadow was distracted.

But Shadow had said she'd be putting aside the matrix so Prossie could read her mind.

Did that mean she'd be putting aside *everything* that protected her?

Susan apparently thought so.

Susan obviously didn't believe Shadow's lies about sending them home afterward any more than Amy did.

Amy quickly turned away, not looking at Susan, very definitely not looking at Susan, looking anywhere except at Susan, and she watched as Prossie gulped air, stepped forward, and vanished.

The stars blazed brilliantly overhead, the rock was black beneath her feet, the cold tore at her like knives slashing at her bare hands and face as the moisture was torn away. She had to struggle to keep the air in her lungs, the pressure here was very low; she had to be careful to shuffle her feet, not to kick, because the gravity couldn't be more than a few percent of a gee, a good kick could send her right off the surface of this asteroid, or moon, whichever it was, and it might take longer than her oxygen would last before she fell back to the bare stone ground.

And as if the physical pain wasn't enough of a distraction, the thoughts of a galaxy full of people poured in on her, the minds of thirteen billion people all going about their own business, and scattered among them the thoughts of the four hundred other telepaths shone like diamonds in sand; she had forgotten what it was like, it was like a cold wind blowing through her, and like steam boiling in behind, it was hard to remember her own identity at first.

But there was Carrie, calling to her, asking what was going on, calling her by name, and she remembered who she was, and why she was there; she was Proserpine Thorpe, Registered Master Telepath, and she was there to read Shadow's mind. She reached back through the . . . through the dimensional barrier, she took the phrase from some unguarded, unrecognized mind somewhere. She reached into Faerie. She could feel her lungs straining, her lips were dry and cracking, and her ears were burning with cold and pounding with the roar of her own blood and roaring with the pressure of her breath.

She ignored Carrie; she reached into Faerie and found minds there, she found the familiar first, the patterns she already knew—Wilkins was still alive in a town she didn't recognize, Sawyer was still alive and halfway across the marsh, and then she found Amy and Susan and Pel and Ted, there in the fortress, and Susan was pulling the gun from her purse, and Amy knew about it and wasn't saying anything, Ted and Pel didn't see, and the other mind there was Shadow, it had to be, a dark, narrow little mind that seemed to go on forever.

And Shadow wasn't planning treachery; she honestly believed she would keep her promises, but down below that, in the tangle of memories and motivations that Shadow wouldn't allow herself to recall, Prossie saw the dark vicious selfishness that lurked in every human mind. In Shadow it was deep and strong, great and powerful, it had been growing unchecked for centuries, as Shadow's every whim was fulfilled.

She was not lying—but she would betray them and destroy them anyway, in time.

And at that realization Prossie panicked and dove back for the magical space warp, aware as she did that Susan's finger was closing on the trigger of a .38 revolver that still held two bullets.

Pel jumped at the sound of the first shot; panicking, he whirled, trying to see what was happening. His first thought was that the building was collapsing, that he had heard a roof beam crack.

Then he saw the pistol in Susan's hand as she fired again.

"What are you *doing*?" he screamed.

She was only about six feet away, shooting Shadow in the back; she couldn't possibly miss at that range. She was shooting Shadow, and then there wouldn't be anyone who could send them home, there wouldn't be any matrix he could use to bring Nancy and Rachel back from the dead.

Prossie had reappeared by the time the second shot sounded, kneeling on the floor, trembling, gasping, frost forming on her hair and hands and the legs of her uniform, and Amy had stepped back to watch, and Ted was just *standing* there, giggling.

"It's coming apart," Ted cried. "I *must* be waking up!"

And Shadow wasn't falling, wasn't bleeding, she was turning around slowly and deliberately.

Susan dropped the revolver; it clattered loudly on the stone floor as she sank to her knees. She bowed her head and waited, kneeling, as Shadow took a step toward her.

This was all mad, Pel thought. This wasn't how it was supposed to go. This wasn't a proper end to the story. He'd all but forgotten about that stupid gun, about his suggestion that Susan might shoot Shadow. He'd thought Prossie would step back calm and whole and confirm Shadow's story, and the fat old woman would choose someone, probably Prossie—she'd been singled out to test the truth, after all, so wouldn't she be the logical choice?

Any sensible storyteller would have made Prossie the hero of the whole thing. After all, she was a telepath, she'd make a great viewpoint character, she'd always know what was going on. She should have come back upright and proud and confronted Shadow.

Or if Susan was the hero, if it was *Wizards* reenacted, then Shadow should be down and dying, and they'd have to hunt down Taillefer to get home, they'd be here for weeks or months yet.

But Prossie was on hands and knees gasping for air; Shadow was turning to face her attacker with no sign she'd been harmed; and Susan was bowing her head, preparing to die.

That was what she was doing, Pel realized; Susan Nguyen, who seemed to be able to survive anything, to calmly withstand whatever befell her, was preparing to die.

"Dost think so little of me, then?" Shadow said, in a voice that was strained and terrible. "Thinkest thou I'd have no protections left without the full matrix about me? Did think me such a fool as that?" She took another step and stood over Susan, who made no answer. "I have endured for centuries, 'gainst wizards, warriors, and time itself; thought thou some simple machine could slay me?" She kicked the revolver aside; it skittered away.

And then Susan slumped forward, fell in a heap at Shadow's feet, and lay still.

"Die, then," Shadow said.

Amy sobbed, a deep, bone-shaking sob.

"I don't understand," Pel said hopelessly.

Shadow turned to face him and glared directly down at him from her throne.

"Dost thou not, then?" she asked. " 'Tis plain enough. This wench tried to slay me, with that device from your world, whilst I was distracted and had set aside much of my power; and this other hoped the attempt might succeed. Thus I've stopped the heart of the assassin, and would slay the other— but I think thou'd have it otherwise and thus I restrain myself."

Pel blinked.

"Me?" he said.

"Look about you, sir," Shadow replied. "See my choices. A corpse, a madman, and two women, the one who longed for my death, the other a trickster who can hear thoughts—and you, who called out in outrage when that weapon spat its pellets at me. Who, then, shall stand in for me, shall hold the matrix in my stead while I venture forth?"

Pel swallowed hard.

He was no hero. He was just a spear-carrier, someone along to help fill out the party.

But then, this wasn't really a story at all. He was being of-fered his chance. If everything was as Shadow said, it was a chance—his *only* chance—to have everything he really wanted.

He glanced at Prossie, who lay on the stone floor, drawing deep, gasping breaths and shivering with cold.

The telepath looked up at Pel, swallowed, and spoke.

"She isn't lying," Prossie whispered, but the expression on her face was a clear warning.

A warning of what, Pel couldn't guess, and without further thought he ignored it.

"All right," he said.

CHAPTER 23

*P*el *had somehow thought that it would all be over in a mat-*
ter of minutes, that Shadow would transfer the matrix to him
then and there, with Susan lying dead on the floor and Amy
weeping and Ted giggling, and Prossie trying to stop shivering
as she brushed the ice from her uniform. He had thought that
he could send Shadow through to the Galactic Empire, and
then she would come back in a few moments, and he could
collect on her promises.

That was nonsense, of course. Shadow, whose appearance
was blurring weirdly as she let her suppression of the matrix's
appearance continue to slip, explained the situation.

Before Pel could even begin to hold the matrix, he had to
become an actual wizard, rather than a potential one; before he
could send her through to the Galactic Empire, he would have
to learn the portal spell. Shadow would teach him, of course,
but it would hardly be instantaneous.

Pel began to wonder if it might have been quicker if Susan
had succeeded in killing Shadow after all and they'd had to
track Taillefer down, instead of going through this abbreviated
apprenticeship.

"How long will it take?" he asked.

"That depends upon thine own talents," Shadow answered
from somewhere inside a halo of shifting colors. "With only a
little good luck, three or four days; if thou hast the true talent,
as many hours; but if thou'rt such a fool as thou sometimes
seemest, then perhaps 'twill be years."

"Are you planning to feed us?" Pel asked.

Shadow flickered, and Pel saw her face glowering through
the colors.

* * *

239

Amy had to admit that the food was good, and the service, provided by odd-smelling black-clad people who never said a word, never opened their mouths at all, was impeccable.

Much of the decor was ghastly, though; she took professional affront at it. She would *never* have allowed one of her customers to decorate a room the way Shadow's dining hall—if that's what it was—was done; she'd have walked off the job first, and to hell with the customer always being right. Punk was all very well, but to line an entire wall with human skulls, several hundred of them . . .

She almost giggled at the absurdity of her aesthetic concerns. Shadow didn't care what the place looked like; she probably had some reason for the skulls. Maybe they were from old enemies, all lined up there as a reminder that she'd killed them all. Maybe they were from servants who'd messed up, to encourage the current crew not to spill anything.

There was no question that they were all genuine human skulls, though; these were not fakes. These were dead people; when Amy thought about it, she had to conclude that to all intents and purposes they were eating in a tomb.

But the heavy, chewy brown bread was rich and filling; the roast beef was tender and had been cooked with onions and some sort of spice that gave it an exotic tang; the wine reminded Amy of the chianti she and Stan had drunk at that little restaurant they'd gone to when they were dating. She skipped the boiled cabbage—she had never liked cabbage. There were oranges for dessert, and nuts and cheese afterward.

Despite the skulls and the gloomy servants, it was unquestionably the best meal she had had since ISS *Ruthless* almost fell on her in her own backyard. She hoped she'd be able to keep it all down.

Ted and Prossie ate well, too.

She didn't know about Pel, though; he was off with Shadow somewhere, starting his training. She saw servants carrying plates past the table on their way to the workshop, for Pel— and Shadow? Amy didn't know whether Shadow ate, or whether she got all the energy she needed from her magic.

And she wondered about the servants—were they ordinary people, or were they monsters Shadow had made in the shape of humans, homunculi, or whatever they were called?

Or were they something else—zombies, maybe? Shadow had talked about raising the dead at one point, and there was that odd odor.

These people didn't smell *bad*, though, and they weren't black—all of Shadow's monsters, from the stovepipe things to the dragon that had chased them up the stairs, seemed to be black, and none of the servants were any darker-skinned than Raven had been, let alone *black* black. Amy preferred to think that the servants were local people who had found themselves in Shadow's service in perfectly natural ways.

She didn't look at them too closely as she ate, though.

Prossie worried about what Pel was really going to do. He had ignored her warning—he *must* have seen it.

Maybe, she thought as she wiped her mouth and winced at the friction on her frostbitten lips, she would be able to warn him once he held the matrix, while Shadow was making her first venture into Imperial space.

She wondered if Pel had thought this through; did he really think that Shadow would ever let him go, alive? She would want to go back to the Empire again and again, she had almost said so—every time she went, every second she was away, she would need someone trustworthy back here in Faerie, holding her matrix together and keeping the space warp open. She would want Pel here forever, and if he ever refused she would kill him and fetch someone new. After all, once she knew that her idea would work, what would stop her from sending her homunculi to kidnap people from Earth or the Empire?

And there was no question at all about Shadow's callousness or ruthlessness. Susan's cooling corpse had still lain on the floor of the throne room when they were all led away to be fed, and the skin was peeling from Prossie's own ears and mouth and fingers from the cold of that asteroid Shadow had sent her to; no one could expect generosity or kindness from Shadow.

Maybe Pel had some scheme of his own, but Prossie did not entirely trust him to outthink Shadow.

She rose cautiously from the table, cast a final glance at the wall of skulls, and followed a beckoning servant.

The privies were primitive, by Amy's standards, but functional; the beds appeared luxurious, but she found that if she stretched out, her feet stuck off the end, and she had never thought of herself as unusually tall.

At least there weren't any skulls in the bedchambers.

She wondered whether Pel was getting any sleep.
She wondered if wizards *needed* any.

Pel never remembered just how the whole thing was done. Whether this was inherent in the process or the result of some spell on Shadow's part, he had no idea. By morning, as he sat on the rough wooden stool in Shadow's workshop, he simply knew, without being able to put any of it in words, just how one drew upon magical currents, how one manipulated and directed them, how one bound them to one another or to one's own mind. He could sense the currents, could feel and see them; he understood what Valadrakul had seen beneath the haze of color and light and knew how to ignore that haze himself, if he chose to. He could see the dull lumps of rock on Shadow's crude wooden shelves as glittering foci for magical forces.

He was, in short, becoming a matrix wizard.

Maybe it was hypnosis, Pel thought when he realized that he didn't know how he had become a matrix wizard. That conjured up unpleasant thoughts of lurking posthypnotic suggestions.

"Have you . . . I mean . . ." He looked across the dim, dusty workroom at the shimmering darkness that was Shadow's current visible incarnation, and decided against finishing the question.

Shadow guessed more or less what he had been going to say, however. The lone candle flickered as she answered, and the room darkened further; there were no windows, no skylights, no natural light in here at all—only the single candle and whatever magical glow Shadow allowed.

"Aye, I've placed a geas upon thee," she said, "that thou shalt never turn my magicks against me, that thou shalt do me no harm with either thine own hand or through magic the hands of others, and that upon my request thou shalt yield up to me whatsoever I ask of thee."

"That's . . ." That wasn't exactly what he had been going to ask, and it hardly seemed fair to have done that without his permission, but Pel decided against protesting. Shadow wasn't much on fairness, and if she hadn't asked a lot of questions of him while he was in her thrall, so much the better. "That's okay," he said.

He got the impression that Shadow was smiling, though he couldn't see anything resembling a face. "Though 'tis wearisome betimes, Pellinore Brown," she said, "yet I'd never wish to be other than I am, if only because none talk back o'erboldly to me."

Then he realized how he knew she was smiling; he could feel it through the magical matrix.

The candle puffed out, but he could still sense where everything was in the little stone chamber, despite the utter darkness.

A warm golden glow flooded across him, pouring from Shadow's face.

"Come, thou hast the foundation," Shadow said, "and far sooner than I'd hoped; thou hast the true talent, Pellinore. Now, let us build doorways upon that foundation."

There were other spells Pel was far more interested in learning than he was in creating doorways—the spell to raise the dead primarily, and secondarily the spells to create homunculi—but he was in no position to argue. Shadow didn't want him to know all that; she wanted him to serve as her doorman between worlds.

She was looking at him expectantly.

He had the true talent?

He slid off the stool and stood up.

She had said he did, and he had no reason to doubt it, really, but it seemed so odd. He wasn't anyone special; how could he have had some special talent all his life without knowing it? How could an Earthman have a talent for wizardry at all?

Maybe he'd been the hero all along, the young innocent who turns out to be the greatest wizard of all time . . .

But he was no innocent, and not much of a hero, even if he did have the talent. It was more likely that *all* Earthpeople had the talent than that he, Pel Brown, was somehow *fated* to have come here.

But here he was, fated or not, and Shadow was going to leave him holding her matrix, was going to teach him the spell to open portals to other worlds.

And he would have time to experiment with other spells on his own while she was away exploring the Empire.

There were no eggs at breakfast, no coffee, no orange juice, but Amy was satisfied with ham and tea and buttered toast; she passed up the sticky little cakes, and the gooey brown lumps that might have been candied dates. She hadn't thrown up that morning, and she wanted to keep it that way.

Prossie ate a little of everything, though, and Ted ate whatever was put in front of him as if he didn't know or care what it was. None of them paid any attention to the wall of skulls; familiarity had bred contempt.

After the meal, the servants either went away or simply stopped moving and stood where they were; no one gave any sign of where the three were to go or what they were to do. For several minutes they simply sat, looking about the room or at each other, not speaking. Amy looked over the skulls, but they gave no clues—she would not have been very surprised, under the circumstances, if a skull had started talking, but none of them did.

The remaining servants simply stood, and Amy tried for a moment to identify the peculiar scent they produced—a faint chemical smell, vaguely reminiscent of doctors' offices—but she couldn't place it.

And nobody was paying any attention to them; she and Ted and Prossie were being utterly ignored.

She wondered if something had gone wrong somewhere, if Pel had died, or Shadow, and that had shut everything down—but there was no evidence of anything like that.

"Now what?" Amy asked at last.

Ted didn't answer, or even look at her, but Prossie shrugged. "I don't know," she said.

"Do you think we missed a signal or something?" Amy asked.

Prossie shook her head. "No," she said, "I think we're being ignored. Shadow doesn't care about us anymore, at least not for the moment. When she needs us, she'll summon us."

"So what should we do?" Amy glanced uneasily at a servant, at the black suede tunic he wore, his motionless hands and expressionless face.

Prossie shrugged. "Whatever we like, I suppose." She hesitated, then added, "But if you were thinking of doing anything Shadow wouldn't like, I wouldn't advise it—she can hear anything, anywhere in Faerie, when she chooses, and she can see through other people's eyes—or for that matter, *anything's* eyes. She could be looking through mine, or Ted's, or yours, right now—or the eyes of a rat under the table, or one of these servants."

"How do you know that?" Amy asked, startled.

"From when I read her mind yesterday," Prossie explained. "I only had a few seconds, and I was sort of desperate, so I wasn't very selective, I just grabbed at everything I could. I picked up a lot of odd bits, so now I know something about how her magic works." She grimaced. "Not enough to be any real use, I'm afraid; you can't learn skills that way. I just picked up a few random memories of using that matrix thing. She's got centuries of memories of that."

"So she might have been spying on us the entire time, from when the ship crashed until we got here?" Amy asked. "She could have watched us through the eyes of squirrels in the trees, or something?"

Prossie nodded. "I don't know any details, there may be limits, and I didn't hit any memories of anything like that, but yes, she *could* have been spying on us. Not just through squirrels; she could have used your eyes, or mine; we'd never have known it."

Amy shivered. "Did Raven and Valadrakul know she could do that? Or Elani?"

Prossie shrugged.

Amy looked around uneasily and still found no clues as to what she should do; accordingly, she just sat.

There was a trick to the portal spell, Pel discovered, even for a wizard; it required one to look in a direction that wasn't there, and then draw enough magic into one's perceptions to make the direction real. It was no wonder that no one had discovered it before Shadow, or that it had taken Shadow herself several centuries to come up with it.

It was, in fact, much harder to learn this single spell than to acquire all the basics of matrix wizardry; he had to work at it for most of the day. Shadow let him pull as much energy from her matrix as he needed, so much power that the air in the stuffy little workroom seemed to vibrate with it, the walls glowed pale green, the stones on the shelves buzzed and chimed—but even with all that power, it still took some time before he began to get the hang of it.

It seemed so strange—as if he had found himself in a fun house, one where he had to learn to work all the tricks just by wishing. Shadow never explained why the walls glowed green, what the stones were for; she forced him to concentrate on the portal spell.

He tried very hard to concentrate, and at last, in a way he had no words to describe, he began to sense how it would work.

Shadow forbade him to make any attempt to contact Earth,

but she guided him in finding the Galactic Empire, in scanning through the worlds therein, in choosing one, and in opening a gateway.

The stone walls fluoresced blue, then vermilion; stones crawled and twisted; but at last he managed to create an opening.

And once the portal was there, holding it open was fairly easy. He simply had to not let the currents of magic slip away.

Colors shifted oddly around him, and he ignored them. He had succeeded in creating his first portal, creating a hole into another world!

Pel marveled at it. He had worked *magic*. He had opened a path between universes! The feeling of power, of accomplishment, and most of all of *strangeness*, was overwhelming; he found himself weeping with no idea why.

Shadow summoned servants from somewhere; the single door of the workroom swung open and admitted one of her silent, black-clad people. She ordered him through the portal, to test it; the man stepped through, vanishing, and a moment later reappeared unhurt. He bowed before Pel.

"Don't they talk?" Pel asked, when the man did not speak, did not say a word about where he had been.

"Not well," Shadow replied.

The remains of breakfast had congealed into an unappetizing mess; no one had ever cleared them away. Amy thought it was time for lunch, past time, though it was hard to be sure when the only light came from a shaft overhead, a square opening in the ceiling that obviously opened to daylight, but which was angled so that she could not see the sky.

No lunch came. Maybe Shadow had forgotten, or perhaps the folk of Faerie only ate two meals a day; Amy could only guess.

She and Ted and Prossie had made no attempt to leave the dining hall beyond visits to a privy that was just up a short corridor; she and Prossie had discussed leaving, had twice almost decided to go back to their bedchambers, but both times they had lost their nerve.

Ted hadn't said anything; most of the time he had just sat there, staring at his thumbs, occasionally glancing around disinterestedly.

All three of them, even Ted once or twice, had walked about the room, stretching their legs; all three had spent some time just sitting, as well. Amy and Prossie had talked a little, and several times Amy had found herself starting to slip into confessions and confidences, only to veer away whenever she remembered Ted's presence. Despite his silence, she thought he might be listening, and she did not care to share her memories, and her concerns about her pregnancy and Stan and Walter and Beth and Susan and all the rest, with a madman sitting a few feet away.

For that matter, while the three servants still in the room gave every appearance of being inanimate, she didn't know whether *they* might not be listening. Amy was now convinced that whatever the servants were, they weren't fully human; ordinary people could not possibly stand so still for so long. These things might be some sort of magical robot, or people under some sort of spell, Amy didn't know; but whatever they were, they might be listening.

And of course, Shadow herself might be listening—any time, any place, Shadow might be listening.

So Amy kept her conversation vague and general, or else trivial.

She was just about to suggest, for the third time, that they return to their bedchambers, when the abandoned servants suddenly jerked to life. Two simply turned and walked out, leaving the door open behind them; the third beckoned for Amy and the others to follow her.

The two of them had moved from the workshop back down to the throne room, where Pel had practiced, opening and closing a portal into the Empire unassisted three or four times, using power drawn from just one strand of Shadow's web; Shadow wanted to be absolutely certain that he would be able to let her back into Faerie.

Pel had discovered some interesting things in the process of this practice.

For one, he had found that Shadow's geas, or posthypnotic suggestion, or whatever it was, worked; if she told him to open a portal, he had no choice in the matter. He began the spell whether he wanted to or not.

There was no compulsion with other requests or commands, but there certainly was with the portals.

He supposed this was intended to insure that he wouldn't strand her in another universe. It seemed there was a problem with this in that Shadow would be unable to give him orders from the Galactic Empire, but he supposed she would have thought of anything that obvious and found a way around it.

He had also discovered that it was very difficult to open a *new* portal—each time, after a moment of wild gyration, the spell tried to settle on the exact same spot he had used the time before, like machinery settling into a well-worn groove, or an animal on a familiar path, and had to be forced away. It was downright impossible to open a portal near, but not at, one that had been used before. That explained why Elani's spell gateway to Earth had always come out through Pel's basement wall.

And he couldn't control *exactly* where a portal would come out; he didn't understand why, and Shadow did not explain it, but even when he thought he knew the exact location where his portal would appear, even when he could sense the shape of the other world so clearly he felt as if he ought to be able to step right through without any portal at all, the portal might come out a hundred feet, or a thousand, away from the intended target.

That might explain why Elani's spell had come out in his basement in the first place, instead of somewhere more useful.

Of course, he couldn't really see where it would come out, he could merely sense certain characteristics of the place, characteristics for which he had no words—he could feel them magically, but had no idea how to explain them in words. He guessed that they might relate somehow to magnetic fields, but he didn't really know.

He knew the spell, though, which was the important part. He could open portals.

When Shadow was satisfied that Pel did, indeed, know the spell, she began making her final preparations for departure; Pel leaned against a wall of the throne room and watched.

Every so often he glanced at Susan Nguyen's corpse, lying in a corner where Shadow had left it—she had had her servants remove Valadrakul's scorched remains, and there hadn't been enough left of Raven or Singer to trouble about, but she had perversely left Susan's body. Each time he looked, Pel shuddered slightly.

He had never seen Nancy's body, or Rachel's; he had grieved for them, but he had also been almost numb in some ways, had struggled through moments of disbelief.

He could hardly disbelieve in Susan's death, when the poor little Vietnamese lawyer's corpse was lying right there.

He hadn't known Susan well; he suspected almost nobody had. She had been so quiet, so reserved, so determinedly self-sufficient—and so brave, to attack Shadow like that.

Pel felt a certain shame at that. He had been trying to make deals with Shadow, trying to get himself home, or to get Nancy and Rachel resurrected—but wasn't it Shadow who had been responsible for their deaths, who was responsible, in a way, for his being here in the first place? It was Raven who had brought Pel through the portal into Faerie, but it was Shadow who had driven Raven to it, who had first made contact with other universes and made that contact a hostile one, of spies and saboteurs and plans for war. It was Shadow who was responsible for the disemboweled corpses in every town and village, for the dead soldiers dangling above her castle door.

And Susan, the survivor, the one who simply lived through whatever life threw at her, had done a brave thing and tried to kill Shadow, and Pel hadn't helped her, he had protested.

How could he have done that?

At the time it had seemed perfectly reasonable, but now he was ashamed and angry at himself, and angry at Shadow.

Shadow was a monster. She might be his teacher, she might look like a bored housewife, but she was a monster, a ruthless conqueror—even, it might be argued, a genocide, the exterminator of her own kind, the other matrix wizards.

And she held limitless power; he had tasted a little of it himself, and he knew how dangerous she was.

If anyone had ever deserved to die, Shadow did; as long as she lived, no one in Faerie was safe—and now, no one in the Galactic Empire was, and Earth was presumably next.

And quite aside from preventing further deaths, or any abstract interest in justice, Pel wanted revenge. Geas or no, he wanted vengeance—for Susan, for Raven and Singer and Valadrakul, for Nancy and Rachel, and for all the others.

And he intended to have it.

CHAPTER 24

The throne room was full of people, but eerily silent. No one coughed, no one spoke; they all simply stood there as Shadow's patterns of light and color played across them. Amy stopped in the doorway and looked uneasily in, her eyes adjusting to the glare, her ears starting to ring with the odd sensation of pressure that Shadow's presence usually provoked.

The unmoving people were more of Shadow's black-clad servants, dozens of them. Amy was more certain than ever that whatever they were, they weren't really human.

Prossie stopped behind her, but Ted ambled on past them and began pushing his way through the crowd.

"Come you," Shadow called, and the servants shoved back against each other, opening a path. Watching them move, Amy noticed for the first time that they all wore belts bearing sheathed swords.

What was *that* about?

Uneasily, Amy followed Ted, Prossie trailing behind, and the three of them made their way to a wide clear space before Shadow's throne.

Shadow's glory was relatively restrained just now, so they were not blinded, and they could vaguely see a human outline within the glimmering matrix. Pel was standing to one side of Shadow's seat, partially obscured by the shifting colors. In front of the throne was an area of open floor about twenty feet across; all the rest of the vast chamber seemed to be jammed full of servants—homunculi, walking dead, whatever they were, there were hundreds of them, all of them outwardly human.

There were no obvious monsters anywhere to be seen, which struck Amy as a bit odd. Shadow used so many monsters outside her fortress, and in that huge entrance hall; didn't she use them in here?

"Welcome," Shadow said, as Amy stepped into the open area.

Amy stopped.

"You see before you," Shadow announced, "my personal bodyguard. Never in this realm have I had any need of such, but I go now to visit *thy* land, telepath, where my magicks cannot protect me."

Amy glanced around at the expressionless faces. That explained the swords, anyway—Shadow didn't have any guns to give her guards. And Shadow's monsters couldn't live in Imperial space, which explained their absence, as well.

"In a moment," Shadow continued, "your companion, Pellinore the Brown, will open a portal to a small, pleasant world in the Galactic Empire; my escort will precede me thereunto and make ready my way. And likewise, you two Earthpeople will step through."

Amy started. "Why?" she asked. "Why aren't you sending us *home*?"

"Because," Shadow explained, "though I have taken what precautions seemed good to me, yet am I wary that our good Messire Brown may not act for love of me. Thou and this madman shall serve me as hostages for his good behavior—an he faults in any way upon my desires, shalt first the madman, and then thyself, be slain."

Amy felt tears stinging her eyes. This just went on and on, world after world, but never Earth. "What about Prossie?" she asked.

"The telepath? Nay, nay, I'm not such a fool as that; an she came, the Empire's soldiers would know my plans and my whereabouts in a trice, and they'd not be troubled by the loss of a handful of you, nor greatly slowed by my swordsmen. I'd flee safely hither, but 'twould be a misfortune best avoided. She's to stay here."

Amy blinked at the indeterminate shape on the throne, and at Pel, there beside it. For a moment she thought an odd expression seemed to appear on Pel's face, as if he were struggling not to smile, but Amy could not be sure through the haze of color.

"Now, Pellinore," Shadow said, "let us begin."

* * *

Pel watched as the black-clad creatures Shadow had called fetches marched, one by one, into the portal he had opened.

Raven had mentioned fetches—weren't they supposed to be the walking dead?

Did that mean that these were dead people brought back to life, or live people condemned to a sort of half death? Pel didn't know.

He didn't know the name of the planet they were appearing on, either, but he thought it was a green and pretty place, and that the low towers of a city would be visible in the distance from the other side of the portal. He could not really explain how he had found it, or how he knew what it looked like—one didn't see through a portal, rather, one put a portal through to what one saw, and Shadow had told him through the matrix, in ways words could not describe, where she wanted this one.

He supposed that this troop of black-garbed swordsmen was really a scouting and raiding party, as much as Shadow's body-guard; he was certain she intended to fight the Galactic Empire eventually, and he supposed she might well conquer it all in time.

And after that, she would probably go after Earth. He really was face-to-face with a world-conquering menace, just as in all those stories, and one that didn't have any ring to throw in a volcano, nor sword to be broken, nor plug to be pulled—but one he wanted to kill.

He couldn't harm her, though, nor ask another to, and he couldn't refuse her instructions regarding the portal.

He could *think* about harming her, of course; he could imagine her hanged and disemboweled, or torched and burning, or beaten to death, like some of her victims—but he couldn't do anything directly to make his imaginings come true.

The throne room was emptying; he could see Susan's corpse again, no longer hidden by Shadow's slaves.

And he could see Prossie, standing to one side, waiting, as the crowd trickled away through the portal, until finally the last four slaves took Ted and Amy by the arms and led them through.

That left Shadow, himself, Prossie, and Susan alone in the throne room.

"Now, Pellinore," Shadow said, "thou shalt hold this portal open 'gainst my return, and shalt open no others lest they distract thee; understood?"

"I understand," Pel said, annoyed that he could not deny her orders about it. He had been wondering if he might be able to maintain two portals at once, once he was holding Shadow's incredible matrix. It certainly wasn't possible with the little dribble of eldritch power he had access to so far, but Shadow's power was so vast that he doubted the limitation would have held. He had been thinking of opening a portal to somewhere else . . .

But she had forbidden it, and the geas was irresistible.

" 'Tis well," she said. "Be ready, now."

And then Pel felt power pouring into him and felt himself spilling out of his body, as Shadow's magical matrix was transferred to him. The line between himself and the huge network abruptly blurred, and for an instant he was everywhere, all through Faerie, in the currents of magic; he felt the winds and the earth, the seas and the forests; he saw from a thousand eyes at once. An entire world was within him and around him, all at once.

With an effort, he tried to recollect himself.

Maintaining the portal, which mere hours before had seemed a major task, and mere seconds before had taken a conscious effort, was now as thoughtless and automatic as breathing.

Light and color were spilling out around him. He realized this once he had managed to relocate himself as being in a specific place, in the throne room of the fortress.

And beside him, a pudgy dark-haired woman rose from her throne and announced, a trifle unsteadily, " 'Tis done. Fare thee well until my return, Pellinore Brown."

He was still trying to gather his wits and get a firm grip on reality and said nothing as she walked, a little unsteadily, into the portal.

Prossie watched the matrix transfer with interest, as far as she could; at first it didn't seem as if Shadow were giving anything up, but merely as if Pel were developing his own shifting and colorful aura.

Pel's aura grew brighter and brighter, however, far past the level Shadow had been maintaining herself, and Prossie had to look away.

In seconds, Pel blazed with a brilliance fully as unbearable as Shadow's had been when first the party—eight of them, then—had entered the throne room. (Had that really only been the night before?) Prossie closed her eyes against the glare, flung an arm across her face, and turned away, pressing up to the wall.

And still the light grew brighter.

Then, finally, it stopped, though it was so intense that Prossie thought she could see the bones of her own arm silhouetted, black against red, right through the flesh and through her closed eyelids, and that was merely from the light that reached her with her back to the source, light reflected from the gray stone wall.

She heard Shadow's voice, sounding oddly weak, say, " 'Tis done. Fare thee well until my return, Pellinore Brown." Although her ears were ringing and blood was roaring through them, she heard footsteps.

And then she heard them stop.

And then Pel's voice roared out, loud as thunder, "Prossie? Are you all right?"

The two men, or whatever they were, pulled Amy forward a few steps, and then released her arms, leaving her standing there in the open air of a meadow; Amy looked around warily.

Shadow's black-clad servants were fanning out across the meadow, stamping down the tall grasses and wildflowers without so much as glancing at them; tiny insects, or at least creatures that resembled insects, whirred and buzzed about as the invaders trampled their habitat, flittering through shadow and oddly dim sunlight.

There were insects, but there were no birds, and no trees anywhere to be seen; just grasses and flowers and stalky things like oversized weeds. In the distance she could see what appeared to be rooftops, but of an architectural style she'd never seen before.

The sky was a peculiarly purple color and utterly cloudless above the gently rolling hills; the sun was far up the heavens but as orange as if it were setting, and its light seemed almost *thick*, somehow—syrupy and rich, but not as bright as sunlight should be.

The air was fresh and cool and spicy, and she felt light on her feet; her back felt straight and strong, and she realized for the first time that it had been aching dully for days, an ache that was now fading rapidly. She took a step and almost lost her balance.

Clearly, the gravity here was less than in Faerie and probably less than on Earth—though it had been so long since she had been on Earth she was not absolutely sure of that. The change took some adjustment.

Ted, beside her, tumbled to the ground; quickly, he sat up again and looked about. The four servants who had brought the two of them through the portal were a few steps away, standing as if waiting for something, completely ignoring the two Earthpeople.

"Am I awake?" Ted asked. "It still looks a little funny . . ."

"No," Amy told him, "it's not Earth." She took another tentative step. "I think the gravity's weaker here, for one thing, and look at the color of the sky, and the sun."

Ted looked up at the purple sky, and his face seemed to cave in.

"Oh, *damn!*" he said, and he started crying, heaving deep sobbing breaths.

"I'm fine," Prossie said, "but I can't stand the light."

Until that moment, Pel had not consciously realized that he was emitting light at all; the light had seemed a part of him, and he had somehow not recognized that it existed outside his own perceptions. He struggled for a moment, looking for some way to control the glow, and found it.

He wasn't really much of a matrix wizard yet, he thought wryly, not if it took a struggle just to stop leaking so much light.

He fought down the leakage as best he could, until he thought he was seeing it entirely by magic, then asked, "How's that?"

"Better," Prossie said, warily opening her eyes and turning to face him. She kept a hand up, and blinked often—he supposed that despite his efforts he was still glowing, but more tolerably.

He didn't have time to worry about it; he didn't know what was happening on the other side of the portal, didn't know what Shadow was up to, didn't even know if she could see or hear what was going on, and he wanted to talk to Prossie quickly, before Shadow could do anything about it. This might be his last chance to ever talk freely to someone who understood the situation, someone who could advise him, someone who could tell him he wasn't making a horrible mistake.

"Listen," Pel said hurriedly, "when she sent you through there, and you said she wasn't lying—did you mean that? Was there something else you wanted to tell me?"

Prossie blinked again. "She can't hear us?" She hesitated, then asked, "Are you sure?"

Pel noticed the hesitation and some little part of him wondered whether Prossie was afraid of him, now that he held Shadow's all-powerful matrix, or whether she was just unaccustomed to not *knowing*, telepathically, how sure someone was.

Or whether it was something else entirely.

It didn't matter, though. "She's through the portal in the Galactic Empire, and I'm holding the matrix," Pel answered. "She can't hear us from there any more than you can read minds from here." He *thought* that was the truth; he hesitated, and then in a fit of partial candor added, "But there might be homunculi listening, and they could tell her what we say—if she comes back and asks them."

The telepath took a second to consider, then replied. "She wasn't lying," Prossie said, "but she could change her mind at any time—instantly. She's selfish and short-tempered and . . . and whimsical. You can't trust her, not about that, not about *anything*."

Pel sighed, and wind whistled around the fortress tower above him. He was aware of it, aware that the matrix had caused that gust in sympathy to his sigh, as he might have been aware that he had blinked, or that his pulse was beating—he knew of it, but it was unimportant.

"I never really thought she could be trusted," he said, "but what choice did I have?" He tried to keep the sound of pleading out of his voice, and could not tell if he succeeded. "She says she can raise the dead—if it's true, she can bring back Nancy, and Rachel."

Prossie nodded. "She can bring corpses back to life," she agreed. "After a fashion, anyway. That's where a lot of those servants came from, I think—I didn't get the memories very clearly."

"The servants?" Light flickered across the walls in the magical equivalent of a blink.

"The ones in black, like the ones she took through the space warp with her," Prossie explained.

"Fetches," Pel said. "She calls them fetches. I heard her call them that."

"That's right," Prossie agreed. "Fetched back from the dead—it's not quite what the word means in the Empire, but that's what *she* means by it."

"Then she *can* bring back Nancy and Rachel!" A surge of long-suppressed hope and joy welled up, and for a moment white light flooded the throne room, forcing Prossie to turn away.

The telepath blinked, trying to clear her vision, and for an instant, inadvertently, Pel thought he looked out through her eyes.

"I know you want them back, Mr. Brown," Prossie said, "but I . . ." She stopped.

"But what?" Pel demanded, the hope turning to ash within him.

"But wouldn't she need the bodies?" Prossie asked. "I mean, to bring back your wife and daughter."

Pel sat motionless for a moment, and sickly reds and violets flickered along the ceiling. "I don't know," he said, finding himself involuntarily looking at Susan's body again. "Would she?"

He hadn't thought about that. Maybe he should have asked Shadow about it, tried to make her promise to revive Nancy and Rachel.

But maybe she couldn't, without the bodies. And what if the bodies had to be fresh? Rachel and Nancy had been dead for some time now; he had spent weeks at Base One and on the long journey from ISS *Christopher*.

He didn't want to think about it anymore, didn't want to kill his hope completely, and he changed the subject. After all, there were other things that needed to be discussed.

"Listen," he said, "I can't harm her; she put a spell on me, and maybe I could break it if I knew how, now that she's there and I've got this matrix of hers, but I *don't* know how. I can't harm her, and I can't ask anyone else to. But I won't stop anyone else who tries."

Prossie blinked at him, not understanding, her hand shielding her eyes against the glare.

"Are you still in touch with Base One?" he asked.

"I don't know," Prossie admitted. "Not right at the moment. And even if I were, it would take time for them to find her and reach her . . ."

"And she'd see them coming. She'd kill Ted, and maybe Amy, and she'd come back here and probably kill *me*," Pel agreed. "I couldn't defend myself; the spell wouldn't let me. I have to give back the matrix when she wants it, I can't close the portal and trap her there."

"If she were killed, she couldn't bring anyone back from the dead," Prossie pointed out. "She couldn't send anyone home."

"*I* could send people home," Pel said. "That much I learned." He paused, as a thought burst through his mind, a thought that he now saw as so obvious that he could not understand why he hadn't thought of it before.

He had learned how to open a portal; maybe he could learn more.

No one had taught Shadow to raise the dead, had they? She had managed it on her own, by virtue of the incredible accumulation of magical power she had amassed.

It might have taken her a while, though; she'd had centuries in which to experiment. And he didn't really know anything about the magic he now controlled.

But there were other wizards out there. They could help. And if Shadow were dead . . .

He couldn't harm her, of course.

But he didn't need to stop anyone else from harming her, if someone could figure out how.

And as far as raising the dead went, he certainly had enough corpses around to practice on; even if Raven and Singer were beyond recovery, Susan and Valadrakul remained, and there were the bodies hanging over the fortress gate.

A sudden urgency swept over him as pieces fell into place. He didn't just want to talk to the telepath; he wanted her to *do* something.

He wished she was still able to read his mind; how could he lead her to the conclusion he wanted?

He would have to try.

"Prossie," he said, "I can't leave here, I have to hold this portal open—go down to the gate, will you? I'm going to cut down the men hanging there."

Prossie blinked at him. "What?" she asked.

"Just . . . just go down and look at them. Hurry!"

He wanted to explain further, but he couldn't. The geas stopped him.

It was too much like asking someone to harm Shadow.

The woman called Shadow appeared from the air; Amy saw the arrival from the corner of her eye.

There was no glare of light, no shifting colors, no darknesses or other peculiarities. Shadow was just an overweight middle-aged woman, standing in a meadow and staring about openmouthed; there was no trace of magic to her—or to anything else here, beyond the everyday magicks of nature, sun and sky and flowers and grass.

" 'Tis real!" Shadow said, and her voice seemed weak and thin without her magic amplifying it.

Amy turned, and started to take a step toward Shadow, but then stopped herself.

Here Shadow was, without her magic, and Amy wanted to kill her, she wanted to beat that ugly head against a rock until it broke, to pay her back for Susan and the rest—but she stopped herself.

Because Shadow still had her guards; the four who had brought Amy and Ted through the portal were stepping up beside her, standing at attention, obviously waiting for orders. Their hands were mere inches from the hilts of their swords.

Amy had not lived through so much just to get herself run through by some semihuman creature's sword.

"Yes, it's real," Amy said. "Now what?"

Puzzled and wary, Prossie emerged from the throne room onto the landing at the top of the stairs. She didn't understand what was going on, whether Pel was cooperating with Shadow or pursuing some scheme of his own.

It would be so simple, back home, to dip quickly into his mind, maybe not see the details but at least sense which way he was going—but here it was impossible.

Did she *want* to cooperate with him? What was going to happen to her, if Pel was cooperating with Shadow? Where would she go?

Return to the Empire meant death; living here, under Shadow, meant constant fear and probably death as well. And would Shadow allow her to go to Earth with Amy and Ted?

Would Shadow ever allow Amy and Ted to return to Earth at all?

Prossie paused atop the stairs and glanced down.

The black dragon was still down there, looking up at her from below, but then, abruptly, its head burst into flame; for a moment Prossie thought her eyes were playing tricks, or it was an illusion of some sort.

Then the creature bellowed, spitting fire; it crumpled, toppling to one side, and fell, twitching once and then lying still, obviously dead.

"I can't really control them yet," Pel's voice, unnaturally loud, called from behind her. "Run!"

Whatever his plans, Pel was determined, she realized, and while it might have been cowardly, she didn't dare defy him, not when she could be incinerated as easily as the dragon, or as Raven and Singer before it. Prossie dashed down the steps, but slowed as she neared the dead beast.

The beam of light above the corridor was dim and flickering unsteadily; Prossie glanced uneasily up at it as she picked her way carefully past the dead dragon.

Sunlight was pouring in through the open doors, and the eldritch glare of Shadow's matrix shone down from the top of the stairs, so there was plenty of light even should the beam vanish completely; it wasn't darkness Prossie was afraid of, but the uncertainty.

The creatures along the ledges weren't moving; that was some comfort, anyway.

She heard several distant, muffled thumps from somewhere ahead, and she stopped in her tracks.

"Hurry!" Pel called from above, his voice weirdly distorted.

Baffled and frightened and annoyed, Prossie hurried, running down the long, long passage and out into the sunlight, where the six bodies lay.

They stank. Maybe they had before, and the height had kept the odor away, but now the stench was overwhelming, and Prossie shied away involuntarily.

And they didn't look very pleasant, either; they had fallen heavily into loops of their own entrails. Decaying blood and damaged flesh were heaped across the threshold, only partially wrapped in ruined purple uniforms.

Why had Pel wanted her to see this?

Was this some sadistic quirk, forcing her to look at her dead comrades? Was he going mad?

Bloated hands, dead faces, staring eyes; torn cloth, scuffed black boots, black leather belts.

Prossie wished desperately that she could read Pel's thoughts and find out what she was supposed to see.

Lieutenant Dibbs's mouth gaped open mere inches from another man's bowel, and Prossie had to swallow hard; she looked away, down Dibbs's body, but that was no better, with his slit-open belly, the severed ends of the waistband of his Sam Browne belt dangling into the cavity within, the empty holster at his side . . .

Empty holster.

They weren't all empty.

And Pel was holding the portal open. He couldn't go through it himself, he couldn't harm Shadow—but Prossie could.

Suddenly, she had no doubt at all of Pel's intentions, and she found herself smiling even as she struggled to hold down her breakfast. She scrabbled eagerly at Spaceman Shelby's holster.

"Oh, 'tis wondrous strange!" Shadow exclaimed, oblivious to Amy; the wizard smiled broadly, taking it all in.

Annoyed, the Earthwoman glanced at Ted; he was ignoring her, too, as he stared at the flowers.

And the men in black weren't paying any attention, either. Most of them had formed a hundred-yard ring, while half a dozen hovered wearily near Shadow, hands on sword hilts.

For her part, Shadow was lifting her feet and marveling at the feel of the lighter gravity, staring at the color of the sky, and trying to look in every direction at once as she wandered slowly in the general direction of those distant buildings.

"And 'twill be mine," Shadow sang, "all mine!"

Amy snorted.

The ring of men was moving with Shadow, and Amy was, reluctantly, moving as well.

Ted didn't notice, didn't move, until the ring touched him, and two of the swordsmen snatched him up by the arms and dragged him along.

A few feet away, as Amy watched, a swordsman vanished into the portal—presumably by accident, since the opening was invisible. The swordsman had been keeping his station in the moving circle when it reached the portal and had stepped through.

Amy waited for him to reappear—surely, once on the other side, he would simply turn around and step through again.

He didn't.

Amy blinked; what was happening back there in Shadow's fortress? Why hadn't the swordsman reappeared?

"Hey," she said.

No one paid any attention.

"Hey, *look!*" she shouted.

Prossie dashed into the throne room, blaster in hand, just as a fetch stepped from the portal; Pel saw her raise the weapon and point it at the black-garbed slave, but of course it didn't do anything.

Ray guns didn't work here; magic did.

He let one little tendril of arcane force free, just as he had with the dragon, and the fetch burst into flame—as Raven had, as Singer had.

He wanted to shout encouragement to Prossie, but he couldn't, the geas wouldn't let him. He didn't need to stop her, Shadow hadn't worried enough about her safety to appoint Pel as her guardian, but the spell prevented him from doing anything to urge the telepath on.

She didn't need encouragement; she ran through the hot, drifting ash and through the portal without slowing.

Amy stared as a figure burst from the portal, a figure in a slashed and dirty purple uniform, a figure with a gun in her hand.

The gun fired with an electric crackle and a muffled thud, and a swordsman fell, headless and twitching, as blood sprayed around him; Shadow spun, astonished.

Prossie fired again as Shadow opened her mouth to speak, and Shadow's shoulder exploded into bloody scraps. Whatever Shadow had planned to say was lost as she screamed and tottered, but for another long second the wizard remained upright. Amy glimpsed her face and saw nothing but surprise; she had obviously not suspected that anything like this could happen.

Shadow had been ready to confront the Galactic Empire with spies and swordsmen and had not realized how vulnerable that made her. In an instant, Amy understood what that meant. Despite all the reports her agents had brought her, Shadow had never *seen* a blaster, nor any other weapon produced by high technology—or Imperial science—except Susan's pitiful little pistol. She hadn't really comprehended how powerful they were. She hadn't known what she was getting into, hadn't realized how vulnerable she was in this universe where magic didn't work.

She hadn't understood that here, the Empire held a scientific matrix just as powerful as her own magical one.

Prossie fired a third time, and Shadow's chest burst into rags; she toppled forward and landed facedown in a patch of strange red flowers, her blood staining their leaves and stems almost as bright as their blossoms.

A hundred blades flashed in the alien sun as the black-clad

men drew their blades and prepared to defend—or avenge— their mistress.

"Run for the portal!" Prossie cried, as her weapon blasted the belly out of the nearest swordsman.

Amy hesitated at the idea of running *toward* that thing Prossie was firing, but then she obeyed; she stumbled once, forgetting the lower gravity, but she quickly recovered.

She didn't know how it had happened, but she knew an opportunity when she saw it. Pel must have arranged it somehow, despite all Shadow's plans. He had sent Prossie to save them.

And he was waiting for them, back in Faerie.

She hoped that Pel had some way of sending them back to Earth, but even if he didn't, they certainly couldn't stay here.

"Ted!" she called. He looked up. "Through the portal!"

He didn't move, and she was almost there; Prossie was picking off swordsmen one by one, starting with those nearest her, but there were an awful lot of them, and some were coming around behind her.

"Ted, I swear, just get through the portal, and you'll wake up!"

Ted hesitated, then stumbled toward the faint waver in the air, but Amy didn't wait for him; she dove past Prossie and through and landed on freshly skinned knees on the stone floor of Shadow's throne room.

Or rather, she corrected herself, of *Pel's* throne room.

CHAPTER 25

*P*el wished he could see what was happening beyond the portal, but despite his incredible power, he couldn't manage that. A way might exist, for all he knew, but if so, he hadn't discovered it; the portal itself seemed to block whatever he had done to sense where it would go before he had created it, and the trick of seeing through other eyes, even if he had known how to use it, couldn't work in Imperial space, any more than any other magic could.

He saw Amy fall out onto the throne-room floor, though; he saw Ted stagger out a moment later, and then Prossie backed from nowhere into the room, still trying to fire her blaster. She was squeezing the firing stud so hard he could hear the clicking over Amy's panting and Ted's shuffling and all the other little noises of their disorganized return.

Then one of Shadow's fetches charged out of the portal, sword raised, and Pel was so startled that the thing was able to take a swipe at Prossie before bursting into flame. The blade cut open one tattered sleeve and drew a line of blood before falling from shriveling, blackening fingers.

Then more fetches came bursting through, mostly one by one, occasionally in pairs or even trios, but each appearing only to flare up instantly and burn away to scattering ash. Amy crawled to the side on hands and knees, out of their path; Ted wandered clear; and Prossie backed away, blaster still in one hand, the other hand shielding her face, and watched as the swordsmen perished.

The stream of burning swordsmen seemed interminable. Since the energy that incinerated them was not his own and needed no actual guidance but merely a point of release, Pel didn't tire of destroying them, exactly, but the simple repetition

264

was wearying, and the accumulated heat of their fiery extinction did become uncomfortable; by the time the last fetch perished, the air of the throne room was sweltering hot, like the inside of a furnace. Amy and Ted retreated up the passage toward the rooms where they had eaten and slept, while Prossie backed out onto the landing at the top of the great staircase.

The whole process quickly took on a surreal aspect—the procession of undead charging forward to immolation, the blackened and melting swords rattling to the floor and lying there in a smoldering heap, all in the flickering, unnatural light of the windowless and underfurnished throne room, had the mindless, irrational repetitiveness of a nightmare.

If any of the fetches ever had the wit to do anything other than charge blindly after the woman who had slain his mistress, he didn't show it—but then, Pel didn't count them and could not be certain, when they finally stopped appearing, that some weren't still active on the other side of the opening.

Pel would have preferred closing the portal and stranding the fetches on the other side, for the Empire to deal with, but he could not afford the concentration to do that as long as the swordsmen kept appearing; he was unsure just how much the matrix would protect him without conscious direction.

At last, though, the stream of attackers paused, and Pel was able to think about something other than burning.

"Did you get her?" he shouted to Prossie, as he struggled to close the portal. The spell did not yield readily, did not collapse the way his portals had in practice. Something was fighting him—the geas, presumably.

"Yes, sir," Prossie answered, sharply. Pel was startled by the "sir" until he realized that she was simply reverting to military habits.

He was relieved to hear her reply; he had assumed as much, but it was good to hear her say it. And she was quite definite, no "I think so," or "Probably," but a definite "Yes."

And then something yielded and crumbled in his mind, and the portal was gone, leaving only charred sword fragments and boot heels and a haze of drifting ash where the fetches had been appearing. The oppressive heat lingered, and Pel could feel himself drenched in sweat, but his mind was clear and sharp—and free.

The geas was gone.

And that, he knew, meant that Shadow was dead.

* * *

The grip of the blaster felt good in her hand. The steel cross-graining bit into her palm as she squeezed it, keeping the still-hot weapon steady despite the slick of sweat—and despite its uselessness here in Faerie. It felt good to hold it, and to know that she had killed Shadow with it.

Her hand wanted to tremble, but she wouldn't allow it. Her long-ago training did that much for her, anyway.

She had never shot anyone before. As a rule, the Empire did not arm Specials; they weren't there to fight. They were trained in the use of blasters, just in case, but only on the practice range, with low-power weapons. Prossie hadn't fired a weapon in two or three years—until today. And she had never before used a full-power blast, or shot at a living target.

But now she had—and she had hit what she aimed at. She had killed Shadow.

That she had killed did not bother her, at least not yet; somewhere inside she thought that perhaps it should.

But this was *Shadow*. This was the Enemy. And she, Proserpine Thorpe, outlaw telepath, had killed it.

It felt very good indeed, and she was in no hurry to put the ray gun down.

The swordsmen had stopped coming, finally. When she thought about it she realized that they had stopped before Pel had asked her if Shadow was dead. In her excitement she had lost track, for a moment, of the sequence of events.

The portal was probably closed, then. She straightened up, out of her gunner's crouch.

Heat was still pouring out of the throne room, while cooler air drifted up the stairs behind her; she could feel her hair plastered to her scalp with sweat. She turned and looked down the steps.

The beam of light seemed a little brighter than before, though still not up to when Shadow had controlled it; by its glow she could see the dead dragon in the hall below, lying headless on the floor. Purple ichor had puddled around it.

Imperial purple, she thought wryly.

And as if that made some mental connection, she heard her name being called.

"Carrie?" she asked.

For a long moment Pel simply sat there, savoring the calm after the storm. The heat was gradually dissipating, the ashes were settling. The matrix hummed and glowed around him and through him, and he could feel it reaching out through all of Faerie.

Just now, he didn't want to think about it. He knew that he would have decisions to make, important decisions, but just now he wanted to savor his victory.

That was what it was, all right—victory. He hadn't just escaped from Shadow, from Faerie, from the Empire; this time, he had done more than escape. He had played the hero's role after all.

He had won.

The throne room was quiet, and the heat rolling up the passage seemed to be lessening; Amy took Ted's hand and called, "Pel?"

No one answered—but she hadn't called very loudly.

"You said I'd wake up," Ted said accusingly; she jumped, startled, and turned to face him.

"Yes, I did," she admitted.

"I'm not awake yet." Then he laughed, not his usual nervous giggle, but a wild, hysterical laugh. "What am I doing?" he said. "I'm arguing with a *dream*? Because it fooled me?"

"It's not a dream, Ted," Amy replied.

Always before, when she had argued with Ted, or just talked to him, she had felt frustrated and helpless; she had been powerless to help him, to convince him of anything.

Now, though, as she tugged him back toward the throne room, she felt triumphant. "Come on," she said. "We have to get you home."

"That's twice now you've reappeared in Imperial space, and then vanished again," Carrie sent. "We all felt it; a new adult telepath turning up anywhere in the galaxy is hard to miss. And when we tried to locate you exactly this second time, we found some of those Shadow things, but now they're gone, too. Prossie, you said you were abandoning the family and the Empire, but you keep turning up. Who's creating these space warps for you, and how? Are you working for Shadow now?"

Before Prossie could answer, Carrie added, in a far more emotional tone of thought, "Prossie, what's going on?"

"I killed Shadow," Prossie answered proudly. She looked down at the blaster in her hand, and her mind was flooded with a tangle of emotions. She had sometimes felt something like it in others, in moments of crisis, but this was the first time she had ever experienced such powerful and complex feelings entirely on her own.

And she was really, truly on her own now. "You wouldn't help," she said, "you didn't want to hear from me, but I killed Shadow."

"What?" Prossie could feel Carrie's astonishment clearly. "But . . . did you really? You're serious? How? You'll have to . . . Prossie, can you get back to the Empire, then? They'll want . . ."

Prossie's grip tightened on the blaster, and she cut Carrie off.

"Fuck the Empire," she said. "And fuck *you*, Carrie Hall."

The throne room was ablaze with color and shadow, and stank of smoke; blackened debris was scattered across a wide area.

And Amy noticed that Susan's corpse was still lying against a wall, untouched by recent events.

The shape on the throne was a mass of light, too bright to look at; for a moment Amy could not believe that it was poor Pellinore Brown. It had to be Shadow; the whole thing must have been a trick of some kind.

Then it spoke, and the voice was Pel's.

"I might as well send you all home, I guess," he said. "If I can, anyway."

"Are you sure you don't want to go back to your *own* universe?" Pel asked again, for the third time in ten minutes.

Prossie shook her head. "Earth," she said.

It wasn't an easy choice, but it was the right one, she was sure.

If she returned to her own universe she would be a criminal, a hunted fugitive, with no way to hide from her hunters—who would be her own family. They were all slaves to the Empire, all bound up in the web of deception and self-deception, shared delusions and identity. They would track her down, steal from her mind everything she knew about Faerie and Shadow and Pel and Earth and all the rest, and then turn her over to the Empire to be hanged.

And if by some miracle they *didn't* hunt her down, if they sided with her, or even just let her slip away somehow, then they would be as guilty as she—they would *all* be risking their lives. The Empire would not hesitate to wipe the filthy mutants out.

She might have disowned them all, cut herself off, rejected them all—but she couldn't ask that of them.

And besides, she had grown accustomed to the oddly liberating mental silence of the other realities, and to being her own person; she didn't think she could fit back in the Empire, didn't think she could go back to being a communication device instead of a person.

As for Faerie—even with Shadow gone, even with the entire world's magic in Pel's hands, it wasn't for her. The heavy gravity was wearing, the watery light was unpleasant, the sanitation was abysmal, the whole place was depressingly primitive and harsh.

And although she hated to admit it, she didn't trust Pel anymore; she didn't trust *anyone* who held that much power. She was not at all certain whether Pel entirely controlled the matrix, or whether the matrix partially controlled Pel, and she also wondered if some part of Shadow might still linger in that great tapestry of magic. Shadow's original body was dead, yes—but how much of her had been bound up in the matrix?

Not the Empire, not Faerie—that left Earth, which she had only glimpsed, directly and through the Earthpeople's minds back at Base One—Earth, with its amazing alien machines, its complex history, diverse society, and strange, rich culture— television and movies, cars and airplanes, books, music, so *much* to explore! The Galactic Empire had been working toward uniformity for a century, trying with mixed success to impose its single central culture on thousands of worlds; Earth, with its fragmented politics and sophisticated communications, seemed to be going to the other extreme, jamming a million different societies together on a single big planet.

Earth looked like far more fun—frightening and alien, but fun.

"Definitely, Earth," she repeated.

The shifting colors swirled for a moment, and Prossie thought that swirl might have been Pel's magical equivalent of a shrug.

"It's your life," Pel said.

Finding Earth was tricky, much more difficult than finding the Empire had been; Pel was not surprised that the Empire's telepaths and science had found it before Shadow's magic.

He would have preferred opening another portal to the Empire first, for Prossie's use—that he could have done in just a few minutes—but she insisted she didn't want to go home, she wanted to go to Earth.

Which meant only creating a single portal, but it also meant that he had to *find* Earth.

And finding the right *part* of Earth was tricky, as well. Nobody had cared *where* on a particular planet Shadow arrived, so long as it was a reasonably pleasant neighborhood and not too far from civilization, but Pel did not think Amy and Ted would appreciate being dumped in the Australian outback—let alone on Mars.

But then, at last, Pel found a place that the portal *wanted* to go, and he realized with a start that he had found his own basement, and the lingering traces of Elani's portal.

His own basement.

He hesitated, momentarily reconsidering his decision to stay.

Then he began the process of prying the portal open.

Ted vanished, and Amy took a step toward the portal. Then she paused, "You're sure?" she asked, staring at the throne, trying to see Pel through the glare.

"I'm sure," he said.

"But . . ."

"No, I'm *sure*, Amy," Pel said. "It's a chance to play God. To make everything better for all the people here. I mean, remember what it was like out there, under Shadow's rule! Those gibbets, the dirt, the squalor—I can do a lot of good. Just teaching these people some basic stuff like indoor plumbing, I'll accomplish more than I would in a hundred years as a marketing consultant."

Amy glanced at Prossie, waiting her turn a few feet away, then back at Pel. She knew perfectly well that that wasn't the sort of "playing God" that Pel was really interested in. Oh, he might do it, and it might be a good thing, but it wasn't why he wanted to stay in Faerie.

He wanted to learn to raise the dead, so he could bring back his wife and poor little Rachel. Amy knew that.

But it was his business, not hers.

Poor Susan's body was still lying against the wall; in all the excitement no one had had time to do anything for her, or for those dead Imperials out front. Maybe Pel would raise Susan from the dead, too. Maybe he would bring Lieutenant Dibbs and his men back to life and send them all home.

It seemed vaguely blasphemous and somehow dangerous,

but Amy told herself she was being silly. She'd never been devout, and any ideas about it being dangerous came more from horror movies than from logic.

It wasn't her problem.

Her biggest problem was an unwanted baby, and she needed to get back to Earth to get rid of it safely. And just getting back to a normal life—which she could hardly do in Faerie.

She didn't want to play God; she just wanted to go home. So why was she still here, arguing?

"Besides, Amy," Pel said, "if I leave without turning the matrix over to someone, it'll come apart, and wild magic will run amok—the sort of magic that cooked all those people, Raven and the fetches and the others."

"It will?" she asked, startled. "I thought that it sounded like things were pretty good before the matrix wizards got out of hand." She wondered whether Pel was just making excuses, trying to convince himself.

She wondered, also, if he had any idea what he was talking about. Did he really know any of this stuff? If he'd learned it from Shadow, had she told the truth?

"Well, yeah," Pel said, "but that was before the magic all got collected. It would disperse out to harmlessness eventually, I think, but if I just turn it loose now it'll be like an explosion."

"Are you sure?" Amy asked.

"No," Pel admitted. "Look, Amy, you go on; I can always open the gate up again and go home. But I can't ever come *back*—once I leave, the portal closes and the matrix comes apart. So I want to do whatever I can here first."

Amy glanced at Susan's corpse and shrugged; it wasn't really any of her business if Pel stayed, and maybe he *would* do some good. She stepped through the portal, and as the throne room's eerie colors vanished she saw Prossie coming close on her heels.

She emerged into the dim light of a single bare bulb—if there had been others, as she vaguely remembered there were, they must have burned out. She stepped quickly to one side, so that Prossie would not walk into her.

Pel's basement was hot and musty; the house had probably been closed up all summer, Amy realized. Ted was sitting on the stairs.

"Hello," he said, as Prossie appeared.

Amy glanced at Prossie, and then, reassured that she was

safely through the portal, turned and blinked at Ted. Her eyes needed time to adjust to the dimness after the blinding glare of the matrix.

"Are you okay, Ted?" she asked, concerned. "I thought you'd be on your way home by now."

"I don't know," he said. "Am I awake? Why am I in some-one's basement, if I'm awake? This is supposed to be Earth, isn't it?"

"It's Earth, Ted, and you're awake," Prossie said gently. "You've been awake all along."

He shook his head. "No, no; that's crazy."

"Well, crazy or not," Amy told him, "you're in Pel's base-ment, on Earth, and you're safe. Open the door, and let's go home."

Ted shook his head, and Amy saw terror on his face. All through their adventures he had smiled, or simply looked blank, but now that they were safely home he was obviously seriously frightened.

"I don't know what's out there," Ted said slowly. "I don't know who you two really are, if this is real and the dream's over. If I'm here, and not home in bed, it can't have been an ordinary dream—so maybe I'm not awake yet after all. Maybe if I go through that door I'll be back in that castle, or the spaceship, or something. There could be monsters, or slave drivers, or anything."

"Open the door and see, Ted," Amy said, annoyed with his weakness. She marched across the basement and up the dusty steps, while Prossie trailed uncertainly after her.

For an instant, as her hand closed on the knob and Ted stared fearfully up at her, Amy thought that he might somehow be right, that *anything* could lie beyond that door—or beyond *any* door.

But then she swung it wide and saw only the Browns' hall-way, dusty and muggy, and she knew it was over.

Pel sat on his throne, staring at the portal, for several minutes after Ted and Amy and Prossie had vanished.

None of them reappeared; they were presumably safely back on Earth, but for all he could see they might just as well be dead, or imprisoned. He considered holding the portal open for a moment longer, just in case, but then decided that was silly.

He let his link to Earth collapse into nothingness, glanced back at Susan's body, and got to his feet.

Susan would have to wait; he wanted to practice on someone or something else first. Susan was a friend; he didn't want to bring her back until he could do the job right.

And after he had brought Susan back to life, he would find Nancy and Rachel. Somehow, somewhere, some way, he would find them.

A world of fantasy and
adventure in the novels of

ABOUT THE AUTHOR

LAWRENCE WATT-EVANS grew up in Massachusetts, fourth of six children whose parents were both inveterate readers, and both of whom read science fiction, among other things. He taught himself to read from comic books, and first attempted to write science fiction at the age of eight.

He was considerably older than that when he sold his first fantasy novel, *The Lure of the Basilisk*, to Del Rey Books, beginning his career as a full-time writer.

He is best known for the Ethshar fantasy series, consisting of *The Misenchanted Sword*, *With a Single Spell*, *The Unwilling Warlord*, *The Blood of a Dragon*, *Taking Flight*, and *The Spell of the Black Dagger*.

In addition to fantasy, he's written several science-fiction novels, of which his personal favorite is *Nightside City*, a twenty-fourth-century detective story. He also writes horror. He has sold more than sixty short stories and novelettes, including "Why I Left Harry's All-Night Hamburgers," which won the Hugo Award for 1988.

He married in 1977, has two children, and lives in the Maryland suburbs of Washington, D.C.

DEL REY ONLINE!

The Del Rey Internet Newsletter...

A monthly electronic publication, posted on the Internet, GEnie, CompuServe, BIX, various BBSs, and the Panix gopher (gopher.panix.com). It features hype-free descriptions of books that are new in the stores, a list of our upcoming books, special announcements, a signing/reading/convention-attendance schedule for Del Rey authors, "In Depth" essays in which professionals in the field (authors, artists, designers, sales people, etc.) talk about their jobs in science fiction, a question-and-answer section, behind-the-scenes looks at sf publishing, and more!

Online editorial presence: Many of the Del Rey editors are online, on the Internet, GEnie, CompuServe, America Online, and Delphi. There is a Del Rey topic on GEnie and a Del Rey folder on America Online.

Our official e-mail address for Del Rey Books is delrey@randomhouse.com

Internet information source!

A lot of Del Rey material is available to the Internet on a gopher server: all back issues and the current issue of the Del Rey Internet Newsletter, a description of the DRIN and summaries of all the issues' contents, sample chapters of upcoming or current books (readable or downloadable for free), submission requirements, mail-order information, and much more. We will be adding more items of all sorts (mostly new DRINs and sample chapters) regularly. The address of the gopher is gopher.panix.com

Why? We at Del Rey realize that the networks are the medium of the future. That's where you'll find us promoting our books, socializing with others in the sf field, and—most importantly—making contact and sharing information with sf readers.

For more information, e-mail delrey@randomhouse.com